CW01645788

superstars

ANN SCOTT was born in Boulogne-Billancourt, and at 16 she moved to London alone where she played drums with local punk bands. At 18 she turned to fashion modelling and was one of the first tattooed fashion models to break through in 1980s prêt-à-porter and couture, walking the runway for John Galliano and Jean Paul Gaultier. Upon her return to Paris at age 21, she started writing fiction. She is also the co-author, with Nicola Sirkis, of the song 'Paradize' by the rock group Indochine. She is the author of ten novels including *Les Insolents*, which won the 2023 Prix Renaudot in France.

JONATHAN WOOLLEN is a French-to-English translator originally from North Carolina, currently based in Queens, New York, and working in publishing. He previously led the in-store author event program at Politics and Prose Bookstore in Washington, DC, and served as music director of the radio station WXYC-Chapel Hill. His work has appeared in outlets including *Electric Literature* and *Asymptote*. *Superstars* is his first published book-length translation.

superstars

ann scott

TRANSLATED FROM THE FRENCH BY
JONATHAN WOOLLEN

pushkin press

Pushkin Press
Somerset House, Strand
London WC2R 1LA

Superstars was first published by Éditions Flammarion in Paris, 2000
First published by Pushkin Press in 2026

ISBN 13: 978-1-80568-059-8

A CIP catalogue record for this title is available from the British Library

The authorised representative in the EEA is eucomply OÜ,
Pärnu mnt. 139b-14, 11317, Tallinn, Estonia,
hello@eucompliancepartner.com, +33757690241

Offset by Tetragon, London
Printed and bound in the United Kingdom by Clays Ltd, Elcograf S.p.A.

Pushkin Press is committed to a sustainable future for our business, our readers and our planet. This book is made from paper from forests that support responsible forestry.

MIX
Paper | Supporting responsible forestry
FSC www.fsc.org FSC® C018072

www.pushkinpress.com

1 3 5 7 9 8 6 4 2

superstars

prologue

shadows on the walls

One night a year ago in January, I got slugged in the face by a bouncer at Rex. I wound up on the sidewalk in a dress without a coat, and with blood all over my hands. L'Entracte, that lesbian club a little farther down the boulevard, was the last place on Earth I would have wanted to go. But I felt out of it enough to disregard that fact—enough, that is, to dissuade the incoming dipshits from getting too close to me.

Right before, I was exiting the bathroom at Rex, having just shot up heroin for the first time in ages, and I already had that pleasant floating sensation as I headed down the hallway to the dance floor. I kept my eyes on the ground as I walked, an elastic band between my teeth so I could tie up my hair, when I came face-to-face with Alex. She had her arms crossed, arguing with the girl who had given me cause to leave her that morning. The girl was wearing one of my T-shirts under her jean jacket, a worn, sky-blue *Jaws* shirt with the title scrawled across it in red, Jaws also being Alex's DJ name. Alex stared at me, amused, all of 5′2″, not yet convinced that our split was for real, used to me always forgiving her when she slept around.

Except that this time, the excuse wasn't "I just wanted to see if you'd be jealous" or "You were bugging me so I needed it" but "I was craving some adventure, you know—we'll be back together in two weeks." So there I was, with Alex standing in my way, acting like a smart-ass, and I remember saying she better tell me where I won't bang into her like this, or things weren't going to end well. And then everything happened very fast, even in my dope haze. I saw a glass going by in someone's hand, I snatched it away, and I smashed it against Alex's head. Back then, she wore her hair up, these short blonde dread things that never stayed pointy for long. The blood, starting to mix in, wound up holding them together better than whatever gel she was always slathering on to no effect. That's the only retort I could manage; in the meantime, I tried helping her regain a little balance. Then the other girl started screaming into her hands. Honestly, she was the only one making a big deal; there were far too many people around for anyone to notice what was going on. Alex simply patted around, delicately hunting for bits of glass, and then, with this psychotic smile on her face, she grabbed my hands, forcing them flat against her hair, which was sticky with blood. It wasn't so much the bouncer escorting me out that set me off, because I basically found that part laughable, this coat hanger of a man a full head shorter than me in my heels, who seemed unsure where to grab me without breaking my bones. What got under my skin was his hissing in my ear, saying, "Catfights get me hard." So I punched him in the balls, hoping to grind them into a million pieces. Hence the slugging.

I had savored every moment, immersed in the thick fog-machine haze of Rex's basement, searching for a little corner where I could enjoy the music in peace. After all, it was my favorite club, dammit. Now here I was at L'Entracte instead, this secondary club that saw almost no action on weeknights, that never even threatened to heat up. As my eyes adjusted to the dim light, I noticed the tables topped with glasses and cigarette packs were all centered around mine. The clatch of trolls wiggling their asses on the dance floor would sooner or later be encircling me when they returned to their seats. But I felt too wasted to get up.

I couldn't get myself to focus on Alex, that mind-fucking worm; after three long years in a power struggle, I still couldn't quit her. Nor could my brain concentrate on all the belongings I'd hastily packed and stashed in her garage, or on wherever I'd end up crashing that night, or on the drafts of air that were passing right through me as I lay there slumped in my slip dress. I even forgot that tonight was the first time I had worn a dress since meeting Alex, that I'd purchased it that same day with some shoes, firmly intending to pick up a man. At this point, I had only one interest: nodding off. Those final moments when your head's weight starts dragging forward and your eyelids suddenly plummet into spiraling dreams—short but searing flashes of beauty, as only dope can provide.

The kinds of dreams that feel all the more amazing after a long abstinence period—and the ones I had that night were really something special. I remember soaring over a vast expanse of barren, cracking land, watching an endless parade of ants stream off into the distance until an imposing monolith rose against the setting sun, dark and metallic like in *2001*, which up close turned out to be a giant Coke-flavored popsicle stick, with dozens of hoses branching off to fill an array of soda cans. A second later and I had turned microscopic, standing at the foot of some immense trees, in a verdant clearing that smelled like melons. Fat drops of pregnant ovular dew pearled from the tips of flower blossoms. As they cascaded down, they distended, hanging in the air in the most abstract shapes, before softly crashing onto the mossy bed below, sparkling for an instant before they were fully absorbed. Kneeling by the banks of a pond, a dragonfly sat combing its hair. Her body was a patchwork, every beautiful shade in the rainbow, her transparent wings reflecting the pond's clear, calm water. Hearing me approach, she shot me a startled look and asked why I wasn't with the others, preparing for her birthday party. And that's when I felt someone sit down beside me.

I straightened up as best I could, ready to cast off the new nightmare before my eyes, but it was a familiar-looking face. Still, I didn't know any twenty-year-olds, much less one who looked like *this*. She was so skinny that her shoulder blades, poking out from under her sweater, gently spread the wool's stitching enough to reveal the color of the underlying T-shirt. And through each lock of black hair that fell around her features, you could see every ridge in her face jutting out from beneath her pallid skin. It was only when she pulled out an old Zippo that I placed her: Alice, little sister to Nikki, the guy I was with before Alex, and the person I had given this very lighter to. I wondered, was she a terminal case or something, and then noticed the vaguely Spanish girl standing right in front of us. She really didn't seem like a regular here, despite her shaved head ripe with fine black peach fuzz. Almost as tall as me—a real rarity in a place where everyone struggles to be seen above their stools—more than anything she looked powerfully feminine in a black form-hugging dress, her olive skin perfectly powdered. That she was deigning to stand in my proximity could only be due to the fact that I also was wearing a dress; her contempt for the surroundings was legible from the haughty, prideful bearing of her head. Alice introduced her as her roommate, Pallas, but Pallas's gaze was so frosty that I refrained from extending my hand. I blurted out that I didn't have a home anymore; Alice replied with something about an impending move, before they departed for the bar and I went back to dozing. This time I was in an aquarium where obese Japanese koi glared at me, perplexed, when I tried to mount one like a steed. Rocks, glittering with gems, were visible in the distance, all shaped like syringes, with golden powder pouring from their gaudy stones, then splashing into lagoons that snaked through the surrounding vegetation toward a smooth, flat lake that had fused with the far-off horizon. Having here discovered the planet's dope reserve, I was ready to dive in headfirst, my heart aflutter, before something touched my knee . . . It was Pallas trying to rouse me. With the music, I couldn't hear anything she was saying, but I forced myself to seem attentive. The whole time she was talking, her eyes wouldn't leave my fingers, which were still stained with Alex's dried blood, and I remember thinking that though I'm sure she wasn't perfect exactly, in certain circumstances she must have been stunning. Sitting at a booth a few feet away, a girl was puking between her feet. I could think of nothing more grotesque than watching some ugly bitch puke her brains out.

Then came the cold—headlights from the occasional car and vapor escaping Pallas's grumbling mouth: "Quit dining out every night, quit foreign friends dropping in for a month at a time." Alice's frail shoulder guided me to the bus stop. In the taxi, Pallas continued: "Quit parties, quit afterparties." Alice gave me a look to show she wasn't paying any mind. "Quit drugs," Pallas went on, while I stuck my nose in the breeze out the lowered window, hoping to stave off the onset of nausea. I could just imagine my coat, hanging all alone on the rack in Rex's cloakroom at the end of the night, and I wondered if I could go by and retrieve it the next day, but more so I wondered whether the rest of the dope would still be there, too. I also thought about Alex's latest fling, the one who now seemed to be wearing my T-shirts.

It was bizarre to be back in this apartment, here with a twenty-year-old girl, with people who were nothing to me, nothing except the little sister of the one guy I'd ever truly loved and this chick named Pallas who already hated me. The latter opened the door to a room that looked huge, empty other than a black leather couch and a massive TV. Alice pulled a drab gray heap from a closet, a quilt with a big black paint splotch, which I recognized from having slept in it for seven years with her brother. With a loud clack, I took off my heels on the hardwood, holding myself up with the back of the couch so I wouldn't look so conspicuously far gone. Alice hugged me good night; Pallas added, "And quit blasting music"; and then I was alone. I sat there wondering if Alice remembered: that's what I did, I made music.

A yellowish glimmer was filtering through the slats of the shutters, somehow both weak and persistent, producing even, slightly fuzzy horizontal streaks along the bare white walls. The light came off one of the blackish cast-iron bells still found on facades across Paris, their feeble gleams sneakily weaving into old buildings through their battered wooden shutters. One such shutter was being held on by a piece of string, and a light breeze was making its shadows tremble. No noise could be heard from the bedrooms. The heat wasn't on, and the room felt frozen in time, like furniture draped in shapeless white sheets. I couldn't tear my eyes from the quivering shadows on the walls. For some reason, I was expecting one of them to actually move. To suddenly form a sentence, like: "Get out while you still can." There were loads of other places I could have gone to get some shut-eye, but the prospect of heading back out into the cold, of hunting for a taxi in a neighborhood with no known landmarks—that frankly didn't appeal to me. So I studied the shadows a little bit longer, and since they didn't want to transform, I let myself get sucked into the depths of the couch.

chapter one

the living-room couch

1.

A year and change later, and I was still slumped on the same couch—the only piece of furniture in the living room aside from the VCR and massive TV sitting right on the hardwood.

For two months, it had served as my bedroom until Alice moved out, when I decided to set myself up with her old space. Now it was back to being a living room, which served no purpose except for the exhibits that Alice organized as her contribution to the rent. Decor was the least of our worries: we were so broke that as soon as any of us had a little cash, the squabbling would begin over who was in charge of what, who was reimbursing whom, and so nothing ever got bought. The result was a lifeless room. We'd visit it ten times a day, because that's where our closets were, plus an entire wall of overflowing shelves next to a wardrobe also bursting with Pallas's stuff, which occasioned numerous fights whenever I had something I needed to hang—but that's about all the room had. The trestle table, stashed deep in the closet beside a half-dozen folding chairs, only came out for the occasional dinner party, while the TV and

VCR stayed put, on loan from one of Pallas's friends—both useless, since everything we needed we had in our bedrooms. The room only felt active whenever Alice had a showing. Every other month, she'd organize an exhibit for someone who didn't have her gallery luck, and so then we'd get forty-some faces rolling in, all of them more or less familiar. It was a pain in the ass to always have to head to other rooms to avoid people, but all things considered I met some interesting folks that way.

The apartment was spacious, but also fucking lousy. It needed a real hallway, not to mention bedrooms that were more spaced apart. Pallas's was by the entrance on the right, then came two doors on opposite walls, one on the right going to the living room and one on the left going to my room, with the washroom, the toilet, and the kitchen also on the left. Pallas's bedroom was bright, with an impeccable hardwood floor, but also tiny. Mine was enormous, even bigger than the living room but more fit for office computers, with hideous white polystyrene tiles on the ceiling and a scratchy, dreary gray carpet underfoot. It also had an unobstructed view of the employment agency below. So it was clear enough why Pallas selected her room instead of mine, but that was fine with me. I wasn't a hardwood fanatic, I didn't spend my days staring at the ceiling—the tiling was actually pretty good insulation from the neighbors upstairs—and anyway, I liked to keep the shutters closed.

The common rooms had their own eccentricities. It was a spacious washroom, with white porcelain surfaces and all kinds of metal accents (all of which Pallas had bought during one of her spending sprees), but the tub itself was stupidly small, and the shelves in the vanity were too close together for a single bottle to stand up inside. The toilet room, capacious but welcoming, with walls entirely covered in flyers courtesy of Alice, had a septic tank that was always running. As for our kitchen, which looked more like a hallway, it was a constant inconvenience. All the outlets were blocked, the sink leaked all year round, and the stove's hood couldn't suck for shit. The space was largely obstructed by an immense couch that was already there before the girls arrived, invincible to our dethroning attempts, flouting any efforts to turn it around the hallway corner, even though it must have gotten here somehow. A red vinyl imitation of Dalí's mouth couch: it may have tickled all our visitors, but the three of us had come to hate it, having stubbed our toes against it too many times.

The apartment was also very poorly insulated, with noise being the worst. Pallas, jammed up against the stairwell, could hear people going up and down all day and night, and I was privy to the traffic taking the Rue du Chemin-Vert toward Voltaire, Bastille, or République. The only real pleasure was the way we chose to arrange our bedrooms. Pallas's, entirely beige from the walls to the bedsheets, had nothing but a big wrought-iron bed with a matching chair being used as a nightstand, while everything else, from the stereo to the VCR, was stacked in a recess, hidden behind an equally beige curtain. The curtain also hid all of Pallas's art supplies, untouched since she left ESMOD, along with her latest purchases (a digital camera and printer) that felt equally useless. The room's only human touch, hanging on the left-hand wall though typically hidden behind the open door, was a large poster of Bowie in the *Heroes* era, with bits of Pallas's own work encroaching over the top, plus countless Polaroids of our group, all composing an impressive collage that always invited examining eyes.

My room was the kind I'd been dreaming of for years, back when I lacked a space to call my own. Sitting on the left as you entered were the mattress, TV, and VCR; the comforter's feathers were flattening over time, and the navy-blue slipcover on top, the only one I owned, had gradually bleached from endless washing; and then on the other side, by the windows, I had set up my "home studio." Shaped like an inverted L, it started with a small computer table facing the left-hand wall, then, blocking the left-hand window, the first folding table supported hardware: a bulky mixing deck, compressor, sampler, DAT, SPX, Groove Box, four-track, and CD burner. My Juno synth was in easy reach up front, and the second table, stretching to the second window, held both turntables, the stereo, and the speakers. Under the two tables were jumbled heaps of jacks, floppy disks, and DAT tapes, mixed with piled computer magazines and manuals, and all together the hundred-something cables and electrical relays looked identical to the heating-duct lair De Niro had to fix in *Brazil.* Continuing on in a straight line from table number two were my five hundred vinyl records, placed right on the carpet, with an equal number of CDs stacked in vertical piles, and capping it all off, in the right-hand corner of the room were eight cardboard boxes of stuff I'd been hoarding. Open but never unpacked, they contained videos, my *Keyboard* magazine collection, a handful of books, and a smattering of other objects that I regularly combed through hoping to reduce the number of boxes. Though I'd been here for a year now, I still couldn't fully unfurl. Because I'd needed to move so often before, I was completely obsessed with feeling like everything I owned could be speedily packed back up when the time came. My only obvious knickknacks were a thick turquoise ashtray made of glass that sat atop a speaker, into which I dropped my small change, and an inflatable silver alien with a wide head and a single eye, which I'd brought back from a trip to New York with Alex. Folded into a seated position, I'd placed him at one end of the records, as if spying on them from above. The room was precision-tooled to accommodate the only two postures I frequently employed back then: sitting (for work) and lying down (for watching movies, fooling around, or going to sleep).

2.

Alice and Pallas had only been living together for a month when I showed up. Pallas had rented the two-bedroom with her girlfriend of the moment, who—shit luck—left her the night before they were supposed to move in. Then Pallas met Alice at a private showing, and the latter, waiting on housing details from the Cité des Arts, decided to settle here for the time being. So Alice and Pallas had only known each other a short time, but they'd developed an immediate camaraderie, a camaraderie based on shared obsessions: fashion, celebrity, and hard cash, spending all their welfare money at Colette and periodically racing out of the bathroom screaming with enthusiasm or incredulousness over whatever articles they'd been reading in *Voici*. Alice, consumed with anorexia, was no longer the sweet little kid I used to encounter with her brother. Now, at age twenty-two, she was nothing but a bundle of arrogance, capriciousness, rage, and uncontrollable weeping, but her issues were easy to take compared to Pallas's princess act. Pallas was just emerging from a four-year fling with a girl who had always taken care of everything, and even if once upon a time she had been capable of fending for herself, now, at age twenty-six, that fling had eliminated any of her inherent street smarts.

Not content with a mere phobia for housekeeping, she couldn't handle dinners either, dinners that she would organize nonetheless, or more accurately where she'd simply drag our table out of the closet. Everyone, Alice and I as much as our guests, came duly warned: she'd be cooking, but nothing else. Therefore, it was only fair that each of us, in exchange, would dip our hands in the sink after—but her ego fooled no one. Any pushover who came to check on the broken TV, free of charge, couldn't expect her to stay and keep him company. When we ate chicken, it was breast meat or nothing. When we rode in cars, she'd only get in if she could have the front seat, and whenever she decided it was time to go home, then at the drop of a hat we'd have to oblige, whether it was convenient for the driver or not. The most minor aggravations (benefits procedures, utilities) completely wiped her out, and she was always hurting somewhere or other. And so she'd wander from room to room in her Versace mules like a weary, resigned old man. But, in her defense, Pallas did have routine migraines, suffered from chronic lumbago, and on top of that had every allergy in the book (dust, mites, pollen, fur, feather pillows). Knowing her as little as I did early on, that side of her personality was by far the most charming.

So in the beginning, I kept my distance. After seven years cohabiting with Nikki, one year spent bouncing around, and three more with Alex and her four roommates, all I aspired to was privacy behind closed doors. That was only possible at the end of the night, when the girls were done messing with the living room closets, but at least it was something. With Alice I was considerate, whereas Pallas I didn't even approach. In their minds, there was no doubt I would claim Alice's room once her studio opened up, but from my perspective, staying behind, just me and Pallas, felt out of the question. She had demanded I pay a third of the rent for what was still a shared living room, and so I found her unbearable. I kept it to myself, but it disgusted me that she wouldn't let me collect my things from Alex's place. Taking up more space in the living room, space that could be used for dinner parties, would have impinged on her mental health. If I stayed rather than find my own efficiency somewhere, which honestly wouldn't have cost me that much more, it was because I lacked the pay stubs and savings for a security deposit. But I wasn't worried about Alice's impending departure; by then, I would already be gone.

That is, until that moment finally came, in only the second month, before I'd had time to squirrel anything away, and so I found myself out on the balcony with Pallas, waving at Alice as she drove off in the moving van, asking myself what the hell I had gotten into. But strange as it might seem, Pallas underwent an immediate transformation. All it took was one phone call and a suitor of hers pulled up in a van to help me grab my things from Alex's; then, as I started bringing boxes into the now-empty room, Pallas drew me a bath, shouting about a mattress she had at a friend's place that I could now retrieve, and that she could loan me a little something if I wanted to buy whatever I was missing. It was like she'd been waiting for this moment all along, as if she knew that we'd only get closer once Alice had left. Alice, without being the direct cause, acted like a trigger for Pallas's more trying qualities, and Pallas could tell that if she wanted to butter me up, then she'd have to cut the crap. The urge to do so felt even more intense because our tastes had considerable overlap (Marilyn Manson, Kevin Spacey in *The Usual Suspects*, potato puffs). This hadn't escaped my notice, but I'd previously refused to indulge it, unprepared for what would result. I allowed her to serve me all evening, amused, expecting that it'd be back to the old Pallas the next day, but the charm didn't wear off over breakfast, which she presented on a tray, nor over lunch while I set up my equipment, and I couldn't tell, was it that she was taking a sudden interest in my work? But that night, as she started to yawn, I even held her back so our conversation could last a little longer, and longer still, until the early rays of morning. And from that moment on, we were inseparable.

Our newfound friendship gave rise to a need to assist Pallas. Naturally, early on I felt tempted to show that the more she delayed in stemming her phobias, the more risk they'd only amplify, but she got so distressed that I always compensated by doing three times as much work. So now I was the one in charge of everything, from the dishes to the laundry to tidying up her room. Attaching myself to Pallas meant taking on a second, even trickier problem: her total lack of ideas about what she wanted to do with herself. Her talent for drawing was left to rot in a corner while she tried all sorts of other endeavors, without ever persevering with any specific one. An exhibit of Polaroid self-portraits for a small conceptual gallery, a performance at a nightclub, vocals for a trip-hop cut that wound up in DJ sets for years: each of her attempts was successful except when it came to generating a follow-up. Sometimes, having multiple talents can be a handicap . . . To change would have required catapulting her into a country where she didn't speak the language, with no friends and no credit card—survival, pure and simple. From time to time, I pointed out that the people she envied, like Puff Daddy and Lauryn Hill, already multimillionaires by her age, had worked their asses off to get to the top. She fired back that she wasn't aiming for the top—at most for a rich husband who wouldn't object if she needed to get with women now and then. What she wanted was the superstar lifestyle, and in many ways she was already living it. From Marks & Spencer muffins to little bottles of Bon Marché orange juice to the latest Le Vernis from Chanel and daylight-hour cab rides, she never refused herself a thing. Whenever the bank sent her a letter, she'd call Mommy and Daddy, retirees from Nîmes who didn't really have the means to help but who always managed to mop things up, however appalled and stressed they were about their only daughter's misadventures. And in a show of solidarity, she would unearth little projects here and there, whether they were focus groups or medical tests—her particular habit, before swallowing even aspirin, of always nervously scanning the instructions for the list of "undesired or embarrassing" side effects . . . But that was Pallas. She'd barge in elated with some brand-new test product, then spend a whole month complaining of nausea, right back to her insufferable-princess ways, and yet one couldn't help but be proud that at least she was trying.

Among people who didn't know her that intimately, she was perceived in two different ways, both equally disastrous. Girls exasperated by her haughty side saw nothing but a pretentious bitch, whereas those fascinated by her inaccessibility wouldn't dare to make moves on her, scared to suffer the defeat of a lifetime. The same went for her occasional hookups with guys. Sex, in her case, was always rather complicated: if she was in love, then she couldn't take things further physically, but if sex came first, then she wouldn't fall in love. And that's how the two of us wound up sleeping together.

It happened by chance one night when we were talking about what we liked during sex. And because it felt so good, we started doing it all the time. But what should have remained recreational curdled into a nightmare when we were stupid enough to make out in front of Alex at the club. Alex didn't care if I had one-night stands, but she blew a gasket if she thought it might lead to something more. So she started turning up at all hours, nuzzling up to me in front of Pallas, trying to demonstrate who held the reins here. It was a funny thing, making her jealous; it altered those few post-breakup experiences when she'd persuaded me to sleep with her again, only to leave me the next day feeling sick and abandoned, ducking out without the slightest clarity about whether we were back together or not. But it completely humiliated Pallas, who it turned out was, in fact, looking for something more, to the extent that eventually I had to tell them both to fuck off. Alex was thrilled to be done, but Pallas was convinced that free of Alex's interference, we might still end up together. Maybe for her that was possible, but for me, even if I totally adored her as a friend, it felt like there wasn't any substance I could cling to. So it all came to a stop, and Pallas went through a pretty little rejection period of obnoxious sarcasm until, through my own patience and tenderness, I managed to tame her once again. And since we had never really said we wouldn't sleep together in the future, the seduction remained, binding us together that much more.

3.

And so, a year and change later, on a particularly damp night in May, I was slumped on the living room couch, where I typically landed when I found myself working too long. Whenever I had kept the bass thumping for hours, with the analog graphics dancing across the screen eventually looking like nothing but a bundle of jerking, tousled striations, like a lie-detector needle gone wild—that's when I'd drop down there to rest. Sinking into its leathery depths, which comfortably embraced the whole of my body, felt like connecting to a brain clearing machine; I got a soft calming sensation that let me review the fruits of that day's work, then joyfully, even impatiently, greet the prospect of doing it all over again upon waking the next day.

But this time, I was there to temper palpitations brought on by too much coke. Lying on my back, I glanced sideways at the huge unlit TV, its edges glowing in the half-light, and I giggled to myself about what a welfare worker would think if he came to check our lifestyle, the two of us benefits recipients—he would flip his lid, for sure. With TVs, VCRs, and stereos in every room, tons of clothing and CDs, monthly magazine subscriptions: all catch as catch can. Stuff that had fallen off the truck, publicist friends who brought us to sales or friends in retail who gave us their discounts. Even the cable hookup had been a ruse, asking Nikki to patch us into the upstairs neighbor's connection. Even with our respective incomes, Pallas and I were really struggling. Our housing benefits covered our shares of the rent, our welfare checks reduced the burden for the first ten days every month, but for the rest, we juggled things as best we could. Pallas borrowed from her credit card, and I borrowed from Pallas. We lived in nonstop anticipation of the next payment or advance, which then inevitably went out the window through repaying our debts.

A lot of things had changed in a year. Most positively, I had reconnected with Nikki, with Alice having sent him back my way; contrary to what I'd always been tempted to think, and which had made me hesitant to call him all these years, the fact that I had gotten into techno when he was still playing rock guitar didn't change any of the respect we had for each other. Whereas the worst change was Alice's anorexia, which now alternated with fierce bouts of bulimia. Alice was making conceptual photos—photos of feet—that met with instant success. Moving from "young fine-arts student" to "young hope for modern art" should have chilled her out some, but strangely enough, it only widened the gulfs she needed to fill. Advertorials for Swatch watches, action shots of Rollerblades, or pictures of Kangol bucket hats on clubbers' heads as they pissed at nightclub urine-troughs: she started to take on all kinds of derivative work.

Some part of her blithely reveled in trend-hopping like this—the reception from women's media slipped the bounds of indecency—but another part of her was truly unwell. That's the part that wanted to binge, vomit, then start back from the top, again and again until there was nothing left. Until the next time, that is. Except that even though she couldn't keep anything down, she was still gaining weight, and that drove her crazy.

I got up to grab a Coke from the kitchen. When I came back, my eyes lingered over the shelf in the entryway where we placed our mail and our keys. There was a pouch full of photos, a Post-it note in Alice's handwriting asking us to hurry up and tick off the ones we wanted to remove. They were pictures of the three of us at a party a few weeks back. Generally, looking back at old photos is how you notice things have changed, like when you stumble across the first season of a TV show and the clothes and haircuts make you cringe. But in this case, it was seeing ourselves in our present forms that called attention to it.

These days, Alice had shoulder-length hair like Björk, with brow-level bangs, but no hairdo was ever going to completely vanquish the sense of bulimia bloat. On her best days, her plump rosy cheeks and bulging electric-blue eyes made her look like a jolly little kid, but in her more troubling phases, like when these photos were taken, her face felt cruelly transformed. Her eyes had been sapped of all expression, nothing but blindly staring marbles, while her mouth, always so cheerful, mutated into a limply skewing orifice always open just a crack, like the stupor after an accidentally heavy infusion. Pallas wasn't really at her peak here either. Her shaved head had grown back into a long black bob with thick, blown-out bangs, like a more severe take on Bettie Page. Whenever her forehead showed, she refrained from wearing makeup or dressing too fancy, making her look young and fresh. But whenever she pulled out her gaudy red lipstick and fluffed up her bangs to accentuate her Spanish features, she looked ten years older. As for me, my expression changed with my hair, which was now very short, very disheveled, as if when I cut it, my gaze also got a trim . . . I looked *gone*. As long as I was working, I felt present, *involved*, but otherwise, from the moment I stuck my nose outside, it was like I entered self-protection mode, afraid things were about to go ass-over-tit . . .

I went back to the living room couch. Yeah, lots had changed in a single year. Alice was blowing more and more cash on clothes, but Pallas, through my intervention, was now making real strides toward limiting her overdrafts. Aside from the occasional dress she bought to refresh her evening wardrobe, she made do with mixing stuff together that she'd found at H&M (everyone, in fact, had started visiting H&M since their campaigns with Johnny Depp and Helena Christensen, whereas previously no one would have dared be seen wearing things that cheap). As for me, the change, which had kicked off with Alex, had been a slow one, but it now felt in-your-face. Gone were my years of '70s clothes, my years with Nikki; nowadays I was always in T-shirts, jeans, and sneakers. I initially resisted by specifically wearing rock shirts, but now I only wore ones that Alex had given me in bulk. Label logos (Ninja Tune, FCom, Giant Step, Warp, Output . . .) or détourned ad slogans—it felt like a competition with Alex: a contest to see who'd be first with a new style or could produce the coolest designs. We made them on a computer before transferring them to whatever cut-rate T-shirts we could purchase wholesale: she'd roll up wearing Cindy Crawford's head, with *supermodels suck* printed just above, and I'd counter with *suck me* over Evangelista's face. But even if Alex still found my jeans "too rock," there was no way I was going to switch to baggy pants like the rest of our scene. Three-sizes-too-big might look sexy with curves, but when you're tall and skinny, it makes you look like nothing. And no way was I forcing myself to buy Northwave skate shoes that gave you duck feet. Sneakers, fine, but not just any sneakers, always leather Adidas, pre-1980.

I wasn't sure if the change owed to a dead-end sort of feeling, or if I'd simply wanted to escape my sense of exclusion from Alex's universe, but there was one thing I felt sure of: my musical aspirations had shifted due to infatuation, not frustration. Before Alex, I played bass. I had only ever played with Nikki, both on record and on tour, and when we split I couldn't find another band. I felt caught in a loop, conscious that the things I liked to play had no future because they were too passé. Then I caught my first set by Alex in a bar, then my first rave, and then everything else transpired from there.

4.

I lowered my eyes to check the time on the VCR. It was close to one in the morning. I had done it. I had *stopped thinking*.

But now, it was already theoretically the next day, and it was time to face things head-on. So I got up and headed to my bedroom, and I picked up the envelope I had left on my bedroom carpet. I had given it a once-over with the afternoon mail: "Virgin" in the top-left corner. I had unsealed it so quickly when I got upstairs that I tore the first sheet inside. The letterhead read, "See enclosed for two copies of your contract." The fucking contract, beyond my wildest hopes, because it had been under discussion now for six months. Three pages with all sorts of clauses, and on the second page, my advanced sum written out longhand . . . Then back to page one, where they asked me to provide a bank account number for the transfer.

I don't know what came next—I think I started crying.

First I called Nikki, but I hung up as soon as I heard his voice. Even though he'd be nothing but extra-excited for me, the contract was a hundred times better than the one he'd just signed, so first I needed to figure out how to break the news. After that, I tried Pallas, who was out shopping with Alice, but I got her voicemail every time and hung up. After that, I stood outside the mailbox on the sidewalk, sticking a stamp to the envelope, with my bank account and signed contract inside. Afterward, I lay in my room, flat on my stomach, my cheek against the carpet, arms crossed beneath me, telephone and answering machine unplugged, afraid of getting a call to say they goofed up the sums. I stayed like that all afternoon, unmoving, listening to my heartbeat, and as soon as I closed my eyes, I saw doors opening onto dusty back-rooms where deluxe TB303s and TR909s, old Prophet-5 synths and Minimoogs all lay dormant just for me . . . After that, I visited Alex in the nineteenth arrondissement, pacing her bedroom up and down, shoving my copy of the contract in her face, trying to get her to lend me five hundred bucks to spend at her coke dealer's two streets over. And then to cap it all off, I headed to Notre-Dame.

There I was at the foot of this hulking behemoth I had always found incredibly moving. There I was telling myself that my time had come at last, that at last I was being given the chance to add my stone to its edifice . . . I was about to be something more than a former French rock bassist allowed to record a few electro sputterings for some crappy compilations. Here I was among tourists returning my smile but keeping their distance all the same, a little leery of my wide-open arms and my face that was drowning in joyful tears . . . A hundred thousand francs. A HUNDRED THOUSAND, HOLY FUCK! DO YOU KNOW WHAT THIS MEANS?

Then I ran back home, ran all the way from Notre-Dame to the Rue du Chemin-Vert, like Denis Lavant in whichever Carax movie, I was literally flying, shearing through the warm late-May air. Pallas had left a note by the entrance: she had stopped back home for a change of clothes and was wondering why I'd called so many times without even leaving a message. She gave me the address for a private showing she was heading to with Alice, then for the restaurant they were going to next, before popping in at Pulp where Alex had a set scheduled. I tried calling her a bunch more, but I kept getting her voicemail, and that's not how I wanted to break the news. I could have caught her in person anytime that night, but despite the obvious urgency, I didn't want to be in a crowd at the moment. I wanted to stay right here bumping coke until I couldn't anymore. So I wound up back on my bedroom carpet, on my back this time, and once again I just listened to my heartbeat. Except this time I thought it might give out, might ironically give up on me now, so close to attaining my goal. And maybe I would've liked that. To still be waiting for victory. To not have to measure myself against the impending outcome. Because all of a sudden, I was scared shitless. But I thought about Nikki and Alex and so many others who would have given anything for a contract like this, and I told myself I didn't have the right. Yeah, as dumb as it sounds, that's what I told myself. And then I tidied up the leftover coke and I made myself lie on the living room couch—that benevolent fucking couch.

Now it was one in the morning and I was standing in the middle of my room, envelope in hand and completely flustered. A hundred thousand francs . . . Wild, wild shit. My phone started ringing. At that hour, it had to be Pallas just now turning her cell back on, but I took my time to pick up. My head was spinning too fast—I needed to move as slowly as possible to prevent from overheating . . .

Right away, she asked "What's going on?" in a flat tone of voice.

I could hear traffic in the background. She must have gone out in the street to call.

"Take a guess."

"No . . . It can't be . . . The contract?"

"Yeah."

"Oh my god! That's awesome! How much? *How much?*"

I wished she could have been right there with me so I could hold up ten fingers, then open and close them ten times more.

"Ten times what I owe you," I said softly.

I could picture her eyes widening and instantly bringing a hand to her mouth to stifle a scream.

"Oh my god," she couldn't help repeating it, "oh my god, it can't be, that's impossible!"

So what if it's possible, I wondered as I heard her go back inside Pulp where the music was pounding, shouting for whoever wanted to hear, "Louise got a hundred-thousand-franc advance! Louise got a hundred-thousand-franc advance!"

chapter two

x-tazy roomalator™ rave on experience

1.

When the taxi finally pulled onto the top of Avenue de la Grande-Armée, I couldn't sit still any longer. I hoisted myself up as best I could to stick my upper body out the lowered car window, trying to catch a glimpse of the Place de la Porte-Maillot below. Beside me in the back seat, Alice and Pallas sulked.

"SUPER-MEGA RAGER!" I repeated over and over, trying to make them crack a smile.

Alice got annoyed by traffic jams, and Pallas was anxious to learn if I had E in my pocket. She hated when I took things, convinced that when I did, I got too blotto to . . . I don't know exactly, to be her friend anymore? She was probably pissed at the inscription on my new T-shirt, too, because the money she had loaned me that morning was supposed to go toward groceries. It was bright orange, just skimpy enough, with "drugs" written on it in white. Fine, five hundred bucks for a cotton sheath, it was a little excessive, but an opportunity like this called for high-level idiocy. I pulled the flier from the pocket of my jeans, unfolded it, and for the umpteenth time I reread its pretentious claim:

Friday, June 2
Detroit—London—Berlin—Brussels—Paris
The best the underground has to offer

It was all anyone could talk about for two months, ever since the flier first started making the rounds. No address, obviously, otherwise the cops would have camped out for two straight months, but also no named affiliations or any indication of sound quality, which was truly unusual. And more mysterious still, no DJ list. Even when you met this or that person who'd been booked, no one could provide the full set list, no one had the faintest idea who the foreigners would be. That kind of secrecy suggested either a wild first-class rave, like in the early days, or a hyper-commercial crapfest with smiley-face T-shirt stands and other baloney. But everyone had decided to go and have a look, just in case.

We were starting to see the Porte-Maillot in the distance, and it looked a mess, cars parked anywhere they could find, people strolling in between. We were still many hundreds of feet away and already things were bumper-to-bumper. I suggested we finish up on foot, but the girls didn't want to hear it. Mostly, they were sulking because they didn't know our final destination, when it was precisely that nothing was clear in advance that made the coming attraction so thrilling. My first rave with Alex . . . A real treasure hunt, that one, choosing which cars to follow by the strange getups of the people inside, stopping at every backwoods intersection to decode the chicken-scratch directions scrawled on road signs, and then, when we got close, dropping silent in the blackest night to suss out what might have been sub-bass or scan the sky for potential lasers. We eventually arrived at a giant warehouse—all it needed were showers to be a concentration camp. There was water streaming everywhere, and especially around the electricity sources, with sheet-metal walls so rusty that I avoided getting too close for fear of catching tetanus. But when Alex started mixing, it all became clear. Obvious. And it had been just the same with every subsequent rave, every night . . . By the edge of the square, we could finally move no farther; we stepped outside at last. Our butt cheeks were sticky with sweat from the leather back seat. On days like these, the pricks selling Coke cans for ten bucks apiece and little water bottles for fifteen made their weight in gold, while the entire city, the entire country even, dopily took it all in.

I made my hand into a visor, trying to pinpoint Alex's car, a metal-gray Ford Puma coupe. People were exiting the metro in clusters, others in cars expanded the traffic jam even farther. Everyone was heckling one another, waving greetings. It smelled like a highway rest stop, tires burning in the heat. Everywhere maps were unfolded over hoods, and everywhere the techno was pumping. But most astonishing were the cops, who were there to try and get the traffic moving, and who didn't even seem interested in the cause of all this mess. Yet these same guys would carry out raids across France, barging in, blithely shoving anyone who wanted to negotiate, barking "shut up or I'll knock your face in," mangling ten thousand francs' worth of gear in the process, just like that, for no reason at all. Unless these things were operating with really shady security, what the hell did they care if we blasted music without a single neighbor nearby? Half an E in your pocket got their panties in a twist, when they had pastis on their breath by seven in the morning. Why even do this job if they hated it so much? For the adrenaline rush they got every time they nabbed some unlucky fuck with skin that wasn't the right shade of white? But here they were, gesturing the cars to inch forward or back, ridiculous in their little pleated jackets designed by who-the-hell-knows. Perfect little sniper targets—watch them dance, tightly clenching their ass. That would teach them the meaning of terror. Nothing felt creepier than getting hounded by a cop, because who could you turn to in that case? I was more afraid of cops than any psycho I met on the street corner at night. The power these guys had was downright obscene. That was one reason, among many, that we all wanted our work to break through. They couldn't afford to force famous people to wait on the shoulder for half an hour, listening to them spout their little threats and dirty jokes. Scumbags.

We eventually located the others, all grouped around Alex, who despite being 5′2″ was always the first to get noticed. Alex, molded into a Marilyn Manson "Dope Show" promo shirt (that fucking bitch . . .), magisterial with her short dirty-blonde hair slicked back to accentuate her pure, angular face. She was there with Inès, her seventeen-year-old girlfriend, whom Pallas dashed over to hug. The entire scene coveted what Alex had with her, but I could barely even say hello, I found her so loathsome. Sort of a Natalie Imbruglia clone: the same unstructured brown bob with longer strands falling over her eyes; sure, she was pretty cute, but she gave off the same contempt as kids whose families might not be well off but who still think they're hot shit because they live in Versailles. Always decked out in low-rise pants fifteen sizes too big, short T-shirts hanging just above her belly-button piercing (as if she were the only one), always standing rigidly erect with both hands on her lower back, effectively thrusting her breasts and chin forward, while the rest of her body—her shoulders, elbows, and ass—slid backward, making her look like a freaky bird. Among the older set, like me, she couldn't stay consistent, acting pathologically shy to the point that she could only look at you from behind the locks devouring her face, which made her that much more unbearable. There was Eva, too, one of Alex's roommates, who, like her, was originally from Montpellier and was her best friend in childhood, and thus the only one Alex never dared treat like a flunky. A short twenty-six-year-old brunette, a little chubby, with soft sea-green eyes, she was different from the rest, and not just because she had once been hetero or because she was the only one of us with a "normal" job in retail. Even if she was the one who went out the most, the one who took the most E and never had a serious thing to say, always with the blonde jokes, schlepping around tons of Hello Kitty kiddie baubles, she was like our den mother. Maybe because she was always cooking up a storm whenever we left the club, but even more so because, as a recent Paris transplant, she had no history with the scene here, and therefore shared no exes, no conflicts, with anyone. And Gayle was there, Eva's girlfriend from London who came for a week every month, her adorable baby face framed by short brown curls, practically sucking her thumb in her sleep, always loopy in an acid haze. And Julia was there, the same age as Eva, also Alex's roommate, who worked the cloakroom at Pulp but more importantly was an unparalleled dancer and juggler, huge and imposing with her heap of red dreads constantly whipping around like a hard rock singer. Your prototypical Midwestern teen: robust, wholesome, and corn-fed, yet a tireless party girl perma-stoned on weed. Little Cyril was also around, already shirtless, already spritzing himself with water. Alex's little brother—he wasn't much taller, but he exercised a lot, buzzed brown hair with a gnarly depilated torso that he sculpted relentlessly, never missing a chance to flaunt his six-pack. And lastly, her brown hair also buzzed, looking tan and rather strong, standing somewhat slouched in a form-fitting black shirt open to reveal a WonderBra that looked ready to explode—this had to be Jessie. A DJ, from Nîmes just like Pallas, who had just settled in Paris to make music with Alex, and whom everyone always talked about but whom I'd still never happened to meet. In the spitting image of hundreds of others pacing the surroundings—except for Pallas and Alice, who were wearing dresses, and me, faithful to my habitual snug jeans and Adidas—our whole little gang wore short, form-fitting T-shirts (whether G-Star, E-Pure, Lady Soul, or Tim Bargeot), wide pants (Carhartt, Dickies, Homecore, Goodvibes, or Kanabeach), and bulky athletic shoes (Northwave, Globe, Oakley, New Balance, Nike, Reebok, or Fila). But somehow it suited them so well that I couldn't picture it any other way.

"How many of us?" shouted Alex, her eyes locked to my shirt's inscription. "I'm taking Eva, Gayle, Inès, and my brother; the rest of you are going with Fred."

That bitch. I was supposed to be taking her shitty ride for once. And now, all because of my T-shirt, she wanted to find this place before I did. I couldn't understand it—hers was cooler than mine anyway. Her Puma was sparkling in the light behind her. Through its open door, I could see the chrome dashboard, the built-in CD player, and the clean floor mat, with the Puma proudly bumping. When the two of us had been together, cars like this had always been our solemn dream. We always figured that one day we'd move to San Francisco and get a house with big bay windows, like Sharon's in *Basic Instinct*, out by Stinson Beach, with two Lotus Elans parked out front. And now that she could get herself something comparable on credit, I still hadn't taken a spin inside it in the entire month that she'd had it. I was mad at her for that, and for so many other things. After all, I had her name tattooed on my stomach, and she had mine on hers (I had "Alex" and she had "Lou," each in the same place, between the navel and our bush, in beautiful, thick, blood-red, black-embossed Gothic letters). Sure, to be fair, it was rare I could see her without getting furious at some point or other. I was mad that she had goaded me into leaving her, I was mad that she never cheated on Baby Inès when she had been fine doing it to me, but more than anything I was mad that she kept periodically letting it slip that someday somehow, we'd wind up together again. The problem wasn't whether I wanted that or not; I was mad because she was making my decision for me.

I was on the verge of calling her out for not letting me in her car, but then Jessie grabbed my arm: "Sick shirt!" in a beautiful throaty voice, a funny contrast with her broad shoulders (which made Alex so exasperated that she pulled Inès in close to suck some face). "I'm Jessie—want to help me load my records?" Alice tapped my shoulder to ask who Fred was. I pointed to a shaved-head guy from Radio FG, wearing a black T-shirt with white letters that read *Home-Fucking Kills Prostitution*, then I looked in all directions to see if I could spot Guillaume, who had said he was going to meet us here. Guillaume was a young skater we ran into anywhere we went, who for a while now had been fixated on me, and fifteen days earlier I had finally let him get a little closer. His too-too-perfect figure, like he'd stepped right out of a Calvin Klein undies ad, bewitched anyone who liked guys, while the remaining few unfrightened by hetero sex couldn't really see why I'd chosen a man so young—even calling him a man was pushing it. But I knew what I was getting into . . . Plus, the deal we made suited me just fine. I had suggested we keep our numbers to ourselves, that we'd only go home together whenever we ran into each other. Possibly he only agreed hoping to get his hooks in me later on, but I could deal with that when the time came.

We went to Éperon, about forty miles from Rambouillet. The hard house was thumping, vibrating our half-lowered windows, and every time the refrain came back around, Jessie and Julia shouted in unison *I-DON'T-NEED-THIS-SHIT!* Jessie was a true paradox, simultaneously vulgar in appearance and terribly feminine, with her breasts springing from her shirt. Simultaneously a teddy bear, with her pale gray eyes and freckles under her tan, and a fucking ball of energy I couldn't wait to see mix. Sitting in front, Pallas stayed turned in our direction but wasn't looking at anyone in particular. She was put off not being in the same car as Baby Inès. Those rare times she found herself around me, Alice, and the little baby, she didn't know where to turn her head. The baby was her favorite friend for dancing and gossip, Alice for consumption and high society, and me for our homey cocoon. Here, obviously the baby was her preference, which irritated Alice, already sulking that she was in this pale-green Clio and not Alex's much flashier Puma. There were moments when I, too, could get jealous about Pallas's preferences, but right now my only thought was the rave. From Fred's refusal to check where we were going on the map, I could tell that he already knew: FG must have been a partner, or maybe even the organizer. So I stared at him in the rearview mirror, trying to frown my way into making him mentally broadcast the info we were waiting for, but all in vain. He just smiled, and I pouted, thinking they had better make sure this all worked out, because otherwise, after so much mystery, they were going to look like total idiots.

2.

From the outside, the setup resembled the yearly Trans Musicales rave in Rennes. Two smaller circus tents linked to a larger one via clear tunnels, like the housing insulation in *E.T.*

"Not very original," I whispered to Fred as we headed for the larger one.

He just smiled. We moved up the long line leading to the entrance, he said something to the bouncers, and they let us in. The big room, already half-full, was awash in juddering strobes; there was heavy, pounding techno. You could barely see the DJ in back atop a very high stage, looking tiny in a blue beam of light. On either side of the stage were large screens projecting multicolored spirals. So far, nothing unusual. But then we lifted our eyes to a big display panel like they have in airports:

HOUSE STAGE

11:00–00:30 : *Markus Nikolai (Ger)*
00:30–02:00 : *DJ Jaws (Fra)*
02:00–03:30 : *Freaks (UK)*
03:30–05:00 : *Herbert (UK)*
05:00–06:30 : *Trash 2000 (Fra)*

TECHNO STAGE

23:00–00:30 : *The Hacker (Fra)*
00:30–02:00 : *Jessie (Fra)*
02:00–03:30 : *DJ Hell (Ger)*
03:30–05:00 : *Kevin Saunderson (USA)*
05:00–06:30 : *Laurent Garnier (Fra)*

EXPERIMENTAL STAGE

00:00–01:30 : *Torgull (Fra)*
01:30–02:30 : *Micropoint (Fra—live)*
02:30–04:00 : *Manu Le Malin (Fra)*

04:00–05:30 : *Liza 'N' Eliaz (Bel)*
05:30–06:30 : *Atari Teenage Riot (Ger)*
Visuals: V-Form, Alien's Mother, 4 Spaces

"FUCK," Jessie roared, "I'm mixing with Kevin Saunderson! I'm mixing with Kevin Saunderson! I don't fucking believe it!"

"Shit," said Julia, "too much good stuff at once."

"Holy shit," I added, "you two and Alex are the only girls."

Fred probed my reaction with a wry glance, but I couldn't think of anything to say. This wasn't some hypercommercial rave with merch stands and posters thanking sponsors. There was the requisite FG notice by the entrance, but otherwise there was nothing but a long initial folding table with water, which four guys were serving into paper cups from plastic jugs, and then a second table with three more sitting beneath a Doctors of the World banner, offering to test your E. In short, only the essentials. Nothing but a big spartan room with incredible sound. And Fred's look seemed to be saying, have a little faith sometimes.

Alice and Pallas asked if Fred could lead them to the others, while I followed on Jessie's and Julia's heels toward the edge of the room. Jessie and I carried flight cases while Julia carried both Jessie's and her own record bags. The flashing strobes revealed and concealed the hair already plastered to foreheads, the torsos already glistening, and I couldn't explain how so many people were here when we must have been among the first to arrive. When we reached the barriers, we set everything down so Jessie could find her pass. The stage on the other side was over ten feet high, with a large space between the barriers and the audience. The security guy was standing guard with crossed arms, as if he could already taste the thrill of sending us packing. Was he brain-dead or something, didn't he see our records? Jessie finally, triumphantly waved her pass and gestured that we were with her. The guy shook his head no. “WHAT?” Jessie shouted over the music. Julia then crouched to rifle through her own bag, pulled out her own pass, which she handed to me, and as she stood back up to her full height, she made her hands into a megaphone to shout in the guy’s face: “YOU’VE GOT TO LET ME THROUGH, I’M PART OF THE SHOW!” The guy calmly asked for her name, spoke into his walkie-talkie, then released the button to await their response. He stared me down with the chilliest gaze imaginable while I slipped the pass around my neck. Maybe it was the “drugs” on my T-shirt that had set the bastard off. His answer came through, and he reluctantly freed a gap for us. Jessie and I went off to the left, skirting the stage. We bumbled our way up a metal staircase with the bags over our shoulders and the flight cases hoisted with both hands underneath. We set everything down behind The Hacker, who motioned to say things were already really hot in here. Jessie checked her watch by the flame of her lighter, shouted that she still had half an hour, then we clattered down the stairs and plotted a course to the green room.

A half-dozen girls were applying makeup before a long table with overhanging mirrors and copious tiny bulbs. Julia was so nearsighted she had to get within four inches of the mirror to draw on her eyeliner. She made a pouty expression, pointing her chin in the others’ direction, at their wild manes, cat eyes, and metallic tunics, like a cross between *Mad Max* and *Quest for Fire*.

“I-fuc-king-can’t-be-lieve-it,” with extra emphasis, “I’m mixing with Kevin Saunderson.”

She took a few steps back, dipped her hand in her jeans pocket, then beckoned us over. I refused her extended pill, I already had what I needed. She gestured to take it anyway. I looked all around before examining the E's design: a hand, my favorite kind—might as well start with this one. Discreetly, I brought it to my mouth, the other girls did the same, and we returned to the green room.

I reflexively marched upstairs again with Jessie, but once behind the decks, I felt superfluous. Not that I needed a reason to be there, but ever since Alex, I felt out of the habit. Jessie had flipped one of the flight case lids down and gestured for me to sit if I wanted, then she started sorting her records. Just like Alex . . . Just like every DJ on the planet: both hands quickly skimming the stacks, pulling certain records out to slot them farther forward or backward, leaving other sleeves sticking halfway out to make them easier to find. With Alex, I always stayed in the booth, or stayed onstage depending on the layout, and my eyes never left her hands. A hundred percent locked in to whatever she was playing, my eyes registering every perfect transition or occasional tempo shift. As soon as she took off a record, I'd receive it and stow it, and by the end, I was so good I could guess what she'd play next, keeping the vinyl close at hand and blindsiding her every time. My goal had been becoming indispensable, and that had happened, but not in the way I'd hoped . . . The back of my neck was starting to prickle, my mouth was getting dry now. Jessie was untangling her headphone cord, shouting that things were about to get mental. I motioned that I was heading down.

I melted into the crowd, which was now substantially thicker. Beams of blue light swept over sweat-drenched faces. A strong pot smell was in the air. I carved my way into the mass so I could face Jessie dead-on; she had put her headphones on and was now lining up her first record. Little by little the audio faded until there was nothing but a vague drone. Some discontented murmuring commenced. Acid sounds started to rise. My feet were already moving of their own accord. The sound started sprawling over its quiet base, swirling here and there, until the low end started taking shape. Slow, watery, I was starting to feel its grip in my stomach. Around me, inchoate stirrings. I slipped the pass back under my T-shirt. A shattering burst of Aphex Twin's laughter exploded once, twice, and then abruptly dropped out, catching everyone by surprise, a tremendous surge of percussion, with a single cry rising from the crowd, the sudden realization that this was going to kill. The strobes came back, accelerating the movements all around me, instantly altering my perception of how far I was from everyone else. My feet were keeping time, my head following the sound. Loops overlapped, unfolded, weaved all kinds of structures, infinite trails, and my brain wanted to follow them all, one after the other. One second the accent was up, and the next the accent was down. The inversions jolted me, twisted me around, brought me back up. On giant screens, spirals morphed to match the sonic whirlwind. I looked at my undulating hands as they opened and closed. My arms were now extensions of the rest of my body, first up and then down and then up again, whipping like cables, and my eager eyes were soaking it all in. Everything around me seemed a little clearer, a little more dazzling. Twinkling eyebrow rings, nose rings, earrings, beads of sweat on foreheads, water drops from drinks pearling on chins, gazing deeply, unbridled, into all their faces. All ecstatic to be there, in this strange place that they'd invaded for one night only. All transported by the magic of Total Music, by the lights and the crowd.

By the time I noticed I needed a drink, I couldn't tell if it had been hours or minutes. The water line up front was too long. I pulled out my pass for the security guy, who still hadn't eased up; I climbed the stairs and found Julia next to Jessie. She was crumbling some pot in her palm. I got my lighter to fire it up, and in three fluid motions she had rolled it, licked it, and tightened it up. She lit the spliff, passed it over, and left in search of water. I stayed to take a drag, nodding my head back as I watched Jessie from behind. She was crazy fit. Her head and her whole upper body were violently pounding. She was super-rough with her records, pulling them out with no regard for the sleeves, which went flying, unceremoniously plonking them down on the turntables. Shrugging her shoulder to knock her headphones back to her ear, she tested the tempo, adjusted it, and then sent it on its way. Julia returned with a bottle. Jessie turned to face her: "TAKE THIS," she shouted. A breather track had transitioned into furious jungle beats, and Julia's body shot straight up; I had to immediately back away if I didn't want to get clocked. She bounded forward and back, her dreads flying every which way as she popped and locked to the ricocheting, disjointed rhythms. Jessie turned to me: "DO YOU KNOW THE NEW DJ RUSH?" I shook my head no while I drank. The beats reached a paroxysm and then cleanly cut away, and Jessie started yelling with the rest of the room as the techno pace returned with shrill force. Then all the sound dropped out again, leaving nothing but the bass and a man's voice, a white-person voice, cold and ironic, whispering *I wanna . . . I wanna fuck you all night*. My entire body drew me to the staircase, hurtling down to reenter the crowd at the very moment the rhythm exploded in full. Everyone's arms were raised. Anyone who says this music is cold and inhuman should have their head checked. The bass kept plowing, a deaf, blind locomotive climbing upward with that voice tirelessly repeating its urge to fuck you all night. I thought about the other room, where Alex also must have been totally killing, and the third room where the live sets meant even more guaranteed hits. I wished I could be everywhere at once.

Someone grabbed my shoulder: Jessie, shouting that she was going to check the other spaces, that with any luck Alex's set would still be going. I hadn't even clocked that we had transitioned to DJ Hell. The plastic tunnel felt cool and deserted, techno subsided as hard house took the fore, less fast, more lugubrious. This room was smaller, and the heat pushed you back. Here they had multiple light beams sweeping the crowd, going from orange to yellow to red to green, and sure enough, Alex was still mixing, tiny as she was on the stage in back. Jessie pointed that everyone must be right up front. It was funny seeing Alex on such a large stage. I had already seen her spin at even bigger parties, but this was the first time I had witnessed her from so far away, here at the heart of the crowd. We inched up slowly, weaving between people, careful not to interrupt their flow. My eyes slipped from one shaved blond head to another, a whole swarm of them, but none had Guillaume's face, my precious skater. And sure enough, the others were all up front. Fred looked unshackled: it was awesome to see him like that, somewhere outside the FG offices, where you'd only catch him coming and going, always running late, frustrated by his lack of freedom and resources. Little Cyril's arms were windmilling so fast that they looked fluid. Gayle was pushing herself forward on invisible ski poles. Eva was taking short steps, dancing and going "woot woot" with her index fingers pointed at Alex. Alice had her arms running down her body with her head thrown back. And Pallas and Inès were face-to-face, hopping from one foot to the other. It was so bizarre seeing Inès in public. I never danced to Alex's sets, I just kept watch. That's how I lost her, and that's how Inès kept her. Something about the distance—that whole attitude drove Alex away . . . I lit a cigarette and stayed in place, taking her in, seven feet above me, with the decks positioned closer to the edge than they were in the other room.

She was in her element now. Always essentially static, always the same delicate unflappability, rewinding the record to stall it in the right position, but her face didn't look nerve-wracked anymore—just dope-wracked. It was always flagrantly apparent when she took it. Her eyes, a shade of brown that would usually make pupil sizes difficult to gauge, would get so shiny that they became teary and golden. Her naturally drooping lids would puff up instead, making her look like a dazed lizard, while her already ultra-white skin started tending toward gray, her features suddenly hollowing out like the triangular inflatable-alien head in my room. And of course there was her breath, her breath that started smelling like Stoptou licorice. Those fetching little candies you find at market stalls lined with countless bags of sweets, where you use a steel scoop to fill one of the little clear bags on hand and then weigh it—candies for kids, innocently named, and which every junkie in Paris sucks all day long to suppress their puke. There she was, really feeling herself in her "Dope Show" shirt, and all that was missing was her giant name flashing up behind her like a music video. But I had to admit: being out of it never prevented her from perfect mixing, it was only on the comedown that her concentration faltered.

Now that my feet were moving again, and without me even realizing, my eyes started lingering on a certain screen. Majestic ripples of analog feedback exploded over manga images, alternating with Hong Kong scenes where shootouts and hyper-athletic stunts played out in their color-negative. The more far-out the video team got, the more sublime everything immediately became . . . My eyes were now back on Alex, who waved to Eva that she'd be leaving it right there after the next track. I wondered how she was taking my contract situation. If our relationship had been less complicated, then I'd have been making this record with her. We made a good team when we were together; the ways I tinkered with her sets from the shadows made her gigs much more original . . .

“Why that face?” Eva shouted.

I shrugged.

“Hey!” she shouted again. “Why do blondes have triangular caskets? Because they’ve always got their legs spread!”

She was so great. What I would have given for a history with her. Aside from being really sexy, she also had something that no one else had. Something healthy, happy to be alive, responsible. Something that made you want to nest in her arms and let her take care of the rest.

“FUCK, WHY THAT FACE?” she merrily repeated, taking my hands to lift up my arms.

Yeah, it was time for that second E.

3.

Later, I wound up back in the big room, still lit only in blue, and once again behind the decks drinking water. Behind DJ Hell thumped tribal techno, spilling over with percussion.

Onstage, the beams had gone to war: serpentine, gyrating fluorescents versus fiery torchlight. I drank a little more and then went back down to find Jessie. She was dancing with a slight hunch in her back, her hands in her front jean pockets, a smoke wedged into the corner of a rapturous-looking smile. I moved only my feet to give the rest of my body a rest, clasping my hands around the back of my neck, elbows spread, conscious of two or three men staring at my tit-hugging T-shirt. I let myself get carried away, eyes wide open and fixed upon the flaming batons tracing figure eights. Despite the deafening percussion, it felt like I could clearly distinguish the sounds of the torches cleaving through the air, even the people’s breaths when they spat out flames. Occasionally emerging from amid all this light came Julia's body, swaying her shoulders, her elbows, her hands, her tensing-releasing fingers. She was also great. But she was also already with someone. A set of arms squeezed me around the waist. A second later I glimpsed Guillaume's naked torso and broad shoulders, his eyes nothing but pupils under the brim of his bucket hat, and his heavy mouth molded to mine, all heat and moisture. My tongue explored his gums, the minty taste. My skin had grown infinitely sensitive to his fingers as they grazed the creases of my arms. He was a good kisser, for a man. Whenever I told myself, *how about a boy for a change*, right away all I could think about was how much better it was with a girl . . . I opened my eyes, wondering how the toilets looked, until I spotted Jessie back onstage, standing behind a powerfully built Black guy with clear headphones. In the audience, the whistles were coming thick and fast. Guillaume slipped around my back and slid his fingertips into my front jean pockets, trying to open up some space so he could get to my crotch. I could smell the sweat from his torso sticking to my tee. Turning around to kiss him some more, I saw Eva forging a path, followed by Gayle, Inès, Pallas, and Alice. I wondered, vaguely, where Alex could be. Maybe in the middle of getting paid, or still listening to the set after hers. Everyone, or almost everyone, had stopped dancing, everyone was screaming. Kevin Saunderson put his headphones on, everyone clapping and shouting at the top of their lungs, and he had a big smile on his face. And why not—all the guys from Detroit, or from anywhere, always got a much better reception here than in their home country. We could hear the first track taking shape behind a mess of percussion that was starting to fade. Pure Detroit techno, minimal but velvety, and complete finesse. People who don't know their shit think the job consists of inconspicuously stringing two tracks together, but it's much more complicated than that. The real magic comes from your capacity to maintain some sonic unity while surging out in all directions. When I thought about what first drew me to this music, it seemingly had something to do with what it did to my head, but also to my belly. Something sexual. Guillaume stepped back to regain control of his arms and I shut my eyes, borne aloft by the flow.

The sound's heart had become a torrent of lava streaming over my brain, clearing away whatever resistance remained behind the private movie playing out across my eyelids. A crystal sea had opened inside me, as far as the eye could see. Beneath my feet, now hovering off the ground, I could see all living things, a world of roots and tiny creatures calmly going about their business, with neither fear nor urgency. I was alone in these surroundings, but I knew that if I opened my eyes, then they'd all be right there. And they were feeling just like me. Each of them on their own trip, but all riding the same wave. All conscious of the one true thing: the rhythm. All there to let themselves get carried away, far away from everything happening around them. Far away from everything we botched before we even tried. Far away from the few things we had, which were completely separate from the things that we wanted. All there to surrender to the here and now, to the music's relentless repetition.

chapter three

e: day two / strap-on god

1.

Face down, I opened my eyes to sunlight flooding the bedroom. At first, I couldn't tell by what unfortunate circumstance my blinds had been left open. Then, little by little, it all came back to me. Guillaume and I absconding from the rave without saying goodbye, catching a ride from a guy so plastered we made him pull over twice on the shoulder and spin around in circles to sober up. The walk after he dropped us off around République, both of us stopping every ten feet to make out against cast-iron shop grates, then setting out again whenever a cop car slowed down. Helping ourselves to pasta and tomato sauce while watching the end of a TF1 documentary showing sandpipers hunting in swamps, and then, at last, fucking for a while before the open shutters. Guillaume wanted to give the employment agency a spectacle, all the workers coming in for a long, mindless day's work across the street: here were two young, free, and beautiful slackers furiously knocking boots . . . Except it was Saturday, so instead all we had was a neighborhood bum catching sight of my ass cheeks, probably red from rubbing against the balcony railing. I spotted him when I thrust my head backward to hang out into nothingness: there he was, directly below, marking the beat with his slow and steady jerking.

I shoved my head under the pillow, leaving my mouth just enough space to cry out, "GUILLAUME?" There he was, bared chest and bucket hat, his beige Dickies unbuttoned with his black underwear peeking out. I softened, asking him to close the blinds, and I watched him carry out his orders before leaving the room. How had I gotten to the point of doing it with a guy like this? Other guys, Nikki and all, had something anomalous about them . . . Whereas with this one, his allure was like any other guy's his age. Probably something in our day and age that called for it, that made it coincide with the music we listened to . . . He reappeared with a tray, which he carefully placed beside me. Cup of tea, glass of orange juice, toasted muffins with Nutella. I sat up. I was aching all over, my ears were ringing. It was just as hot as the day before; I immediately smelled my sweaty armpits as I rose.

"Is Pallas around?" I asked, grabbing for the orange juice.

"Don't think so. I gotta go, need to test the new rail in La Défense, it's supposed to be sick."

I suppressed an itch to burst out laughing, don't get home too late, darling, the kids don't see you much these days! Joking aside, he was legitimately good: fourth in rail-grinding for whatever X-Games competition, and other young people in the street would sometimes stop him to ask for advice. He buttoned his pants and bent down to kiss me. "I've got five minutes, though," he murmured, gently tugging the duvet to expose my legs.

"Oh, well, if you say so!" I giggled. "I think we can make that work!"

We had already done it so much that this was starting to feel like one long session.

"OK, cool," he replied, faux-indifferent.

I watched him sit in the computer chair and bend to grab the socks from his sneakers. I liked his round shoulders, his skin that was golden from all the hours of skating. Most of all, I liked his pants: their pliant zipper went down easy while he sat. I pulled my robe over and slipped it on before getting up and shutting my bedroom door. His green eyes and fleshy lips made him look like a little kid. But there was nothing little-kid about the rod beneath his fly. I only had to graze it to feel it getting hard. He pulled the bucket hat down over his eyes, indulgently reclined in his seat, with his hands crossed around the back of his neck. "What are you thinking?" I purred as I exchanged my hand for one of his. They always say a woman's never going to do it as well as another man, unless they do it exactly the same way, with the same hand that they use, with the wrist tilting on the same axis—or at least that's what they say. Me, I've always loved to watch men handle it themselves, that ecstatic bond between them and their own hand, it gives them this air of smugness that I honestly find intoxicating. I also knew I wouldn't endure long enough to get him there under the wire . . . I knelt to take him in my mouth for a few seconds, just long enough to hear him start sighing shorter and shorter, enough to see his abs contract with his body stretched out in his chair. Then I straightened up to sit on his knees. I held my robe just open enough for him to see how ready I was, but I waited to sink down on him, aware that the chafing was going to burn. I was also holding out for his gaze to become slightly supplicant, at which point I went to it, all the way down, gently, and it burned like crazy, but this was what I'd been banking on. The moment when those child-eyes would widen, his blood-red lips bitten, his hands no longer knowing where to grasp to make me move a little faster. Except with the more durable ones, the ones more expert with their hands, fucking guys would probably never be enough for me, but either way it still felt good, and besides it gave my head a break from girls, who I always fell too in love with too quickly, for the better sometimes but far more often for the worse.

2.

Out on the landing, I tried to keep my robe shut while I waved goodbye to Guillaume. I saw his bucket hat turn and disappear, as the crackly audio from his Walkman's digital hardcore started fading. Farther down, a hand was steadily slapping and grabbing the handrail coming up, and then I saw Alex appear, climbing the stairs two steps at a time. Her hair, still slicked back from the night before, had a mind of its own now: a little hurricane fit for a Muppet, in a black T-shirt with pink punk lettering—*Goldorak's Not Dead*—with big Northwaves and spiffy gray American cop pants with black bands running down their sides. Except, as was often the case, whatever brand this was didn't carry them in her size, so she was really swimming in them.

"So! You screwed your skater!" she burst out as she shot into my room.

She dashed straight for my CD piles, where right away she found what she was looking for and popped it in the stereo. "You silly little slut, you," she added, going back to slam the door. I crossed my arms, deadpan, watching as she slipped her sneakers off with her heels. She hated when I slept with other people but, at the same time, she loved it. It made her feel bad and she loved it. I sat on the edge of my bed, flapping my robe back over my thighs, and my ears pricked up with the rising noise, the repetitive beats, like something being hammered, the intro to "Mr. Self Destruct" by Nine Inch Nails, the same thing she always wanted to hear when we fucked.

"I have one hour," she was very precise, while she whipped her legs from her pants, dangerously teetering on one leg.

"What are you thinking?" I said, shoving a pillow behind my back. "I've already dosed."

She bit into half a muffin.

"What are *you* thinking!" she exclaimed, her mouth full, as she climbed on top.

Sitting on me, she pinned my wrists behind my head, gently rocking to the heavy, stabbing machine-music. "You were so hot last night," she growled, "who told you you could do that?" and then she fixed me with a smack. Before I knew it, her face was already buried in my neck. Her teeth sank into my throat. I had to ball my fists in her hair before she loosened her grip. For a second she sized up my shoulders, sliding her gaze down to her name's tattoo on my stomach before her bony hips wedged between my thighs. Our bellies were already gluing together with sweat. Her lips hunted mine and shunned them at the same time. I pretended the struggle to get back on top was for real, wondering how I found the imagination, every time, to make this seem like an actual fight, when all it would take was lifting a knee to send her flying, she was that light. Once I managed it, her hands instantly tugged on my shoulders to pull me back down. Then came another slap, and another, and another, until I complied. I ignored her belly-button ring—I hate those things: fiddle with them once and they get infected—and I ignored the red-black letters of my name on her skin, and I circled her clitoris instead. Her nails tilled through my scalp amid guitars that were all saturation, with Trent Reznor's degenerating voice, belligerent and sharp. When I finally touched her, she involuntarily moaned, and then nothing. Our whole deal was holding it all back until the other person's gone nuts, legitimately violent, and that's when things really start. I acted like I wanted her on all fours, and so she turned around, I collapsed onto her back, and she understood all too late that I still had the dildo. That it was under the mattress like it used to be. Old habits, hard to shake, yeah, yeah. It wasn't hard to attach it while restraining her movements. My teeth kept her spine in place, long enough for me to coat the dildo with lube, then the tip of my thumb started playing with her anus. I was going to wait here calmly for her emptiness to feel intolerable. She knew she'd only be entitled to it if she asked, that she had to dare to say it out loud. She turned her head to one side and I saw her lips tremble, but I pretended not to hear anything and now I was the one doing the slap. She said I had to, I had to fuck her up the ass. So then suddenly I went for it, eliciting one short whine and then nothing else, just like before. I restrained her hands to prevent her from touching herself, and when I say I went for it, I mean I really went for it. She must have had a prostate to like it this much—how else? And that asshole Reznor bellowing about total control. She yelled about hating me, all so I would say I loved her, but I had stopped saying that kind of nonsense ages ago. I swiveled us to have her forehead against the wall. With every pelvic thrust, her head came that much closer to bursting right through it. Eventually, I released her hands, and she hastily spit on her fingers to make them a little slicker. She let me know she was about to come, her body tensed to its breaking point, and then all at once she asked me to stop, but I kept going even harder, like that would teach her for bailing whenever she pleased. She started coughing, choking, trying to keep from bashing into the wall. Without removing the dildo, I unstrapped the belt to instead use my hands. That got it moving even faster, even deeper, all the strength in my arms being put to the test. Tears started streaming down her cheeks, her hiccups matching the rhythms on the record in the background. I managed to get her to face me, and at that very second, nothing mattered in the world except this undone face before me.

We rested side by side on the soaking sheets, short of breath. She was the first to crack, to get up and grab the Coke bottle off the stereo. I patted around for the remote and brought the music all the way down. I could feel the trickling sweat in my armpits. It was the early afternoon; it would only be getting hotter. The occasional slammed doors in the street, reaching us through the open windows—they felt labored, fatigued. I eventually rolled onto my side to get up. The Coke tasted warm and flat. I drank another swig anyway, and ignoring Alex's pleas, I recapped the bottle and left it by the stereo. She elbowed me in the stomach, and it almost made me spit out what was left in my mouth. By the time I transferred it to hers, there wasn't much less. She spat it out on the sheets, whining about the temperature, then crawled over me to grab the stereo remote—things were only just beginning.

Her plan was a direct assault, because with me that's just how things were done. Sitting on my back, she pushed my face into the sheets, which were now damp with Coke, and it was easy to picture her in a movie shoving a six-shooter barrel into some guy's neck. She twisted my arms, tied my wrists together with what must have been a knee sock, and then I felt the cold lube being indiscriminately applied. The dildo went in gently, pulled all the way out, then went back in, this time to the end, making me clench my teeth, wondering about a sudden impulse for the bathroom. She raised the music's volume, and we were on our way. A slow, sustained in-and-out, rending me a little more each time. I could already tell, the sheets beneath me were all I could rely on to bring me to a climax. With my nose crushed into the mattress, I felt the residual surges of E. My entire body was levitating, I couldn't feel the house, the bed, anything around me. But I could feel Alex there beside me, or no doubt on top of me, and Reznor was there, too, calling out to me, bellowing anew of his omnipotent control. I knew from experience that things were far from over. She had gone maybe six months without cheating on Inès, but if this was how she started seeing me again, there was no way she was going to leave me in peace. It was important that I meet someone else . . . With every shift of my pelvis, searching for any fold in the sheets, she balled her fists in my hair and tugged my neck to its bendable limit. Did she act this way with that seventeen-year-old kid? She pressed her mouth to my ear and said that one of these days, she was going to show up with all her gear, and then I wouldn't be able to refuse. Like any pure white: all it needs is a little bloodstain. She withdrew the dildo, unbound my wrists to let me turn around, and then she settled in the other way round. My hands groped for a pillow to elevate my head. Early on, I had struggled to adjust to her height, but soon enough it just became another fact: a perfect fit for one another. So that when we split, at first adjusting to "normal"-sized bodies felt frankly unpleasant. Maybe that was the reason we lasted so long, because we fit too well. She called me "bitch," I called her "motherfucker"; in the club we would circle each other like panthers, or violently tear into each other for the whole world to see, but back home, once sleep took hold, we cradled one another all night . . . I constricted my body to delay the climax, long enough for hers to initiate as well. She needed to give me a break about the dope. She knew how much it sucked watching her do lines for three years, when I had been into that shit for a long time before I met her. But she knew full well that I'd never help secure her first fix, not in another lifetime even. Long-term addicts always get confronted with nonsense like that: "You've got to do it for me, because if I do, I might mess up." A lot of talk—not false exactly, but also not honest. What a heavy responsibility, deciding if a person's merely entertaining a whim or if she's actually set on it, in which case it's better to handle it yourself than to let the first available idiot butcher the job with an overdose. The prospect kept sending shivers up my spine, but I was determined to convince myself: this wasn't my problem anymore . . . I squeezed her ass the better to spread her cheeks, and she let out a violent groan that made me grip her waist, and I closed my eyes as hard as I could so I wouldn't yell out that I still loved her.

Afterward, the fun died down. She was already on the phone as she dressed, she took down dates as dictated by her agent, and I—I didn't exist. Then she called Baby Inès, who was apparently out shopping with Pallas, and to forestall any guilt about the little one, I wandered to the bathroom, erasing all trace—all trace of anything that could fuck things up with Pallas.

3.

Saturday afternoon dissolved into a groggy night. I lay beneath a mountain of comforter, half out of its slipcover, feeling beaten down by the undiminished heat. I had MTV on with the sound cut, the remote in my hand in case a track came on that I wanted to hear, but it wasn't meant to be. Nothing but clips for new jack swing and some bargain-basement rap—pubescent yappers barking with their fingers pointed right at you, or oiled-up strutting groups, encircled by bombshells in miniskirts that left nothing to the imagination (and they wondered why your average yokel saw nothing but "gangsters" or "lecherous hulks"). I had the stereo remote, too, but I wasn't planning to use it. Humming in the background was Marilyn Manson's leering voice, which Pallas had left on repeat before heading to the kitchen to make dinner. She had spent the night at Alex's, and we had escaped the worst: she could have easily rolled up with Baby Inès.

Slumped there, I thought of the others, who were going to Batofar later. I didn't even have the energy to shake my legs and stretch my thighs. My lack of sleep had me feeling grimy, foggy, but more than anything it kept me in an unpleasant liminal state. With every second, I drifted away a little more, but never managing to actually doze off. My lids drooped of their own accord, but my brain remained beset by all sorts of images that were constantly pulling my eyes back open. Images so fleeting and disordered that I couldn't retain a single one.

A second day of E: not bad compared to a good old-fashioned speed or acid crash, and yet there was nothing I could do to hinder the depressive process. I ultimately told myself that maybe I just had no place anymore within a gang this young. Two sleepless nights in a row was beginning to be too much. Not that turning thirty makes that huge a difference, but it felt like the others still had all the time in the world to laze around without asking too many questions, whereas I, at age thirty-one, felt like every day that amounted to nothing was a day wasted toward constructing my future. *The future*: what an alien concept . . .

I should have been working, or at least contemplating what would go on the record. It had been how long since I'd received the contract—two days? I couldn't remember a time when I'd felt that excited . . .

I didn't even muster the courage to get up and grab a nice cold Coke. I listened to Pallas, busy in the kitchen, knowing we were about to watch Tuesday's *Ally McBeal* that she'd recorded, and not even that could lift my spirits. If I could have, I would have asked if we could do it tomorrow instead, but I had already disappointed her enough by having snuck out of the rave. Ever since she got back, anytime my phone rang she mischievously walked in to listen to the voice on the answering machine, then sniped at the machine that whatever this invitation was, there was no way I was picking up, because tonight—tonight was for me and her.

Alex had called three times to convince me to come to Batofar. The third time, she swore that I was obviously there since she had got a busy signal just before. Pallas got a good laugh about it, but I had nothing to say for myself that afternoon. Beyond her own jealousy, she would've hated to learn that Alex had cheated on her little protégée. This had been everyone's big topic of conversation those last six months, how Alex was like a different person since meeting that kid. Except apparently the winds had changed again . . . But I didn't want to think about that.

Eva also called with her joke of the day: "There's this blonde who goes to the doctor. Doctor, doctor, I hurt all over. I hurt here, and here, and here. She points all over her body, jabbing her skin with her finger every time. Doctor, doctor, what's the matter with me? And the doctor says, I think you've got a broken finger!" That one really sent Pallas, she practically skipped around the room, like, "Oh! That's what you should do! A record sampling blonde jokes! Or maybe that would cause too much laughing on the dance floor!" I wished that Eva could be there, she knew how to be gentle and calm when someone was in the throes of an E crash. Yeah, I wished that she could be there. But not so we could fuck each other, just for her soothing arms. Because I could still feel the keen burning sensation in back and in front from too much sex in one day, and instead of feeling flattered by surplus desire, or sated with variety, I felt uncertain, unseemly, like a beached whale.

Jessie also called, though I hadn't thought she would find my number so fast. Her first message said she had just arrived in Lyon, where she had a set scheduled, and she was asking if I knew someone there who sold E. In the second, she mentioned looking up and down for anyone with an Internet connection—the girl dog-sitting for her had a webcam, and she wanted to see her dog. Then she called again to say how amazing her dog was and that I was going to love her. Pallas burst into more guffaws, but I paid no attention.

For a second, I turned up the sound on TV to hear Puff Daddy's rework of Led Zeppelin. It was far from the first time I had seen this clip, but this time it made me feel a certain way. Like some kind of sadness had swept over me, reminding me that I had spent years trying to master the "Whole Lotta Love" riff . . . Maybe it was just sleeping with Alex again that had got me feeling sordid. I pulled on the burgundy Talkin' Loud tee that Guillaume had left on the bed. He didn't wear cologne, just Kenzo deodorant, whose scent lasted a long time. Pallas came in with a tray and rolled her eyes when she saw me sniffing his shirt. I dropped it and straightened up as best I could. Pallas just stood there, waiting for me to arrange the sheets. I smoothed them flat over here and over there, until I pretended I couldn't take any more.

"Is it your skater that's got you like this?" she asked, setting down the tray.

I didn't bother to respond that it was the E doing me in, or else there would be an anti-drug monologue, and given the timing, how awful would that feel. I poured myself a glass of Coke, drained it to the last drop, then gently shook the glass to hear the ice clink. In places, their perfect transparency revealed a formidable mass of tiny veins, frozen and entangled within. A crystal sea as far as the eye could see, available to my eyes whenever I took some E . . . the Pure World, flat and infinite, where all I could hear were my own resounding heartbeats. This piercing wish for silence felt totally contrary to the music I made . . . I raised my eyes to Pallas, and something about her looked different. Her bangs. She had just made them shorter. Now she looked like Jacquouille from *The Visitors*.

"How goes it, Jacquouille?" I asked as I offered her a pillow.

She was frozen in place, a spoonful of tomato salad lying half across her plate.

"If you ever call me that in front of anyone, even once . . ."

I burst out laughing, trying to keep my expression sympathetic. She was right: if anyone else caught wind, then she'd be hearing it left and right.

"Can I ask you something?" said Pallas.

I nodded as I started to eat.

"That guy, are you in love with him or what?"

I waited until I'd swallowed to answer no, that it was nice but nothing more. Which was true. But what I didn't say was that I slept with him to feel something else. To prove that I wasn't like most girls in the scene, girls whom I looked down on. To prove that if I really wanted, I had an exit waiting for me . . . Why I couldn't just accept seeing girls exclusively, I truly didn't know, but my earnest fantasy had me passing for straight. So I slept with him, and it was cool and all because it felt good to please a man, but otherwise it left me indifferent, much like the other occasions there had been since Alex. I wanted to find one who'd hold on to me for good, someone like Nikki. And that's what was eating at me. Realizing that wishing for something wasn't enough to make it so.

chapter four

vox ac30 / miss pallenberg / a little kurt weill

1.

When I woke up the next morning, I put on a record I hadn't listened to in ages. I put it on without thinking, only conscious of sitting on the mattress to lace up my tennis shoes. I was sitting and watching my fingers loop around the laces, absentmindedly humming the words, when all of a sudden I had a vision of some boots. Black boots with heels, walking close beside me in the night, stumbling over rain-slick cobblestones. Anello & Davide boots, with some trim suit-pants—dark gray with thin bands in a lighter shade—falling over them perfectly. They were Nikki's boots, and I was listening to "Gimme Shelter" by the Stones, the first track I ever heard Nikki cover on guitar. I slowly raised my eyes to the turntable where the record spun, felt an urge to cry starting to burn in my nostrils, and then and there I understood that something wasn't right. Pallas was puttering around the entryway, and I didn't answer when she went out on the landing to ask where I was dashing off to like that. I raced down the stairs, as if gripped by an unexpected instinct to puke that now threatened to explode ahead of schedule. I only stopped once I was out on the sidewalk, panting for breath. Unwashed, hair a mess, standing in the already-blinding Sunday morning sun in a T-shirt, pockets empty, no money, no cigarettes, not even my keys. There was a good chance Nikki wouldn't even be home. I lingered there for a few seconds, staring at the door to the building opposite—I could see him coming out to meet me again . . . But another street, another time . . . I gave Pallas a short wave—she was calling to me now from the window—and I started down the street.

Nikki lived at the far end of the Boulevard Rochechouart, a good forty-five-minute walk from Parmentier. One side of my brain wanted some time for honest reflection before arriving, while the other, a little dizzy, just wanted to get a move on without any thoughts at all. But everything before my eyes reminded me of Nikki. A couple in a car with their kids recalled the family who, every morning, couldn't believe it when they saw us walking along in our tight clothing and shaggy hair, heading back home for bed. A guy on a bike, in a somewhat nice suede jacket, recalled Les Puces, where we rummaged through heaps of clothing for hours, looking for jackets with this neckline here, shirts with that neckline there. And every shuttered storefront window recalled any number of strolls on the day after a concert, in whatever provincial town, on whatever Sunday . . .

I eventually stopped and looked around, blinking away tears that wouldn't be stopped, choking back saliva to hopefully clear the lump in my throat. There wasn't a lick of shade on the sidewalk, but moving to the other side of the street felt beyond me. As I came back to my senses, it felt like I was emptying myself out, like when you stand up too fast after a blood test. And so I decided to keep my hands locked in my back jeans pockets, and I hurried along with my head down, avoiding both the sun and the eyes of the few sporadic pedestrians. With every intersection, it felt like the path ahead lay undiminished. Same with the lump in my throat. A genuine, painful lump. A real rarity, much more rare than tears. A lump so undeniable that I felt I needed to drop down on every bench I saw and stop moving. That I needed to spread my legs, hang my head forward, and cough, to cough and cough until the lump was expelled. But I carried on—no succumbing until I arrived, no succumbing in the middle of nowhere, with no one around to pick me back up.

Nikki and I met in the coolest way possible. One day, when I was going on nineteen, I was lying on the mattress in my garret apartment, napping on a quiet summer afternoon, when music broke the silence. And not just any: "So You Want to Be a Rock 'n' Roll Star" by the Byrds, the Patti Smith cover of which I had been playing on a loop, having taped it by holding a recorder near the TV during a rerun concert, seeing as I couldn't find it on CD. Naturally, I immediately jumped to look out the window. In the alleyway, which was always deserted, the face of the building opposite was only about fifteen feet away, and I could tell the music was coming from three floors down, but some sort of net curtain prevented me from peering inside. I waited patiently for the track to end before putting on my Patti Smith rendition and hiding behind the open window shutters. I saw a long-haired brunette poke his head around the edge of his curtain. He looked down, then up, then over at me. His hair was in his eyes and hanging down to his shoulders, and he was wearing a purple shirt. I held my breath, wondering if he could see me through the shutter slats, which prevented me from getting a good look at his face. At the end of the track, I pulled out the tape, wondering what to put on next, but he beat me to the punch with "I Can't Explain" by Bowie, from the covers album only a real fan would buy. Without even waiting for it to end, I responded with the Who's original; he poked his head back out, with this manic expression on his face. Now he was the one who couldn't wait, piquing my interest even more with the Shadows of Knight from the *Nuggets* album, which even fewer people knew. I responded with a different track from the same compilation, and this time he grabbed his curtain with one hand and pointed his finger with the other. I was being submitted to a test, pure and simple. He would drop an intro, and every time I'd have a few seconds to choose a reply from anything I owned. When he threw out "Alabama Song" by the Doors, it felt like billion-to-one odds that I'd know Kurt Weill and Bertolt Brecht. But I did know them—I had just bought *The Threepenny Opera* after reading a Bowie biography that mentioned it in passing. So I cranked the volume to the max to make its old melody pervade the whole alley, a sublime melancholy halfway between a waltz and a polka, and with that, he ripped his curtain fully to one side and cried out, "Fuck you, show yourself! You better be a girl!"

Instead of showing myself, I went downstairs; when he saw me down below, he instantly fled his window, and a few seconds later he was standing right in front of me. He had a slight hunch, a little bit shorter than me, even with his boot heels. He was twenty-six and gorgeous, like Syd Barrett's little brother but dressed like Keith Richards. He started circling me, enthusing about my outfit. About my shirt that looked like what's-his-name's on whatever album cover, my pants, my belt buckle, my boots. I could only smile, but inside, I, too, couldn't get over running into this guy. Soon enough, I was hunkered in a room that was drowning in amps and guitars, flipping through his records, and now it was his turn to smile, as meanwhile I gradually came to understand that this was the former frontman and guitarist for a group I had kicked myself for missing back in the day. Then we ended up in bed, trying to undress without separating our lips, and three days later my old garret was a thing of the past.

2.

When I finally arrived, I wasn't crying anymore, I just felt weary. And in the alley, standing beside the intercom affixed to the outer wall, I paused. It was much too early for me to be bothering Nikki, he might not be alone, and plus I hadn't seen him in almost two months. That wasn't a huge problem—we sometimes went a while without catching up, before one or the other of us would call and it was like we had seen each other just the night before—but this time it felt different. Even if I was almost certain that what was happening to me wasn't just a passing thing, I wasn't very sure I had the words to explain it. I could have sat for a moment, gathered my composure in the shadows, and then headed back out, but I also knew that if I really wanted to foil my trip down memory lane, all I'd have to do was turn the corner. So I eventually pressed the button. After a few long seconds, a sleepy "Who is it?" crackled into the quiet alley. I cleared my throat, and as seriously as possible, I said:

"Anita Pallenberg."

"Ah," he went, "well, in that case."

The stairwell was cool and dark. I laughed under my breath as I mounted the steps. Anita Pallenberg, longtime companion to Keith Richards, "real *classy dame*, that one, to put it mildly," as Nikki used to tease when I coldly informed him, for some reason or other, that he'd never be Keith Richards. When I got to the doorstep, the entrance was open a crack. There was no sound in the apartment, just the wafting smell of faded tobacco. I gently shut the door behind me and crossed the narrow hallway, carefully avoiding the edges of the giant Ramones poster, which inevitably ripped whenever shoulders brushed against it. I bypassed the small bathroom on the right, where I could sense Nikki's presence through the tiny gap, bending over the sink with his longish mass of brown hair, a green towel wrapped around his waist, and I entered the living room. Nothing, or almost nothing, had changed since the first time I'd been there. Thirteen years now. It made me smile, but just as easily could have made me burst out sobbing.

Nikki had lived in this apartment ever since leaving Rennes around 1985, upon the dissolution of his second band. An uncle had died here, and he was supposed to take care of it before it could be sold, but ultimately his family let him keep it. The living room was on the right, the kitchen farther in, the "music room" across from it, and the bedroom in the back. In the bedroom, where I could hear someone lighting a cigarette, there was just enough space for a mattress with an ashtray on either side and a chest of drawers behind the door. I went to the kitchen to get Nikki's coffee going, the kitchen being just as tiny, with the sink that was always overflowing with dirty dishes, two hot plates, a mini-fridge with the coffee machine on top, and along the wall a tray on top of a stool contained any glasses and silverware that wouldn't fit in the only cupboard beneath the sink. The bathroom was hardly any larger, while the living room—where I popped in to grab a cigarette from the coffee table and watch Nikki slip into the other room, waving that he'd be right back—was an appropriate size but was more a continuation of the hallway than anything else.

Nikki rarely spent time here, aside from answering phone calls. When people came through, it was rare to have two people there at once, and it invariably concluded in the music room, where he was always busy with something or other. All the same, there was an old, and very comfortable, dark-brown leather couch, and a heap of crap on a waist-high shelving unit that stretched all the way to the kitchen. The bottom shelf was starting to sag from all the piled music magazines, not to mention the sheer tonnage of sheet music, all more or less in tatters. The middle one housed nothing but books, and the top one had a little bit of everything: a white TV from the seventies that was shaped like a mushroom, a prehistoric VCR, fifty-something ashtrays full of change and other useless objects, sunglass sleeves, and multiple lava lamps. It served to hold a towering stack of mail, still mostly sealed, since Nikki was only interested in checks and contracts, which were conspicuous from the letterhead on the envelopes.

He returned with his thick brown hair somewhat tidier, slicked back with a healthy coat of gel, a little like Nick Cave. He was buttoning a wrinkled white shirt over some ribbed black-velvet Levi's that didn't look any fresher. In her heels, the girl looked two heads taller than him, barely twenty years old, blonde with long stiff hair and big, blue, closely set owl eyes. The kind of debutante-model they say has an "interesting face." I helped myself to a timid smile before she slipped out the front door without a word. I gave Nikki a wry interrogating glance, but he didn't pick up on it, too sophisticated to disparage a girl even after she was gone. He sat on the couch to put on his boots. I stubbed out my cigarette in an ashtray on the coffee table and entered the music room.

It was spacious, entirely lined in gold. A writing desk, a wall with something like five thousand pieces of vinyl on wooden shelves, another taken up by Fender Bassman headstocks in stacks of six, a half-dozen more amps, an upright piano, and a final wall dedicated to his guitars, with about ten of them hanging by their headstock from a rack affixed to the ceiling, all of them vintage.

I knew the contents of this room by heart, and Nikki often called me a philistine whenever I failed to recognize a certain model, when I could only tell what was new and what was missing. His formidable Gretsch White Falcon and his little Silver Jet weren't there anymore. Same with his Epiphone Casino, sanded white just like Lennon's. Instead, there was now a big red Gibson 335, and of course his Gold Top, one of his favorites. He was also missing his black Jimmy Page Danelectro, and his white-and-red Fender Mustang, but the red Stratocaster L-Series remained, as did the spangly Teisco Del Rey, the plexiglass Dan Armstrong, and the Burns Synchromatic with the "sunburst" design (a gradient from black to orange, which I always called "sunset" even if it got on Nikki's nerves). He also still had a twelve-string Rickenbacker made of light oak, a "sunset" Fender Jazzmaster, a Jumbo acoustic, and obviously, his favorite, the cream Gibson Junior TV, found in New York for two hundred dollars when he was eighteen years old. Propped up in one corner was a "sunset" Mosrite Ventures that had two strings missing, and maybe there were others in some of the six flight cases stacked against the wall. His black Vox AC30 amp was still there—the one he lugged around wherever he went—along with his red Marshall Plexi Combo, an equally red Kustom with its funny trim, like a fluffed and bedazzled sheepskin coat. Ten or so Electro-Harmonix pedals were gathering dust beside various Fuzzes, Wah-Wahs, and Cry Babies, along with an old Revox four-track and a cluster of jacks. And then his "sunset" Precision bass, also still there, set apart from the rest with his Ampeg bass amp as well as mine, a yellow Mustang he was adamant I never resell.

But what really brought back the lump in my throat was the mirror over the writing desk, hanging between two windows. A faux-gilded oval mirror with a fantail of pictures all around. Pictures of Nikki onstage with his first and second bands, with me and other musicians while recording his two solo albums, a few pictures of friends, but mostly pictures of me and Nikki in all kinds of situations. In one of them, done up like princelings, he in a suit cut with bottle-green velvet over a dark-yellow satin shirt, and I in a plum silk shirt, white Danton-collar jacket, and black Levi's. Anello boots on us both, of course, and Keith Richards haircuts. And then another picture taken just before, of me trying to learn guitar, before I chose bass as a backup. Me seated on a Marshall amp, in this very room, in panties and a black Stooges shirt, a red Hohner on my knees, my face visibly sulking from having been dragged out of bed at eight for my daily lesson, so early because, apparently, there was much I had to learn . . .

Nikki placed on the writing desk a steaming cup of coffee with a second cup of tea, then I felt him against my back, sliding his arms around my waist. Turning around, I threw my own around his neck, and I burst out sobbing.

3.

"Wait," Nikki sighed, sinking a little farther into the living-room couch, "I don't understand, start over."

His poorly slicked hair had cowlicks all over, and his shirt was misaligned two whole buttons. I wanted to laugh, but he looked so somber that his eyebrows were almost touching.

"I don't know any other way to put it," I sighed. "I was listening to 'Gimme Shelter' and all of a sudden it felt obvious, that's all."

"But what did, what felt obvious?"

"Everything. The guitars, the boots, all of it!"

"Yeah, you're right, they're pretty classy, I know."

"Yeah, well, I had forgotten how much."

"Well, so what?"

"*So what?* I should stop pretending!"

"Pretending what?" Nikki was irritated. "I don't see what you're getting at. You want to pick up the bass again? Is that it?"

"No, no. Or—I don't know!" I added, annoyed. "I just don't want to do a techno record anymore."

Nikki stood up, but not fast enough that I wouldn't catch the ironic gleam in his eyes. He picked up his cup and headed to the kitchen for more coffee.

"And at the same time," I continued, a little louder so he'd hear me still, "I know how lucky I am to get the contract."

"Yeah, you could say that again," Nikki spat from the kitchen.

"Come on, don't snap at me. I finally just told you you were right all along—just because your guitar stuff isn't working out doesn't mean you should give up."

Nikki came back and sat down. Really thinking about it, this seemed like the first time we had ever discussed these things right here. Clearly this stuff felt important, even more than I'd imagined.

"Alright," he said, gulping down some coffee and setting his cup back down, "I feel like you're missing something. First, your contract's with a Virgin imprint that's only techno, right? So those guys are gonna be seeing red if you show up with a rock thing. But even beyond that, I don't know that you really get it. It's not my own records that bring in money, it's what I do on other people's. But I've got twenty-three years of guitar behind me, which means

I'll basically always have work. So you, I mean, you played bass for what—three, four years?"

"Six."

"Yeah, OK, six. But you don't sing, and you don't write lyrics. So, what, you see yourself onstage with Cabrel or Jean-Louis Aubert?"

"Fuck that, I could start a band!"

"Did you just turn twelve or something? Rock's not a *thing* anymore."

"Not true! What about Radiohead, Placebo, Marilyn Manson . . ."

"Pff, exceptions. And they aren't French."

"So you're saying there aren't any good French musicians?"

"No, I'm saying there are loads, too many even, but not many with the charisma you'd need to start a band that'll stand out, and the system DOESN'T WANT ROCK anymore."

"OK, OK. So what's your point, then?"

"I'm saying you need to calm down and let's think this through."

"Yeah, well, while we're thinking it through, why don't we go next door," and I stubbed out my cigarette, getting up to transition us to the music room.

I rifled through the Rs until I found the Stones' *Satanic Sessions*, the thing I'd been listening to at home. I was careful not to press my fingers to the disc itself, and I fast-forwarded to the start of "Gimme Shelter." Then I went for my bass, softly stroked its dusty knobs, and turned to face the guitars.

"Which of these can I use?" I asked Nikki, now standing at the doorstep, cup in hand.

He shook his head, sighed, then placed his cup on the writing desk. I was so out of practice, who knows what my goal was when I grabbed his outstretched Strat. Then he unhooked his Junior, placed it gently against the Vox, and crouched beside the cluster of jacks. He pulled out one, then another, he stood up, he walked to the desk chair, pulling it closer to the amp, he sat, grabbed the Junior again, and he motioned for me to cut the music. I plugged in some headphones and cued the track to the start. As Nikki brought both guitars into open-tuning, I just stood there, listening to the track, incessantly cuing up the intro. I knew that for Nikki this was a cross to bear, that I was going to bungle notes galore, and even more so that I couldn't maintain a proper tempo. But listening to this track is what had gotten me started in the first place, even if I abandoned guitar for bass only a year later. To say I could play "Gimme Shelter" after just a year's practice would be joking, but I could successfully fiddle with the notes in the long intro, and after that I just followed the chords. Nikki was goddamn lucky he could still play here, with no one on the floor below—ground level: a two-story workshop-cum-warehouse that hummed all day and night; upstairs neighbor: an old fop who raved about Nikki's riffs and Nikki's clothes whenever they crossed paths on the stairs. But Nikki was the kind of guy who found it normal to hook up his amp wherever he saw fit. It was all he ever did. Here, sitting on a table edge, or anywhere, just scribbling out lyrics. The track concluded, and I heard Nikki shouting. I took off my headphones.

"Want a strap?" he asked.

It felt ridiculous to play standing, but what the hell, might as well go all the way. I nodded, switched off the stereo, and he bent over to collect a rolled-up strap that he hurled in my direction. When he didn't grab a second one, I smiled and said he couldn't just sit while I stood there making a fool of myself alone. He sighed and bent for another strap. Mine was mottled like a python, stupidly gaudy, whereas his was black, complete simplicity, which made me feel even dumber. He pulled a pick from his pocket, handed it over, then grabbed another off the floor. The Vox and the Marshall subtly purred while Nikki waited, half-amused, half-pitying. My hands were trembling; I signaled him to start.

There were two different guitar parts in the intro. The first was busier but felt more prominent, and since Nikki kicked things off, I was going to come in with the second part, less ornate but more difficult with all the bends and slides. Soon enough, Nikki was having to insert filigrees all over the place to make up for the notes I missed. I was shocked he hadn't butted in to make me take it from the top until I finally got it, as he'd done while teaching me to play. I had to keep my right foot forward to elevate the guitar on my knee, and my eyes needed to focus on the neck. I had lost all my dexterity. My pinkie felt like it was always in the way. My right hand was mixing up strings. The guitar was laying heavy on my shoulder, the strap cutting into my lower neck. And I felt silly in my T-shirt and tennis shoes next to Nikki, looking immaculate in his collared shirt, which he'd finally, correctly rebuttoned over his black Levi's and boots. But fuck it felt good, not full-volume but full enough for my ears, with Nikki's voice starting to hum snatches of the vocals here and there to keep me on tempo. He played with his eyes closed, head slightly back, motionless, with just his left shoulder gently rising and falling, marking every other beat. But even just a glance at him made me lose my bearings on the neck. Eventually I sat in the chair to feel more comfortable, and Nikki shot me a faint smile, his eyes still closed, still keeping time with his shoulder. Little by little, I stopped playing anything but a few scattered notes, disgusted that I could do no better. What Nikki kept playing solo now sounded perfect, but at the same time a little monotonous without the second guitar, or the bass, or the drums. He ended up transitioning into

"Susie Q," and I got the message. I shut off the Marshall to hook up the Ampeg instead, and I moved my strap from the Strat to my Mustang bass. It was more or less in tune; I settled into the sequence Nikki had underway, and immediately everything started sounding much better. The ultra-prominent bass on "Susie Q" helped structure the track, a call-and-response with every guitar lick. Nikki started singing over top, "Oh say that you'll be true . . ." His voice so clear, so right, with no trace of an accent. Now I was the one keeping time with my foot, with both heels, like Jagger when he mimed marching in place. Since this time I could pull things off without a bum note, Nikki could freely devote himself to a lengthy solo, and since I no longer needed to watch the neck, I could look at him instead. Still practically motionless with his eyes closed. As if inhabited by whatever he was playing. But he didn't seem to just be summoning old favorites—the tracks themselves seemed to be summoning him, swooping in and taking possession. Transformed—that was it. Even in normal life he was a sight to behold, but get him playing and he was utterly radiant. Goddamn magic. Even his crotch looked sexier hidden behind a guitar. How many times had I enjoyed playing the Pamela Courson to his Jim Morrison, slinking to my knees while he sang standing or at his piano? But it never came out like the Morrison on film, he couldn't summon that same stunning voice—no, he'd stop cold or shout about how now wasn't the time. I ended up cupping his face in both hands; the sudden silence started filling with feedback as my bass rested against his guitar. He let me kiss him with open eyes and then stared at me amused when my head pulled back. I stripped the bass, set it against the amp, did the same with his guitar, and then leaned against the wall. He looked quizzical, like you're sure this is what you want? I reached out my hand to grab the bottom of his shirt, gently tugged it over, his body pulled in close, and that's how his hands seized my hips, totally different from my skater.

4.

He lingered expectantly in the entryway, had already seemed to be filling it before he even got there. We were going to rise together, cling together atop a huge impending wave, and it was going to feel incredible. The wave seemed as expectant as he did. The breadth of his shoulders, the calm, flat strength of his chest, and the power of those depths that were beckoning with all their might. A gulf waiting to be filled. Fantasy, desire, lack—all, at last, to be filled. All this time spent feeling not like a woman . . . spent feeling . . . *neuter*? Up in the air from ages fourteen to nineteen, exclusively hetero with him, then equally homo with Alex—what did that make me? Bisexuals don't exist. There are hetero girls who sometimes get with other girls, homo girls who sometimes get with guys, gay guys who sometimes loosen up around girls, and hetero guys who maybe, once in a lifetime, loosen up with other guys. But no one gets with both sexes indiscriminately. People always have a preference, and anyone who says otherwise is lying to you. Maybe I had gotten with Alex because I couldn't find another Nikki, but I wasn't now returning to Nikki because I couldn't find another Alex. I was returning *just because*. Maybe those last several years were ultimately nothing but an overwhelming fear of other men. Apprehensive that I couldn't match them. Unsure of how to handle their bodies, their minds, their differences. An irrational fear that practically verged on paralysis. A fear of the unknown. A fear of life itself. Ultimately this was all about trust.

That's what made things stick in the first place. Because I trusted him. Our shared music was just a distraction, there to lighten the load whenever I was feeling weighed down. We broke up because we had gotten too close, and now it seemed like enough time had passed for us to start from the beginning. I knew it from the way he smiled, hunching over me with his hair in his eyes. I was smiling, too, couldn't help myself, smiling and saying go ahead, I guess I'm yours again! That fucking charm he had, working overtime yet again. He was going to search me—inspect and take possession of his claim. That stupid thing with men: always so convinced they've got a gift from God, and that they're the only ones. The guy next door—maybe he's been gifted, too, but no way could his ever make the same impact . . . In everyday life this felt exasperating, facile, laughable, but in moments like this, there was magic. That confidence, even its inquisition aspects, floored me. I melted. My heart, my guts. I finally moved my pelvis a little closer, and he entered in a single thrust, slowly, to the very end. I held my breath, enthralled by the violence of it. He stilled, and my nerves released in spasms. Without the condom, I could feel it all. I was toward the end of my period and we had never used them before, and so it wasn't even in question. Some things can't be done halfway. I didn't just want to feel the discharge, I wanted to feel the grain of his skin. I tentatively stuck a finger inside. To touch what cinched our union. Otherwise fully still, he started gently moving his muscle. My own contracted. I didn't dare breathe, I was swooning so hard. I could feel it all. Every millimeter of skin. The now-hypersensitive, irrigated texture. His living skin. That perfect moment when everything fits. And my closed eyes were shining on another world.

5.

Night had fallen, the only light coming from the music room where a lamp was still lit. Naked, lying next to Nikki with my cheek against his chest, I was gazing sidelong at the wardrobe obstructing the window. The gap between the panels gave a peek of the burgundy velour jacket sleeve within, a vintage Granny jacket. It felt good seeing these clothes again—so difficult to find for myself . . . A sudden realization shot my body straight up, like a slap in the face. I was now sitting there with my mouth open, like a fish ripped from its tank. Nikki raised an arm, faintly opened one eye before falling back asleep. I massaged my face up and down before lighting a cigarette and slipping on my T-shirt. In the room next door, I grabbed an ashtray, sat on the little piano seat, and among those heavy, silent record shelves, with the amps off and the guitars hanging motionless from their racks, I let an anxious laugh escape.

My nerves lasted for only a second, but even so . . . A few hours before, dreaming of how lucky I felt reconnecting with Nikki again, I plainly hadn't grasped the full extent . . . Now it seemed much clearer why no guys I'd nailed since had ever stuck: my tastes hadn't evolved, no, they still perfectly coincided with whatever unlocked inside of me at fifteen years old.

Beyond Bowie, I'd only ever had three idols: Syd Barrett, first singer and guitarist for Pink Floyd; Keith Richards, guitarist for the Stones; and Johnny Thunders, guitarist for the New York Dolls, the Heartbreakers, and solo. The first had entered orbit circa 1967, his neurons fried from a mythical Mandrax shampoo job. The second was married, and then the third, when I finally had him right in front of me, proved too close an acquaintance with Nikki, whom I'd already started dating by then. But besides that they were all geographically out of reach, and beyond the fact that they'd have found me too young and insignificant next to their usual girls, now they had become too old for me. I liked the way they looked on my record sleeves, not the way they looked today in the twenty-five, thirty years since. Nikki combined the three: the first one's appearance, the second one's attitude, and the third one's soul, not to mention a whole host of his other things, which had made them both inseparable until the latter's overdose in '91. But before meeting Nikki in '87, it had been four years of one-night stands, only ever meeting pale copies of the originals. Legends from the sixties, icons from the seventies, and punk-rock survivors—unfortunately those were the only kinds I liked. I liked guitarists with long brown hair who had read their Byron and Oscar Wilde, the kind who were prone to flirt with the abyss, inhabited—or haunted—by a certain penchant for junkie imagery.

I stubbed out my cigarette and squeezed my knees between my arms. Four years of sleepless nights at Gibus, copious fistfuls of Dinintel and other amphetamines before moving on to the mellower intravenous stuff that everyone administered in peace on the shitter, taking care to stash their gear deep in the club so they wouldn't have it on them during one of the regularly scheduled narc raids. That small room with the low ceilings, sculpted in stone, with the proud, oval Gibus logo over its scarcely elevated stage. The groups stringing together one after the other without a break, all more or less inspired by whatever albums were the present hot-ticket items in collector store bins. I was fifteen at the time, there with my best friend Monica (as in Monica Vitti, but actually named Cécile); we were always worming our way into the little green room off to one side. Monica already looked "high femme" with her long bleached hair, six-inch heels, and big black Jackie O glasses. Whereas I was going for Edie Sedgwick, with the same crop bleached to the roots, the same smoky makeup, and the same fashion sense, like a kid borrowing her mom's clothes, blending short, slight dresses with a grab bag of kitschy accessories. I affected the same mannered drawl of an haute-blasé teen, alternating unspeakable tantrums with excessive amounts of charm, going as far as imitating her exaggerated, graceful hand movements. Monica and I, then, as always, worming our way into that green room, with her sights set on the singer and mine set on the guitarist. Sometimes this carried over to the hotel, or to an apartment not even they were familiar with, snuggling up while listening to their host rhapsodize about that evening's concert. A chain of such nights, any sense of time having flown out the window, and waking up comatose in the midafternoon, gazing deep into their fevered, smoldering eyes—all of them hooked on the sixties and seventies (and, of course, on the fifties), all of them hungry to simply travel back in time . . . Monica had fantasized about Nikki, whom she'd often seen in concert but who still lived in Rennes at the time, though I was the one who eventually bagged him while she was off pursuing some New Yorker. We stayed in touch until their wedding—I couldn't find enough cash for the trip—and then one day she just stopped responding to my letters.

I set my feet back down and slid my hands under my ass. Yeah, nothing all that serious before Nikki. At the time, I was already basically aware of my slight preference for girls, but I marked that down to a lack of boys that suited my taste. Now I knew, it was that boys simply didn't please me *enough* for me to fall for them more easily. Whereas with girls, it didn't really matter what they wore or what they listened to—just one smile and it was sealed. That felt very "rock 'n' roll" in our scene, two girls kissing. It reminded people of Anita Pallenberg and Marianne Faithfull: Keith Richards and Mick Jagger would frequently catch them sucking face after they'd stepped away to bash things out in the studio. Except that in my case it all felt so meaningful, perpetually coming away from the experience bitter when, after a few hours, I got gently shoved aside to make way for their man's return. Still, there were some of these that lasted a little longer, but nothing serious compared to the three years I'd just spent with Alex.

I went back to the bedroom, looking for another cigarette. Nikki had flipped onto his belly and was now emitting a wheezy snore. I leaned back against the wall, slid down to sit on my heels, and I stayed there in the half-light, smoking and watching. I hadn't chosen it exactly, shifting to girls when I left him. It hadn't been a choice at all. I had simply landed on a friend's couch, and out of a lethal sense of boredom I tagged along to her usual lesbian clubs. Early on, I couldn't even imagine things getting physical, given how dispiriting I found the banal mechanics of it, until I started getting hit on so incessantly, hearing how I was the coolest thing they'd ever seen, that I finally went along with it. And from that point on I fucked anything that moved, the pretty-enough and the low-down-and-dirtiest alike, finding a sick desire out of driving them wild with passion, only to drop that they should be mindful of the competition. There had been dozens of them, all scowling at one another and then breaking down in tears when I left the club with someone else. And coolest of all, I was more into dope than ever, constantly calling Nikki in tears, getting back together, not getting back together, regretting leaving my bass at his apartment, regretting all the places I couldn't visit anymore without the risk of running into him, then taking it out on these girls of such depressing plainness, and with the nerve to think they could ever make me happy. It went like this for a year before I stumbled onto

Alex. Nothing had conditioned me to latch onto a girl of only 5′2″ if not for the massive dose of perversity in her eyes. And nothing had conditioned me for the pure jolt of seeing her mix for the first time. But there was actually some logic to it: somehow, she was like Nikki, possessed by her turntables like he was by his guitars. It was also my first time making it into *the room where it happens*. In 1983, everything I loved was already dead and gone, whereas now, these new duds I'd started wearing, this new music I was listening to, I encountered them everywhere I went. Rave meetups were like mod rallies on the beach in Brighton. The atmosphere on the streets of Marais was just like Carnaby, with silhouettes tailored to the music that was blasting from every bar. Except it didn't take long before I was hearing people say the movement was already changing, that it was starting to leave the underground, that raves were already losing their greatest strength, which had previously resided in their very refusal of any rock 'n' roll schematics. Like how punk rock in '76 was already nothing but a shadow of itself the following year, techno was already becoming this gigantic corporate fraud . . .

So it was back to square one . . . What that meant, the wheres and hows, I hadn't the slightest idea. I felt condemned to be wandering through a labyrinth of ghosts and outmoded riffs. But now that I was back with Nikki, at least I could escape from a second form of wandering. Of wandering through an emotional wasteland. Because, of the scattered few survivors from the early-'80s scene, those who hadn't succumbed to ODs or popped a bullet in their brains, could any intrigue me the way that Nikki still did? Review copies of their debut solo records washed straight into the clearance bins at Gibert. Some had veered into "experimental electronica," but others, who no longer even earned royalties on their records, records no one even bothered to keep in print—these others had absolutely nothing going on. Unable to evolve, or lacking some guru producer to give them a chance—that was their own wasteland. Days and days of silence punctuated by cold sweats, waking from cosmic nightmares, Faustian bargains, with Armageddon-touting newspapers serving as their blankets. And a handful of these guys had been so gifted, and so beautiful, that it almost made you cry . . . Of course there was a bevy of young guitarists sprouting up around the world, ultra-gifted and ultra-cool, but there was only one who had listened to his first Stones record at eleven (in '72), started wearing his first boots at thirteen, formed his first band at sixteen, and now at thirty-nine was still enacting that last true myth, of "teenage rock 'n' roll," and he was right here in front of me.

Then I stubbed out my cigarette, climbed onto Nikki's back, flipped him over as best I could, threw off my T-shirt, and since he was only just beginning to open his eyes, I straddled him from above and set myself to reviving the "toy" of my once and future betrothed.

6.

Around one in the morning, we got dressed to grab something to eat. I borrowed one of Nikki's button-downs for the occasion. One he didn't wear anymore but that summoned countless old memories: lime-green satin, rather form-fitting, only four buttons, the top three of which were missing. He put on his white shirt from the day before over some black velvet Levi's, with a matching jacket fitted just right and, naturally, his boots.

For a moment we roamed the triangle of Abbesses, Blanche, and Pigalle, linked arm in arm. At this late hour, naturally everything was closed but a few bars, and as was often the case, anywhere that held meaning for Nikki, in the fifteen years he'd been a fixture in these parts, no longer existed, something that only ever kicked in for him when it was already too late. We eventually settled for a Moroccan hole-in-the-wall around Anvers. The room was empty aside from one of its managers, who was eating all alone at a table by the entrance. We walked to the far back; I gave Nikki the booth, as he was looking pretty spent. Sauce marks on the table kept our elbows away; the place reeked of hot oil, but even with the upsettingly violent overhead lights, we were pleased to be there. Pleased because we'd been hungry for a while now, and finally we were here among these edible aromas, no matter how appetizing they turned out to be, ogling the waiter as he came to take our order. Nikki, his eyes closed and arms crossed and his head slumped against the backrest, had a mirror taking up the entire wall behind him. I could see the room in reverse, with the door open to the street outside, to the sounds of traffic and pedestrians, still plentiful even now, the tour buses . . . parked along the island in the median, and the neon lights of nearby sex shops reflected in the buses' doors and windows. I could see myself, too, looking pasty and twiggy in this light-green shirt, whose neck dropped far too low what with all the missing buttons. It was weird seeing myself in this shirt with my hair cut short. Because I knew, if I stood up, I wouldn't see low-waisted pants and boots, but perfectly ordinary 505 jeans and sneakers. And the crazy thing was that nothing, aside from the hair, would have made you guess that I was nothing like I used to be. Nothing to signal that some six years earlier, I had changed my life completely. My look, how I carried myself, the way I lit my cigarettes and stashed my lighter—gestures that now seemed hyper-femme—were all in no way different than if I'd kept on seeing Nikki. If we'd tried, back then, to envision what we'd look like later on, it would've been an image of two old lovers starting to resemble each other over time, two formerly longtime junkies now more or less in shape, still devoted to their rock 'n' roll and their greasy little hole-in-the-walls in Pigalle. Nikki was too prudish for me to voice this out loud, and he had fallen asleep anyway, so I kept my mouth shut; I drifted off observing his hands. His long, tapered, slightly crooked fingers, alarmingly white and basically hairless, the fingertips callused, like little bits of hardened candle wax. Those magnificent guitar hands that he refused to dunk in water for too long whenever we were at the beach, because he couldn't risk dissolving those calluses. I stayed motionless and quiet, but on the inside I was stunned by how dramatically everything could change in only five minutes, the time it takes to distractedly, sleepily listen to an early-morning Stones track . . .

I turned to eye the waiter who still hadn't dumped our plates high with couscous and veggies. I tapped my wrist to show him he was lagging, and he waved his hand to say it wouldn't be long. I lit another cigarette. Nearly forty years old, and despite all the wrinkles that would henceforth mar these slackened sleeping features, still Nikki had a baby face. And at the same time, it was a man's face now. Probably from the turn that his professional life had taken. Everything now, essentially, seemed on track, no real possibility of financial or social ruin, as he'd long been dreading. Outside his own records, he always had something on deck. He helped some people with their recordings or tours, while with others it was just a one-off without any follow-ups to speak of. His own record sales were nothing spectacular—refusing to sing in French presented a major handicap—but Nikki had considerably more clout when it came to other people's work. His albums, ultimately, were mere tributes to the things that he loved. The voices of Scott Walker and Alice Cooper, the guitar lines of Mick Ronson and Jeff Beck, that's what made him happy. Everything he released always felt flashy and technically faultless (he played everything himself but the drums), yet also unoriginal. It was through other voices, or within a band, that his creativity flourished. It was sort of a tragedy, but he seemed used to it by now.

What a funny lot, singer-guitarists . . . These guys always looked for the same thing: the girl they could land through their songs, who would have something to keep them going or would be connected to record labels and were, in all cases, blonde. Regardless, the girl they really wanted didn't exist anymore. She belonged to a race that went extinct around the time Jagger started dressing for aerobics. A race of groupie-muses like Anita Pallenberg, Marianne Faithfull, Miss Pamela, and Cyrinda Foxe—all of them larger than life. Even now, I couldn't quite say if Nikki deviated from the norm or if he merely acted more realistic . . .

The waiter finally arrived, depositing our steaming plates, and right away Nikki opened his eyes, a childlike gleam peeking through the fatigue. He had highly unusual traditions around food. He'd wait until he was literally famished before even bothering, but once the time came, he left no room for talk until he'd consumed his final bite. So we started out eating in silence, cutting our merguez and shoveling up forkfuls of veggie-laden couscous, washing it down with an ice-cold Coke apiece, and once again I felt shocked to find my gestures getting slower, lighter, more graceful . . . A thousand times in the past, I had wondered which of us would be first to die of an overdose. Then, once we unhooked ourselves for good, me via Methadone and he via Subutex, which he actually still took, I started wondering how he might age. But not one hair had changed. In the twenty, thirty, forty years he still had left, he'd go on eating whatever he wanted, smoking close to three packs a day, wearing the same clothes, and making the same music.

It felt good being back together. I didn't know where this would lead, and that didn't even matter to me, I just felt relieved: it seemed like a missing piece had just discovered, or rediscovered, its place in the puzzle, and many things were about to get much simpler. But more than that—most of all—I was grateful to him for reawakening me to myself. I was conscious of my body's transformation, of the blunt-force femininity I gave off, and wholly naturally, as if it had always been there—and that? That was the most refreshing sensation I'd experienced in a long, long time.

7.

Nikki couldn't be the one. I realized it when I got up to find him already plugging away in the music room. He was sitting at the piano, hunched over some sheet music that was resting on his knees, and which he was slowly filling out with a lead pencil he'd clearly been chewing on. I leaned back against the doorframe in my button-down and panties. He couldn't be the one because nothing had changed. Back together, we would only be picking things up where we left them . . . Eventually he noticed me and smiled, but I couldn't think of anything to say. There were tears in my eyes, which he saw, and when he forced his way through a smile all the same, I understood: not only did he know this, too, but he had recognized it first. I walked over to grab a cigarette from the piano. He was diligently scrawling his chicken scratch over the score. I bent down to empty his ashtray into a plastic bag he was using as a trash can, I kissed him on the top of his head, and I returned to the bedroom.

It was so dark in there, you would've thought daytime was over. There were gray skies outside—and it was cold, too, maybe. The last few days of heat, the rave, all of that seemed so far away. I thought about Pallas, surely wild with worry not knowing where I'd gone off to. I thought about my bedroom with my gear and the contract lying somewhere on the carpet. The expectations made everything feel unresolved. Weighed down with misgivings. But what kind of expectations? About the insane sum landing soon in my account? It hadn't even crossed my mind in these last twenty-four hours . . . I slipped on my jeans, and then I crawled across the bed to grab the ashtrays on either side so I could bring them to the kitchen.

The grayness outside lent the living room the ambience of a winter morning, when I would rouse myself from bed to confront the cold, unheated apartment alone, the cold shower tiles, and then the same cold outside. Dark and rainy Monday mornings spent poring over the classifieds in *Le Figaro* or *France Soir*. Those shitty ads on the last page, the only page designed for the unschooled, a place for offering petty cash, the sole info being an address for a same-day appointment. Flyer distribution by the metro exits, say. I'd last two hours before, utterly depressed by my anonymous ranks of fellow workers, I wound up shoving my bag down the first available trash can. And as I raced into the metro, I'd feel quite proud of my integrity here, but then as the stations filed past, that sentiment yielded to humiliation that I hadn't lasted longer. This was a time when Nikki visited Gibus or wherever every night to see if someone might call him up onstage. This mental torture, by the time he got back home, would clearly have absorbed any lingering effects from his initial waking shot of dope, and so without my even asking, Nikki would set his guitar down to go out looking for a score. As he heated up his spoon, I'd see his anxiety spike at the thought of prematurely sapping the portion he'd set aside for that night, but he wouldn't say anything and just put a bass in my hands instead . . .

Today was a Monday, an empty gray Monday, and I felt the same as if I'd been scouring the news racks again. I felt pathetic. Turning up in Nikki's life again like this, without seeking his thoughts on the matter, and all of it for nothing . . . I caught myself crying when he put his arm around my shoulders.

"I'm sorry," I wept, burying my face in his neck. "I'm really sorry."

"It's nothing," he sweetly said.

"I just can't." I hiccuped. "You know?"

"I get it."

He slipped his other arm around me for a hug, and again I burst out weeping. We easily could have resumed our lives together, he was exactly what I'd been looking for. But I couldn't return to a situation that would only prove enabling, however perfect it might seem. I couldn't return to him expecting someone totally different. And snuggling up to him as I was right then, I only cried that much harder, disgusted it could never remain this easy . . .

By the time I finally called Pallas, she was much less worried than I'd have thought. She said that when she'd heard what I was waking up and listening to, she'd suspected what was coming; she just didn't think I'd be spending the night. I could make out traffic sounds behind her. I asked where she was, and she answered she was store-hopping with Alex and Baby Inès, and it was weird to think that in the span of two days I had just slept with two exes, and all for nothing. After an extended silence, Pallas finally asked what was up. I could feel the tears coming on again, and since I was sick of bawling and blubbering every five minutes, I said that everything was fine and I hung up. I held off on checking my voicemail, then figured that if it was a message from Virgin announcing they'd transferred the sum, I'd be getting the same news soon enough back home. At the moment, though, I didn't want to be back home. I just wanted to stop thinking for a while.

Later, sitting on the floor of the music room, I was listening to records on headphones while Nikki, back at the piano, was playing notes here and there and then jotting them on his score sheet. Every now and then, he turned to smile at me with a knowing expression, nodding to assure me I was making the right choice. Despite my headphones, he could still hear what I was listening to, or at least could sense it whenever I got carried away by a certain track and raised the volume several notches without realizing. Here we both were, just like before, and it crossed my mind that if my being here prevented his concentration, then maybe the simple fact was that he barely even noticed me. As used to me as I was to him? Maybe ultimately he was the one who fell out of love first. After all, he hadn't tried to keep me when I left . . . Our past kept flooding into my ears, and I was trying to understand its impact: a violent thrill mixed with an intense feeling of frustration, because there would never be enough hours in the night, or in the month, or in the year, to rediscover all these tunes. I had no more than thirty of these records at home. At most a few best-ofs, a few Stones, Bowie, and Patti Smith albums. All the rest were techno, house, and electro imports, plus a wide range of '80s synth stuff. How had I managed these last few years, satisfying myself with all these "faceless" records? Albums, and especially maxi singles, with practically interchangeable sleeves—either black or white—and with almost nothing written on them, not even on the sticker. Tracks that could last for hours on end without a single story to tell.

chapter five

dépôt—pulp—shit

1.

It happened on a Tuesday. The location: Le Dépôt. The boys' club on the Rue aux Ours, which sometime recently had started opening its doors to girls once a week.

The craziest thing was that initially, my even being there seemed out of the question. Home from Nikki's the night before, already running on zero sleep, I spent a whole night and day burning CDs from the stack of his LPs I'd borrowed. And so when Pallas curled into my bedroom doorway around eight o'clock, asking what I was waiting for, it was time to get ready, my only wish was to close my eyes and finally sleep for twelve straight hours. Besides, techno didn't sound appealing right now, even less so poking my head outdoors given the recent heat wave. Unfortunately I had this foggy memory from a week before, outside Le Dépôt on a different outing with Pallas, laughing hysterically while she confessed to having fallen for the barmaid, and in a pinched voice I unmistakably had promised to return the next week and to offer her my input.

Le Dépôt is a cramped, steamy club with a stone front. The layout has changed a number of times since, but at the time it was done up in camouflage fabric hanging from the walls in long strips, with a low red light accenting the various intimate nooks and crannies. Heading for the main room, you first came to a grand staircase that descended to the "back room," a basement that seemed to be twice the size as the ground floor but was off-limits to girls. As if we gave a fuck about watching men wank, suck, and fist each other. (Back-room access required constant surveillance, earning a steady five-hundred for anyone with the stamina to stand there for five straight hours, and ironically it was always girls who got the gig.) Off to the right stretched the dance floor, with a long copper bar around back, while immediately to the left another staircase spiraled up to a metal gangway overlooking parts of the main level. To the gangway's left came a succession of banquettes with the DJ booth in back, plus another staircase, steeper and narrower, descending straight to the bar, and that was where you'd find the "back room for girls": three doorways, all in a row, leading to compartments barely larger than personal changing rooms at the pool, but for my part I never saw any girls sneaking in or out.

Wednesdays at Dépôt—dubbed "Ladies Room" by La Chocha, a Cuban woman from San Francisco fighting to update the mainstream's image of lesbian culture—had nothing in common with similar nights at other clubs. To start with, the music was exclusively house and techno; your more standard-issue dykes couldn't hang, out of their depth without their Eurodance hits or Mylène Farmer medleys. Plus, male promiscuity often stressed them out; quite frankly, the place's "hardcore" rep on other nights of the week scared them shitless. So given the basically all-boy clientele, any girls you met were something altogether different. More or less the kinds you'd find wherever Alex or the other girl DJs were mixing: gay, but first and foremost techno fans, which meant crazy getups and easy attitudes, aware they were coming here exclusively to dance.

Opening at nine and closing around two, it also attracted people who wanted a glass before heading home, and others who came to dance for a bit while waiting for the other clubs to open. For us, Alex's sets—she was a resident DJ—felt like popping into the corner café where you knew the manager. The upstairs had become like an HQ: we'd drop off our belongings in the booth, squat all the banquettes (even lying down on them horizontally), drink on the house tab with tickets La Chocha passed around, and if we wanted to dance, we did it right outside the booth, where, given the monitors, the sound was the strongest. Anyone who ventured upstairs was swiftly scared off by our air of privacy, immediately retracing their steps. This limited any chance encounters, at least for me and Pallas, the only singletons in our crew, but newcomers were so rare that scoping out the dance floor downstairs amounted to a slideshow of familiar faces, like perpetually recycled air-conditioning.

So that's where we found ourselves that Tuesday. Me, Pallas, Eva, Gayle, Jessie, Alex, Baby Inès, Little Cyril, Guillaume, and Julia, who was rolling through before her own shift at Pulp. The spot was just about to open, and there was a late-afternoon-on-vacation atmosphere, with daylight streaming in below through the open doorway to the street. Alex hadn't started mixing; an easy-listening group was playing while she sorted through her records in the booth (bopping around like a nut in a T-shirt reading *Last Night a DJ Fucked Your Wife*), and we were just hanging around sipping our icy Cokes, savoring the chilled indoors when compared to the furnace outdoors. We were arguing, each taking turns stroking Jessie's awful dog, a somewhat jumpy white bull terrier she had named, simply, Dumbass. Eva was regaling us with the indignities of the retail grind, having to be on your feet all day without talking to the other cashiers; Julia was showing us the drawing of a dragon she wanted to get tattooed across her back; Cyril was testing Guillaume's skateboard on the gangway; and then, a little ways off, Pallas was chatting all hush-hush with Inès, most likely about her barmaid. Me, I was waiting for that fucking chick to show up so I could get home and go to bed. I could feel the sleep wash over me, slumped in whatever patched-together garments I could find. I had on Nikki's shirt, the one without the top three buttons, while on the bottom I had wrapped myself in a long sheath of ecru fabric, which I had knotted into a makeshift skirt, and on my feet I wore some old white sandals that some visitor had forgotten at our apartment. As it happens, I'd been lounging in my undies all day, and once I gathered that I couldn't not go to Dépôt, I had this impulse that was equal parts delightful and thoughtless that I would meet Pallas's challenge: I'd come naked if I wanted to but I'd hop to it either way. In retrospect, this ensemble was nothing but an awkward attempt to seem more feminine, and if I'd been in my right state of mind, I would have borrowed one of Pallas's dresses rather than wind offcuts from her bedroom curtains around my waist. And there was burgundy nail polish on my toes. That was the first thing I'd done upon getting back from Nikki's; I wondered why I'd stopped wearing this stuff the minute I started seeing girls. Nobody commented, but occasionally I felt intrigued glances sliding up and down my outfit.

"OK, so there's this blonde who's going to the hairdresser," Eva began, "and she's got these headphones on her head from her Walkman. So naturally, the hairdresser asks her to take them off, but the blonde, she says that if she does, she'll die. The hairdresser tries explaining that if she doesn't take them off, he won't be able to cut her hair, but the blonde, she doesn't want to hear it, if I take off these headphones I'll die. After a while, the hairdresser's getting fed up, so he rips the headphones off the blonde, and she falls down and she dies. Still, the hairdresser, he's feeling pretty pissed about it. He doesn't get it, you know? So he picks up the headphones, he brings them to his ear, and he hears: breathe, breathe, breathe!"

Eva was laughing so much that she fell onto Gayle's knees. Then she started rifling through her bag with the flashlight she used to help her find her cigs when the lights were too dim; everyone joked she needed a second flashlight to help her find the first one. So there we were, cracking each other up—I never imagined that a few hours later, one harmless sentence would be enough to fuck it all up, that things would never be the same again.

Pallas had tugged my arm many times so I'd make the rounds with her downstairs, but her bartender was nowhere to be seen. I needed to get some sleep; I kept having to retie my DIY skirt and shoo away Guillaume—I was never brave enough to fess up that I wanted him to stop—yet Pallas insisted I remain. I wound up resting my elbows on the banister, watching the dance floor down below. It honestly wasn't bad just listening to the techno. It was everything anyone could wish for from a place like this. It's just I would've rather been with Nikki and company talking guitars and Granny jackets. Even knowing that it wouldn't lead anywhere, I wanted to get back to all that. Or maybe I didn't feel like being somewhere maximum-homo. I watched the smattering of girls on the dance floor downstairs, wondering how many had even bothered to try out men. And I watched the men, too. Some were hostile to the girls' very presence, with those haughty little pouts that gay guys flaunt so well, but otherwise their eyes just glided right past us like we were nothing but doorknobs. No one masculine enough to stimulate my arousal, but even so, it bothered me to not be getting noticed, not when everything inside me felt so different now . . . Pallas came over and rested her elbows next to mine. For once, she wasn't taking seriously what I'd told her upon getting back home. Like: What the hell do you need? A little time to get used to the idea, or what?

Baby Inès joined us and started ribbing Pallas about her barmaid, saying she was probably the type with an Amélie Mauresmo poster in her bathroom. That she was probably boozing her brains out somewhere trying to forget her latest defeat. Pallas, unamused, shot us both withering glances before wandering off elsewhere. Baby Inès—a baby in age but not a baby in make—wordlessly stayed behind, her elbows rested just like mine. This was the first time I'd ever been this close to her and just her, but weirdly enough, that didn't bother me. In profile, beneath that brown middle-part, with locks falling into her eyes, she looked a little like Leonardo DiCaprio. The same mildly jutting nose starting high between her sunken eyes, though Inès's eyes were darker. The same dullardly aspect, too, her cheeks a little full, but most importantly they had the same arrogantly bent chin. Something about her belonged here, proudly gallivanting with that cute little face of hers, but something else made it seem like she was only passing through. A kid only just beginning to emerge into the world, who had landed here at random and was giving it a once-over before embarking for further destinations. There was no ambiguity to her femme side, the honest girly things that only heteros do, and maybe, subconsciously, she was waiting to transition to greener pastures where guys would really make her blossom. For better or worse, that felt impossible to know. She asked if I was thirsty before drifting somewhere else. Pallas returned, and I told her that for a change, I thought Inès was looking pretty. "Better late than never." And she shut her mouth. I was on my way out until Baby Inès came back with two glasses. Pallas's eyebrows raised. Inès and I each offered our drink to Pallas, but she scoffed them away. She looked disgusted, ran a hand through my hair, declared that I needed a serious chop before she wandered off again. Inès quietly laid her elbows back down. I vaguely recalled this one day when Alex said that she saw a lot of me in her. But I couldn't really see it—I mean, sure, I at that age sported the same superior affect, when on the inside I was quaking in my boots around all these people much older than me. I noticed Guillaume was waiting by the stairs, with his skateboard in hand. He was a good thirty feet away and yet those intense eyes of his seemed to glimmer through the darkness. As if the sheer fact of his staring at me could relay a message so he wouldn't need to pantomime it with his lips: "I might as well pass the baton." As that sentence formed in my brain, it echoed somehow, though I didn't know what any of it could mean. And that's when I noticed Alex thundering past behind me; Jessie waved goodbye from the decks, Eva and Gayle converged on the staircase, Inès asked if I was coming along, and before I had time to even question it, I found myself hastily descending, holding onto my makeshift skirt as best I could. I ran right into Pallas. I said she was in luck: she needed to get a move on and grab her things from the booth, because we were all going to Pulp. She said she wasn't coming. Her face had turned to marble; meanwhile, Baby Inès quickly kissed her on both cheeks. Inès backed away when I signaled I was coming, and Pallas crossed her arms.

"I thought you didn't want to go out?" she sneered, and then before I could answer she added, "If whatever is happening here actually happens . . ."

I still felt shocked. I was about to say *What's the matter with you* but then Eva came and grabbed me by the elbow, and the next time I turned around to face her, Pallas was gone. "You should wear a skirt more often," Eva said as we marched down the hallway to the exit, and trying to suss out whether this was a compliment or the very opposite, I didn't realize that we were leaving Pallas all alone.

I didn't want to go to Pulp, I think I just seized on any opportunity to leave. Maybe I considered getting dropped off along the way but then I simply forgot to ask. Eva slid into the back seat between Gayle and Inès while I climbed in up front. The seats were low like a sports car. The leather smelled new, the floor looked spotless, not yet cruddy and littered like her old set of wheels. Alex hit the ignition, and the sound system roared to life with Suprême NTM's "Ma Benz." She bent over to open the glove box and pulled out two bucket hats. A black one with "Iron Maiden" on it in yellow, which she tamped over her own head, and a second, white one with "Trust" in red, which she tossed back to Eva. On the sidewalk, all eyes were on us, with our music pummeling through the lowered windows. Twisting around and donning her "Trust"-y bucket hat, Eva bobbed her head like those dashboard dogs in redneck cars. Everyone was rapping at the top of their lungs, imitating Joey Starr's deep ogre-voice, repeating "dans ma Benz Benz Benz" over and over, the only intelligible lines in the entire song. I followed along with a wry expression on my face, used to seeing Alex parody all sorts of things with Eva, and I wondered if these people, whom I liked, would ever accept me outside their scene. Again, no indication that this would be my last time riding in this car with them.

2.

The room, just before opening, was deserted except for the staff, and there was the potent, wafting odor of ammonia and stale tobacco so particular to all nightclubs: clean, sure, but the air smells no fresher.

Before it gets livelier, Le Pulp, formerly L'Entracte—and actually still going by that name in the afternoons when it's a dance hall for the olds—is a little like a fading cabaret. The walls up front are bedecked with mirrors; then comes the bar to the right, while on the left a head-high partition guards what feels like a raised den, accessed by a short stairway. The dance floor opens straight ahead, with the DJ booth in the center-back, with assorted low tables, tight banquettes, and footstools all around it, matching the thick, faux-red-velvet wall hangings.

Back when I was seeing Alex, I always joined her for her sets here, but at this point I would only set foot in the place on the odd nights out, and only ever at others' insistence. The girls who owned the club were two of Alex's roommates, and I respected them, but no matter how drastically they'd transformed the place's look, it was still such a buzzkill. Despite their alterations—from a range of good DJs trying to hip their clientele to anything other than French pop and disco, to the go-go dancers dancing (and dancing really well) with their tits out, to the staff who looked straight from the pages of a Shop catalog, with "streetwear," tattoos, piercings, and trendy haircuts—but despite all these details, which could rival New York or London nightlife, and which were starting to attract a real nucleus of "in" girls, those standard-issue dykes were still a hefty slice of the clientele. The club's refusal to impose a strict, selective door policy was honorable, sure—first and foremost, this *was* a spot for girls like them—but me, I couldn't take it anymore.

Inès, Eva, and Gayle had claimed a banquette near the DJ booth, where Alex had already started unpacking her records. I stepped away to use the restroom. The tiles were still dry, but that wouldn't last for long. Who the hell knows why these girls were always pissing on the floor. It wasn't that hard to be careful. What the fuck was I doing here?

Whoever turns them into a card game, "Seven Families"-style, has a real shot at making a fortune . . . From the "butch family," I'll take the cruder options, sad that they were born without a dick but acting as if they were, including some who were openly looking into transplants. They'd bark at you like junkyard dogs if you were lucky enough to tread on their toes, and theirs were the fists you'd see flying in any minor scuffles that brought the black bouncer inside. Next came the ones who'd have loved to be guys but settled for just being really masc. They constituted half the clientele and modeled themselves after guys from the sticks, of the "cheap suit" variety, stumbling in for a glass before heading back home to their bachelor pad. They lit your cigs and propositioned you for slow dances, utterly mortifying events you were never fully cleansed of and which left me grievously on edge. After them came the ones who didn't want to be men but who were masculine nonetheless, too timid to accentuate their femmeness because, not being straight, they felt afraid it wouldn't seem that convincing. They constituted the other major half of the clientele, and occasionally there were some cuties, but all in all they were faceless and nameless. Then came the eternal thirtysomethings, ten or so girls who for some reason all looked a little horse-like: long hair down to the middle of their back, all around 5′9″. They thought they looked ultra-femme: pantsuits over open button-downs, and rings upon rings upon rings. They always kept to themselves, acting high and mighty, flashing credit cards over the heads of all the dwarfs clustered by the bar, ordering bottles that they sipped around a table, criticizing everyone they saw, but all ultimately just as masc, with their jacket sleeves rolled to their elbows and their cigs between thumb and index finger. Next came the half-dozen true femmes, who, like Pallas, were obsessed with fashion or, like Eva and Julia, were laid-back girls who had started out straight and still looked like it. Then, to conclude: a flock of young, green tomboys, some of them charming and others just uncomfortable in their bodies. But didn't that apply to everyone here more or less? Otherwise, how would you explain people confusing them with men from afar? And a similar handful of girls like Alex—or me—who were neither that feminine *or* that masculine. Girls chiefly focused on the music they listened to, and who when they weren't at places like this just seemed like "modern" girls, all short hair and unisex clothing.

Yep, like a deck of "Seven Families." A dispiriting comparison, for sure: for every five hundred girls, four hundred of them were shit, eighty were whatever, another ten weren't bad but had already been "used," and the ten left over were—or basically were—our best friends' girlfriends. So there was just one question: Would you agree to go home with her or with her, both of whom you'd already spurned a hundred times before? There was one mercy, at least: the answer to that didn't concern me anymore.

When Pallas arrived, we were stationed around the booth. We shouted her name, we waved and waved; I must have been the only one to notice she was ignoring us on purpose. I eventually got up to corner her. She was seething so much she couldn't even meet my gaze. She kept saying it made her want to puke, that she didn't think something like this would ever happen. I had to drag her to a private booth to escape their spying eyes; everyone was already copping a look at my improvised skirt, with the wide-open shirt and flip-flops. I assumed that she'd finally seen her barmaid and that it hadn't gone as she'd hoped; I was stunned to find out that it was all about Inès. It pissed me off, her fixating on something so absurd, but it disturbed me too, her feeling so much *hatred* for me. It took me a while to convince her how cuckoo she was acting. To thaw her out, I had her spill the beans about her barmaid. Meanwhile, my eyes were locked on Eva and Gayle dancing—but Pallas assumed Inès. "Fine!" she spat and stood up. Obviously I wanted to restrain her, to put an end to the ridiculous mix-up, but I wasn't trying to be like the others, making a scene by settling scores. Not for the first time, I wondered what the hell I was doing here—until Baby Inès came and dropped down beside me, completely breathless.

"I can cut it for you if you want."

"What?"

"Your hair!" she shouted over the music. "I can if you want! I cut it for my sister!"

I gestured *Why not*, my eyes hunting for Pallas. I tracked her down staring daggers at me from the other side of the floor. Inès handed me a cigarette, lit it, and then she pointed to a mixed-race girl who had just come in, and she asked me what I thought. I fixed my skirt flaps—my thighs were bare—and I bent over so she could hear me better. I said that that chick was off her rocker, that there was this one night when she'd come straight up to me to say I didn't have a chance, when I hadn't even been looking at her! Inès struck a shocked expression, moving in next to me with one leg folded under her ass, then she got real close to my ear:

"I can't imagine anyone not wanting you."

I wasn't sure I'd heard correctly, I had to ask her to repeat.

"I can't imagine anyone not being attracted to you."

She pulled her head away to shoot me this innocent, inquiring look. I smiled, amused, wary.

"I mean it," she added.

I dragged on my cigarette, felt the smile widening at the corners of my lips but struggled to contain it, conscious that Pallas was still glaring at me. Inès was wearing a little white tank top from Petit Bateau, and when she turned her face to me, her bare shoulder grazed my breast. She wouldn't stop staring in my eyes, so I finally burst out laughing and asked was she on E or something? She nodded but was quick to insist that it didn't make a difference.

Ultimately, I said, "I'm very flattered," fixing my wayward skirt yet again. "But that's hard to hear coming from you, especially with Alex right there."

"She knows, though!" Inès shouted, scooting across from me again, lifting her knees and feet to the table's edge.

"What?"

"Fucking yeah. She asked me what I thought one day and I told her."

I bent over, and without looking at her I said:

"Alex is the last person on Earth I'd want a threesome with. So don't get any ideas."

"I didn't mean to make you uncomfortable," she said in this placid affect. "It's just an opinion, not a proposition."

We were silent for a while. Julia had just left coat check so she could dance for a few seconds, which she did whenever she got the chance. Tonight she was wearing some acid-washed denim overalls over a black bra and nothing else, looking more than ever like Cindy Crawford in her cornfield days. When she reached the middle of the dance floor, everyone stepped aside to enjoy the show as much as to avoid getting hit. She furiously gyrated her hips like a giant octopus, swinging her long, naked arms up and down through the air, shaking her mountain of red dreads. I saw Inès's hand go up and her cigarette butt land somewhere far away. I felt dumb for having acted so aggressive. I turned my head in unison with her, and this time I held my gaze. Her eyes were so dark that it was impossible to gauge her pupil size.

After a while, I said, "I'm sorry."

She straightened up, slid her hands beneath her thighs, then started rocking back and forth—gently, very gently—lost in thought. I saw her hair, her straight hair parted just off-center and a little uneven. She ran her hands through it and left the locks behind her ears, a habit I was only noticing for the first time, and suddenly she'd stopped exuding any little-girl shyness, she was sweating pure sex. Her face was barely six inches away. I could see her smooth skin, her fleshy lips, so full and soft, her lips drawn back to reveal the impeccably white teenage teeth. I watched her mouth subtly twist as she bit the corner of her lower lip. I could have stayed like that for hours, swimming in the heat waves rolling through the bottom of my stomach.

"Who knows," I finally said, "maybe in another lifetime."

"Yeah, another lifetime," she said at once, and then she sank back into the booth. Someone came to say hi to her, and as she stretched out her neck to offer the girl her cheek, I caught a side glimpse of her breasts, flattening beneath her straining top. Breasts that stayed aloft without assistance. The other girl walked away and Inès dropped her arm down the backrest behind me, then tilted her cheek onto the backrest as well. She was staring at my mouth, the tip of her tongue poking through her teeth now. Another surge shot through my belly, and my mouth parted. Her gaze lingered, and lingered, while her mouth parted too, a little further, until her eyes rose, they sank into mine, aroused and glassy all at once. We stayed like that, barely six inches apart, our faces at the perfect kissing angle, on the verge of suffocation. And then I noticed two other bodies—Eva's and Gayle's—sliding in across from us to sit on the other side of the booth. "Another, distant lifetime," I mumbled, getting up.

I ran into Pallas on my way into the bathroom.

"Stop hitting on her!" she barked at me.

Luckily, aside from the washroom attendant, this was a deserted location.

"I wasn't hitting on her, I was defending myself."

"Yeah, right! I know that look. That's how you look when you're into someone. You've been that way since Dépôt."

"What? At Dépôt? Hold on, to be clear, she was the one hitting on me!"

"You're disgusting."

"Oh, fuck you—but . . ."

But Pallas had already left. I caught up with her heading out into the street with a firm grip on Inès's arm. I had to peel her fingers away so I could drag her down the sidewalk. A half-dozen girls were lined up to get in, and they couldn't stop rubbernecking. I was mad at Pallas for forcing a scene, but she needed to calm down before the drama turned real. I patiently explained that Inès had spilled some secrets; she was on E, she hadn't been thinking. When it seemed like Pallas understood, I let her go, but she instantly careened toward Inès. Then Jessie appeared, sans dog, and when Pallas had to let her pass through with her flight cases, I saw my moment to corner Inès.

"Whatever she says, deny it."

"Huh? What does she know?"

"Deny it, understood?"

And I grudgingly drifted back inside, with Jessie tapping me on the back and saying she was happy to see me.

When Pallas and Inès finally reappeared, Alex, whose set had just ended, immediately asked the latter what she was trying to pull, moaning that she'd been looking for her everywhere, that *she* had to get to Queen, that *she* had work to do. Inès bent over and kissed my cheeks, not one look, not one hint to suggest what she might have said before. Pallas asked Alex if she could drop her off. I got up to join them, but Pallas sat me back down.

"You," she bent over and hissed in my ear, "you forget it, you've got that kid completely traumatized."

I was flabbergasted. Eva just shot me this quizzical look, but I signaled she shouldn't pay it any mind. Then I turned to face the dance floor, trying to look somewhere, anywhere else. I should have been furious with Pallas, and with Inès too, for confessing who knows what, but most of all I was worried that this would all make its way back to Alex. But as it stood, the only thing on my mind was that if this was all anyone could think about, then for once I was ready to tell the whole lot of them to fuck off.

3.

When I got back out on the sidewalk around six, closing time, it was already light out. Silence all around, only barely disturbed by the sounds of early traffic—that's shock enough when you emerge from a long night of blaring music. But even more disorienting are when the days begin to lengthen, when the morning light starts to feel eternal. It was Wednesday or whatever, some day like any other, and I felt this vague urge for aimless roaming. Who cares where it came from—I just knew. That feeling of suspension I'd experienced at Nikki's: it was only just beginning. Detaching from girl-world, not yet returned to boy-world—no attachments at all for the moment . . . "This fucking headache," came a voice behind me, and there was Jessie, also stepping outside, immediately sticking her sunglasses on. But unlike the old days with Monica and Nikki, when we'd always have a pair in our pockets, I didn't have any. Jessie offered to join me for a cab ride home. She had two bags of records on top of her flight case, but she wouldn't let me carry anything as we stumbled our way to the taxi stand: a little marker along the boulevard, right across from Le Brébant, the brasserie . . . Monica and I had been regulars there, hoping the beer would help us brave the short, sluggish trek only yards down the right-hand alley to Le Palace, dreading whenever Marie-Line was working the door, who knew that respectively, we were only fourteen and sixteen. Monica, now in New York—undoubtedly vital to some uber-hip scene, whereas I didn't even know where I was anymore . . .

With the flight case by her feet and the bags on her knees, Jessie napped while we wove through the still-deserted streets. The house we were traveling to had been put under quarantine. By the day's end, I'd probably be sick as well, but for now that all felt ludicrous. It's just that I'd have to sponge off Pallas again if I wanted to buy a carton of smokes . . . On the sidewalks, people were starting to get into their cars, or were wandering toward the metro and bus stops. When must they have gotten up if they were already dressed and ready? Packing themselves into cafés, the scent of perfume and halitosis. Holed up in some office with the fresh air and blue sky calling to them, saying come to the park, come and lounge in the grass. Crammed around a table, with the commotion and smell of grease, or managing the lazy line outside the bakery with the prix-fixe menu: a tasteless sandwich, a scoop of sauce-drowned carrot shavings, and for dessert some three-day-old flan. In the wintertime, how do they keep from sticking a bullet in their brains, waking up and finding that it's basically still night out? I never had a cent to spare on any passing fancies, but at least I didn't have to deal with any of that shit. Someone should make a *Falling Down* sequel where, this time, Michael Douglas's target is taxis between five and seven in the morning. He'd be lurking around at dawn, spying on passengers from the back seat, and then whenever he found one under thirty, he'd spring up and strike, drag them from the car and strangle them right in the middle of the street, exacting payback for the indecency of having to slip out of bed at a time when it feels like the entire planet's cutting loose. And as we crossed the Place de la République, I spied a bus parked outside the Holiday Inn; from afar, I thought I saw a band stepping out. Or, at the very least, four hunchbacks dressed in black with bleached-blond hair. For a second, I almost asked the driver to let me out right there. Hey, where you coming from, what kind of music you make, oh yeah, that's cool—when Monica was around, we used to do that all the time . . . But by the time those thoughts had passed, the square was already far behind us. So that's what I'd been reduced to: my heart leaping in my chest anytime I saw a couple sets of blond tourists! We were only two lights away from the house when Jessie straightened up, loudly coughed, and then asked me what was wrong.

"What do you mean?" I asked.

"I mean, you didn't dance at all, you basically didn't talk to anyone, you got into it with Pallas, and yet you stayed at Pulp until the end. Unless my set was really that mind-blowing—so what's up?"

"Nothing," I said, both touched and annoyed that she was involving herself in my affairs when she had only met me three times. I reiterated: "Nothing major. Oh, here's great," I added to the driver.

"Hey," said Jessie, scribbling her number on a slip of paper. "I'm guessing I'll be asleep until noon, but call me after if you want, we could grab a bite, I'm not leaving till six or so. Fuck," she sighed, "tonight I'm in Le Mans, tomorrow I'm in Reims, and then the next day I'm in Besançon . . . Wait, hang on," opening a bag and extracting a CD, "tell me what you think."

I got out, clinging to my wayward skirt; through the car's lowered window I thanked her for coming along, and when I backed up to let the taxi dart away, I smiled just enough that it wouldn't give her false hopes. People in this group always interpreted things wrong.

I found Pallas asleep in my bed, flat on her stomach with her dress riding up around her ass. I was about to tiptoe off when she jolted upward, rubbing her eyes. She smiled tentatively in a way that seemed totally innocent, so I walked over to sit on the edge of the mattress. She averted her eyes, saying she didn't know what got into her. She had been afraid. Of what, she wasn't sure—just afraid. I ran a hand through her hair, whispering that all was forgotten. She asked what was in my other hand, and I showed her the CD. If Jessie was already giving me CDs, she said it meant she had a crush on me. From my perspective, it seemed more likely she had some tracks she wanted me to listen to, especially given the lack of a case.

Dressed in my bathrobe after taking a shower, Pallas prepared us some tea, and sitting across from each other, I opened up.

I confessed that as soon as I noticed Inès's interest, it instantly triggered something reciprocal in me, like who cared if Alex was nearby? At the same time, it seemed like I should clarify: it was only her behavior that turned me on, not at all that she was Alex's girlfriend. And since my candor seemed to satisfy Pallas, I cut to the chase: I would never do that to Alex, and besides, I was serious when I said that I wanted to be with guys again. Besides, teenage girls had never been my thing.

"You know," Pallas said, standing up, "I don't want this to upset you, but you were imagining things. She wasn't hitting on you at all, she was letting you hit on her because it was easier than saying stop. She didn't want things to get out of hand. She was really shocked that you would stir shit up between her and Alex—that was the problem. I've never seen her like that. She's young, you know. So let's hope she doesn't say anything."

I did everything I could to keep my jaws clamped so my mouth wouldn't widen to match my eyes. Before she was out the door, Pallas turned around and added, "It's funny, you turned so fucking girly all of a sudden. I was watching you at Pulp, and now it's in everything you do. It actually fucking fits you." My lips tested a smile, hoping to express a "thanks, how nice," but as soon as Pallas was out of sight, my shoulders slumped and I stared into the distance. Sure, I might have literally ordered "the baby" to deny it—clearly she was gifted at denial! But could she honestly have been shitting me the whole time? But when people exhibit denial to that extent, they're surely hiding something, right . . . ? My thirty-one years of experience hinted that I needed to nip this in the bud. But Pallas's attitude had left a bitter taste in my mouth.

4.

Later that afternoon, while I was asleep with Pallas watching TV beside me in bed, her cell phone rang and it was Alex. I asked if I could speak with her, but without really knowing what to say. At the moment, she was sorting through her records for the trip she and Jessie were taking to Le Mans. She started to catalog their next fifteen days of gigs, saying Inès wouldn't be tagging along because she needed to prepare for her big exams. So for as long as they were apart, I was welcome to any and all temptations. The bait had now been set, and I could still hear Pallas as she moseyed to the bathroom, but I didn't care and I let it fly:

"So wait, does she actually cut people's hair? Because she said she would cut mine."

"Hang on, I'll grab her for you."

And so I found myself, for the first time ever, on the phone with Baby Inès. From shock to embarrassment in the span of only three seconds—she started asking me questions about the haircut I wanted. Her voice was so quiet I had to stick a finger in my ear. A voice like no one else's. Very young, very cheery, but with this slow, blasé diction that dipped into the bass register at times, as if she'd only just opened her eyes. She was probably standing somewhere with the house cordless, but who knows, maybe she was lying across their bed with her head thrown back into thin air, dreamily contemplating the ceiling.

"Is Alex with you?" I asked after a while.

"No."

"So what did you say to Pallas?"

"I mean, you wanted me to deny it, right?"

"Yeah, but not like that . . . Anyway. I just wanted to know—what you said last night, did you mean that?"

"I mean, what about you?"

I let myself slouch backward in bed.

"Well, I asked you first."

". . . Yeah, I meant it." (Silence.) "You?"

"We're in deep shit, aren't we?"

"I mean, I guess so, yeah."

I heard Pallas flushing the toilet. I straightened myself up.

"Listen," I whispered, "I can't really talk right now, OK?"

On second thought, she must have been lying down, was maybe even naked in Alex's bed, with just the sheet up to her shoulders, because I could hear her breathing lengthen as no doubt she reached for a pen and paper. She slowly repeated the number that I gave her, and honestly I had never heard someone's voice sound so blasé.

"If you get the answering machine, don't leave a message. Thinking of you, OK?"

"You, too."

I hung up just as Pallas was entering the room again. My heart was beating fast, and I had a smile that reached my earlobes. Pallas cocked an eyebrow, and I felt my blushing reaction. I pulled myself together and I chuckled that Alex wasn't ever gonna change, always needing to charm the pants off people! So far, everything was running smoothly.

When nighttime rolled around and my phone started ringing, I just knew it was Inès. If I let it reach the answering machine, I'd lose my chance to speak with her, and how could I be sure that she would ever call me back; plus, I couldn't run the risk of Pallas hearing her voice down the line if she decided to leave a message. I leapt up just before the machine could kick in, greeted her once, then twice with a "Hello?," catching only the subtlest breathing sound until, right before Pallas's unbelieving eyes, the conversation transpired as follows:

Inès: I love your voice.
Me: Oh, yeah, uh.
Inès: You must be a really good kisser.
Me: A poll? What for? Can you call back a little later?
Inès: What a start!

Me: Thanks, OK, goodbye.

After hanging up, I sat back down with this glum expression and told Pallas that when I was at Nikki's, I used to always get these survey calls, from the days of dragging myself to work in Montrouge—market-research stuff at Sofres. Pallas gave me a wincing smile; so far, everything still was running smoothly.

When the phone next obliterated the one A.M. hush, I instinctively sprang out of bed to pick it up after the first ring. "Hello?" once, twice again before remembering the short silence that preceded Inès's voice the last time; I sighed and said that I was happy she was calling.

"Same," she said, her voice both muffled and utterly present.

"Where are you?" I asked, walking to the doorway to make sure every light was off in Pallas's room. They were off, but naturally her door was open wide, just like every other night, and I couldn't close mine because it squeaked too much. Another knock against this apartment: if I wasn't smart enough to close my door before Pallas went to sleep, things could go irretrievably haywire. "Huh? Where are you?" I asked again.

"At my parents' house."

I grabbed my smokes and my ashtray and sat down by the window on the far side of the room.

"Shouldn't you be asleep by now?" I whispered, lighting myself a cigarette. "Don't you have school or something?"

"Very funny."

I gently laughed, but I clearly didn't have the slightest idea how to talk to a teenage girl.

"If I hang up all of a sudden, it's 'cause my father's coming in."

Her voice was always so low that yet again, I had to shove a finger down my ear.

"Anything you want to talk about?" she asked, clearing her throat.

"Huh? Oh yeah, for sure."

But what? I knew nothing about her. I didn't even know how she was doing on her exams, or if she always lived with her parents when she wasn't over at Alex's. I knew absolutely nothing, and knew even less what she could possibly want from me.

"Just now," she butted in, "I was fantasizing about you," sharp inhale, "just a hickey, you know, right here, right above my belly button," another inhale, "and I came."

". . ."

"And it happened really suddenly, you know? I wasn't expecting it to happen so fast."

I felt speechless; I had to remove the receiver from my mouth so she wouldn't hear my sputtering breath. When it seemed like my voice had stopped trembling so much, I said that maybe it was someone else, I wasn't much of a hickey person. Then I froze because I'd said it too loudly. But the apartment was silent.

"I really want you," she said. "You?"

". . . yeah."

"Can you say it?"

"I do too, I want you too."

And right then I heard Pallas's door slam shut—and hard.

5.

"Babe, you're being paranoid, totally paranoid—you should really get your head examined. That was Nikki calling. I mean, if you couldn't tell, we almost got back together last weekend. So he's got a right to call at one in the morning if he wants to. He's got a right to whatever he wants whenever he wants because he's the only guy I've ever loved. That clear enough for you?"

Pallas was paralytic, but now her eyes were starting to widen more and more. Like she couldn't believe what was happening, like she was going crazy or something. She was sitting ramrod straight, her hands locked around her naked, shaking knees. Losing her marbles was her greatest fear; her mother had these violent fits of paranoia, and was subject to lifelong treatment. I felt bad making her doubt herself like this, but I had no other options. Later, if she thought it over for just one second, she'd realize that I was clearly hiding something, provided how fiercely I was acting, but we would cross that bridge when we came to it.

I walked into the kitchen, didn't even flip the light switch, and I grabbed myself a Coke. I lingered in the dimness, gazing out the window. There wasn't a single light on in any building off the courtyard. Usually it felt exhilarating to be the only one awake, but now it just felt isolating, like agony. I walked away, sat on the edge of the couch where the plastic squeaked. I could clearly hear Inès's voice outlining that personal moment, imagining things with me . . . Where had she been calling from? From her bedroom? Her parents' living room? I couldn't picture it, but I could see her there regardless, sitting just the way she had on Pulp's banquette, staring at my mouth through the wisps of hair in her eyes, gently nibbling her bottom lip. And I could see Alex, who for six months now, whenever she was at the turntables, would raise her eyes any chance she got to watch Inès dancing in front of the booth. And now, sitting in the gloomy, silent kitchen, I surrendered to the obvious: I had never felt so flustered in my entire freaking life.

chapter six

waiting

1.

The next day, I opened my eyes to find Pallas opening my door, and even in my sleep haze, it was instantly clear that nothing had improved. She who, like me, never emerged until late in the morning was already dressed and ready to go at 8:45. Standing in the doorway outside my darkened bedroom, she was glaring straight ahead, out the window, raising a cup of steaming tea to her lips and then returning it to the saucer in her hand. With her eyes fixed in place, she started listing the various spots she was planning to shop at with Alice. Her tone was alarmingly smooth, like she was talking to herself. She didn't look at me when she asked if I wanted to come, nor when she heard that I couldn't. She kept sipping little gulps of that visibly scalding tea, running her tongue over her lips to soothe the sting every time. Some of it, evidently, had spilled onto the saucer, because it dripped whenever she lifted her cup. When I noticed it falling on my carpet, I felt a cold surge of fear. I wouldn't have flinched if she were anybody else, but with Pallas, so loath to ash her cigarettes anywhere other than the center of an ashtray . . .

This was like stubbing a smoke out on her plate. It wasn't like her, it wasn't like her at all.

I should have forced myself to go shopping. To show her that everything was normal, or else to make her feel that no matter what happened, our relationship wouldn't change in any way. But I didn't have a choice: I hadn't thought to take down Inès's number, and if she called, not being there would give her an entire day to decide that it was probably better to just let this thing go. So I pretended I wanted to work, and Pallas bobbed her head like "yeah sure, I understand." I finally got up, but only to lean back against the entrance while she stormed about, making doubly sure that she had her cell phone, her keys, and her shades. Meanwhile, I tried figuring out some way to bum a little money from her for cigs. I just came out with it as she was opening the front door: "Listen, I know I already owe you a lot, but I'm running low—is that OK?" She bobbed her head a little more, she didn't have any cash, if I wanted some I'd have to walk her to the ATM. I quickly dressed, and I raced to meet her downstairs. When I reached her in the lobby, I said I'd visit the bank as soon as my advance came through and I'd withdraw everything I owed, all at once. And I added, when that miracle came at last, we would shop to our hearts' content. We would hit Colette in the morning, then every Étienne Marcel that afternoon, and everything I found, I'd get an extra one for her, on top of her ten thousand bucks. Pallas wasn't listening, even with that head still gently bobbing. My words themselves couldn't crack through enough that she'd weigh what they really meant, or even grasp their tone; I was using my sweetest inflections. On top of wanting to work, I said, I was too beat to go shopping, I wanted a little peace at home. When we reached the ATM, I capped it all off by asking how long it had been since I had had a true night's sleep—like an entire night, not three or four hours here and there. It was not since the rave: a week to the day. And then this funny expression washed over her face as she handed me the two hundred francs. A vacant, almost dumb expression that deep down, very deep down, seemed to register that only a week ago, *on the dot*, everything had been going just fine. A microscopic glimmer so intense that I averted my eyes, rattled by a sudden wave of guilt, while Pallas simply walked away.

Back upstairs, I was in a silent apartment once again, taking in the panorama of Nikki's fifty records all strewn across the carpet. I remembered it all . . . The sensation of pressing up against him in the music room early on, and then the rush I felt when he slowly pushed inside. I remembered every fleeting thought, like dozens of comets exploding in bouquets across the stratosphere, sprouting only to fade into the distance, forming even more bouquets, smaller but equally potent. Dozens of these detonations all morphing into a single mass eruption, an echoing rumble that bound every image and feeling together, an unending power-wash complete with a rainbow—a feeble, timid rainbow, perhaps, but auguring the kind of sunny spell I hadn't experienced in ages. So long that I couldn't even remember. Since the last time I'd allowed a man into my heart . . . Yet here I was, feeling heat pulsing through my loins whenever Inès's face came up.

I wasn't an idiot, I wasn't even blinded by physical lust, not at all. I was fully aware that she was the last person on Earth I should approach, and that this wasn't just my rational side speaking, because I felt it through my entire body, like a brutal rain of whips cracking down whenever those sensations started roiling in my stomach. It was more concrete than that: I knew that even a one-night "misstep" meant instantly losing it all. Our whole posse would go up in smoke, nothing less than my emotional landscape for the past four years.

Because even beyond the scenesters who loved sticking their nose in things, happily taking roles they had no business in, the whole crew was going to side with Alex. Weren't they all her friends more than mine? And suddenly I could tell that this went deeper, much deeper: everything I'd experienced in those past four years I owed to Alex, all of it. The music I made and listened to, the clothes I wore, the places I went, the flings I had (always with Alex's friends, exes, or future lovers who I'd been scoping out for her), up to and including the dope I now shied away from, largely so I wouldn't indulge her quest to feel a little less alone about doing herself in—absolutely all of it connected back to her.

But I knew it was too late to turn back now. If Alex hadn't dumped Inès after six months, that meant she was really something special. Alex and I had the exact same taste. So, if this was good enough for her, then she was good enough for me. As simple as that. I couldn't start backpedaling now; even if Inès changed her mind, I would needle her till she relented. Because I was already possessed by an attraction, was choking on it even, was hungry to spread her thighs, to press our sweaty bellies together, to feel her deep inside—and only from the front, knowing Alex, *no question*—and to spurn it all now would be like firing a bullet in the brain of someone you just fell madly in love with. And I remembered what Alex said when she copped to our similarities, me and Inès: "Your birthdays are a day apart."

A baby Scorpio. Baby Scorpio, meet adult Scorpio. We were jetting off for a planet billions of light-years away. A planet where not even someone as determined as Alex would ever get her grubby paws on us . . .

So there I stood, clothed in the middle of my bedroom at a little after nine in the morning, when for months now I had chained myself to an anti-restorative sleep cycle—and now I was up and about. If I could just force myself to stay awake, maybe I'd fall asleep earlier than usual and disrupt the rhythm, but of course my eyes started hovering over the bed, and the thought of not slipping back under the covers felt totally inconceivable.

I flopped down, watching MTV with the sound off before I finally fell asleep. First gradually before suddenly sinking all the way down to the deepest layers of slumber, where it hits you like a sledgehammer, where dreams, even if they start to coalesce, simply evaporate into another mysterious realm where memories never make it out alive. But when the phone started ringing, I had no trouble getting up to take a peek at the alarm. It was half past ten, so it could only be Inès; everyone else had been instructed to never call me before noon. My heart skipped a beat; I listened for the second ring and then the third, and it wouldn't hurt if she had to try me several times before she got through, but then my inner weakness made me pick up right before the machine could kick in. A hoarse "Yes?" emerged from my parched throat, and I immediately had to pull my ear away from all the crackling street noise in the receiver.

It was Pallas. She and Alice were at Girbaud, and she was wondering if I'd be interested in this black cross-back dress now that I was luring boys again. As nice as I could, I said I'd rather wait for my advance, that if she was really being rational then she'd think of doing the same. Her "yeah, you're right" sounded reassuring, like she was back to reality.

My cheek greeted the pillow like an old friend, and yet my lids refused to droop. It was already too hot out. From the heavy air alone, oozing through the shutters, you could feel how muggy the day was about to be. I was craving a McMorning. Despite the horrible ad—a couple who only saw each other over breakfast because she's a night nurse and he's got a day job—I really wanted to try one, but I never managed to get there before they stopped serving them at eleven. Judging by my clock, I still had a little time, but I was too much of a couch potato to get up and get dressed. Lying on my side, I watched the images coasting by on MTV. They were frankly unbearable, the endless ads they'd pelt you with for mail-order comps. "Greatest hits" box sets, three, four, sometimes even five CDs apiece; anthologies meant to encapsulate a given period (fifties, sixties, seventies, eighties) or to fit a given purpose, music for driving, music for a romantic night in, music for vacuuming or wiping your ass. Track intros soundtracking bargain-basement skits while titles scrolled along the bottom of the screen, context-free and often incorrect, all enhanced by some scumbag's preening voice explaining how good a deal this was if you ordered this limited-edition gem right away. The ads lasted five minutes, easy, and you were treated to them, what, like ten times an hour? Then, after about two or three months, it was on to the next one. Hearing the first notes from the latest selections always made me smile, tracks tangibly connected to this or that memory I had, but by the second time around they were already starting to grate, until by the third time you were reaching for your remote to stop yourself from throwing something through the screen. Who bought these things anyway?

Again the phone started ringing. Eleven thirty. This time it had to be Inès; it felt right that she'd be rising late that morning, fitting for a high school student without any classes that day. For the second time now, I waited to answer, my heart skipping a beat just like the first time before I finally picked up, all the saliva absconding from my throat. Pallas again. This time she was at Patrick Cox: Any chance I'd wear beige mules with pearls along the top? Again,

I'd rather avoid spending at the moment, I said, after which, nicely, I repeated "See you tonight" three times in a row until she hung up.

Now, on MTV, we were being treated to Britney Spears doing some ridiculous robot dance. It reminded me of this one Fête de la Musique with Alex, I can't remember which, when we were trying to reach Bastille by car; 2Be3 were writhing on the main stage, pulling off this string of backward somersaults without ever stopping to sing. As if moving like that had no effect on their breath control . . .

Once again the ringing removed me from my sleep, which was steadily getting shallower, and my heart, if possible, was pounding even stronger than the first two times, knowing that at this point it truly had to be Inès, because it felt even more fitting that she was getting up around noon. No, still Pallas, wanting to know if I honestly didn't feel like joining.

"What the hell are you up to anyway?" she shouted over music audible in the background (2Be3 perhaps?).

I told her that maybe I'd make a decision if the phone would just stop ringing. I giggled saying it, though my impatience must have shown through, because her "fine, I won't bother you anymore" sounded more like "got it, I'll keep the line open for you."

When it started buzzing again a few seconds later, I answered with a teasing "What now?," except that this time, clearly, I hadn't picked up on the subtle silence preceding Inès's subsonic voice.

"Where are you?" I spluttered, my index finger jammed all the way into my ear so I wouldn't miss a single drop.

"Calm down," she said, amused. "At my parents' house. I'm prepping for my bac, don't you remember?"

Remember what? It's not like she told me that herself, and Alex had barely mentioned it.

"Oh yeah, right," I conceded, hoping I would sound expertly detached. "Yeah, I'm working too, so five minutes is all I've got."

A deep drag on a cigarette, followed by a lengthy exhale.

"That's weird," she said slightly louder, probably aiming for gentle sarcasm but sounding just plain unfriendly, "you never seem like you really like techno deep down. Didn't Alex teach you everything you know? I mean, that's the deal, right? That you wound up in this at random?"

Touché.

"A hundred percent," I said, humbly enough to try to make her feel stupid. "She taught me how to mix, and then I learned the rest after that."

". . . Yeah," sounding resigned, again so muted that even having my finger so far in my ear that it hurt, I also had to smash the speaker into the other, "see, that's what kills me is—I'M COMING! TWO SECONDS!—that's what I keep telling Alex. Playing other people's records works for, what, like five minutes."

She had obviously just woken up, and I couldn't get over how low her voice got, how drawling and laid-back.

"I mean, that's a real skill if you can do it well," I said, thrilled that I'd given her an excuse to deride Alex.

"I gotta go," she whispered, "I have to make lunch for my little sister. You want my number?"

Naturally, some part of me wanted it, but another part preferred it that she was the one who was having to keep calling.

"I don't have a pen around—so you've got a baby sister?"

"And a mother who's kind of a wackjob, and a father who's a real dick; I'll tell you about it later, though."

With that implication of future intimacy—something of a shift in our power relations—I felt I ought to cede a little ground:

"I'd love that," dropping my voice as low as possible. "That and a whole lot else."

"Same," in a breathy exhale. "I'll call you."

I was dying to keep her a little longer; I had to really squint before I could say:

"Alright, well, later then."

"Hey, wait . . . I love your voice."

I hung up without a goodbye. She was really sprinting for it now. I was lobbing up the ball, and she was sprinting for it.

2.

I was lying on my back, drenched from not drying off after a cold shower, but why bother when the sun could dry me just as quickly? Except that in this case I wasn't reclining in the sun's sweet embrace, droplets evaporating beneath its sumptuous flame, tickling slightly, like flies climbing up and down my calves and my thighs—no, instead I was baking in an oven. It felt like sticking your skin under a gas-station dryer. The only option in times like this is to cease all exertion.

And so I was resting flat on my back, raising my head on a pillow with a glass of warm Coke in one hand and the TV remote in the other; without even bothering to lift up my arm, I was shuffling from one channel to the next. On TF1, Citroën was doing an *Invisible Man* parody with a couple walking down a road: they were invisible, they had no faces, necks, or hands, but somehow no clothes, either, only a hat for the mister and a handbag for the missus. I didn't get it: Were they supposed to be buck-naked? I wanted to put on a record but wasn't brave enough to move. How come no one had figured out some kind of telescoping arm that could pull an LP from its sleeve or a CD from its case? I eventually managed without, crawling on all fours to stick on some Iggy: Nikki's copy of *The Idiot*. The phone started ringing. I had been acting so lifeless that it startled me, and so oblivious that it might have been Inès that I started out in Iggy-voice, approximating his zombie-baritone:

"I don't care who you are, I don't need a vacuum, and I've killed three Jehovah's Witnesses already."

A puerile laugh burst out, and I started laughing too; however imperceptibly, my heart had started beating faster as I bounced up to kill the record.

Finally she asked, "Are you working?"

"Yeah!" I said loudly, falling back onto the mattress, once again screwing a finger in my ear so I could hear her a little better. "So your dad?" I prompted, reaching for my cigarettes.

"Huh?"

"A real dick is what you said."

"Oh . . . yeah, my dad's a real tub of lard, so sad—he's like a senile old tomcat with his balls cut off."

I snorted with laughter again, but this time she wasn't laughing.

"Sorry," I said, hoping to soothe.

She sighed: "It's fine, but sometimes I just wish I were anywhere else."

"My bedroom—it's the number one hiding place on Earth," I offered with a wink, immediately conscious of how mental I was acting.

"Isn't Pallas there?"

Her voice was so low . . .

"If Pallas is gonna faint, she'd rather do it outside—easier to meet people that way. She's got this real thing for firefighters!"

Which didn't make her laugh. But she should have—I was telling the truth.

"So how's this gonna work?" she asked with sadness in her voice. "Does she ever sleep anywhere else?"

Her voice was like a dying wheeze.

"We'll figure something out," I answered, as kindly as I could.

"Are you gonna take me to a hotel?" she exclaimed, excited.

Well, well . . . Had Alex already spoiled her with luxury hotels like she used to do with me? How obvious could she be? How unoriginal, Alex, zero points for originality.

"Is that what you want?" I asked.

"No," she muttered. "I want to see your room. Your bed. Oh shit," dropping her voice even further, "my dad's coming, I'll call you back."

Did her tomcat castrato work from home or something? Now on TF1 they were offering Herta sausages: a little boy carving a hunk of wood, fashioning a little boat and then setting it out on the water, watching it drift away with a mixture of hope and nostalgia. With trees all around him, a riverbank, a patch of gravel—and all this for some industrial, vacuumed sausages . . . I stubbed out my cigarette and stretched out on my side with both hands under my cheek. She wanted to see my room . . . but then what was she going to think? She knew the apartment itself from her regular visits picking up Pallas with Alex, but she had never caught a glimpse of my bedroom except from the doorway, and only for a second even then. I closed my door whenever the two of them arrived; afterward, when Alex knocked to say hi, I could never stop myself from prodding her that I didn't have any coloring books or lollipops for her little friend. But my bedroom. Everyone in our crew whose homes she might have visited had really sick bedrooms and apartments . . .

Julia's room, for example, in her shared house with Alex in the nineteenth. It was twice the size of mine—you'd have thought you were in the practice room from *Fame*: hardwood as far as the eye could see, and with one wall entirely covered in mirrors for dance practice. There was nothing in the room but a mattress and our so-called "standard survival kit" (TV, VCR, and stereo), but it wasn't bland and impersonal like mine. Eva's, meanwhile, was like a country cottage: tiled floors, scented candles, and plants spilling off a picnic table. On top of that, there was a bed she'd adorned with a panoply of little cushions that all beckoned you to snuggle in, the opposite of my ancient blue duvet. Alex's little brother Cyril, still living with their parents, had something like a drug den turned rapper's paradise, with its sparkling new gym equipment and a thick navy-blue carpet that your feet blissfully sank into as you wandered to his bed. David, Alex's graphic-designer friend who dealt coke among his other pursuits, had a room painted turquoise with a red bulb dangling from the ceiling, and across the red-painted hardwood stood an assortment of thirty globes in all sizes, all connected to a single switch, a wild display whenever we rolled through after a party in the wee hours. As for his living room, it was like a furniture catalog had vomited up its best and blackest contents, like Mickey Rourke's place in *9½ Weeks*, up to and including the blinds. Take one look around, and you would learn what it meant to make steady dough hand over fist. Then came the apartment Alice had obtained through the Cité des Arts: entirely silver, including the hardwood, with two huge Cindy Sherman photos framed over her bed, while the other room had three lined-up clothes racks, with basically only black apparel, and below them a row of shoes, fifty pairs equally black. And finally there was Alex's . . . a real teen paradise. A Freddy pinball machine, snowboards, collectible paperbacks arranged on metal shelving (every Ellroy, Stephen King, and Anne Rice), a hundred manga tapes, a king-size bed with matching sheets, typically silk in burgundy and gray, and with action figures any which way you looked. The tallest ones were hip-height—Goldorak and *Dragon Ball Z*, Darth Vader and Spawn, *Alien* and Chucky and the Silver Surfer, a giant *Scream* mask, Spiderman in every pose—and many of them talked or roared or blinked somehow, like the tentacle-beast that unfurled as you walked by. When anyone under thirty starts really raking it in, assuming they're still awash in childhood fantasies, then they invest it all on toys. But the craziest things were her clothes, which took up an entire wall. An immense array of cubbies reached up to the ceiling (one for uni-color tees, one for solid whites, one for whites with graphics, etc.), even bigger than Nikki's record shelves, and with a ladder that slid on a rail so you could reach the higher cells. And in the wardrobe in the middle, you could see how every item, from the quilted parkas to the lighter summer jackets, had been bought in twos and threes, however many colors were available in that style. Not to mention the sneaker collection down below, or the record collection, five times bigger than mine, beside the turntables in the living room.

Whereas my room . . . The only thing that might impress Inès about my room were the electronics. The phone started ringing. Her again, and it struck me how no one else was calling me that day—and how Pallas still hadn't returned.

"You can work in this heat? I dunno, with these books I've got to read, I feel like my fingers are sticking to the pages."

"What are you studying?"

"Don't even try, this stuff would take you back ages!"

I couldn't tell if she was calling me an old maid or if she was trying to say she felt young and dumb.

"Are you seeing Alex tonight?" I asked, depressed all of a sudden.

"Not sure yet. If I do, I'll be thinking of you! Shit, what's his fucking problem? Sorry, I gotta go again."

At this point, this was more than just bad luck, this was a total Scorpio move.

Little by little, I was starting to remember things I'd heard about Inès. Her school was close to her parents' house in Versailles or somewhere near. Early on, she only visited Alex on the weekends, but over time Alex had convinced her mom to let her stay past Sunday night, promising to make sure that she actually went to class. I could still hear Alex saying how it wasn't too bad having to get up at six in the morning to walk her to the train. But I also remembered Eva confessing to me and Pallas how there had been whole weeks when Inès hadn't set foot on campus. Alex had to start insisting she get a diploma, but then little by little her ego gained the upper hand again, similar to when she'd been teaching me to mix. She found every possible excuse for company in the things she was too lazy to do alone, or reasons to keep us hanging in her bedroom while she felt shitty from all the blow that she'd snorted. I remembered it raising Pallas's hackles that Alex was slipping Inès increasing amounts of E, when early on she hadn't taken anything at all. And I remembered Alex wouldn't stop showering her in presents. Back home from a day they'd spent store-hopping, Pallas would tell me everything, or Alex would brag about it herself. All the stuff I used to be entitled to, except that now Alex was earning loads of money, and so the items were getting costlier and costlier . . . The phone rang, and I couldn't tell if I felt grateful or deep down in it.

"I had this crazy dream the other night," Inès began, once again in a voice so low I had to jam a finger in my ear. "This was after Pulp and Queen the last time. I was in this desert, on the edge of an oasis. It wasn't that bad, it just wasn't very big—like, barely any water.

And I could see how, way off in the distance, there was this other one that seemed a lot bigger, and a lot prettier. So I went to check it out from afar, and I realized it was everything I'd ever wanted. But I figured it was possibly a mirage. I couldn't tell if I should risk the trip and watch it vanish before my eyes."

I cleared my throat, uneasy.

"I don't know what to make of it," she went on. "Shit," she sighed, "it's no big deal—I've just got to get to work. Thinking of you."

I was still in shock when I put down the receiver. Had she really just implied what I thought she had?

3.

Nightfall had fully settled in, and it felt like feeling my way through a fog. I dozed at regular intervals, laid out by the Efferalgan Codeines I'd swallowed, four of them, to stave off a headache—but was that the only reason? More than anything, it felt like I was sloshing around, savoring the codeine's side effects, which weren't powerful enough to get completely wasted, but still sufficient for numbing my limbs and mind, dragging me into inertia, like eyelids getting heavy in the sun after a feast. Outside, a string of dark, fat cumulus clouds had stalled over the neighborhood. The air had turned so thick that on top of having to open my own shutters, I had to do the same for the windows on the other side of the apartment, desperately hoping to create some kind of current. Still, now and then I could hear the wind start picking up. It rustled the leaves of our kitchen plant, it gushed against Pallas's curtains, but in my room it could barely even stir my shutter-cord—no breeze to graze my face and sweaty body.

There was jack-shit on TV at the moment, nor could I bring myself to stick something into the VCR. But succumbing to a movie, any movie, might have helped me slough off the suspicious weight I felt while ostensibly relaxing; to switch the light on and cue up some music would have cut the reigning atmosphere, the heightened surreality. I could feel myself sliding down a gentle, infinite slope, proceeding ever deeper into the night with every tick of my digital clock, yet at the same time I felt like I was hanging, imprisoned in an endless moment. Hanging on Inès's latest call, six hours before, like the clouds outside hung over the city, still unsure if they should finally break or just continue along their way.

Why wasn't she calling back? I didn't mind if Alex was out mixing somewhere and she had tagged along and was now dancing beside the booth, but if they were alone somewhere together, in Alex's bed for example . . . That was a distant possibility, but her presence sporadically would surge back through me and suddenly drown me in a discomfort I couldn't quite shake. A prettier form of oasis . . . I refused to let this send me off the deep end.

Around one in the morning, I jolted awake from a cascading echo of thunder. I was still sitting there listening to its reverberations, the wind violently thrashing another window in our building, when I heard a roar of rain start tumbling down, and I stood up to close our shutters. The wind had toppled our plant in the kitchen, strewing soil across the tiles, and the rim of our toilet bowl was fucking drenched. In Pallas's room, it felt odd she wasn't back yet, still. Even if she hadn't bought anything, after a full day of shopping, it puzzled me that she hadn't passed through again, at least to change before heading out.

I lasted ten minutes, sprawled in front of MTV with the sound off, before I grabbed the phone and called Alex. The answering machine engaged at the second ring—some nasal forties actress saying, "I didn't sleep, so this had better be good"—so I instantly hung up. I tried again on her cell, but then I cut the line with my finger, deciding I needed an extra-sturdy reason to be calling her at one in the morning. All I had to do was say I missed her. It rang into the void for a minute—a minute that felt like an hour—before the voicemail kicked in, and this time, Alex was singing some Françoise Hardy, first sweetly, "*Mais si tu crois un jour que tu m'aimes,*" but then morphing into a braying stuck pig, "*NE LE CONSIDÈRE PAS COMME UN PROBLÈME-UHH, ET COURS ET COURS JUSQU'À PERDRE HALEINE-UHH, VIENS MEUHHHH RETROUVAYYYYYY,*" concluding with a powerful belch that lasted till the beep. Laying the phone back on the carpet, I couldn't help but laugh. Alex only didn't answer when she was mixing, and that's when I remembered: she had just set off on that series of gigs with Jessie and so therefore was in Reims. Which reminded me: she'd said Inès wasn't going because of test prep. And instantly I felt soothed. But didn't Inès also say that she couldn't tell if she'd see her? Reims wasn't exactly far away . . . Unfortunately, that could easily explain the missed call. I tried again, in vain.

So this meant Alex's set must have started, and her cell phone was in the car, or else it was on the bed at her hotel, assuming she had one. I was reminded of all the times that I'd been there at her side, in towns across France and beyond . . . Typically she only asked for accommodations if the trip was too long to hit the road again right after. So now was our chance if we wanted to fuck as loud as possible, bearing in mind the shoddy soundproofing in Paris apartments. And so I impulsively hit the redial. Nothing. But even if Inès *was* there, even if they were staying overnight, it was highly unlikely that Alex and Jessie had booked two separate rooms . . .

Those Hôtel Ibis shoeboxes, with their hideous ribbed duvets, their little toothbrush cups straight from a school cafeteria (complete with a space down below to write a number for your age), and a wooden wardrobe with three sad plastic hangers—it was like they were winter sports themed. First, Alex always drew a bath up to the brim while I test-drove the TV, irked at the lack of choices. It was cable, sure, but there were only ever two or three channels, like BBC Prime (a snoozefest—those interminable snooker games, and not even any holes for the balls to drop into!), Rai Uno (their sitcoms looked even shittier than AB Productions stuff), or ZDF (where the news sets were always as drab and depressing as *Derrick*). And otherwise it was just TF1 and France 2, not even Canal+ or M6. So when we got back after Alex was off, there was nothing we could do but fuck on every surface, in the bathtub, on the carpet, against the windowsill watching the day break over some gray provincial town—a town just like all the others we'd ever seen. And with that on my mind, I hit the redial once again.

The receiver hadn't even reached my ear before a crazy ruckus started erupting from the speaker. I quickly cut the volume on TV, and hearing Alex shouting over music, I felt forced to do the same, feeling slightly dumb to be hollering all alone in my quiet bedroom. Yes, she was in Reims with Jessie, they had already called it off; first one of them had quit and then the other—a total nightmare. The local yokels only wanted Eurodance, clearing the dance floor for any slightly cool track she played, to the point that the promoter eventually came and whispered in her ear: maybe she should try the venue's own records instead. Going by what was audible behind her, I had to take her at her word. I asked if anyone else was there, but she didn't understand the question. "Oh, I dunno, maybe you took Eva along or something." "No, no," she said, "just Jessie and I." The relief I felt. She kept describing the scene, how all the guys had ski jeans and crew cuts with mullets down the back, and the girls all had dresses showing leg hair like Portuguese fatties. And how everyone was giving her strange looks; with her exaggerated slurring and those drawn, alien features of hers, practically a skull-and-crossbones, I could only imagine the effect she was making. I asked when she'd be coming back, but there was someone else talking to her at the same time. I doubled down and asked again and, annoyed, she asked me why. "I don't know—stupid question, I guess." A brief silence ensued, if silence is the right term with all the music in the background. Not so long before, it would have royally pissed me off for her to think I might have missed her. I heard Jessie asking if she'd been able to reach Inès, and Alex saying no, still nothing. "So?" I cut back in. "When can I see you?!" She said she didn't know. They still had to check the map for how far they were from Besançon, for the next day's gig; maybe they'd head straight over instead of cutting back through Paris. There was something funny in her voice all of a sudden. What if she knew? Inès might have cracked and confessed, or even just broached the subject, afraid that either Pallas or I was going to do it soon enough. Or maybe it was Pallas who blabbed. She wasn't the kind to betray me, but she always acted so strange about Inès. And if Alex knew, then she wasn't going to confront me directly; no, she'd wait and find a more subtle approach. So I said something about my cell bill going through the roof, and she hung up without a goodbye or anything, and it made me feel that much more paranoid. I forced myself to calm down: judging by how dosed she sounded, I doubt she even noticed the phone in her hand.

I lit a cigarette and stared at the receiver after setting it back down. It served me right for always refusing Inès's number. If Alex was trying her this late, then that must mean she had a cell. I was so tempted to learn why she hadn't reached her. Maybe Inès was feeling too ambivalent to talk right now. A prettier oasis indeed . . .

4.

When I woke up around noon, Pallas still wasn't home. Her cell: another ring into the void. I could just picture her, holding it right in front of her, staring at my number on the screen, unable to decide if she wanted to answer me or not. Why did it feel this way now when her calls the day before had sounded calmer once again? I was just about to give up when I heard a frosty "Yes?"

"It's me. What the fuck is wrong with you?"

"*What do you mean* what's wrong with me?"

"You couldn't have warned me you weren't coming home?"

"Why?" she asked, equally frosty and now with an added ounce of skepticism.

"Because I was too pissed off to get groceries," I lied. "That's why."

"Maybe you could give me a heads-up yourself if you know you're going to Pulp."

"OK, don't even start with that," I wearily sighed.

"What do you want?"

"Nothing," I said, another exhale, just as frosty. "I just wanted to make sure nothing had happened—that's all."

"The answer's no—happy now?"

"Yes, I'm happy," I grumbled, restraining myself from saying all her bullshit had made me miss my golden ticket with Inès. "Alright, well, have a good day," I said and hung up.

Had she deliberately gone AWOL so I wouldn't suggest our place to Inès?

Ten minutes later, I called her back, sitting cross-legged on my bed with a cup of tea.

"Yeah, still me," announcing myself as cool as could be. "I'd just like to know when you think you're coming back; I'm trying to see if I should run some errands or not."

"I don't need anything," Pallas said, sounding perfectly detached.

That doesn't tell me when you're coming home . . .

"Listen," shooting for earnestness now (and in all honesty), "I'm sorry I spoke to you like that the other night, I really am."

". . . I know," she finally said, sounding sweet. "You're not the reason I left—I am."

So there it was. Watching me banter with Inès must have triggered something. And just like every other time she fell in love with me again, she started things off by acting like crap, then got livid with herself for how poorly she concealed it, and then she just turned distant, like she'd actually stop giving a damn if she could only affect the right airs. And in the end it left her a miserable wreck. And me, I had to witness every phase without even batting an eyelash.

"Listen," I said, with renewed, unfeigned sincerity, "let's just forget it, OK?"

She gave a nice, long sigh.

"Will whatever you bought yesterday keep until tomorrow?"

"Why tomorrow?" I asked, suddenly alert.

"I'm in Honfleur right now."

"Where?"

"You know, Alice's gallerist's house."

Oh, I knew: an ultra-crib, complete with a pool she was always using but I was never invited to. But what the fuck? How long had she known she'd be there?

"Come on, you could have let me know!"

"Why?" she asked, getting suspicious once again.

"Uh, I dunno," I stammered, aware of having essentially just betrayed myself. "I might have gotten worried. Whatever. When are you coming back?"

"Why?" she asked again.

"Come on, stop with all the whys—I'm your best friend, remember? I mean, shit."

". . . I don't know yet," Pallas answered, with some residual wariness. "Tomorrow afternoon, I assume—Alice has to be in Paris that night. But maybe tomorrow morning, or could be as early as tonight," and then she wished me a pleasant day and hung up.

She really must have taken me for a fool. No one gets home from a weekend away on Friday night or Saturday morning.

It was four in the afternoon, Inès still hadn't called, and I was pacing around in circles, walking from one room to the next in our deserted, static, deadening apartment. I couldn't stay in place, couldn't think of anything else. Alex must have decided to come back and Inès had gone to meet her and they were definitely in the middle of some incredible fucking sex. Alex always used to fling herself on me the moment she got back from a gig I couldn't attend. Maybe they'd even done it on the phone in the middle of the night, Alex loved that shit. And maybe Inès was going to join her tonight in Besançon, and maybe Alex and Jessie would each have a separate bedroom, and maybe Inès would even spend the whole weekend with them. I needed to calm down, but there was only one way for me to do that. It wasn't exactly classy, but it was really the only way. I paced around a couple minutes before I finally just gave in. Alex answered her cell on the very first ring:

"Fuck, you can't get enough of me, can you!"

"Listen," I said, "I really, really need a haircut, it looks like garbage right now and I've got something super-important tonight. Could you give me Inès's number?"

"She probably can't this weekend, she's at her parents' right now, studying. But call her anyway, maybe there'll be time this week. So, when's the next time we do it again, you slut?"

I laughed. "I dunno, where are you?"

"Besançon."

"Ha, well, sucks to be you!"

If you only knew, Alex . . . but I didn't want to think about that right now. With my back against the wall, I stood staring at Inès's number. A number so easy, I already knew it by heart. The prospect of calling her, informing her the coast was clear—that should have sent me over the moon . . . but I wasn't over the moon, not even slightly, I was worried. Calling meant losing the upper hand, if I'd ever even had it, whereas not calling meant passing up an outstanding opportunity. And I had another reason for putting it off: that thing inside me saying Inès would never give me a simple "OK, I'm coming over." Every time I hunkered down to dial her with the phone down at my feet, my heart would start beating too fast and I'd hang up. Maybe I could wait a little bit, see if she'd call me herself, but it seemed like she wouldn't, or wouldn't until much later, when it would be too complicated for her to come to Paris. And so, still in a crouch, I dialed that fucking number, and this time I let it ring, so petrified that I almost wanted to puke.

"Hello? Inès?"

"No, it's her sister," in that exact same voice.

"Oh, sorry—is Inès around?"

She shouted my name—with all her might, it seemed, enough that I wondered what kind of house they must live in—and I felt myself fighting a violent urge to hang up.

"Hey," came her lifeless wheeze.

"How's it going?" I asked, like a moron.

"I hear you were looking for my number?" she asked, amused.

"Alex, haircut, yeah yeah. I just wanted to say: Pallas is away this weekend."

"You sure?" she asked, all casual-like.

No, I wasn't sure, I wasn't sure of anything.

"Until at least tomorrow afternoon."

". . . yeah—honestly though, I don't know. I'm not sure this is a good idea."

And there it was. I closed my eyes, felt a familiar knot in my throat, just like the one I felt that morning I went to Nikki's . . . And then the tears started coming.

"That's fine," I said, hoping I might sound dignified. "All good—I'll see you later then."

"Wait, hold on!" she cut in. "Don't take it so hard!"

"I've got work to do, I'll see you later."

"Hey," her voice mellowing, "hang on, OK?"

Hang on for what, I wondered, as I blinked to ward off tears that were making it hard to see. I tugged the phone's extension cord so I could slip into the living room; I suddenly couldn't stand my bedroom.

"I don't know," she went on. "It's really nice to think about, but actually doing it . . ."

With my back against the living room closet, I felt my anger coming on. So what was her plan? Just your average Scorpio mind games—were things really going to be that stupid? Testing if Little Scorpion could best Big Scorpion? Was that the deal?

"I just can't imagine leaving her, you know?"

"What the fuck, who said anything about leaving her? I never said anything about leaving her!" Then, trying to mellow out, "It's a one-night thing, that's all."

"I think I'd better stay," she added.

So then why wasn't she hanging up? Did she want me to insist, was that it, to make it that much better when she flung herself on me? Well, she could go fuck herself.

"You know," I started saying, walking to the couch so I could sit down on the armrest, "I really do want to see you, because I really want to know you. I can't imagine why, but it's sincere. I thought something was happening here."

Silence.

"But it turns out you're exactly like I thought, nothing but a shitty seventeen-year-old, completely full of yourself. And honestly, you're right, I don't see what the point would have been, us getting together. So don't worry, alright? Next time we run into each other, it's like it never happened. I'll hang up and it's like you never existed."

She still wasn't saying anything, so I really did hang up.

I let my body slide onto the couch, clutching the phone against my knees. I felt humiliated for getting so worked up; she didn't deserve all that. But deep down I also knew that if I hadn't done it, it would have gotten worse. I would've spent all my life wondering if the risk would've made a difference. And I was annoyed that I'd called her without even taking the time to calm down first. I had thrown so much negativity her way, which made her retraction feel inevitable. But it was all good—it was over and done with. Now

I just needed to stay in for a while . . . That wouldn't be too hard, right? I was getting back into guys, right? That hadn't changed. Plus, girls like her with that "special sauce," they were a dime a dozen, right? So many of them, in fact, that you could stoop down and pluck them up! The tears were returning with a vengeance, and I bent over double, crushing the phone against my forehead. Holy shit, did I weep. The telephone started ringing in my ears. I slowly straightened up. Was it her? To tell me what? No hard feelings, let's be friends? Probably. But of course I picked up. Because you never know. Because there's never any way to know.

"What's the code to your building?" she asked in the tiniest voice imaginable.

She was sniffling—had she been crying too? I let my head drop back against the couch. The tears in my eyes were drying; staring at the ceiling, I listened to her breath while she awaited my response.

"Wait, so what's the deal?" I finally asked, gently.

"I think about you all the time!" she shouted and started sobbing.

"Shhhh," I whispered, "shhhh, I'm here."

"One hour," she hiccuped, "give me an hour and I'm going to be there in your arms."

Afterward, I would often wonder what might have happened if I hadn't picked up. And I would wonder when it had actually all started. But maybe that was something no one would ever really know. Except, perhaps, for Guillaume: "I might as well pass the baton."

chapter seven

clean sheets

1.

I hung up and immediately felt ambushed by the worst anxiety of my life. Sitting on the edge of the couch with both hands latched around the phone, I could already see the scene playing out: inevitably opening the front door . . . Inevitably opening to find her there, and I blushed at the slightest thing so no doubt was about to turn *scarlet*, and there was no way to hide that in our entryway. This was going to be pathetic. My heart racing a hundred miles an hour, incapable of meeting her gaze, no clue what to do with my hands, or my entire body for that matter. If there were only a way for someone else to open the door . . . and then she'd find me busy elsewhere. My eyes were nailed to the VCR. If it really took an hour to get here, then there were only fifty minutes left.

I frantically pulled out the vacuum. My gray carpet was a wreck, as were the polystyrene ceiling tiles. And my old blue comforter sapped any lust you had. I let the vacuum keep running while I ran and rummaged through the living room closets. Pallas had a set of whites on her shelf for clean sheets. A huge sigh of relief—she would have to forgive me. I stripped the bed and remade it, with the vacuum howling away to an audience of none. Everything reeked of cigarettes, so I pushed the shutters open. No way would it air out in all this heat, but something was better than nothing. I grabbed the vacuum again to finish on the far side of the bed, and then I wrenched it from the socket and hustled to the living room, leaving the closet open just long enough to return my dirty sheets. I plucked up my various ashtrays and brought them to the kitchen, washed and hastily dried two of them, then opened up the fridge where I had myself a shock: nothing but a half-drunk Coke, some of Pallas's leftover fish dip, and a single jam jar. Shit. When you've got someone wallowing in bed with you, you always want some nourishment on hand. I didn't even have time to crib a little cash for groceries. But who could have even lent it to me? Usually Pallas handled that . . . I wished I could have canceled the whole thing, or postponed it at least, but she was surely on her way by now. Wallowing in bed with me . . . That prospect felt miles away. All I knew was how gross and uneasy I felt about our impending alone time. I closed my shutters again while leaving the window open. Even with the risk that she might find the room too dark, there was no way I was going to allow any extra light. What kind of music to put on? A crucial decision for anyone's first visit. What did she listen to besides Alex's hard house? Massive Attack, Björk, Air? No harm in sticking to the basics—the things you always heard at people's homes—but so unoriginal. The alarm clock was cloaked behind a fold of the comforter. I cleared it with my foot: only forty minutes left.

From the bathroom cabinet, I grabbed anything I could get my hands on. What about perfume? I just wore what Alex wore, and Pallas's never worked on me, too heady. Sitting in the tub, I washed my hair, and then, while the conditioner settled, I applied a quick facial. I shaved my armpits and here and there on my calves, then stood to exfoliate my ass and thighs. I would have just enough time for makeup, and maybe for a change of nail polish. Fingers crossed that the dresses Pallas had in my size weren't all at the dry cleaner's; I only had one dress, and it had a stain problem, but just where the stain was I couldn't remember. Finally, I squeezed half the bodywash into my hands, hoping the vanilla smell might linger on my skin, and as my hands slipped under my breasts to lift them and massage, I suddenly realized: I was prettying myself up for a guy or something . . . I gave up and sat on the edge of the tub. This date was with a *girl*. What was the matter with me? Whatever this was, these past few days had had me feeling different . . . That ingrained belief that I was turning a page, which at first had felt like blissful liberation, and ultimately felt unsurprising, before long had started seeming like a given, so entrenched that I didn't even need to think about it. Except in those moments on the phone with Inès. And then things just went back to . . . back to being like before, I guess. It felt so strange, grasping this only now as I stood up to drain the bath. But it felt even stranger that the girl coming over was only seventeen years old . . .

Butt-naked outside the living room closets, dripping all over the hardwood, I had lost all sense of what to select. With girls, I never wore things too femme. Half of me wanted to break the absurd habit, while the other half instinctively gravitated toward a T-shirt and jeans. It struck me: maybe it was the Tuesday before, that super femme night, that had caused me to see things differently. But how could I be so sure? "Unisex" stuff would feel like a total rupture after the past few days, but at the same time, wouldn't a dress make me feel like a *lady* standing in front of a teenager? I pulled out my heap of T-shirts and crouched to spread them on the floor. Which ones hadn't she seen me in a hundred times before, and which didn't Alex own as well? I tried on four, rising each time for a look in the closet mirror. Impossible to gauge without the lower half. I went to the bedroom for my 505s. I rifled through, hunting for some panties. Nothing clean. In Pallas's I'd be swimming, and I had stopped feeling good in boxers. So what were my options? How about nothing, nothing underneath . . . And I'd keep my feet bare, too. I went back to my T-shirts. I finally narrowed it down to a final contender: *Liquid Sky*. She must have seen me in it countless times, and no doubt it would remind her of Alex, who had the same one in navy with the little yellow alien, but mine was much nicer, black on black. Among the rave gang who had traveled to New York that time, I was the only one who bought it in this design, and now that they weren't printing them anymore, everyone was always asking if I wanted to sell it. I felt stupid wanting to flaunt a dumb collector shirt, but with Alex involved, I had some fierce competition.

So I was dressed and washed, my hair was drying into its standard flattering mess, my bedroom was in order, and the rest of the apartment was, too; so now all that remained was the music. And that's what I'd be doing when she buzzed—i.e., twenty minutes from now. I could already anticipate an overwhelming urge to vomit, I felt so tense. But another solution suggested itself . . . and why not? I returned to the bathroom and took my jeans off but left my T-shirt on—it was short enough that it probably wouldn't get wet—and once again I stepped into the tub. It was common for guys to drain their balls when expecting a woman if they didn't want to come too soon. So there was that, and also, beyond delaying my physical urges, it would help me to relax. Wedging my back against the lip of the tub, I adjusted the water temp and screwed off the showerhead. I had left the bathroom door open. If Pallas came back now, she'd be in for quite a show—which honestly would be far less dramatic than if she arrived a little later. I was also risking another call from Inès, and if so, this time I'd be beet red. Holding the nozzle in both hands, one finger obstructing the stream for added force, I tried fixing her in my mind's eye. But too many different images were coming up; I couldn't linger on any in particular. Better not to think, to just do. But the water was splashing the bottom of my T-shirt, so I bit it between my teeth. A few minutes in, I realized this was utter nonsense: orgasms left me so sensitive that I couldn't take it again for a long time after. But it was already starting to happen, and clearly I wasn't brave enough to break things off, with my eyes finally honing in on Inès's mouth, the way she nibbled the corner of her lip . . . I was prostrate for a few more seconds, catching my breath, eyes closed, assuaged at last, drained. Maybe a little depressed, too. Then I did the difficult work of extracting myself.

I instinctively sat at my computer for a cigarette; pressing my foot against the floor to swivel my desk chair back and forth, it felt decided: I would stay right here in this room until she arrived. The only thing she knew was I was working on a record, so why shouldn't she find me at work? The music itself would be my own, the latest track I'd been slaving away on. For the time being, it was just a bunch of layered audio, the kind of airy progressive-house bed you didn't hear much anymore, acid notes stretched to effect something similar to Aphex's trademark laugh. I was just going to use a temp track for the beat so it wouldn't sound too dull for her baby ears. I switched on the computer, and while it booted up, I made some adjustments to the synth on my right. Playing my own music felt potentially fraught—what if she thought it sounded shitty? But if so, if she didn't like my room or my getup or how my bodywash smelled or my music, then honestly, what would we have to talk about? Take Nikki's records scattered on the floor near the turntables: no way was I going to stash them somewhere. To most people, "sixties" and "seventies" meant "hippie," like rock was old-fogey music now. But if she saw things like that, then that was her problem. Deep down I knew: I had a super-cool room, a high-end home studio, and me, I was a pretty awesome chick, thirty-one with a better body than the average club dweller, with an awesome gig and an interesting life. So if anyone wondered what we saw in each other, my appeal should have been obvious.

2.

When the buzzer sounded, I forced myself to take a deep breath; I stubbed out my cigarette, lit myself another, placed it in the ashtray, and then I went to let her in. My cheeks were burning slightly, and my hand was trembling on the doorknob; I opened it slowly to discover her rifling through her shoulder bag. Her face was blocked by her hair, which was falling down in front. She lifted her head just long enough for a quick peek, her way of saying give me a sec, I'm looking for something. Uneasy just like me? She was wearing an overcoat despite the heat, a fitted three-quarter-length in dark red suede; it was a new one for me and had a seventies vibe, which made me wonder if Pallas had heard about my recent backsliding. Underneath there was a blinding white V-neck, some light grey Carhartts, and a pair of plain white Nikes with red stripes. Her ensemble wasn't new or expensive enough to have come from Alex's arsenal of gifts, so she must have gone with things she'd owned before . . . She pulled out a cell phone and stared at its screen for a while, then stowed it with a shrug, finally raising her eyes with an intimidated glance. Even in bright light, her eyes looked very black; I had never noticed how much. It imbued her with a subtle sadness that instantly softened me up. I wanted to fling my arms open, squeeze her to my chest, and whisper I was with her now. But I was stupidly dawdling, simply pondering how pretty she looked, and how young, and how innocent, so she finally flashed me a smile and a glance over my shoulder, like: Should I stay out here or do you intend to let me in? There was something surly in that smile, wry with a touch of chilly, preoccupied disdain. All of a sudden she was exuding this intolerable sense of freedom. Free to leave in five minutes flat if that's what was in the cards.

"Hi," I finally uttered, turning tail to let her shut the door herself. The bass was pumping in my room, acid lines going through endless warps, growing increasingly strident, and as I sat at the computer again, I refrained from raising the volume past the point of bearability. In my peripheral vision, I watched her make her entrance before my eyes immediately returned and fastened themselves on the screen.

"You working?" she casually tossed out. "Pff, fine, I won't bother you long, OK? Is this your music I'm hearing?" she asked, suddenly right behind me.

My stammered "yes" faded when I caught the rustle of her bag slipping over her head and then her coat sliding down to the floor. One of her knees cracked as she prepared to bend over; I heard a clicking lighter being tested multiple times, and then I sensed her straightening up behind me. My eyes were still anchored to the screen, I couldn't even reach for the ashtray. I watched her bare arm slowly enter my field of vision, and I froze even further. Her breast cushily flattened against my shoulder until, just as slowly, her profile appeared, now bending down to grab my lighter. There was a nice detergent scent from her T-shirt. Her cheek stayed close to mine while lighting her cigarette. I didn't breathe, couldn't even hazard a peripheral glance at her mouth. Her breast unstuck itself, and I faintly sighed feeling her body depart, then letting out a little "shit!" when I saw I'd started ashing on the keyboard. I blew it away as best I could before risking a fleeting glance, but she wasn't paying the slightest attention. Standing at the foot of the bed, her eyes were staring downward at the silent TV. With the cigarette at the corner of her lips, she was standing in her standard pose, odd-looking, with her palms flat against her lower back. Her avian qualities were actually pretty charming. Her shoulders were looking lovely in that T-shirt, which didn't flaunt her navel for once. Shoulders broad and loose, the kind good swimmers have. My slim build and heightened pallor surely reminded her of Alex, whereas she was the opposite, with a slight tan over a rounder, plumper, more muscular frame. The body of a healthy kid, but more so very feminine, with a pronounced arch in her back and a curving ass. Eventually her hand went up for her cigarette, and she sat on the edge of the mattress. Again I watched as she bent toward the ashtray, then averted my eyes the second hers returned to mine.

I thought I'd keep pretending to work for a while. I wanted her, too, to have time to scan me without my knowledge. And I felt it, her lingering gaze. With my right hand on the mouse, I clicked through all sorts of adjustments, altering the sonic texture. Anyone who knew a thing or two could have seen I was doing absolutely nothing. I stubbed out my cigarette so I could shoot her a quick look, and I saw that she was actually eyeing my hardware. There was clearly a sadness behind those dark eyes as they slowly examined my gear, unaware that mine were watching her head lightly bobbing to the music, and I flattered myself to think that the comparisons with Alex had begun. It felt disgusting to rejoice at that, but I couldn't help myself. Alex had everything I lacked. Notoriety, material comfort, a sports car, ostentatious habits, a home fitness instructor and all. She had ample opportunity to take Inès on trips, plus the option to support her if she chose to cut ties with her parents. But what I envied most of all, despite how heinous it felt, was that she refused to let love affairs eat at her. No way would she screw up a gig on account of feeling down, nor was she the type to hassle you with endless questions, and the fiercest arguments were forgotten only fifteen minutes later. That wasn't true for me . . . But I also had everything that Alex lacked: the profile of a real musician, whereas Alex was still just a DJ, one who dreamed of putting things out but was too lazy to record, thereby limiting her chances for further success, whereas I was putting my all into it. And I handled my everyday habits pretty well, as opposed to Alex who was as fucked about feeding herself as she was with the bureaucratic stuff; case in point, she always had roommates so she'd have someone to slip her rent to without having to confront the landlord directly. And most importantly, I was much more adult about relationships. I was equally able to hear "I love you" and to use those words myself; my appetite for power struggle never stretched past the preliminary stage. I was faithful, I didn't goad my girlfriends into getting high, I didn't systematically repeat everything I'd done with my old partner with my new partner, and whenever there were problems, I brought them up. True, I brought them up too much, but where I simply wore people down, Alex straight-up drove them nuts, fleeing any attempts at communication. To fall for her meant finding yourself in a spiraling power struggle where your dignity lost out to frustration and jealousy. So next to her, I must have looked like a water fountain in the desert. "A prettier oasis . . ." My eyes locked on my computer screen again, while Inès stood back up.

She meandered her way to me and stubbed out her cig in the ashtray, ignoring the one beside the bed. I felt her hand delicately rest upon my shoulder, and once again I froze, my breath cut short. Her hand was exerting a gentle pressure, and since I wasn't reacting she simply pulled it away, which I took as my cue to shift focus to my hardware. Her hand returned, but this time I ignored it, reaching an arm to one side to grab the cigarettes by my computer. Again her hand retracted, and I watched as her profile bent down to blow out the flame of her lighter. I looked at her sideways, like: How old are you? As I fiddled with all sorts of made-up adjustments on my mixer, her hand came back, and this time a little firmer. I felt her palm slide up the back of my neck, then her splayed fingers climb into my hair and form a loose fist. I let her scale my head from behind, I watched her mouth crack open as she bent down over me, until at the last second I lightly pulled away. Then her arms looped around my throat, and she grazed her burning cheek to mine, and my eyes closed. I felt her lift the cigarette from my fingers. She wasn't doing anything but rubbing our cheeks together, but with my eyes still closed, the dizziness got so intense that I felt like I was falling, and then I knew that not only would I never forget what she was doing, but if she didn't leave Alex for good within the hour, I was going to be entering the biggest nightmare of my life. I brusquely grabbed her wrists to shove them aside. Then I pivoted in my seat so I could face her directly. Her mouth was wide in shock. I crossed my arms.

"Sorry," I said, thick with irony, staring her up and down, "but I'm not actually into you," and I turned to face my hardware, bending down to rifle through a box beneath my table.

I could sense what was going on behind me, but I took my time to straighten up. When my back was vertical once again, she had already donned her overcoat and shoulder bag and now was clearing a path across the room. I watched her walk out of my bedroom and proceed to the front door. I caught up with her right as she opened it and seized her by the shoulder, pushing the door closed with my other hand. She slowly spun around, I loosened my grip, she raised her eyes to mine, and what I saw made me recoil against the wall behind me.

Never had I witnessed such suffering in a person's eyes. Such despair. A bottomless well in those teary black depths. Her mouth was still cracked, beseeching now. I wished I could have found something to say, could have told her to wait a few seconds and I'd be ready for her. But no sound would come out. All her pain bowled me over, this pain I was an integral part of, and which she was letting me see. Was consenting to let me see. Was she starting to understand just how much I needed her? I knew the word for this feeling, and I knew what it did to the other person, but I didn't know how to behave any differently. It was only when I closed in on someone from a great distance that I could settle in and start a proper exchange. I needed to see the other person accept her own dependence, needed to harm her before I could be nice. She took a step forward, but my hands lifted to signal "no." Her arms dropped—a show of impotence. Tears were pooling in her eyes, which had anchored themselves to mine. It was important for her to know that there was a purpose in all this waiting. That feeling we'd feel, clasping bodies, locking lips for the first time: that was something we would never recapture. It was a onetime thing, and a second later it would already have transformed into something else. The second embrace, however magical, was always fated to be less astonishing than the first time. I hated the irrefutable logic of it. And I hated time itself, and everything else that ensured that despite your best efforts to maintain a state of love, the moment of truth was long gone, and now there was nothing but the quest to retrieve it. Most of all I hated the fear, the decree that every new beginning required thoughts about its end.

Eventually, with a sniffle, she said, "I'll die if you don't touch me," drying her runny nose on the back of her hand.

I waited another second, savoring the unspeakable fever brewing inside me; then I sweetly spread my arms, and hers immediately slid inside. Her body perfectly fit, pressing into me, with her shoulders wedged under mine and her forehead nestling right into the hollow of my cheekbone. The whiff of gratitude that swept over me made me reel, slightly teetering us to the side. Her arms squeezed my waist a little stronger, while my own locked around her neck. "Never again," she muttered, with her damp eyes caressing my cheek, "let's never be apart again." Pressed up against the wall, my eyes were rolling backward amid the waves of heat through my intestines. I was rattled by her scent, a scent as sweet and moving as the skin of a newborn baby. She lifted her head, her lips started quivering, but before things could go too far, I clamped my hand over her mouth. She couldn't keep saying things like that. She needed some self-restraint. For as long as possible. Until it felt like she was choking on three specific words. And then, only then, could she let those words escape, even shout them if she wanted. From her look of resignation, I could tell that she understood, and my eyes answered: this was going to be just as grueling for me as it was for her. Still with a tight grip on my waist, she tilted her forehead to my temple, and we slowly returned to the bedroom. I helped her slip her bag over her head and take her coat back off. I made her sit on the edge of the bed, crouched to remove her sneakers, and then I crawled onto the mattress to settle in at the far end. I lay on my back, I opened my right arm, and she snuggled in close.

Stretched out beside me, almost flat on her belly, she had her cheek nestled into the crook of my shoulder. One of her arms was lying across my chest, while the other was beneath her, and her knee was folded over my thigh. I, meanwhile, had my cheek against her hair and both arms around her, my hands meeting atop her shoulder. We stayed like that, motionless. We needed a chance to breathe. My heart was pumping fast, and I could feel hers against my chest. Her eyes were closed, while mine were watching but not truly absorbing some new-jack-swing video, with my own music feebly carrying on behind it. Pallas's white sheets had a nice detergent smell. I could only imagine her if she showed up; I wouldn't even be able to move from the panic, I would be fixed in place with both my arms around Inès. We were already so far gone at this point that there was nothing anyone could do . . . Well, here I was: some girl's new lover. My first since Alex. Except that this time was the real deal. I had found the ultimate. Someone just like me. Whose only requirement would be finding herself reflected in my eyes. I never thought I'd needed a girl this young, but that's the way it felt. Her age made everything virgin territory. Alex must have reached the same conclusion . . . Everything welling up inside me was going to make for an incredible record, and all that thanks to her. Yes, a record that was going to rake in some fucking dough, and then the world would be ours for the taking . . . My shoulder twitched, tender with numbness. She lifted her head, assuming I wanted to free up my arm, and then she dropped it back in place. For those three seconds, her eyes looked totally gone. She could have been completely wasted and it would have felt the same. I felt out of it, too. Her fingers started futzing with my cuff, started rolling it up and stroking my skin. Her wrist was imperceptibly brushing back and forth across my breast, and I inflated my chest for a sigh. Her hand immediately descended to the hem of my T-shirt, grabbed and lifted it, and with the contact of her mouth around my breast, I groaned so deep that my belly made a violent scrunch. Her body slipped onto mine, clearing a path with her knees between my thighs, and I let out another groan, feeling her pelvis pressing into me. Her hands rose and took my face while her mouth moved a little closer. "Wait," I whispered, trying to smile but unable to. Her lips closed around my earlobe, and her tongue slid into it with a loud exhale, then I did the same to her, triggering an equally powerful groan. Her mouth was wide and panting; her eyes—only the whites were visible now—closed of their own volition. Our cheeks now slippery with saliva, our mouths approaching one another in such a way that whenever they pulled back it felt that much better. And then joining with hers at last. I could die. My brain asphyxiated, my eyes popping out of my skull. Finally I heard a hoarse voice saying, "I can't take it anymore." "OK," I whispered, testing if maybe this time I could smile. I briefly ran my tongue along her lips and closed my eyes, praying that if my heart actually exploded, hers might do the same so she wouldn't be left behind. I could feel her shaky breath beneath my nose, her lips mere millimeters away, and I kept thanking her internally for allowing us this respite, however brief. And then our mouths sweetly collided, and I lost my footing altogether.

It was like the bed gave way beneath me. However much I welded my arms to her neck, I could feel myself falling down an abyss. Her tongue swirled around my tongue, and when her piercing made contact, it was enough to drive me crazy. My brain was pumping up with air. The pressure was building around my temples, in my throat; my heart was leaping through my rib cage, and everything between my thighs was going liquid. I hadn't even known about the piercing. I had kissed loads of girls with tongue studs, but none of them knew how to use it, were all too timid, too careful, whereas she—she let my tongue lift the little ball, let my lips suck it and my teeth close around it. She started unbuttoning my jeans.

"Wait," I panted, "not so fast." "I can't—I can't take it, I can't wait." If only I could have told her this was going to take us hours, given the shower I'd just taken. She was going to think she was terrible at it, and I was going to have to pretend because I didn't want to hurt her, but that wasn't my fantasy, not with her. "Wait," I said again, but now my jeans were sliding down my ankles, and she lifted them one by one so she could pull off my pants completely. Her fingers wormed their way into my thighs, drawing a deep sigh; she smiled to see how wet I was. She mounted me, and her tongue returned to mine, feeding on it. I pictured Alex, or anyone, showing up that second and mowing us down with a machine gun—we'd never be apart again. She lifted her head: "If we died right now, this second, then we'd never be apart again." My eyes widened with shock, while her mouth raced forward, mimicking mine. She wiggled her hips, unbuttoning her pants and pulling them down. When I saw what she was doing, I almost felt like crying. There was no way. I couldn't come like that. Never. This wouldn't work for me. This didn't work for anyone, dammit! I shifted my mouth to speak, but no sound came out. I was *really* going to have to pretend, and with that now decided, my eyes started filling with tears, which trickled down looking for any kind of purchase. I felt her bush press into my shaved groin, and she started some tender motions, a slow, sustained rotation. Her pants were baring her ass, and she had squeezed her legs into the space between mine. Unless her clitoris was up around her waist or something, how was this ever going to work? "What's the plan?" I asked. "This is the quickest way," she said, panting, "we just need to relax, we're not going to stay like this." It took a few seconds but then she lost control of her breathing; there was choking in my ear. So not exclusively vaginal, I guess . . . The fingers of both her hands were toying with my nipples, pinching and twisting them this way and that, exactly like I'd taught Alex to do. So now I was heating up, and heating up quickly, with my nipples stinging more and more each second. I spread my legs as wide as they'd go, knees bent, and my hands traveled downward, gripping fistfuls of her ass, extracting a moan. She was drenched. She gobbled my ear, and my middle finger, slowly, inserted itself from behind. My finger up this teenage ass. My finger in the ass of a kid completely wild for me, who was wailing like a banshee. Now was my moment to locate her mouth and thrust my tongue inside, which she instantly started sucking on as hard as she could, and with some hiccuping jerks, I suddenly came. With the motion still going, she released her hold on my breasts and started inching her way up onto her elbows, her lips mutely quivering. Maybe I hadn't heard her, but I had just seen her mouth saying it. I had expected it, but this was still a major shock. Like she'd plunged a hand through my chest and ripped my heart out. A vital warmth, but also a gaping void. All the immensity of life suddenly concentrated in this moment. With my eyes wide, I squeezed my jaw, suppressing a grimace from all the rubbing still at work around my crotch, my now unbearably sensitive crotch. My hands returned for more fistfuls of ass, my forefinger made a second insertion, and her hands joined in, spreading her cheeks a little wider. Then her shoulder blades started peeling backward, jutting her breasts toward my nose, palpable even through the coarse threads of her T-shirt. Tossing her head back as far as it would go, she offered up her throat, protruding tendons and all. With one hand, I grabbed the back of her neck, and I brought her mouth to mine again. "I want you to watch," she panted; "Later," I hissed, tugging fistfuls of her hair. She resisted; I found a better grip, and I tugged even harder, as hard as possible, and a flash of utter blankness stole over her face, so the pain must have coiled into her brain.

With a steady grip, the other hand stuck a finger back inside, and then another. “FUCK I LOVE YOU,” she cried, seizing my face with both hands, her fingernails shoving into the hair behind my ears, and her tongue penetrated deep into my throat; she was howling to the moon.

For a second, she stayed like that, caved in on top of me. With my arms around her neck, I gently stroked her nape. Had she been like this with Alex, right from the jump? She finally raised her head. Pure dishevelment. Her eyes were bulging, glassy. She’d look absolutely divine with some heroin in her system . . . Her lips were puffy, her cheeks grooved with drying tears. And still that adorable babyface, but now with something else painted on top. Something ultra-sexual and clammy and almost bestial, but at the same time as calm as could be. The seraphic poise of a woman who’s just been fucked. But still that shade of sadness in her eyes—her black eyes—but now with a shine as well, inhabiting her and oozing from every pore. Oozing her feelings. She started stroking my lips with her fingertip.

“I love you,” she said in a murmur. “I love you. I’m leaving her tomorrow.”

“Not tomorrow,” I responded, like a fool.

The day after tomorrow, Alex was going to be in the hospital all day getting a cyst removed from her ovaries; it had her totally freaked out.

“Not until after the hospital,” I said.

“Oh yeah . . . true,” she sighed.

She stared into the distance for a second.

“I can’t even picture her face.”

Her locks were plastered to her burning, sweaty forehead. I delicately parted them, then stretched my neck to kiss her on the tip of her nose.

"I know I'm only seventeen," she said, again stroking my lips with her fingertip. "But I want to be with you. For a long time. For years. Maybe my whole life even."

She stopped talking so she could lick a bead of sweat off my temple.

"Something feels right," she purred. "Something in here feels right to me."

3.

"I won't even be gone three minutes," I said, laughing.

"Oh yeah?" she said, also laughing, and she started pressing on my belly.

Alex used to do this all the time. When you hold it for a bit with steady pressure, the sensation becomes pleasure. I could take it like that for hours, but it's the kind of thing you can only do alone, not when there's someone there who can get you off for real. I kept allowing it for a while, gratified by her smile, which grew larger with every grimace, before I gently pushed her hand away to stand up. She stood along with me, and our heads were spinning so much we needed the wall there for support. And then I saw the tattoo under her navel piercing. "Alex" it read in blood-red letters outlined in black shading. Same colors, same size, same location; only the lettering was different, rounded and sloped like graffiti. Her eyes traveled down to my own "Alex" and she smiled, but I wasn't smiling one bit. Alex must have had her name somewhere, too; I couldn't picture where and hadn't noticed it on her recent visit . . .

"Stop thinking about it," Inès muttered, "I'm gonna get it touched up."

Yeah right, but what with, I wondered, given the size. She walked me to the bathroom. She came in and joined me, and I smiled to see how she was already tailing me everywhere, that impulsive jealousy about someone intimate. But as she straddled my lap on the toilet, I saw that this was something else. How had I not seen this coming? What did I think the two of them had been doing those past six months? She was going to stick her hand down there, just like Alex—and that's exactly what she did. Except instead of squirming around like Alex did, searching for an angle so her eyes could catch a peek at what she was up to, her gaze was locked on mine. She was waiting with her hand glued in place, unlike Alex who always ventured a little lower so she could collect it in her palm. I had done this too many times to feel a mental block around it, but I pictured her doing this with Alex and it didn't feel right. Still, I really needed to pee, so I eventually let it flow, holding her steady gaze, but wondering whether she was doing this for the sheer audacity, the taboo of it all, or if she grasped what acts like this ultimately signified. Sure, she was young, and this kind of thing, above all, must have been *a total trip, man*. Submission from the relieving party, domination from the goading party. But not really a power trip, either. More like a demonstration of trust. Like allowing your partner to have a knife at your back, without checking first to make sure nothing was going to happen. Most of all, it was one step further into shared intimacy. I pretended I needed to twist my body for TP, though I knew she was going to stop me, which naturally she did, just like Alex, seizing my wrist with her other hand, the dry one. But then she did something that Alex never did, not with me anyway: she sucked every finger, one by one . . . She stood up, and then I stood up; I lingered for a second, and sure enough, she gently pushed me back against the wall and knelt down in front of me. She pretended to bite the skin around Alex's name. My hands traveled downward to stroke her hair while her tongue started sweetly licking the contours of my crotch, careful to not graze my clit, which was still feeling sensitive. It was really going to be something when she started doing me for real . . . She got back on her feet, slipped her arms around my neck, jutted her chin toward my mouth and I nodded, and her wet lips gently started playing around with mine, the piercing on her tongue jabbing into my tongue. They don't taste like anything—those who know, know. She gently pulled her head back, to bask in my eyes:

"I want to do everything with you that I've never done with Alex."

"Like that's a first!" I chuckled.

"She did that to me. I never wanted to."

"Why not?" I asked, sardonic, not believing it for one second.

"I dunno," she said, staring at my mouth. "Maybe I wasn't ready?"

We walked out arm in arm, bumping against the walls on either side as we made out down every step of the hallway. She dragged me to Pallas's room, but we pulled up short at her threshold. Again, it felt so strange: the stillness in there, from the night before all the way to that morning.

"Whatcha thinking?" she asked.

"Um. Can't say fucking in Pallas's bed really turns me on."

"Yeah, me either."

We wavered at the edge of the living room while she eyed first the couch, then the hardwood floor.

"Here?" she asked.

"Um," again, "been there, done that a lot with Pallas."

"Oh yeah? Well, you're going to have to stop or you'll be sorry. With that skater guy, too—you've gotta drop him, too."

"And who are you gonna drop?" I asked with a laugh.

"Me?" she asked, suddenly distant.

But I put my hand on her mouth. I didn't need an answer, I knew what she'd be giving up. She dragged me to the bathroom, stole a glance inside before shaking her head no, finally dragging me to the kitchen. She sat me down on the plastic couch before making her way to the window. I couldn't care less what anyone saw from the other buildings, but whatever we were gearing up for, they were going to need some popcorn. She stepped back over me and balled my hair in her fist to shove my face against her tattoo. And this time I actually bit her, and she immediately tugged my hair back to get free. Then I started burrowing my mouth into her navel, sticking my tongue out to nudge at the piercing. She flinched, which made me lift my eyes, to an uncomfortable look on her face. Sure, this reminded her of Alex—Alex also had a thing for belly buttons—but why was Inès the only one entitled to remind us both of Alex? She was the one who started it, no? How could I possibly *not* do the same things as Alex? Everything Alex did, I was the one who taught her. She was only a mental pervert when I met her; the physical stuff had all just been a shallow pretense, and not even a very skilled one at that. I pondered the bush in front of me. If it was this long, she must not have slept with Alex in a while; Alex, by now, was too accustomed to shaved pussies to be into something like this. "Sorry," she sighed, "I didn't have time." I grabbed her hips and brought my mouth a little closer, while her face delicately shifted to the counter. She put her hands on the ledge and propped herself up, bent over so much that her shoulders touched the ceramic surface; she shuffled her feet apart, spreading her legs, and both hands moved back to open her cheeks in my face. I'd watched Alex do this dozens of times, but this time, my breath caught in my throat. A dark ring, imperceptibly breathing . . . I kept staring at it, again thinking: this was a seventeen-year-old, a kid who was crazy about me and now expecting me to stick my tongue in. For once, the kitchen being narrow felt useful—and the couch too: comfortably seated and everything. My hands swapped in for hers, and I dove in. First one long, slow lick that made her moan, and then another, and then another, and then I stiffened my tongue and I stuck it straight in. Her hand knocked my chin as she started touching herself. My tongue was already getting tired but I kept going. I rested my free hand on the back of my neck so I could push my mouth even deeper. Her legs were bending; she released my head to secure some more leverage from the wall. And then I pulled out to watch her. She instantly turned around and climbed on top of me, straddled me, sitting right on top of my throat. She gently stroked my tattoo, pinching the skin between her thumb and forefinger, like she was jacking off a micropenis, then started touching herself only inches from my eyes. The fingers on her left hand were splayed and fondling her alert clitoris, while with the middle finger on her other hand she was tracing quick little circles over top. I craned my neck to bring my mouth a little closer, but her knee started pressing into my throat.

"Oh yeah? You want to play like that?" I spat, and I grabbed her by the arms, toppling her onto the couch, and then sat on her chest with my knees pinning her shoulders down. I lowered my gaze to my crotch and let a thread of saliva trickle down, then started touching myself just like she had, with my fingers spread wide enough that she couldn't miss a thing. Immediately her neck started stretching out to me, but she was too far away for that. She had stuck *her* nasty little tattoo in my face, so now she was going to get a load of mine. I sought out her tongue, held it by the piercing, trickled saliva on it from above, and then I bent down over her and forced her to lick Alex's name. She did so only reluctantly, both eyes closed, as if she didn't want to see it. But then I shifted my knee so I could press it to her Adam's apple.

"So," I asked, cold as ice, "you've never done this before, have you?"

"What?" she sputtered.

"This?" I repeated, sinking my knee a little deeper.

Her eyes suddenly filled with fear; she slowly shook her head no. So this game of hers: she wanted to remind me of Alex? Fine, she was going to get what was coming to her. Except that this was something Alex always tried but never successfully. This was going to be a first. My right hand went back between her legs from behind while the left went to the space between mine, and I started focusing all the pressure from my knee upon her throat. This thing had to be done with expert precision. I needed the oxygen in her brain to dwindle, without it going out entirely. And I needed it to be a gradual increase, riding the curves of pleasure. Too much pressure too soon and we were fucked, everything nice giving way to something merely intolerable. Eventually my left hand replaced my knee for better calculation. I could feel whenever she had to swallow spit. Her eyes, bolted to mine, were again glinting with spurts of blankness like before, back when her hair had gotten a tug. She wasn't here anymore—I knew from experience—and now I just needed to make her come as quickly as possible, before we reached the point of no return. Even as I sank down, I made sure to maintain a firm grip around her throat, and my tongue swapped in for my finger between her thighs. Her breathing felt more labored now, a hoarse, steady groan like an asthma attack. Her arms, free from my knees, weren't even trying to move; only her torso was jerking in little spasms. Her inflamed clitoris was now the size of a fingernail, ready to pop. Instead of a soft lick, I pushed on it as hard as possible, compensating for all the intensity happening above. Beneath my hand, her Adam's apple was rising and falling in overdrive. I wished I could have looked up to watch, but the play was afoot so I couldn't. So I kept going, arms pushing with all their weight, down on her chest, preventing too much movement. I felt her throat double in volume, and then her pelvis violently thrust against my jaws, a cry of agony erupting from the silence. I immediately climbed back onto her, grabbing her face in my hands for a kiss.

"Oh fuck," she sputtered in my mouth, "fuck—fuck that was good! Fuck, I wanna learn how to do that!"

I smiled, squeezing her tightly—and then I smiled a little more.

4.

I opened my eyes, lying flat on my stomach, and saw her naked body hopping over me and vanishing down the hallway. I turned my head in the other direction, searching for my alarm clock, and what I found was a bloodstain. A pretty large one right beside my pillow. I sat up, almost calling her to ask what was up before reconsidering. Better not start mothering her. Given her age, it might just set her off, and I knew where that would lead. Anytime I lost control, I needed Alex again . . . I lit a cigarette, fluffed a pillow to sit on, and pulled the comforter up to my chest. The clock read noon. She came back with her hair wet, her long locks parted down the middle and pulled back behind her ears. I could tell something was off right away: she was avoiding my eyes. She picked up her T-shirt and slipped it on, then her panties too; she lit a cigarette and placed it in the ashtray, and then she sat to collect her pants. She stuck one foot in before giving up, looking around like she was searching for something.

"Nosebleed?" I asked, my voice softening.

"Yeah," she mumbled in a daze, her eyes still scouring the room.

She must have been looking for her socks. I could see them balled up on the other side of the television, but I didn't say anything.

"Happen often?" I asked, still soft.

"Never," she mumbled, still dazed.

She picked up her cigarette.

"So," I asked, even softer, "what's the matter?"

She didn't answer. I stubbed out my cigarette. I couldn't bring myself to make a move in her direction.

"What's the matter?"

"What's the matter? This is a sign," she mumbled, lowering her eyes. "It's a sign I shouldn't be here. I never get nosebleeds."

"Wait, what? What are you saying? Come here. Come here," I repeated, opening my arms.

She wouldn't budge. I slowly edged my back upward on the wall.

"Then what's wrong?" I asked again.

"I don't know anymore. I don't know if I should leave her. I don't know anything all of a sudden."

"Um," I went, sticking out my hand to free a lock that had fallen in her eyes. "No one's asking you to decide right now."

She looked up at me, squinting, visibly skeptical, like she wondered if I was serious. It almost seemed to disappoint her that I might be, and I got that. Fucking Scorpio shit.

"Right," I scoffed, aloof. "Well, see you around."

She averted her eyes. Fuck, now she was thinking of what she'd just said . . . I grabbed my T-shirt.

Sticking it on, I announced, "OK, I'm taking a shower, and you should be gone by the time I get back," and stood up.

Her hand immediately lunged for mine. She was still looking down, with her hair falling in front.

"Anything else?" I asked, icy.

Her hand exerted a subtle pressure.

"What?" I asked again, trying to make her scram. "Wanna stay with her? No problem. See if I care."

Again her hand lunged, this time squeezing tightly around my knuckles. I slithered away so I could sit down beside her. I folded up my knees, rested my elbows on them, and took her face in my hands.

"Alright, listen," I sighed. "If you think it's better for you to stay with her, if you want to get as far away from here as possible, then go ahead. But if you're not sure, then shut up so you don't make things worse."

"You're right," she muttered, "I'm sorry."

What a fucking relief . . . She stubbed out her cigarette, and her arms hugged my waist, and her head tilted sideways into mine.

"What are you doing to me?" I asked, slipping an arm around her shoulders. "We can't start like this. We're like conniving little rats—we've got a knack for this stuff. Let's not get carried away playing around, or this is going to end horribly."

"I know," she said, raising her head and kissing the corner of my mouth.

She bent and pulled her bag over. She rummaged through it and extracted a scrap of white paper. As she unfolded it, I felt utter horror wash over me. I sighed as inconspicuously as possible when I realized it was only coke. But even so . . . Why was she getting mixed up with this? Again she rummaged in her bag and this time pulled out a McDonald's straw.

"Want some?" she asked, ripping the straw's tip with her teeth.

Did I want some, at that moment? No! My goal was to fall asleep just as soon as she left, but mostly, except on rare occasions, I didn't take that stuff the very moment I woke up. She pulled out a mass-market Shakespeare and laid it on the ground, dumping the contents of her packet over the top and then rummaging some more, pulling out an organizer and a debit card. I watched her sort her little heap. I was dying to ask if Alex had given it to her. But what was the point—of course she had.

Still, I asked her, "Do you do this stuff often?" struggling to be light about it.

"No, no," she cooed, putting the finishing touch on her lines. "Just for now, for my exam prep."

The two lines she'd traced weren't huge or anything, but they weren't exactly small either. She folded her legs beneath her to hunch over the book. I watched as she shoved the nibbled straw-tip up her nostril, and then I listened as the straw traveled the line in one continuous sniff.

"Do you do skag, too?" I asked, hoping to sound even more detached.

She lifted her head, drying her nose between her thumb and forefinger.

"Heroin?" she asked, mildly squinting her eyes again. "No, no," she went, aloof.

"Listen, I'm only going to tell you this once: don't ever touch that stuff, OK?"

"OK," she said, a little amused. "So, you want some?"

I gestured no, then as she hunched over the book again, I brought it toward me with my foot and picked it up to wedge it between my knees before grabbing the straw still in her hand. It was good coke—definitely Alex's, the same kind she'd scored for me the day I got my contract. She took the book back and ran a finger over it, gathering whatever particles were left and rubbing them into her gums. I wanted to say that if she really wanted to get fucked up, why not just inject it, because that was the best—but I held off. She stowed the book and started straddling me again, her arms around my neck. I grabbed her ass to bring her closer to my belly. The tip of her tongue gently started lifting the edge of my lip, before enthusiastically shoving its way inside in search of mine. My hands climbed upward, massaging her shoulders through her T-shirt, while hers slowly clawed at my ears. The telephone started ringing. We both froze with our eyes open, our tongues caught in the act, waiting to hear whose voice it was.

"Yeah, hey, it's Nikki. OK, well, there's this thing at Les Halles—no biggie, though, not like there'll be Granny jackets; I mean, you're not gonna find those anywhere. Anyway, um, take a look if you want, it might not be that bad. So, I don't know the exact address but it's near Beaubourg, the street with all the retail. You know, the green door."

"What green door?" I asked; Inès giggled into my mouth.

". . . and there are boots you could try at Barracuda on Rochechouart. It looks really cheesy from the outside but it's this old-timer who's been there since 1971, so you know—you can imagine. Zippers and everything, you know, classy shit. Anyway, come by whenever. I'll be back in the studio in ten days but, anyway, I'm here now. Alright, cool, see you later."

We listened to him hang up, or rather try to hang up, the receiver failing to slot into the cradle, hearing "fucking shit," and then Inès busted out laughing and at the same time rammed her mouth into mine.

"So what's the plan?" she purred between kisses. "You gonna keep living here?"

"Good question. I've got to think about it."

"Not sure there's time for that," she cooed, her palms pressing flat against my breasts. "Everything's exploding so fast."

"I know," I said, sneaking my hands up her T-shirt and hunting for her breasts.

"If I pass my bac," she went on, lifting her arms so her tee could come off, "my parents are getting me an apartment. The idea was I'd go in on one with Alex in September."

Alex passing up the advantages of roommates and shacking up solo with her? I knelt down to give a long lick between her breasts.

"After that," she kept on, taking the tip of my tongue between two fingers and starting to suck on it, "mmm . . . after that I'm supposed to go to college . . . mmmmmmm . . . but I'd rather . . . I'd rather travel for a while."

"Where to?" I asked, slithering my thumbs down through the elastic of her panties.

"Mmmmmm . . . I dunno," she said, contorting her body to shed them and kick them away before snuggling up against me once again. "Mmmmmm . . . San Francisco?"

What else had Alex said about me? I happily sighed; she was getting so wet.

"Mmmmmmmm . . . we could . . . New York and . . . ooooh . . . a road trip."

"I don't have a license," I said, starting a gentle to-and-fro with her clitoris.

"Oooaahhh . . . I can . . . I can handle that."

"What kind of car?"

"A . . . oh fuck . . . a Buick . . . aaah . . . a white Buick, it's got to be white to . . . oooaahhh . . . so it looks good crashing into the Bay . . ."

"White, got it."

"So I, I . . . oooaahhh . . . I pass my bac and you, you . . . fuck . . . and you . . . you get going on . . . oooh . . . on your record . . . and after that . . . after that we're outta here . . . slow down a little, I'm gonna come."

"And till then?" I asked, not slowing down at all.

"Aaaah, stop," she was panting, "stop!"

"Till then?"

"Till then . . . mmmmmmmm . . . till then I'll be calling you all the time."

Till then, most importantly, we would need to keep a low profile. A low, *low* profile.

5.

Pallas was right in front of me, sitting on the edge of the mattress, whereas I was stretched out on my crappy comforter in a nightie. She couldn't not see it. My wet hair was the hair of someone who'd just rinsed off, my cheeks were too flushed and my eyes were too glittery, but most of all my lips were blood-red, swollen from smooching Inès all night. Plus, with the heat coming in from outside, I'm sure you could just smell the sex in here. But Pallas was oblivious, dourly recounting her weekend by the sea. Alice, once again, was in the throes of bulimia; she'd spent the whole time gorging on diet cream cheese and then instantly regurgitating (it was strange how she only binged on things that, in theory, had little risk of making her fat—bulimia with an anorexic's logic). And though it felt good getting some nice long laps in at the pool, Pallas ultimately would have rather stayed here and watched some videos with me. She asked if I'd thought to record *Friends* for her. My hand on my mouth signaled no. She shrugged, then said her lumbago was coming on. I gently prodded: her heels were too high, so this was nothing new. I said I'd borrowed her sheets, that I'd been putting off taking mine to the laundromat. This was a first, but somehow she didn't seem to catch on. Lucky I'd thought to flip them around so the bloodstain would be by her feet. She rested her elbows and I expected a moment when she asked me for a pillow and no doubt picked up Inès's scent.

Finally, she said, "I'm really sorry."

"Don't worry about it," putting my arms around her.

She looped her arms around my waist, leaning her head on my shoulder, and I congratulated myself for at least taking pains to wash my face . . .

"I wouldn't want you to think you're not allowed to see people," she said, softly pulling away. "I'm not in love with you anymore, OK?"

"OK," I said, taking her hands.

"It's just that when these things happen, it feels like we're going to stop being friends. That we'll stop having time together. And Inès is like a little sister to me. So even if I know that it was all in my head, in the moment it felt horrible. Besides, thinking I was going to lose you both, I didn't know what it would do to me; even just imagining you together felt excruciating. I mean, don't take this the wrong way, it's just—that kid is really special to me. She's so cute. I'm sure Alex isn't just holding her hand and all, I'm aware she's got her kinks, but she's really calmed down a lot since being with her—but you . . . I mean, don't take this the wrong way, truly, but imagining *you* doing those things with her, I swear, it makes me want to puke."

chapter eight

a postcard from notre-dame

1.

Sunday morning, and impossible to find alone time for calling Inès. I wound up getting Jessie on the phone to suggest returning that CD of hers I'd just listened to. She was blasted on coke, not yet in bed from an all-night set at Pulp. "Chop chop," she said, she was going to make me listen to some wild new shit, and afterward, we should pop by Tintin's, the tattoo guy, where Julia was about to get started on her dragon. Jessie lived right next door, and Tintin too. How convenient—so I could call from her place and then probably again from Tintin's. But I hadn't anticipated Pallas having this obsessive itch to tag along.

I forced myself to act present on the street, offering spirited responses to her multiple questions about the record, but deep down I felt sick to my stomach. If we had had a "normal" friendship, I might have called from my own fucking phone. Or borrowed her cell without there being any problems if I started wandering away to speak in private, and with no reason to freak out about her number saved in the call log. Yeah, if things had been cleaner, then I'd be telling my so-called best friend all about this crazy business . . . Was Inès finishing her test prep or, like me, could she not stop replaying certain scenes with her eyes closed anytime heat surged through her guts? And how were things between her and Alex, probably listening in on the other line?

Jessie had been rooming with three guys while she waited to find her own place. The door opened to a wide hallway that they'd converted into a living room; farther back were a kitchenette and bar, while on the left stretched a hallway with three bedrooms off it. Jessie slept in the living room. A common arrangement with ravers, typically free of any personal effects that would clutter up the living space, just the standard survival kit arrayed right on the carpet, with stacked CDs and videotapes, a few fliers on the wall (Global Tekno, Soma, Magic Garden), a few magazines (*Crash*, *Coda*, *Tribeca*, *Self Service*, *Wad*, *Technikart*, *Nova*), and two couches around a coffee table for whenever a squad rolled through. And obviously there were the usual futuristic accents: a little bottle of Paic Excel degreaser, with its sunshiny liquid colored a bright, condensed orange; a cask of Extra cognac, with its blinding blast of red; some gray, metallic energy-drink cans. Your run-of-the-mill techno-partment.

Pallas and I were at that table now, with tea and croissants that we'd picked up on the way, while Jessie was on the phone in the kitchen. There wasn't any way to disappear with the cordless without Pallas asking questions. And I wouldn't be able to call from Tintin's either . . . Jessie was pacing back and forth, that weird thing where you can't stop pacing if you're talking on a cordless; her top was off, with a black Plassier bra to match the boxers peeking out from her skintight A.P.C. jeans. She had this eclectic aura that was nothing if not distinctive: both loutish and sexy, overeager child and hyper-professional. She was talking to her agent, same as Alex's agent . . . Alex who had never gotten used to being dumped, but losing Inès—that felt even heavier than losing me, and to be losing her *because* of me . . . My eyes fell upon the copious vinyl Jessie had lined up on one side. I was going to have to remember to bring Nikki his stash back. The Sunday prior, at this very moment, I had been in his music room playing "Gimme Shelter" . . . and now I was here nodding along to Aphex Twin once again, the CD whirring away at low volume. And in a T-shirt and tennis shoes again. Impossible that the events from last weekend were already over . . . But I still felt this craving for boots and a velvet jacket. Maybe I just didn't want to wear anything else anymore. Same with music. The only thing I wanted was Inès there beside me, no matter where, doing whatever, just so long as we were never apart . . .

"What the hell?" exclaimed Pallas.

"Huh?" I asked, sitting erect so I could grab another croissant and split it in half.

"All these pages are stuck together!"

I ran my eyes over the three or four magazines lying open on her knees and off to her side. Jessie walked over and placed her hand on the receiver.

"It's Bruno," she said. "He doesn't like ads—pisses him off when he's looking at something, so he tapes the pages together."

Pallas rolled her eyes, but I thought it was funny. Everyone with their own little compulsions. Nikki always bought stuff at second-hand shops so he'd never have to provide his address. Alex always needed to know how many hours of sleep were ahead of her because she really liked to sleep. Eva couldn't dance anymore without her backpack on ever since this one night when her bag's very presence saved her ass from a catastrophic acid trip when she lost any feeling of her feet on the floor. Compulsions, I had tons of compulsions, with a real cherry on top: getting into deep shit any chance I got . . .

"Fuck," Jessie said, hanging up. "Sometimes I just want to stick some pantyhose on my head and throw myself in the Seine!"

She picked up and slipped on a black T-shirt with *Reservoir Dogs* stretching across it in letters dripping blood.

"Damn straight!" I replied as she flopped down beside me to grab her chunky black Reeboks. "Swimming in twelve million turds!"

Jessie guffawed, running a hand through my hair to muss it up. Pallas smiled approvingly, happy to be getting along, though she'd been talking about herself for a while now, and even still she seemed slightly annoyed.

"Seriously, though," Jessie said, standing up and tugging her T-shirt down until her nipples looked like bullet casings, "what's it mean to you: being an adult? My dad's giving me all this grief, saying that adults aren't DJs."

"Being an adult?" asked Pallas, shutting her magazine (buying herself some time?).

"Being an adult," I said, standing up, "being an adult is developing a taste for savory desserts, knowing how to drive, and wearing a watch with the right time on it."

Pallas stared at me out of the corner of her eye, like: *We all know you're bad at all three.*

"Hmm," Jessie cut in, "don't you think they've changed the taste of Coke?"

"The glass bottles tasted better," I said, hoping Pallas might serve as my witness.

But Pallas was ignoring us; she was standing now, too, smoothing the flaps of her skirt, sighing, annoyed by the dog on its hind legs, aware that we were on our way out.

"Totally!" said Jessie, sitting down again. "Plastic bottles are total shit—you crack one open in the morning and by nighttime it's already flat. Uh-uh, no, I wasn't talking to you." (To the dog.)

"Yeah," I went on, also sitting down again. "And have you noticed how they're always rock-hard when they're closed, but as soon as you open them, they get so soft you start spilling everywhere!"

"Totally!" exclaimed Jessie, standing up again. "It's so we're forced to keep buying them over and over!"

"And have you noticed," I continued, also standing up again, "that they never fit in the baggies at the supermarket—like, the bags we put our trash in."

"Fuck yes!" said Jessie, sitting down again. "Coke must have this deal where they make bottles that stick out so we have to buy actual trash bags!"

We could have gone on like this for hours, with the dog bouncing up and down watching us sit and stand and sit and stand, but Pallas's silence was starting to weigh on us, so eventually we put ourselves on mute.

2.

Naturally, Tintin was closed on Sunday; we had to knock, and whose face appeared behind the glass door but Eva's.

"What? You're here, too?" asked Jessie, in shock.

Without the lights on, and without the usual crew around, the waiting room felt frozen in time, even darker with the gray outside, with its walls bearing the most conventional posters.

"I cracked," said Eva, lifting her sweater to show a bandage.

"What did you do?" asked Jessie. "You fucking idiot—stop!"

"What do you think . . ."

"Holy shit," Jessie whistled through her teeth.

"No, you really did it?" added Pallas.

"Did what?" I asked, eager to be in on a secret.

She lit a tiny lamp on the counter, then, with the bottom of her sweater pinned beneath her chin, she started peeling back the Band-Aid. The bandage covered part of what had already been on her hip: a five-inch black panther leaping out at us. Then we saw "Gayle" appear, temporarily smudged beneath a thick coat of Vaseline, with its black letters stretching backward as if sprouting from the creature's gaping maw. It looked awesome.

"Holy shit," repeated Jessie.

"Yeah, it's really, really pretty," Pallas added.

"So?" Eva asked me.

I concurred, a little vacant.

"No pressure, of course," Eva said, pressing the bandage back down.

Aware of my thing for her, she must have assumed I was pissed about her situation with the English girl, which was getting more and more serious, but that wasn't it at all: I was losing interest in the very idea of name-tattoos—but who was I kidding, I was clearly dying to have "Inès" on me somewhere . . .

Eva switched off the lamp, and we followed her footsteps down the hall leading back into Tintin's lair, where you could hear his machine whirring away.

"Hey," she said, turning around to face me, "what's a blonde say when she sees a banana peel on the sidewalk? Well shoot, I guess I'm gonna fall again."

I was pretty into this habit of hers, addressing her blonde jokes directly to me, her way of showing I mattered to her in spite of it all. I felt like saying I might finally take her up on her offer of "mere" friendship.

"Whoa, the whole posse!" Tintin shouted as he watched us hurtle in. "Fuck, you girls are too good—I should cut you a foursome deal!"

With his legs spread in a swivel chair, he was leaning so far forward that all his weight was on Julia's back, who herself was leaning forward on a backward-facing chair with a pillow wedged between her chest and the backrest. She was smiling with her arms crossed as we walked up to kiss her cheek, one by one, but we could see the tension in her smile, that her fingers were tightly squeezing the pillowcase. By the light of the curving lamp above, the black ink was turning purple with her blood. And Tintin's sweaty, smooth scalp glistened in the light as he poked out his tongue. He interrupted himself long enough to offer us all his cheek. Going by the felt-tip outline, the dragon was going to cover her entire back, with the tail ending between her ass crack. It was going to look incredible, but she wouldn't be able to show it off for months. That, plus the cash involved, dissuaded me from getting a backpiece of my own. If somehow there were some way to get your entire back done in one sitting, I would have replicated Crying Freeman's, with the animal tail reaching down and encircling my thigh. But then, spontaneously, I wondered where I should put Inès's name, what kind of lettering, and most importantly, should I wait first and see if she was up for getting mine done, too, or just plow ahead and really knock her socks off.

"You got a phone card?" I whispered to Jessie.

"Nah," she whispered back, "but I can lend you my cell if you want."

"Whatcha need?" asked Tintin, lifting his head.

And here I was, hoping I'd go unnoticed.

"Nothing, I've just got to make a call."

"Cool—take it in there, though," he said, jutting his chin toward the waiting room.

I hesitated before saying thank you, feeling Pallas's eyes on me as I walked back into the hallway. Fingers crossed it wasn't her dad who picked up, because then I'd have to ask for her and risk them hearing me. Dialing the number, I felt a rush of anxiety. But why, unless she might have changed her mind . . . ?

Hearing her voice, I spoke softly: "Hey. Any nice dreams?"

"Don't remember," she yawned. "Where are you, I tried calling."

"You and Alex have the same number of letters in your name."

". . . wait, you would do that?"

"You catch my drift?"

"She wants me to sleep over tonight but I can't, I've got too much studying to do; I'm heading over first thing tomorrow morning. Seriously, you would do that?"

"Going where first thing?"

"Uh, the hospital."

"Oh right," I sighed, "yeah."

"But seriously," she murmured, "you would do that—for *me*?"

"Get to work, no one wants a lazybones!"

When I returned to the other room, everyone was howling with laughter.

And Tintin was braying: "That guy! The only way he'd make his wife scream is jerking off and wiping his dick on the curtains! But man, talk about screaming—she can really scream! That chick, with those nostrils she's got, fuck, it's like she's got a resonator!"

I eyed Pallas for a conversation update, but she smiled to say she had no clue. I whipped out my cigarettes and walked over to give her one. She didn't even ask whom I'd abandoned them to call. I would have given anything for the chance to spill it then and there. Including my plan for an Inès tattoo. But now wasn't the time, so I just sat on my heels and focused on the side of Tintin's face.

This was the first time I'd been here on an off-day. The decor was the same, with superhero action figures all over the place, just like at Alex's, shelves full of paperbacks and tattoo magazines, temporary tattoos from all around the world, and a terrarium for Esmeralda, the hairy fucking tarantula that Tintin was always bringing out for the pleasure of watching girls scamper away screaming. The calm in here felt bizarre when compared to the usual circus. Tintin and Luc tattooed in this room while two other guys handled the room out front, and the four of them spent their days yelling about this and that over blaring music, with ever-replenishing spliffs and buddies constantly rolling through. Anytime strangers walked through the door, they started wildly ribbing them, and if they were girls, then they would take things even further. Even we were still rattled by it. All the fat jokes became a drag after a while, and it was impossible to leave without getting extra-high or extra-drunk, but visiting Tintin's was always a thrill. We often ran into him at Pulp, where he liked to listen to Alex. He'd be there all night long hitting on basic dykes, freaking them out while he just died of laughter. And his laugh was insane, hee-heeing like a tweety bird—highly infectious and a funny contrast to his ripped body. Whenever the mood started tanking, he'd shout, "MY WHIP!" and then lift up his T-shirt to show off his belly with the actual "my whip" tattoo on it in large, gothic letters. And he did, in fact, have a sick ride, the latest drop-top Mercedes coupe, colored black. He was a hot dog, pure and simple, always with those little sunglasses shoved halfway up his forehead, tattooist to the stars, getting photographed all over the place, but back when we first knew him, he was this big softie who just wanted to take you partying. What fascinated me was the grace that crept over his body whenever he got down to business. There was such rigor in how his hand gripped an arm, really tightening the skin, while the other worked the machine like the daintiest of quills. The way he sprayed cleaning product after, lightly dabbing a Kleenex to sponge it all up and then getting right back to it, overflowing with this infinite sense of delicacy.

Yeah, this was the biggest oaf we knew, but when you had him doing what he knew how to do, he turned into a fucking prince. Like when Nikki picked up a guitar. Like when Alex cued up a record. Like when Inès walked into a room . . . ?

3.

After we all returned to Jessie's—sans Julia, who'd be under the needle till nightfall—Jessie pulled me aside in the kitchen.

"So who is it?" she asked.

My eyes goggled in feigned surprise.

"Stop," she muttered, "it's written all over your face."

"I can't talk about it."

"Fine, I see how it is."

"You see how what is?"

"It's someone who's already with someone."

I was about to respond, but Jessie had walked back to join the others, all presently on the couches.

"We're about to buy some cigs," she yelled for everyone in earshot, "anyone need anything?"

And before I had time to protest she had opened the door, gesturing for the dog to stay put. I didn't need to turn around to feel

Pallas's eyes tracking me. Jessie took a seat in the stairwell one floor down. I sat too, with this feeling that whatever was on the tip of my tongue clearly wasn't a good idea.

"OK," she said. "I'm not forcing you to talk, you just look like you need to spill your guts, so all I'm saying is, if you want to, you can."

I sighed, grabbing her offered cigarette.

"It's the girl of someone I'm close to, isn't it?"

I slowly nodded.

"And she promised she would leave her, right?"

Again I nodded, as if the very fact of not responding out loud might limit the damage. Jessie sighed too.

"You know," she kept going, "even if you're going to piss off someone I love, I would never judge—these kinds of things happen all the time. So, if you're *in love* in love, you need to make a move."

"I mean, it's really great. Too good to be true, even. It's just so invasive."

"OK, I know who it is."

"Who?" I asked, holding my breath, split between fear and relief at the thought of finally sharing it with someone.

"I mean, if it's invasive, then it's Alex's girl."

My eyes went wide, trying to pretend it wasn't true, but my smile gave it away.

"You shut your fucking mouth," I whispered at once. "Swear you'll shut your mouth . . ."

"I'm going to say something to you: I won't say a word to anyone because the less I get mixed up in people's love lives, the better I can take it, but I hope you do the right thing, because Alex is super-hooked on Inès."

"I know," I sighed, "I can't stop thinking about it."

"But can I just say something? Inès hits on everyone. Me, Eva, Pallas. That's who she is. So try and think where this is going before getting involved."

"What do you mean she hits on everyone?"

"Come on, the girl's completely fake. No one wants to believe me, but I'm not feeling it. Anyway, beware—I like you a lot, and it's gonna get under my skin if you screw this up."

I stayed there for a second, staring into the distance, listening to my internal clock, processing if anything was coming unglued. But everything was still in place. No rising panic. Just an itty-bitty voice calmly saying don't dwell on it, Jessie must've hit on her one night and been rejected.

"Fuck," Jessie cut the silence, "this is going to be a mess anyway . . . You know they've got a trip coming up."

"What do you mean?"

"Down south. Alex leaves on Thursday for this set in Montpellier, and Inès is supposed to join her post-exams. Alex's scheduled back here for Fête de la Musique and Pride, but otherwise they'll be down there all summer. We've got a full slate—renting a pad with Eva, Gayle, Julia, everyone; even Inès's little sister is coming."

"Well, I'm sorry but that's not going to happen," I gently floated, uneasy with Jessie's edginess.

"OK, hold up! It's going to be a nightmare working with Alex if she's pissed off! And she's leaving in four days, so I don't know when you plan to tell her, but it's in your own interest to make a choice here, because she's already putting money down for the rental!"

I wanted to respond, to let Jessie know that besides making me sick, besides informing me of all these things I didn't know about, she didn't have to put so much pressure on me. But I didn't have the heart to be cold with her, not when she was the only person I could share this with. It was my own damn fault, I shouldn't have said anything. I just needed to trust it. Just have some trust, dammit.

4.

The ringing telephone jolted me awake. My hand instantly shot out to pick it up; meanwhile, my eyes searched for the alarm clock: five after nine.

"Hey," came a little voice. "Asleep, huh? I know, it's super early, but I wanted to hear your voice."

"Hold on a sec."

I stood up to slip on my robe, and I poked my head into the entryway. Pallas's bedroom, with its door open wide, was still cloaked in darkness. I tried gently closing my door, which—lo and behold—promptly squeaked.

"Hold on," I said again, lighting a cigarette before sitting at the far end of the room. "Hey babe," I whispered, "how's it going?"

"Fine," she said, morose.

"Where are you, are you already at the hospital?"

"Yeah," she sighed, "I finally just stepped out for some coffee. I don't know what's going on with her. She's been sticking to me like glue. I swear, she's so pathetic. Anyway, I've gotta go . . ."

Our service cut out. I hung up with a sigh. What's going on with her, I thought, is that she senses something's amiss, and now I'm sensing that you're going to start treating her like shit . . . I kept sitting there, flipping the phone upside down hoping I'd find some nonexistent button somewhere that might tone down the ringing. It was a little late to start worrying about Alex's impending role in our affair, but either way . . . And then there was her tone: that airhead schtick was going to bother me all day. It was obvious how young she was: no one accompanies someone to the hospital if they're not going to be present. It started ringing again.

"Sorry about that," she said, sounding bored, "I didn't have enough coins."

"You don't have your cell?"

"I forgot it, we were running super late."

"Uh-huh . . . so you ended up spending the night?"

"Well . . . she came and got me, because she said I wouldn't get up in time otherwise. I need some coffee, I'll call you right back."

I stayed there glaring at the receiver, which I'd finally laid to rest, a little disheartened; then I took off my robe and placed it over the telephone to muffle the ringing before I started getting dressed. In the kitchen, I put some water on to boil, trying to make as little noise as possible, and I sat on the lip of the couch. I could picture us here from two days ago, and I didn't want those images flooding back. Last night . . . Alex was going to require lots of rest, and of course she was the type who needed to get her fill in advance. A night of hellish fucking; maybe Inès was delaying so she didn't have to break the news over the telephone. Or not tell me at all. Honestly, if I'd been in her shoes, I wouldn't have risked compromising a burgeoning affair by confessing that sort of thing. I wasn't feeling her today, not even a little.

"Sorry about that," came the same little voice, "I didn't want to talk to you like that."

"Listen babe, you need to go right back in there and act really cute."

"Yeah," she sighed. "It sucks, though; it's been dragging out so much that, in my head, I'm, like, already out the door. Plus, I'm going to have to stay at least for tonight—I don't even have my notes with me."

"Hasn't that happened already?"

"What? No, Thursday. Thursday and Friday. And she isn't even getting out until noon, so what the hell am I supposed to do with all this time?"

"Sounds like you should send me a postcard."

"Oh yeah?" she asked, tenderly, "you'd like that?"

"Listen, I've been wanting to ask . . . last night . . ."

"We just kissed."

". . ."

"I didn't have a choice, it was either that or she'd yell at me till I fessed up. Are you really mad at me?"

Alex, asking questions?

"What would you do if I said I'd kissed Pallas?" I asked, ironic. "Would you be really mad at me?"

"I hate you," she scoffed and hung up on me.

I felt amused for a second or two, but the image of her and Alex together—it was lingering in my eyes . . . The phone started ringing again.

"Did you?" she asked again.

"No. But you did. So, you know—just call me back once you've got it all sorted. If you ever get it sorted."

"Fuck, you don't think I'm gonna leave her, do you? I'll do it right now if you want, I'll do it right this second!"

". . . cool it. Calm down. I take it all back."

"I'm totally crazy about you. I'll die if you leave me."

"Shhhh," I said, a little short of breath. "Calm down. Everything's fine."

“I sent you your postcard,” she mumbled. “But don’t expect something pretty.”

“I can’t wait to see your handwriting. OK babe, I gotta go, Pallas is getting up.”

I had just heard her cell phone ring. I lit a cigarette, cocking an ear, but all I could hear was her voice droning on. I waited for her to hang up before I wandered to her doorway. She was lying there sprawled in the dark with her curtains drawn.

“How would you feel about getting some food?” I asked with a smile, waving the smoke away from her room.

“I don’t know,” she said, looking sad. “I’ve gotta go, Alice is expecting me. You think you’ll be here around two to let Donna in?”

“Donna?”

“She’s hanging stuff up—you already forgot? For the private viewing this Sunday.”

She sighed, with the implication, “Yeah, I mean, everything’s slipping your mind these days.”

“Listen . . .” I started.

“I’m running late,” she cut me off, gently, “but how’s eight sound?”

5.

The Donna in question rang at two on the dot. Now that chick was really something. This gorgeous Canadian with short bleached hair and beady blue eyes that looked too clever by half. We only saw her every now and then because all she ever did was work, to the point that some people close to her only caught up with her at night, the only time she wasn’t getting interrupted by phone calls—every time she picked up, the real world came flooding back in—but that didn’t stop her from showing up to the club. She’d sidle up to the bar for the length of a drink, invariably clad in this long, well-oiled, black leather coat, German boots, jeans ripped to shreds, and T-shirts sized for twelve-year-olds, whose slogans were always even crazier than anything Alex and I could come up with (the one today read *I want to be plastic*), an ensemble occasionally taken up a level by S&M headgear clamped tight around her eyes. She'd stay as long as it took to down a glass and clear out. No one was ever good enough for her. Me, I wasn't attracted—too sterile—but we could have been friends, we had the same work ethic, the same ambition. Except, as bizarre as it sounds, she really wasn't trying to make friends wherever she went; she kept to herself and asked nothing of no one.

So she hung it all up in silence in the living room while I observed her in action from my place on the couch. She produced all sorts of mind-blowing pieces—books that talked when you opened them, cushions that moaned when you adjusted them, chairs that vibrated when you sat on them—but her greatest success, soon to be consigned at shops all over, were magic pills. They came in twos and threes, shaped like tabs or gelcaps in clear little plastic pouches, the size of a pack of cigs, spruced up with some kitschy-as-hell labels that explained their given purpose: pills to become a supermodel, to be hairier, more muscular, more in touch with one's vagina, for becoming the best at tongue-play or ovulation—countless options blithely mocking all the girls in our scene. This time it was a series, twenty varieties of "fame pills": fame pills for artists, actors, rock stars, footballers, basketballers, etc., with a celebrity's head on every label and a saying like "become as famous as Dennis Rodman's big dick."

She wasn't the kind to put everything on hold because she was falling in love . . . but I was, and I ran to answer my ringing phone.

But it was only Pallas wanting to know if Donna had come and if everything was running smoothly.

When she got home around eight, I had already been out for Chinese takeout. She was sitting on my bed, posture rigid, waiting for the food to reheat. MTV was playing the video for Marilyn Manson's "Dope Show," a track that usually made us start dancing and singing along. But this time she was barely even bobbing her head.

"Have you seen how French it's been getting?" she said, her eyes locked to the screen. "It's so stupid, we used to watch MTV for the English stuff." And she added, "It seems like you want to talk," her eyes still riveted to the TV set.

"Seems that way, yeah," I quietly answered.

She cut the volume and turned to face me. I offered her a cigarette and lit it, selected one for myself, and then I tamped the pillow down behind me.

"First," I began, "I want you to know how much I adore you, I really do, and this whole time I've been missing you a lot, it's been super hard."

She nodded slowly.

"OK, so look. We got together just once . . . while you were in Honfleur . . . and we thought that was going to be it . . . but then . . ."

"Please," she quietly interjected, "spare me the details, just tell me what's going on."

"Sorry. OK . . . so, she's going to leave Alex. That's all."

In her gaze, still fixed to mine, there was no apparent anger or fear. Only sadness.

"Do you hate me?" I asked abruptly.

"I knew, you know. I knew it right away."

"Listen," placing my cigarette in the ashtray to grab both her hands. "You mean a lot to me. And to Inès, too. So you're not going to lose us, nothing's going to change."

She took a deep breath in before slowly pulling her hands away.

"Dear god," she said, "I don't think you realize what this is going to do."

"I do," I sighed. "Tell me the truth: do you hate me?"

"Of course not," she said, with more than a little resignation. "I love you both too much to ever *hate* you."

"I feel bad I didn't tell you sooner. I didn't know how . . ."

"I know," she said, trying to smile. "Alright, can we eat now?"

She smiled. There was my Pallas, smiling at me. Somewhat sad but still sincere. I scooted closer to wrap my arms around her neck, and the tears just started flowing. Joyful. Grateful. Relieved.

And then later, I was lying in her arms, watching TV—my rented copy of *Face/Off*—we were glued to one another like we hadn't been in ages, me pressed up against her on my side, the way Inès pressed up against me. She was stroking my hair, absent-minded. Now and then, her hand would stop, and I could sense her staring off into the distance, but all and all she seemed to be finding some enjoyment out of the Travolta and Nic Cage performances, each one having stepped into the other's skin. I, too, was keeping up with the movie, but at times I couldn't help wondering how things were going over there with Alex. Alex knew how to turn on the charm when she wasn't feeling well. I wasn't afraid that Inès might succumb—given what she'd said earlier, it would probably just annoy her—but then I thought of all the little pretenses she must have been forced to keep up if she didn't want things to get too conspicuous. It's not like Alex would be trying to restrain her post-operation, but if she only needed to butter up Inès somehow, then how would she go about it? Did I really have a right to blame Inès if she gave in to keep the peace? And also, would it *really* just be pretending? Even when we don't want someone, if the performance is good, inevitably there comes a point when the pleasure kicks in anyway. In the six months they'd been together, Alex inevitably must have learned how to sweep her off her feet.

"What's going on?" Pallas asked, pausing the movie.

I straightened up into a seated position.

"It's killing me, not knowing what's happening over there. I want to call. You think I could, like: just checking up and all?"

Pallas sighed.

"I guess you would have if everything were normal."

"Exactly," I said and grabbed the phone. "You can start the movie if you want," dialing the number as I said it, and I got up to position myself at the window.

"Alex? Yeah, it's me. I just wanted to see how it went—at the hospital."

"Really well," she said, in the weakest possible voice.

"Didn't hurt too much?"

"No, I'm starting to feel it more now," she said in a voice that sounded truly, decidedly gone. "Bastards di'n't wanna gimme morphine."

"Next time!" I joked. "Cool—you got anyone there taking care of you? Is Inès there?"

"Yeah, yeah, she's here."

"Nice, and she's being really cute?"

"Yeah, yeah, she made me dinner and everything, and she's been tickling me and stuff."

"Nice, nice—well, rest up, I guess."

I hung up. Was I feeling any better? That's what Pallas asked, and I smiled to tell her no.

"Come here," she said, patting the space I'd left behind.

I came and lay beside her, wriggling my fingers up the bottom of her T-shirt. Her hand started stroking my hair again. I was dying to ask what the deal was with Inès hitting on everyone, but I couldn't—but who could I turn to?

"You afraid they're sleeping together?" Pallas eventually asked. "Is that it? I mean, in that state, Alex had better not."

"I know," I sighed, "but I can't stop thinking about it."

"Would doing it with me take the edge off?"

I lifted my head to stare at her. Would it take the edge off—make me feel less dumb—to get even, as it were? Probably yes . . . But then there was the Pallas of it all . . . we needed to cut it out, even after everything we'd been through together. I cleared my throat.

"Listen," I said, "I don't know what I'm thinking, but I do know, and you know: I'm extra, extra faithful, so if there's gotta be the last time between us, then it might as well be tonight. Or in the next few days at least, because after that, you know I won't be able to."

So we started kissing, really tenderly, and then the sex. It was the sweetest we'd ever done it. A real love thing, almost. One last goodbye. At several stages I felt tears coming on, thinking how hurt Inès would feel if she could see me right now. But I didn't have a choice in the matter. I wasn't going to process her doing it if I didn't also do it myself. And so on. Meaning, it would prevent me from getting so mad at her I'd leave her. And if she hadn't done anything, well, too bad. The ifs and maybes and questions kept coming.

6.

I kept the alarm set for nine so I could go downstairs and grab the mail before Pallas. It had been nice doing it again—our relationship felt more relaxed. Now she just hoped I could be happy.

And there it was—the card. A shot of Notre-Dame. I waited till I was back upstairs with a cigarette in bed before reading it:

I got married here five months ago, full of hopes and dreams . . . but now her voice goes in one ear and out the other, there's no passion when we kiss, no desire. I only feel a residual tenderness, mixed with pity. I feel like a serial killer in some sadistic game, kindly offering to help a man who's broken down on the side of the road only to fire a bullet in his head three minutes later—and you're there, too, not far away, monitoring the scene through binoculars, aware that I'll be coming for you next. But I digress.

What have you done to me?

I don't get it . . .

She'd forgotten to sign it. At first I paid no attention to the contents aside from their affect, so dreadfully lovelorn, and the fact that it all made me giddy. It was nice, that shot of Notre-Dame, given how much the site itself moved me. I figured Alex must have made her read Ellroy's *Killer on the Road*, which she gave to all her girlfriends. Yet I wondered how Alex could have "gotten married" without me hearing about it, and most of all how she could have ever agreed to it, given that she was always taking the piss out of anyone who broached the subject. And could the choice of location have been hers, some sort of perverse wink to all my respect for it?

On my third or fourth read-through, I absorbed the message. Influenced by the book, of course—she herself never could have done such a thing—but even so . . . It didn't make me sad for Alex, because this was all in keeping with her own perversions. No, I was sad for myself at the thought that someday Inès might send a similar card to someone else about me . . .

Midmorning, the phone started ringing, but it was only Jessie.

"Listen, you do what you want but I wanted to say, last night I went to see Alex, to see how things were going, and those bitches were attached at the hip. Like nothing out of the ordinary. So I was wondering if . . ."

"I just got a postcard."

"Saying what?"

"Saying she's clearing out of there."

"Ah well, in that case. I mean, what do I know. She's even faker than I thought. Because honestly, you should've seen her yesterday . . . Whatever. But still, you should know: Alex is gaga for this other girl right now, so Inès might just be doing this to piss her off."

"Who's the girl?"

"Who cares. Whatever, look, I wanted to tell you because, like I said, I really like you a lot, and it would piss me off if you fell for something. OK, tata."

Who was the girl? No—couldn't be. Not before the postcard, not now. Jessie was going to have to stop this right now. Pallas was on my doorstep, blinded by the sun. The phone rang again.

"It's me. I just got home, my dad's really letting me have it, everything sucks, I can't even study in peace so I'm gonna grab my notes and come over. I know Pallas is probably there, but soon it's all gonna be out in the open anyway so I don't see the point in not."

"Uh-huh. Can you call back in ten minutes, babe?" and I hung up.

"What's happening," asked Pallas, "was that Inès?"

"She wants to come over."

"Here? Now?"

"So, she can't get any work done at home and she needs to study."

"Uh-uh, dear, impossible, it's too early."

I heaved a sigh.

"I understand," I said, "but I can't tell her no, can I?"

"Uh, yes, you can tell her no, it's pretty simple."

"So where would you have us meet?"

"Not my problem, you'll figure something out. Why not take her to a hotel with your advance."

"Stop . . ."

"You stop! If she comes over, she's going to spend the night, and tomorrow, tomorrow's my birthday in case you forgot, and I want some peace at home!"

I had, in fact, forgotten. The phone rang again.

"Don't try and stop me, I'm coming, it's been four straight nights, I can't take it anymore."

"Fine, come."

Pallas got up. Her bedroom door slammed. I went to knock, she shouted, "GO FUCK YOURSELF." I turned the handle, I cracked the door, and I tilted my head back just in time for it not to slam right back in my face. I loitered in the hallway, leaning my back against the wall. The door opened again and Pallas was clothed now. I tried grabbing her by the shoulder as she headed to the living room, but she brusquely shrugged me off. She slipped on a jacket. Again I tried touching her as she opened the front door, but again she shrugged me off. I exited onto the landing, called out to her, and again found myself treated to a "GO FUCK YOURSELF" as she hurtled down the stairs.

chapter nine

blood on the sheets (press *)

1.

Lots of pretty, pretty ones, they wanna get you high, she whispered in my ear, *but all the pretty, pretty ones, they leave you low, and blow your mind. We're all stars now, in the Dope Show . . .* She had been playing it on a loop ever since arriving. Just like Alex always put on NIN's "Mister Self Destruct." No doubt they'd just spent six straight months knocking boots to Marilyn Manson. But it was making me slightly uneasy, like I was doing something plastic. She was on top of me, dancing a little and digging her fingers into me at the same time. Whatever she was doing felt great, but no way could it match how *real* it felt with Nikki. This honestly wasn't something I'd ever need to do again, not when she simply could have held my toe for it to have been enough. Or almost enough. I would have caught terminal cancer for her, like Kenneth Branagh tells Charlize in *Celebrity*. The upsetting thought was she might not have the right experience either. That the hysteria of it all would be the sum total. No matter how perfectly wielded, double-headed dildos never functioned the way they were meant to; unless you rocked your hips like a madwoman, the smaller part that goes into the wearer didn't work in tandem with the other part. But no big deal, soon it would be her turn for it, and I knew in advance that it was going to make my head explode. To have a seventeen-year-old like this . . . And the blood everywhere was going to flip my lid. A total thrill, seeing it all over her, like I had hurt her somehow while her gaze kept pleading more, more . . . The only aspect I found odd was how unfazed she was about three periods in one month. She moved alarmingly well for a girl who'd never had it up the ass before, not really. A little depressing to think that this would've been her method the first time around. With a dildo. With Alex. But I guess if I had been in Alex's shoes, my brain would've melted . . . "Ever done ketamine before?" she purred, lifting one of my arms to give a long lick under the armpit. "My best friend has a hookup. Imagine how it feels to fuck on that . . ." How awesome would that be with a man: that was my first thought. What would happen when she finally felt tempted by it? It wouldn't be fair not to grant her that request . . . "I want you to get me a little model Buick. I'll work on it a little every day, and once it's painted and everything, that'll be our cue to leave. You think I can keep coming here with Pallas and all? No, I want a house with beach access, like *Melrose*. A fridge with an ice maker. And . . ." "Hey," I laughed, "don't you want to finish what you've started?" "Sorry, it's just, I feel like I haven't seen you in a hundred years. I have so much to tell you, so many stories. Every day, when I open my eyes, you're all I want to see. You're everything I've ever wanted. You're gonna get my name tattooed, and I'm gonna get yours too, and I don't know if I can take it . . . ," and she buried her face in my neck, back to gentle motion. I doubt anyone had ever done me so calmly, without any rough stuff. I couldn't tell if I liked it as much, but right here, right now, it all fit, from the music being low to the streetlights glowing through the open shutters. Serene. Like windows over San Francisco Bay. Maybe that's what it meant to be happy with someone: serene. "Hey," she said, lifting her head again. "You're not lying, are you?" "How so?" "I mean, you really like me, right?" I smiled. "Why, are you lying?" She stared at me intensely, so many things buried in those black depths, and she cupped my face in her hands—"How could I lie to you when you look at me like that?"—starting the motion once again. Stronger and deeper this time, with her hands beneath my ass cheeks grabbing them, and my arms welded around her nape; and with my heart drowning in pleasure, I shoved my entire soul down her throat.

2.

The sun woke me as it crept into the room. Inès was still in my arms, her cheek resting under mine, with one knee atop my thigh. Tiny dust motes were floating in the air, suspended in a ray of light. Life could have ended right there, I thought. We could have frozen in that instant. Like approaching nirvana on a drip, like lying back with some really good dope, watching the clouds meander by and smiling at how beautiful, how radical everything was, in every direction. I tried adjusting my shoulder slightly, and she opened her eyes. "I love you," she instinctively purred before burying her face even deeper into my neck. I tightened my arms; she smelled sweetly of sleep. "You hungry?" I asked her in a low voice, stroking her hair. "Mmmmm," she went, lifting her head, and her mouth met mine. Her lips were so nice and soft, it drove me crazy, the feeling as they crushed against mine. "Sleep OK, honey?" she mumbled, and she crawled on top of me to grab a cigarette. It was strange to see a girl so young light up right upon waking, but what could I say, I wanted one as well. She rolled onto her back to puff out the smoke, and since I was just ogling her, amused but showing no signs of coming any closer, she came and pressed herself against me once again.

"Ooh, I love this stuff," she said, lifting her head.

On TV, still running without the sound, Britney Spears was leaping about like a Power Ranger.

"I know it's trash, but sometimes I like trash!"

I grabbed the remote to raise the volume, refraining from mentioning my weakness for Céline Dion . . .

"I've gotta head back," she sighed, "I won't get anything done if I stay."

"Don't you have your notes with you?" I asked, shifting the cigarette into the corner of my mouth as I tugged the comforter up.

"I won't get anything done!" she repeated, climbing on top of me and pinning my arms into a cross, ignorant to the smoke stinging my eyes. "If you want to help me," she said, placing her cheek against my chest, "you'll force me to get up, I can't get out of bed myself."

I took a final drag on my cigarette before stubbing it out, gently pushed her off me so I could find my footing, and offered her a hand up.

We got dressed side by side.

"I really like this shirt," she said, watching me pluck Nikki's shirt up from the ball that I'd left it in. "I really like stuff from the seventies."

I smiled knowingly. There was something so imperious about her goofy stork posture, with her hands on her lower back, looking around to make sure she wasn't forgetting anything. Somehow proud and terribly determined and yet, at the same time, like such a child. I couldn't get over that she was mine. At her age, there's a tendency to want your freedom rather than settling down like this . . . How long could she picture us together? I had no idea either. All I knew was it worked, just like it had worked with Alex: wanting it to last as long as possible, for this to be the final hookup, that from here on out my car would be pulling off the highway for good . . . That had been the plan with Alex. Two or three years living the coolest possible life—recognition, cash, dope, all the passion you could want—until it all came crashing down in an instant; there hadn't been enough time for things to degrade, to soften, to turn stale. And when our heap of metal finally tumbled into the ditch—slowly, like in *The Things of Life*—we could watch as those two or three years paraded past our eyes, and we could say to ourselves, how cool, how goddamn cool, thank you . . . Yeah—it took me back. But I didn't know if she was in that car with me or not. In light of her age, she still had things to do, to experience . . . I folded the comforter back over the blood-stained sheets. She hadn't just gotten it everywhere, she had smeared it across my throat and face and mouth, crying and moaning about how we should try to find a way to have a kid together . . .

"Can you leave me your cell?" I asked.

"Oh, right. And you know what you need is a sofa in here, so I can read while you're working."

She crouched for her bag, pulled out an organizer, scribbled down her number, then tore out the page and placed it near the computer.

"Now, make me leave," she begged, gluing herself to my side once again.

We coasted our way to the wall; again, she cupped my face in both hands to kiss me. As if it scared her that my mouth might turn away. Maybe she really would be in that car with me. As unfortunate as it was, she seemed ready to follow me to the bitter end.

She dissolved watching me gather up my jean jacket so I could walk her to the metro: "Where have you been all my life . . . ?"

Her hand gravitated for my hand when we exited the building. It was my first time holding a girl's hand in the street. After a few yards, her arm slipped through mine, and then she capped it off by stopping us for a kiss. Now this I had done before, many times even, but I had always felt embarrassed by it, whereas this time I didn't care. Before we went our separate ways, I commented how all the people we passed had turned their heads, but all of them were smiling. Two pretty girls, madly in love, what could possibly be wrong with that? It had been that way the entire way down Avenue Parmentier, before she caught the metro at Place Voltaire. We couldn't stop making pit stops to kiss, to whisper blandishments in each other's ears and laugh, then resume course, arm in arm, bringing smiles to every staring face.

Outside the metro ticket booth, our bodies crashed into the wall for one last round of kissing. We didn't dare eye the cashier too closely, because this time, it felt like a little too much; Inès's hands were lightly massaging my breasts, hardly concealed by my jean jacket.

"I love you—*you*," she whispered, finally detaching our mouths.

I watched her use her transit pass and navigate through the turnstile. She looked radiant. She froze on the other side, turned around to face me with a frown to show how little she wanted to leave. I didn't know what our future would bring, be it San Francisco or a grubby garret on the Place des Fêtes, but it was coming for us either way.

3.

Back home, I ran into Pallas, who had only just returned. She was alternating between the couch and the living room closets, stowing away her purchases.

"Hey," I offered timidly, "happy birthday."

She rolled her eyes, like: *yep!*

"Listen," I started, "about tonight . . . I don't think . . . I don't think I can make it to Pulp. I'm sure you understand, it wouldn't look great if I acted like nothing's going on, given the Alex situation. It'd be hypocritical . . ."

Pallas didn't answer, continuing to stow her stuff.

"And, uh . . . Inès said to tell you that she might not be there either."

"Excuse me?" Pallas exploded.

"She's got her exams," I proceeded in lulling tones, "she's almost out of prep time."

"Ha, well, she found time to come and jump your fucking bones!"

"She's got her bac *tomorrow*."

Pallas slammed the closet, then went to her bedroom and slammed that door as well.

I was rooted in place, eyeing her empty bags on the couch. A Gucci, a Prada, and a third one from Le Shop. Pallas's door opened, and she stationed herself in the living room doorway.

"You really think no one's going to notice you aren't there?" she asked, hands on her hips.

"I mean, I don't know . . . Everyone knows Inès has got her bac, and for me, just say that we've been fighting. They'll believe you," I added with a timid little smile.

"Fair enough!" Pallas yelled. "I don't know what you two are playing at, but it's really unhealthy."

"How so?"

"Uh, baby girl going on sleeping with Alex while also claiming she's about to leave her."

"Excuse me?"

"Alex mentioned it today, that the hospital was ultimately a good thing, because it got her so fragile, she had to get head for three hours straight before Inès would let her come."

"Um, she's lying," I sighed.

"Um, we'll see!"

"She lied, I'm telling you."

"And *why* would she lie?"

"I don't know, do I? Because they're actually not fucking anymore and she's flipping out? How should I know! But you're a piece of shit for using that on me! You're just trying to piss me off—it's disgusting!" At which point I walked into my bedroom and slammed the door.

I immediately dialed Inès, hoping she hadn't switched off her cell on the train; it started ringing.

"It's me. Listen, Alex is telling everyone that yesterday you two spent the night fucking."

"Um, she's lying."

"And *why* would she lie?"

"I don't know, do I? . . . Maybe because we aren't doing it anymore . . . I'm having a hard time hearing you, I'll call you when I get there."

She called back an hour later and acted as cute as ever, saying she understood, that it would really piss her off if she had heard I'd been sleeping with Pallas again, for an example . . . She sounded a little miffed, but I chalked it up to stress about the next day. The tests began at eight o'clock and would last until late that afternoon. She said she'd call back just before bed, or the next morning at the very latest, before heading out, so I could buck her up.

"I can't wait," she added before hanging up, "I can't wait for all this to finally be over and we can just be glued to each other. Or, in my case, glued to the sofa watching you work."

4.

I woke up around eleven feeling somewhat dejected that Inès hadn't called before leaving for her exams. I'd already missed hearing her voice the night before. But no matter, surely she needed all her focus at the moment. I got up to locate her digits. And naturally, I reached her answering machine; it was my first time hearing it, and I recognized the DJ Rush track Jessie had dropped at the rave, *I wanna fuck you all night*. It felt off in this context. If Alex had a copy, too, then they must have done it to that track countless times by now . . . But I summoned all my energy and told her to pick up, adding that as soon as my advance came through, I was going to keep my eye on the ball and not drop too much money on new gadgets; that way, we'd have plenty left over for the peaceful life. I hung up and dialed the answering service at my bank. Just checking. "Press star." Yeah, yeah, press star and hear you've got forty bucks left. But fuck me, there it was: YOUR CHECKING ACCOUNT TODAY SHOWS A BALANCE OF ONE HUNDRED THOUSAND FORTY-TWO FRANCS.

"PALLAS!" I shouted, hanging up. "PALLAS!"

I raced into the hall and started knocking on her door. No response. I remembered she must have gotten back super late from her birthday, so I turned the knob as gently as possible. The room was floodlit and the bed looked flawless. I went back to my room and called her cell. It rang and rang for a while until the answering machine kicked in.

“Fuck, I don’t know where you are but you’ve gotta wake up! My advance came in! I got my advance! So I’m rushing to the bank and I’ll call you from a phone booth to see where I should meet you!”

Then I tried Inès’s cell again: “It’s here! We’re rich! Call me as soon as you’re done, I’m gonna pick you up in a limo!”

And I called Jessie’s place and reached the voicemail, then hung up to try her on her cell, where I got the answering machine again: “Fuck, Jessie, I got my advance! I’m gonna buy a G4!”

And I called Eva’s place because the store she worked at didn’t let her take calls: “Fuck, I got my advance! I’m gonna increase your commission, that’ll shut the bastards up!”

I was dying to call Alex too, obviously, but that—that I couldn’t do, I knew full well. I redialed Pallas and this time she answered, sounding frosty.

“You get my message?” I asked, shaken that she would act like this after hearing the news.

“Yeah,” she said, “and not a day too late.”

I didn’t catch on.

“So where can we meet?”

“We can’t, I’ll be back later.”

“When?”

“I said later.”

“Fine, fine, I’m rushing to the bank, then.”

In the taxi to the bank, I was floored: Pallas hadn’t reacted *at all.* She had sounded hysterical on the phone when I informed her I’d finally landed a contract . . . She must have been really mad I hadn’t come to Pulp, but once she saw the wad of bills, everything would be swept under the rug. After the bank, I was going to call Nikki and get the exact address for that store he liked in Beaubourg; I was finally going to snag myself some seventies gear!

It really was my lucky day. I found a fitted black-velvet jacket with a slit down the back, plus an awesome plum-colored shirt, tailored just so. I found multiple other things that were too big for me but might work for Inès, except it would have been better for her to pick them out herself. Then I stumbled into another vintage store that apparently had just opened and was even more seventies, and there I found this incredible pair of boots that were just my size. Not Anello & Davide but equally classy, with a zipper and four-inch heels; I had to have them even if they made me too tall. And to top it off, on my way past a little junk shop on the Rue du Temple, I saw the most important thing of all: a little club chair for Inès.

Now I was out on the sidewalk, and despite the armchair and all my bags, I felt I could go just about anywhere. To Fnac and buy tons of records for Inès, then make the rounds at Étienne Marcel. But I wanted to wait for Pallas. I needed to hit up Colette, but for once I would have the means!

5.

The indicator on my answering machine showed I had a single message. I dropped my bags to kneel beside it; I pressed the rewind button, and when I saw how long the message was, I pressed play to get a sense of who was speaking: ". . . whatever you do," in Inès's voice, "I take full responsibility . . ." I pressed stop. There it was—she had just left Alex . . . I froze, staring into the distance, wondering if this was terror I felt but no, I was just filling up with this incredible liberation. I took off my jean jacket, lit myself a cigarette, and wound the message back to the start.

"Hey, it's Inès. So, um, I tried calling you a lot, you weren't there . . . So, the thing is . . . look, I love you, I don't think I can deny it . . . but the thing is, I also love Alex . . . somehow . . . I don't know . . . and I can't . . . I'd rather we didn't see each other . . . didn't call each other . . . all of it . . . I'm sorry . . . This isn't going to be easy for me, too, but I can't . . . I can't, I can't, I can't . . . I know I'm chickening out, I'm whatever you want to call me, I'm an idiot, you know, I'm sure I am, in some ways, but I can't, and . . . look . . . So the card, I mean, do whatever you want, show it to her, don't show it to her, whatever you do I take full responsibility . . . OK . . . I'm sorry to do this on the answering machine . . . but it had to come out somehow . . . And I'm sure you're never gonna talk to me again, and, look . . . that's fine, but . . ." and then it cut out.

Obviously, I instantly called her cell. It rang. My heart was pounding. She answered in the tiniest voice.

"It's me, please don't hang up."

"Listen . . ."

"You didn't really mean what you said, did you?"

"I did, you know I did. I've gotta go, there's another test about to start."

"Inès, I'm begging you."

"I have to leave."

"Fuck, I just got the advance!"

"I'm thinking of you, OK?"

I immediately tried her back but she put me on voicemail. I was about to start talking when the front door opened. I hung up and got to my feet. Pallas was standing there rigidly with her bags.

"She's leaving me," and I burst out sobbing.

Pallas lingered on my doorstep wearing this funny expression.

"She's leaving me," I repeated, walking over to encircle her in my arms.

Eventually I felt her hand ride up my back but I instantly stepped away. The room wasn't big enough for me to disappear. I wanted to vomit. I hated believing it, but I knew that what was happening was permanent.

Then Pallas, her voice suddenly icy, said, "Are you always going to be like this?"

I turned around, feeling numb. The corners of her mouth were turned up in a rictus of pure contempt.

"No," she added, "because that would be impossible."

I slowly dried my eyes on the back of my hand.

"Can you let me be in love for five minutes?" I asked.

"Oh stop, you really think we're so stupid?"

"Excuse me?"

"Come on, you know you were never in love!"

"Yeah? So what *were* we then?"

"Ha, you were nothing at all! She was never going to leave Alex for you! You honestly couldn't tell? No one knows you, you're flat broke. Sure, you've got this advance, but I honestly can't see how you managed it; your music's shit, and you've got this ridiculous little cheapo, sixties-revival thing going on."

She was giggling now.

"Be real," she kept going, "Alex has the dough, the car, the guest lists, the professional home-gym, the house down south. Look at you! Would you quit someone like her for someone like you? Aw, you poor thing, I pity you."

"What's *this*, then?" I said, brandishing the postcard in her face.

"Yeah, yeah," Pallas grumbled, knocking my hand away. "She told me all about that—it's a passage she nicked from some book."

"What? She told you about it?"

"Of course—I saw her! It was my birthday, remember? You thought she wasn't gonna wish me a happy birthday just to make you feel better?"

Not true, those words weren't Ellroy's, they just imitated his vibe. I folded the card in half and shoved it in my back pocket.

"We went to test out some swimsuits for her trip! Alex has a set with Aphex Twin in Montpellier, you really think she's gonna miss that?! And you know what she says? She says you're mentally ill, you tried to strangle her, that she's been forced to pretend this whole time because you're a piece of shit! Believe me, I had to pretend, too!"

I opened my mouth, no words would come out, and I shut it. As I slipped around Pallas, I pulled ten thousand bucks from my pocket and I let the wad fall at her feet.

6.

"But what happened?" I kept asking, sitting erect on Jessie's couch, my eyes misty with tears.

"I don't know," Jessie sighed. "All I know is they had this big falling-out on the phone last night and Alex left her. So maybe Inès freaked out or something?"

"About what, though?" I sniffled.

"Really, I don't know, but either way, Alex is hip to the two of you now. When Inès was at your place a couple nights ago, Alex ran into her mother who said she'd gone off to spend the night with some Louise. And it's not like there are ten thousand Louises running around."

"Why didn't you tell me this before?"

"Because I only learned about it today. Anyway, Alex got her revenge already—she banged that chick she was crushing on."

"Yeah?"

"So, you know, now they're even."

"And Inès knows about that?"

"How should I know? But it's not your business to tell her."

"Like hell I won't!" I said, standing up.

"Hold it," Jessie said, stretching her arm out to bar my passage. "I wasn't supposed to tell you that."

"Fuck that, you don't understand! Inès bailed because she thinks she still loves Alex, but if she learns about this . . ."

"Nope, uh-uh," Jessie retorted, "that's not gonna change a thing. Alright, listen, if you really want to know everything, Alex says she saw the whole thing coming from the start and thought how convenient if Inès sets her sights on you, because then she could bang that other chick, only Inès's part was starting to get on her nerves, so Alex pretended to leave her to try and get her to chill out."

"Wait, when did you learn all this?" I asked, practically suffocating.

Jessie heaved a deep sigh.

"Listen, I tried to warn you but you didn't want to hear it. Inès isn't the little saint you think she is. She's fueled on coke right now; last month she was taking heroin every day."

My eyes widened in horror.

"Yeah!" Jessie sighed. "I mean, she's with Alex, what do you think? Those two are made for each other."

chapter ten

steribox / mcmorning

1.

I woke up in the fetal position on Jessie's couch, and I could already feel the pain. It had been a long time since this had happened, but once you've felt it once, you never forget it. The pain would be in place before you even opened your eyes. It didn't vanish or dwindle overnight. It was fine with simply pausing your mental and physical energy, only to return with a vengeance, dunking you right back in the situation the very second you awoke. There was no escape, nor even a moment's respite. No matter where I slept—in bed, on a couch, in any room where Inès was not—from the first instant I opened my eyes, the tears would start streaming and the knot would tighten its hold. Then my whole body would start screaming, reintegrating that spiraling sense of lack, and the only option would be proceeding with the day's schedule. Then, come phase two—the next week or week after—my exhausted brain could finally repel the initial attack, enough to make some moves at least, to develop a few thoughts before the wave crashed down on me again. For the time being, I could scarcely open my eyes; I could feel the situation still there. It had actually happened; it was still happening now. It wasn't so much the pain that rattled me but the panic. The outsized vertigo that only needed seconds for the absence to spread the walls around me, the ground to give way beneath me, and lack to steal my every breath. I sat to grab my tennis shoes, first drying my cheeks on my hand.

"Hey," came a masculine voice behind me.

I swiveled my head and found a guy with a buzz cut and a Prozac-branded T-shirt.

"Jessie went to get some croissants, she won't be long."

"Thanks," I sniffled.

I slipped on my tennis shoes, laced them, and stood, collecting my cigarettes and shades.

"Aren't you gonna wait?" the guy asked, surprised to find me putting on my jean jacket.

"Tell her I'll be back—back soon."

Outside it was drizzling. I put my sunglasses on and gazed down the street in both directions, but Jessie was nowhere to be found. I wasn't abandoning my plan, I just wondered the best way to do it. I couldn't show up at Alex's dealer's without her. Nikki's old reliable near Goncourt was still in operation but would have needed a warning the night before. And the last place I'd gone, back behind the Pompidou, that guy never had anything but nasty brown. But why give a shit when he was so close and I still knew the number by heart. Some dealers have numbers so easy to remember that you'd think they had a deal with France Télécom.

The best phone booth for it was the one at the animal fountain, which his windows looked down on from above; if his blinds were open, you had a green light. There were four people in line. One of their wrists read 10:45, and I figured I'd start hunting for a McMorning, now that I had the chance for once. McDonald's is the best spot in the world when you're hungry, except that everybody knows that now, and it can be ten in the morning or four in the afternoon and there'll always be an ungodly line. It was only 10:50 when I barged into the franchise on Place Sainte-Opportune, but both the open registers were slammed behind a cluster of thirty yellow raincoats—Germans or something—and it's not like I could yell at them for stealing the ten minutes I had left. I snaked a path to the cashier, this rudely pouting blonde, and I asked, nicely, if I could cut all the people, I knew what I wanted and it would only take me a second. "No, ma'am," she said, "all these people are ahead of you." Thanks, bitch, I didn't say. Opening my mouth the first time had returned me to reality, and I felt attacked by images in flashback; I kept having to dry my cheeks, and the ever-present lump in my throat did away with the urge to eat. When it was finally my turn, the girl didn't even compensate me with a smile. I don't know if it was my shades that annoyed her or just the assumption that I was on holiday while she was slaving away through July and August, nothing but grease wherever she looked; I wasn't treated to a hello or a goddammit or anything. She simply waited for my order with this glazed expression on her face. I asked for the McMorning sweet version, with a Coke instead of something hot. She turned to face the kitchen: "Hey Momo, we stopped the McMornings, right? Yeah, those are done."

I took a deep breath:

"Listen, for months I've been getting here too late every time, and this time I was good for once, and it's the line that took ten minutes."

"Yes ma'am, but there's nothing I can do."

"Ever watched *Falling Down*?"

She looked at me like a total idiot.

"Yeah, well, if you had, you'd remember," I mumbled, turned around, and walked away.

Outside, it was still drizzling. It would've made an impression, Michael Douglas threatening to empty a clip into a girl who didn't want to serve him breakfast at 11:01 . . . If I had his arsenal, there would've been no hesitation. What could it possibly cost them to serve McMornings all day if that's what speaks to us? In the gutter, a tiny dog was helplessly staring up into its master's eyes as it strenuously shat out a dense yellow turd. It was the very definition of "a dog's life": yellow dumps for the entire world to see, without even the option of dissolving a little Smecta to settle your stomach. I avoided the first pharmacy I saw for a different one a little farther. If I had my buddy Michael's ammo, nor would I have hesitated to decorate the shop fronts of every pharmacy in France that refused to carry Steriboxes. What good was it making a perfect junkie kit if nine pharmacies out of ten refused to stock them? Same for individual hits of insulin: was it always so necessary for them to dawdle before handing them over, sometimes even going so far as wandering into the storeroom and making it seem like they were calling the cops. Who did they think they were discouraging? It was such a waste of time. And a bad process psychologically, too: the less grief addicts get, the less likely their inner demon will awake. The pharmacy I chose was lax enough to hand out three Neo-Codion boxes at a time. Was it actual solidarity or just not having much of a choice given the local specimens? Either way, it was cool of them. Whenever I needed a Steribox, I felt a little uncomfortable asking for it aloud in front of other customers, though they generally never knew. The pharmacist this time was young, and he put the box in a baggie, quite a change from the type who'd push it to you from across the counter like they thought it might get their hands dirty.

Back at the phone booth at the fountain, there wasn't a line anymore, just two fat girls squeezed inside. Phone booths: like a jungle unto themselves—sometimes you'd see people stringing together a never-ending newspaper full of classifieds without a second glance at the people around them, even taking the time to chow into their sandwich before picking up the receiver again. Shocking, the lack of phone-booth-adjacent murders. The phone booth world needed its own militia, complete with a crane that could clamp down on the cabin roof, lift it off the ground, and lug away the bastard inside—street-level so his shame could be seen by every passerby—dropping him into a barn-turned-courtroom where they'd instill a sense of collective conscience, screening painful imagery like in *A Clockwork Orange*. The two inside it now, English by their accents, were a breed in between: not in any hurry to leave but flashing me big, apologetic smiles even so. It wasn't classifieds for them, they were doing their whole Rolodex, taking it in turns, repeating the same thing to each new contact: "We're in Paris! Yes—Paris, France! And we're right by this fountain with an elephant! Yes—an elephant, with a trunk! No, it's raining! What about you, what's the weather like there?" Come on, girls, I thought, smiling despite myself, buy your postcard and beat it . . . Eventually, I abandoned ship for the Rue Saint-Denis, hoping to find a bandanna to use as a tourniquet.

The guy didn't remember me. I tried stepping out of the booth so he could see me from the window. Mostly, he was stunned that I was calling this number. It took me a while to realize that he'd transitioned to a cell phone a year ago like everyone else, and this line was only for his mom, who called him once a month to see if he needed anything. Phone calls with dealers are always a slog, especially when you haven't talked in a long time and don't know their new procedures:

"Am I clear?" I repeated myself. "I thought I'd come for an hour."

"An hour?"

"Uh, yeah, just an hour—you know."

"An hour?"

"An hour, yeah."

"You want to come over *for* an hour?"

"Yeah, an hour. Not fifteen, not thirty, *an hour*."

"Ahhh, an hour . . ."

All set? One gram? Catch my drift, dumbass?

He already had a girl on his living room couch. Some drab blonde in the Gwyneth Paltrow mold, like a young model fresh off the boat from her native Estonia, pale and dim like a calf fresh from the stable. As I sat there waiting next to her, I wondered if the guy had picked her up at some club the night before, or if she'd gotten his address from the agency for her list of daily go-sees . . . Her eyes were locked on the TV, where Ophélie Winter's "Dieu m'a donné la foi" was playing on MCM. Thank god it wasn't Britney Spears (that already was a win), but the girl was lightly nodding along to the beat and, lighter still, was humming to the lyrics; it felt surreal watching her—here of all places!—tripping to that perky choreography. The guy gestured for me to retreat into the other room. Usually, that meant you were getting top-shelf service, but in this case there was clearly something flirtatious going on, quite the nonsensical reaction for this scuzzball to be having, some kind of childish glint in his eye that made him momentarily forget who he was: a smack dealer people *only saw to buy smack*. I almost felt offended that he wasn't trying to con me while he was at it, but I was radiating pure urgency, I was nothing but a husk begging for a fix. I told him I wanted to see it before I paid. He called me a pain in the ass, said he didn't have time for that, but he started unpacking the little parcel regardless. Brown, ultra-brown, no question.

"Alright," I said, "I'll take a quarter to taste, and if everything's cool, I'll take a gram."

"I don't do quarters," was his flat reply.

"Well, too bad then, next time," I said, and I made him think that I was leaving.

"OK, fine," he spat, "but do it in the bathroom, and don't hang around in there."

What did he think I was trying to do, OD?

Sitting cross-legged on the tiles with my back against the tub, my hands were slightly shaky. But it's like riding a bicycle, it never really goes away: fiddle around for a second or two and it all falls into place. Smelling that powder heat up, I felt the usual urge to use the toilet from the sheer rush of excitement and fear. The Steribox, no question, was the invention of the century: two syringes, two vials of distilled water, and two alcohol swabs—as clean as a clean drug test—except now there was something new: another little vacuum-sealed packet labeled "Stericup," where I discovered a spoon. But not just any spoon. A minuscule, stainless-steel receptacle uncannily like a Big Jim camping bowl—like a toy. I read the instructions listed on the plastic, and I thought I was hallucinating: by taking the cap off the syringe and connecting it to the spoon, you could create a handle to avoid getting burned! There was also a new cotton square for "halting the blood flow." What had gotten into them—we weren't playing with dolls here . . . "Steribox 2" they called it. Aha, so Steribox had generations now. The stupid box was so gigantic that it still felt better to transfer everything to your pockets. And why was there only one condom when everything else came in pairs? We only had time for a single fuck before we died? With a flick of the wrist, I wrapped the bandanna around my arm, and then I pushed my shades up so I could see what I was doing. Clenching the ends of the cloth between my teeth, I pierced a beautiful blue vein in my elbow bend. It stung a little, but god it felt good. Sweat was pearling around my eyes. I drew a little blood to make sure I was in the vein, then unclenched the cloth and started drifting away. "How could I lie to you when you look at me like that?" That whole month, on heroin . . . Impossible—my brain refused to register. I folded my arm and let my head drop back against the tub. The heat surged and expanded. I lit a cigarette, and then slowly, appeased, I started gathering the utensils that had scattered between my legs.

2.

No matter how long I knocked at Jessie's, it was clear there was no sound inside. I didn't want to go home. Maybe I wasn't in control of my reactions, but now that I wasn't in shock, I felt a wave of pure violence, a desire to bash Pallas's head into a wall. The heavy stone staircase beckoned. Solid, enveloping, each step sweetly called to me, to my body whose only aspiration was to curl into a ball. So that's what I did, I cocooned myself in a corner of the next-to-last floor, and I pulled my knees into my arms to have them rest against my chin. I was proud I hadn't called Inès yet. I knew I would eventually, but I was forcing myself to put it off as long as possible. If there were even one shot in a million that she missed me, I shouldn't ruin it through endless calls. And yet, wasting away in this roomy stairwell, I would have given anything to hear her voice. To hear her say calm down, I'll think about it. That was all I needed and I would have filled with unprecedented strength, so calm that it might make her change her mind. And who knows, if I kept at it long enough, maybe she'd end up calling me, saying it's impossible, I can't live without you . . . I would have given anything. My hundred thousand francs, my gear, my records, anything. My hand mechanically unbuttoned my jean-jacket pocket. Clearly things had taken a nasty turn if I was here in this stairwell, like I'd regressed ten years, but what else was there to do? My only option was to steadily re-up, waiting for the sliver of strength I needed to start facing things head-on. It felt inevitable—I had taken two grams. The worst thing, I thought while warming it up, ears pricked to the silent walls around me, would be someone showing up and saying he had something that would stop my thinking altogether. I might not have said no . . . And with that I felt my anger mount, while the staircase blurred into a fog. Because living was our whole problem. Living in ways we'd never had the occasion to before. That whole last month, on heroin . . .

Inès appeared, climbing the stairs with one hand on the banister. In the other she held a large flower. "Look," she said, sitting next to me, "it's an iris." Carefully grabbing the stem, I instantly felt the sap stir within, an infinitesimal, palpitating vegetal energy. "Look," she repeated, cupping her hands around mine. The small upper buds were fine, white porcelain, faintly veined throughout. I couldn't feel the nerves in my finger, but as I brought my lips close to graze them, I received a sharp thrill of delight and relief. "Look," Inès continued, pointing a finger to the lower petals unfurling from the sides: blue shading into violet, so tightly grained that it looked like microscopic fur, like the texture of butterfly wings. The base was all tiger petals, and erect at its center were its genital whatsits. "Look," Inès said, taking my finger to trace them. They were almost transparent, covered in frigid hairs with frosted tips. "This flower," Inès muttered, encircling my hands, "this is perfection: what we find most beautiful," and slowly she brought it to my nose to inhale. Typically, irises smell green—a fresh and delicate green—which progressively turns sweeter and sweeter, like a split fruit, until it's violently saturated your nose. But this one smelled like nothing. Not even a plastic, artificial scent. Because once there was nothing left but to hold it in my hands, that's what it became: a plastic flower. Inès was still beside me but her eyes were looking elsewhere, toward the windowpanes flooded with light. I moved my fingers to caress her cheek, but her skin started melting in broad white streams, viscous like paint being poured into a bucket. I opened my eyes to find the dog panting and licking me all over.

"Dumbass, stop! Where'd you come from? How long have you been there?"

I discreetly pooled my jacket between my feet to hide the scattered paraphernalia, then pocketed the lot just as Jessie opened the door, before I struggled to my feet to follow her into the apartment.

"I just checked this new record store," Jessie shot back, as she steered me to the kitchen, "and the clerk, I'm not exaggerating, he knew jack-shit. I wanted to say: beat it, prick, go work at Fnac if you listen to recycled shit!"

I collapsed onto a couch and pulled off my shades to dry them with the bottom of my T-shirt.

"Help yourself, if you want," Jessie said, pointing to the coffee table, with a platter of croissants and jam.

"I'm not hungry," I answered, folding the arms of my glasses and setting them on the table.

Jessie bent down to take a good look in my eyes.

"Yeah, OK, I see . . . Fuck, you started early. Is it good at least?"

I shot her a surprised, questioning glance. Aha, another user . . .

"Can I stay a little longer?"

"You can stay as long as you want," she said, smiling empathetically, sincere.

"And, uh . . . can I use your phone?"

"She won't be there," Jessie sighed, "she's taking her bac, remember?"

Her bac, right . . .

"Fuck, I'm not gonna make it—I'm not gonna make it, shit!" and I crushed my palms into my eyelids.

Jessie sat down beside me.

"Yes, you are," she said, starting to give my back a nice massage. "We'll find you someone else, a real sweetie, someone who's actually yours."

But I don't want anyone else, I felt like shouting. But even if it's what I felt like doing, that wasn't something you said to a twenty-five-year-old when you yourself were thirty-one.

"Can I use the bathroom?" I sniffled.

"Don't you want to give it a bit before the next time?"

I shook my head no.

"Fine, go ahead," she said with a sigh, "but leave the door open at least."

It felt strange seeing the worry on her face that I might OD or something. Not because she was showing concern but because we barely knew each other. Or what got me was that, if she'd refused, I'd have merely taken it somewhere else, simple as that. Nothing and no one had a hold over me. And that scared me shitless.

3.

"How are you feeling?"

"Like a zombie," I said, arduously sitting up.

I saw that I was still there, and instantly the tears returned. The VCR read 17:35. I had almost slept through the entire afternoon on that couch, and I would have kept going if the door hadn't slammed.

"Hey, I salvaged something," Jessie said, and she popped in a VHS. "It's a mix I made for MCM last weekend; they didn't even warn me, the bastards. You didn't catch it, did you?"

I shook my head no and stretched, then lit a cigarette before starting to gather my gear that was lying out in the open on the coffee table. Jessie acted like she didn't notice. On-screen I saw her hunched silhouette behind the MCM decks. Detroit techno—the usual—but the superimposed visuals were, frankly, pretty lousy. Bargain-basement neon CGI wrapping around a negative of her body, with zoom effects timed to the beat and some lame slow-mo of her hands cuing a track. Like, "Let's juice this up a little because otherwise it'd bore you to tears." If it bored them to tears, then why even bother filming DJs? This kind of music did something strange to me. All it took was a beat over 110 and I wanted to hit the town. Get dressed in the mirror, roll up to the club, do a quick round of hellos, and then finally get down to business. Posting myself outside the booth and getting swept away . . . Could I say the same about anything by the Stones? "Gimme Shelter"? No, that sent me out into the street with a band of cooler-than-thou, snazzy-dressing men . . . a feeling just as strong but different. Did I really have to choose?

"Can I use the phone?" I asked.

"Listen, this is what I was thinking: we watch a movie, and if you still want to call after two hours, then go ahead."

"What's that gonna change?"

"Listen, she's not even back yet, or if she is, she just arrived and this is gonna throw her for a loop."

I looked away.

"Honestly," said Jessie, crouching beside a flight case and starting to pull out some records, "I just saw her, and believe me, you should drop it."

"You saw her?"

"Uh, yeah," Jessie said, rifling through the case before putting the records back. "She called to grab some coffee—it was next door to her exams."

Next door . . . Jessie came over and slumped on the other couch. She unfolded a little packet, placed it on the coffee table, and pulled out her credit card. I watched her trace two lines, then bend down to tackle one and then the next. I could picture Inès sitting on the edge of the bed with her coke. That whole last month, on heroin . . .

"It's like Alex says," Jessie said, wiping herself with the back of her hand, "one line for danger, two lines for safety!"

"You do this often?" I asked, suddenly disgusted.

"Nah, just when it's like this, you know? To relax after a good set, or—you know—when I'm kicking it with you, right?"

"Did she talk about me?"

"Who, Inès? Yeah . . ."

"What'd she say? Fuck, what'd she say?"

"She said there was a moment when she believed it, because everything you were saying felt cool, but then she realized that she actually wanted to hear that stuff from Alex, not you."

"Really—she said that?"

"Yeah, but don't get ahead of yourself. She just doesn't want to seem like a slut. Because, you can imagine, I wasn't embarrassed to tell her what I thought of her behavior."

"Wait, that's not a bad sign, though . . ."

"OK, but what is a bad sign is that she left to buy herself this fucking huge horse-dick dildo, specifically for getting it on with Alex."

I reached for my jean jacket, preparing to stand up.

"Are you going to the bathroom?" Jessie asked. "You don't have to, you know—I really don't mind."

Of course I didn't have to, but I didn't feel like seeing her anymore. I was fed up with all the harshness. Fed up with feeling like an overgrown toddler around her.

Sitting over the toilet, the tears were bubbling up as I shut my eyes to really feel the needle go in. The tears returned whenever they felt like it, and I didn't even know why I was crying. I couldn't tell anymore if this was about Inès, about everything hitting the fan—Pallas and all, which felt like it was only getting started—or about what I was doing that very second, for the fifth or sixth time that day, which was far too much. To be honest, I couldn't tell much of anything at the moment, I felt so wrecked, and stiff, and exhausted from feeling it all at once. All I knew was that Inès was still alive. That she still had a life, that she was still playing a role in other people's lives, like Jessie's, whom she'd seen, maybe even at the café across the street while I—I was here, six floors up, choking on how much I missed her. Here in this apartment that stripped me of my coordinates, of anything I could use as a guardrail before the yawning gulf below, nothing but this postcard I felt folded up in my back pocket; and now there was nothing to do but keep filling up the spoon.

For a while, I stayed behind in the bathroom, unconscious, which earned me a full-on tantrum from Jessie: "Fuck, no, this can't happen! You're nuts! Do you know how spooked you just made me?" "It's nothing," I responded, "I just fell asleep." "Yeah, but seriously, don't ever do that again! Fuck, you really suck, acting so pathetic! I swear, if you could see how little of a shit she gives—like, she says you act like Alex in bed, only ten thousand times worse! Come on—fuck, react to that! Jesus!" But I could only chuckle—yeah, only chuckle, musing how the Good Lord above must really be getting his wrinkly balls off forcing me to hear all this unbearable shit . . .

4.

"Hey, wake up. Come on, wake up."

I opened my lid. It was broad daylight, I was still lying flat on my stomach on the couch; Jessie was hunching over me, touching me on the shoulder, and the trampling on my back was the dog on top.

"Come on," repeated Jessie, "shake a leg, we've got things you need to buy. Dumbass, shoo . . ." and she took a seat on the other couch.

The dog hopped down, and I struggled my way into a sitting position. Time enough to take in the entire room before the tears began prickling.

"What *things*?" I asked, stunned that the VCR read only 10:03.

"Your G4 and stuff. You can't just stay here acting depressed. Dumbass, leave her alone."

"I wasn't acting depressed," I said, nudging away the dog who was now trying to sit on my feet. "I was asleep . . ."

"Same thing. Here," Jessie added, pointing to two steaming mugs on the table.

"I don't drink coffee," I sniffed.

"Yeah, but you need some," she said, lighting up a cig before tossing me the pack and the lighter.

"Oh yeah?" I said, amused.

"Yeah."

"Alright."

"Yeah."

"OK, zip it!" I said, testing a smile.

I felt like I was in that movie where the guy starts waking up every morning and it's the same day starting over. I lit a cigarette and pushed away the dog, who now was nuzzling my calves.

"Alright, so," Jessie began, bending forward to put her mug on the table. She picked up a felt pen and a magazine, ripping off the corner of a white page. "So, we're going to grab you a G4, and it's gonna be sick. Dumbass, beat it. And then a Cubase, which is really killer—it's got everything, every drum machine you could ever want, every synth!"

I *knew* all that.

"So, the G4 runs about fifteen K—DUMBASS, WHAT THE FUCK, SCRAM!—and then you're gonna need a screen. My advice would be the . . . Hey! Just tell me if this is boring!"

I now vaguely remembered telling Jessie I was going to purchase loads of gear with the advance. I appreciated the energy she was putting in. Sincerely—I appreciated it. It's just that now wasn't the time . . . But then, as if she'd been reading my mind:

"Oh yes you do, you've gotta pull yourself together—that's all it takes."

Jessie, thank god, was a partisan for taxis, the kind that pick you up right on your doorstep. As we crossed Place de la République, I asked the driver to pull over at McDonald's. Jessie told him to ignore me. "Goddammit, it's ten forty!" I exclaimed. "This is my first fucking chance to get a McMorning!" Jessie sighed and told the driver to pull over (and also, why was he only listening to her?). I ran inside and then I ran back out. I was so groggy, I don't even know how I stayed on two legs. Climbing back into the taxi, I was sweaty, completely wiped, but I instantly started chowing down. I went for the savory stuff first. "OK, so," Jessie started again, reviewing her scrap of paper. "G4, screen, vocoder, mic, Minimoog, Prophet-5 . . . You sure you want to buy all those synths? You know 'cause Cubase already has these." I wiped my mouth with a napkin before moving to the sweet stuff. Not bad. Not really what I'd imagined—a little dry, not as tasty as they looked in the ads—but I was utterly famished. "Alright," Jessie continued, "but you're sure you have a Cubase hookup? 'Cause with all the plug-ins, that's worth like sixty K, so I'm still a little shocked someone would lend it to you for free." I took a long sip of Coke to wash down everything I'd just devoured. "'Cause otherwise, this guy I know . . ." Outside it was cloudless but already much too hot. Muggy even with the windows down. The smell of exhaust. The smell of dog breath at Jessie's feet, its drooping tongue drooling all over her jeans as it ogled my knees full of packages. The driver didn't instantly react when I shouted for him to stop—I really thought I might spray all over his seat. I barely had time to open the door, which almost hit an old lady trying to cross the street. When I finally raised my head to stammer an apology, I saw she was already several strides away. "I knew you didn't need that," Jessie sighed, handing me a Kleenex. "Nah, it's just the coffee," and we set off again. "OK, so, Cubase . . ." Jessie carried on. Whereas I was trying not to look at the dog, who just kept drooling, while the driver's eyes remained in the rearview, probably worried I'd gotten it all over the back seat.

5.

We headed to Backstage on Place Pigalle, the best spot for what I needed, but we were barely over the threshold when I started feeling dizzy. The ceilings were too high, there were too many aisles extending in all directions, there was too much variation between the A/C inside and the furnace outside. Plus, it was the Saturday crowd, where you always had to step aside to make room for their package-laden arms. And then with Jessie yelling at the dog to shut up. We eventually found an employee, who immediately grasped how much grief he was about to get, at least from Jessie, because if I remained there a minute longer, I was going to pass out. So I slipped Jessie my card and PIN number, and I took the dog off her hands. The little bastard darted off like a madman just as I was starting to turn around. It felt like people were intentionally trying to block me. I had less and less feeling in my legs, heat was surging up into my throat; it was a no-brainer, I was about to start puking again. I basically sprinted the final yards between me and the entrance, grateful for the smeary light draining down from the sun. I rested for a moment on the sidewalk, catching my breath, before I went back inside to lean my back against a wall. Only in the movies did dogs obey; this one didn't give a shit about me, he just wanted his master, tugging on his leash, rearing up to try to get closer. I finally started sliding my ass down the wall to sit on my heels, and I pressed the dog's butt down to make him do the same. He had foul hyena breath, his gaping mouth now level with my nose. Across from me stood a huge robot greeting every customer. Almost ten feet tall, like the Gottlieb Silver Surfer or a cyber version of Rodin's *Thinker*—real future shit. We'd been discussing an old Buick, a white Buick crashing into San Francisco Bay . . . and then again with the dog tugging on the leash, pressing my free hand against my face to keep it from shattering into a million pieces. Out in the street . . . how beautiful she'd looked out in the street, hooked around my arm. "You don't think I'm gonna leave her, do you? I'll do it right now if you want, I'll do it right this second!" Why hadn't

I let her? And then the dog bounded forward and the leash flew out of my hand. I hustled to my feet, but everything was fine, he had only dashed toward Jessie, who was finally coming back with the employee right beside her, both of them loaded up to their chins with boxes and plastic bags. The other guy dumped it all at my feet and then wordlessly departed. Jessie must have talked enough for his entire monthly quota. "Yeah, yeah, I'm here," she said to the dog, who was leaping all around her as she bent to put packages down. Her fuzzy scalp and forehead were shimmering with sweat. She ran her wrist through the dog's leash, pulled my card from her pocket and handed it over, and then she put her hands on her hips and caught her breath. Besides the G4, the screen, the keyboard, the vocoder, and the mic, there were also a heap of manuals and a fuck-ton of cables. The heating ducts in *Brazil* again, when it starts acting up and hoses begin oozing and spraying shit everywhere . . . Jessie said that now we needed to hit the Rue de Douai to see if we could find the Moog and Prophet-5. I gave a hand gesture to say, for me, the road ended here.

"But it's just next door!" Jessie shouted.

"I fucking know where it is! That's where my boyfriend used to buy his guitars!"

Jessie went to the sidewalk, stuck out her hand, and a taxi screeched to a halt; I was being forced into compliance.

The idiot upstairs must have wanted to make amends, because at the first store we visited we came across a Prophet-5 immediately, and in the second we found the Moog. All in all, even with Jessie's various bargaining ploys, I'd spent 48,740 francs, and I was petrified. In the last taxi, which brought us back to my place, Jessie finally shut up, gently stroking the dog who was panting between her feet; I, meanwhile, watched the sidewalks hurtle past, unable to get over having flown through all that cash in a single go.

Back home, we ran into Pallas, who was lovely to Jessie but ordered her not to stay because of her dog allergy. I insisted, saying we would close my bedroom door, but Pallas wouldn't hear it.

I exploded: "You've gotta be kidding! What's next, I'm gonna need permission to enter my own house?"

Pallas shot me a dirty look, like, you really suck talking to me like that in front of Jessie, and then she vanished into her bedroom. I returned the favor by vanishing into mine, waiting for Jessie to enter as well before I violently slammed the door. My answering machine indicated no messages.

"Ambience 2000," said Jessie in a stage whisper.

"Seriously—you should stay, though," I said.

"Nah, I'd rather not."

"OK, fine, I'm leaving too."

"You don't wanna stay and install everything?"

Her eyes surveyed my equipment, switched on as always, and I knew what she was thinking: not only could her apartment not accommodate all her hardware, which was still down south for the time being, but she also had less than half this amount of gear. I went into the living room, where Pallas was hanging around near the open closets. We kept our lips sealed as I rummaged through my T-shirts. Sealed even when she noticed that the one I was putting on was a shirt that she had given me. A short, electric-blue tee with an orange collar and orange cuffs, with "17" written on the middle in big velvet orange digits. I lingered on those digits, smoothing them with my finger. Inès's age . . . And Pallas slammed the closet door before she left.

"Alright, I'm gonna call," I announced as soon as we got to Jessie's, and disregarding her protests I brought the cordless into the kitchen. My heart was beating a hundred miles an hour. Her parents' number rang into the void. I tried again before ambling back into the living room.

"No one there," I said, avoiding Jessie's gaze. "I lost her cell—do you have it?"

"Drop it, she's gone."

"What? When?"

"Just now."

"Why didn't you say something?"

"What were you going to do, head for the train station?"

"But . . . her bac . . . did she pass at least?"

"She doesn't know yet, but she thinks so."

And just like that, she was actually heading down south . . . Not even a message on my answering machine. Not even a message telling me everything went fine. And I had nothing left of the two grams I'd bought the day before.

6.

All night long, I weathered the storm. I refrained from asking Jessie for Inès's cell again. I didn't call her parents about it. I didn't call Alex's parents down south, or did so only to hang up after verifying that their number was the same. Still, the sheer fact of knowing where to meet them down there, if and whenever I wanted, that relaxed me. I didn't even call the station to ask when her train would be arriving in Montpellier. And yet even the mere option to mentally track her movements, that too relaxed me. I didn't even remove the postcard from my pocket to reread it. I forced myself through some pasta with Jessie. And I forced myself through conversation with her roommates whom I'd never met before and who were now dining with us, returning tanned from who knows where. But when they all went to bed (Jessie included, who used the absent roommate's bedroom on the weekends) and I found myself alone again with a pillow on a folded-up duvet, I just couldn't. This was going to be a long night, too long. Panic set in at the thought of her train gaining distance from Paris, from me. So I rummaged through Jessie's flight case. There was still half a gram; I took half of that and scribbled "sorry" in felt pen on the packet before putting it back in place. I bent my arm and things instantly grew distant, more bearable, less dramatic. I kept sitting there for the length of a smoke, remembering Charlie Parker in *Bird* telling Dizzie he doesn't get why he should see one doctor for his liver, another for his kidneys, and then another for his head, when he could just line up ten bags' worth—a pretty little dose—to handle them all at once . . .

I went footloose into the night, and the air was nice and warm. An image of Inès, lying stretched on a train bunk, was etched in my mind, but the panic had gone away. I hacked into her mind, forcing her to see what I saw. The streets nearly empty on a Saturday night, walking these streets alone and yet walking them all the same, at a steady clip, lost without her? Not at all. I told her I understood her being on that train. Ultimately, it was all just a matter of time. She was leaving to patch things up with Alex, whom she was so afraid of losing, but once the reassurance kicked in, then she'd realize that she'd been duped. Whatever had just happened wasn't going to change anything between them. Things would mellow out for a few days, but as soon as Alex also felt reassured, then she'd go back to being herself in a snap; I knew the blueprint, I had been treated to it myself a hundred times. And now that Inès had caught a glimpse of how things could have gone with me, she would never be able to forget. She only needed to muster the courage and take that giant leap. As for those perks she may have thought she'd lost forever, my advance should obviate any concerns. So I walked and talked with her in my head. I told her, "Look, I'm strong, I can handle you because I can handle myself. And I'm legit, I give as much as I get. I'm not trying to keep you for myself, I'm trying to share you. I'm offering you my hand, whereas Alex is always going to keep hers to herself. Think it over while you're tossing and turning on your bunk, unable to sleep. Think it over, what you want from your life. Think it over, if you even want a life."

Around République, that's when things really started heating up. The neon signs, the loud brasserie patios, the lines at ATMs, the cars double-parked outside McDonald's, the delinquents. Delinquents up and down. At République, they squatted outside the video arcade to try to snag a little something to game with. At Strasbourg–Saint-Denis, they squatted outside the other McDonald's to try to snag "some ass," while at Bonne-Nouvelle they tried to hawk bottles of E. They were a rare sight around Rex and Pulp, shooed away by bouncers, but a good portion of both clubs' clientele preferred arriving by taxi anyway. Me, I had no problem with these guys: they whistled, sometimes taunted, and I taunted them right back with a smile, but whenever one of them started following me a couple yards, it never went beyond "Hey, hang here for a bit, well OK, good night then." The only reason I didn't stay and chat was that with them, a simple "hi" could last three hours. But most passersby got tense when they saw them, hastily stowing their cell phones or tossing away their cigs, used to the idea that as soon as they stopped to bum them one, half the pack would be gone, assuming those dudes didn't snatch the whole thing right out of their hands. But those guys were always too fucked up to be a danger. Nowadays, getting stoned wasn't a big-money issue. All the loiterers outdoors were hammered on something: E, pot, beer, sometimes heroin, maybe ether, stain remover, or glue . . . The only thing that was strange, down the entire boulevard: there were never any cops.

On the way into Rex, the door guy, Valéry B., kissed me on the cheek, then grabbed me by the shoulder to ask how things were going. Was it really so obvious I was out of it? He'd been present at the slugging a year ago . . . "Doing well," I responded, "heartbreak, nothing serious!" I wandered off to dance—to dance to the verge of exhaustion, the verge of total disorientation. And that was the entire point: cutting loose in "fun" clothes to stand out from the other dreary garb, getting through the week as quickly as possible if you weren't lucky enough to have a job that you liked, and when the weekend finally came, you let it all out. You ingested something that transported you somewhere else—where you were more sociable, where you hit on people, where you could tolerate the crowd or simply dance without shame—and then it was game on. Pre-games, clubs, raves, open invites, private events, after-hours, tea dances, and so on, all the way until Sunday night. And sucks to be you when Monday morning comes around. Sucks to be you with that hole in your bank account. Sucks to be you risking "memory, attention, and vision disorders; psychiatric unrest; dehydration, hypothermia, and neurotoxicity." Fuck you for wanting to live to old age . . . Who wants to see which cancer's going to kick in first? By the time I reached the dance floor, I was sorely disenchanted. This was Saturday, not Friday, which meant it was house grooves, not techno, pumping through the PA. Impossible to go buck-wild to that stuff. And the genre meant there wouldn't be a single face I knew—I couldn't tell if that was a relief or if it made me feel abandoned. The first thing I did was to head off to pee. A guy smiled at me as I was leaving the toilet and he was entering. Pretty cute, blond, average build, about twenty-eight, in a navy blue T-shirt with nothing written on it. Looking mildly uneasy like: it's my first time here. I smiled back, but I didn't hang around; the last thing I needed was a shrinking violet. I went to the bar and ordered myself a Coke. The guy from the toilet came and planted himself beside me. He offered me a cigarette, which I accepted, then he insisted on paying for the Coke as it was placed down in front of me. I let him, and I listened as he talked my ears off. He said he usually stuck to the outskirts of town—those big clubs lining the highways? those were Eurodance factories—, so this music was a little too *weird* for him. So he was wondering if he might just head out and go to bed, which he thought was kind of dumb because over dinner this friend of his had slipped him some coke, and since he wasn't usually in the habit, he wanted to put it to good use. Just my luck: an imbecile. Since I was staring at him, not saying anything, he spontaneously added, "Oh no, I'm not trying to talk you into coming home with me! I'm talking to you because you look sad. You're not my type at all." I cocked my eyebrow in amusement. "I'm into more demure girls," he added, so yeah, he was clearly by-the-book, a choirboy, missionary position only, "you look like the kind who likes slapping! Maybe that's why you look sad, because you're not getting any tonight!" What did he think I was going to do, tell him my life story?

Well, half an hour later, that's exactly what I was doing, leaning back against a parked car. I vented it all. From Nikki thirteen years ago to now. That night. Inès on the train. When he said we just needed to go down there, it made me laugh: "Sure, five hundred miles only to get myself thrown out!"

"You're kidding," he retorted, uber-serious. "When a girl's got me like this, I drop to my knees!"

I bullshitted him that I didn't know the route. He said he had a glove box full of maps, he was a traveling sales rep. I bullshitted that once we were down there, there'd be little chance of finding the right spot. He said that in towns that small, everyone always knows where the other people live. I bullshitted that I didn't have enough money for gas or anything. He whipped out his credit card. I bullshitted that I was a junkie and couldn't make it far from Paris without dope. He said he knew someone who knew where we could get it, even as late as this.

"But why would you do that?" I finally asked, crossing my arms. "Huh? Why would you do that for me?"

"Because I wasn't gutsy enough to stake my claim when my girl left me for another man."

"When was that?" I asked.

He sighed and averted his eyes.

"Well?" I asked, starting to laugh. "Was it ten years ago and you still haven't gotten over it?"

"Six."

Now it was my turn to avert my eyes. I uncrossed my arms and let my hands slide up the hood of the car behind me. OK, so: here I was talking to a perfect stranger, two in the morning outside Rex, he on coke and me adrift on heroin, and the guy might be a madman about to rape me or cut me up into little pieces. That's the truth: Ted Bundy, by all appearances, seemed totally normal . . . More rationally, if he drove with a lead foot or had taken too much coke, we might wind up in the ditch. But that was fine . . . In a previous life, I made a little music and not much else, and now, in my present life, I didn't make much of anything at all. So riding five hundred miles in search of some kid who didn't want me anymore, it was par for the course in this new life . . .

7.

We stopped to fill the tank at the big station at the Porte d'Orléans. The car was—well, it was brown: adult wheels, sturdy but not pretty. Inside, it smelled like vanilla to absorb the tobacco stench. Everything spick-and-span aside from the paperwork all over the back seat. Not the classiest way to roll into the Cap d'Agde, but nothing to be ashamed of either, not something with a plate from '93 or an old lemon with huge rust patches on the doors. The Cap was super ugly anyway . . . He—François—was outside, topping up the gas. He was deathly pale under fluorescent lights and had lockjaw from the coke, but all in all he seemed relaxed.

So, we were really going to do this. We were going to take the ring road in search of Chartres-Orléans, and we would be taking that fork for almost five hundred miles. We were starting the drive at night, riding a line as black as ink, content with simply guessing at the surrounding landscape, a landscape I knew by heart from having made this trip so frequently with Alex. He would drive us along with this serene look on his face, probably without too much chatting—he hadn't been very chatty since leaving Rex. We'd start out listening to Radio FG, and then, when we lost the signal, we would pop in a cassette, or else we'd check the other stations. As always with Autoroute FM and other outfits in that vein, we'd be treated to a range of square French oldies like "On dirait le Sud" or "L'Été indien." Songs that start pissing you off when you really try and catch the lyrics . . . If the great cocksucker in the sky really wanted to test me, it'd be Céline Dion's "Pour que tu m'aimes encore," or maybe Britney Spears. Firmly cradled in my seat, I'd keep nodding off, before eventually falling asleep for real. My head would rest against the vibrating window and trigger marvelous or terrifying dreams, depending on whether my convictions remained or were starting to weaken . . . Later, maybe he'd get a little tired and I'd suggest swapping places. Without slowing down, he'd let me climb in over him; my foot would instantly botch which pedal was which, lightly braking, and I wouldn't fess up that I didn't have a license. I wouldn't tell him that outside this particular feat of acrobatics—acrobatics Alex had introduced me to—I had only ever driven once in my life, the summer I was nine, on flat terrain and only for a few seconds before ramming into one of the flower beds lining the street. I wouldn't tell him that I was only familiar with the wheel once the ride was already in motion; maybe I'd enjoy it, being behind the wheel like that. It's not so much the destination that matters, it's the ride itself that exhilarates . . . No doubt we'd have to fill up again around Clermont, and the station would be like any other station in the world, with fluorescent lights and a pungent gasoline smell. We'd hop out to wake our legs amid families of strangers looking for the restroom, bikers checking their tire pressure, and young couples sagging under the weight of backpacks, while farther away, at a rest area, tractor trailers would be parked with their drivers hidden behind drawn curtains, taking their scheduled break. We'd obviously go in to pee, and then we'd roam the snack aisles, waffling first between chips and pastries, then outside fridges of perfectly aligned cans, unless we chose to put a coin down for fake cocoa, fake tea with fake lemon, or some fake tomato soup. The lights inside would be even whiter than the fluorescents outside, a funny contrast with the black night. Raw, cruddy light that would only accentuate the rings around our eyes and our pasty complexions. Maybe we'd buy a tape for the car, something by Michel Delpech or Joe Dassin to match the mood on the air. Maybe we'd even find some Mort Shuman, like the soundtrack to *Holiday Hotel.* How did that song go, "Un Été de porcelaine"? Total crap designed to get you bawling from the intro alone . . . By the first light of day, we'd have to fill up once again and maybe François would need to sleep a bit. So we'd slot into the space between two long monsters, and I'd hop out to get some blood into my legs. I'd smoke and walk through the damp, dewy grass, and my heart would seize with the urge to escape, but not in a positive way, just at the thought of being lost in the middle of nowhere. Then we'd pass through a lunar landscape with hills as arid and lifeless as granite. Then a series of highland pastures with not a single tree, until the highway reached its end; there we'd take the national toward Lodève and then Sète. Beginning in Pézenas, the salt smell would emerge, and all of a sudden the ocean would open up before us. Right in front of us, looking placid and immense—maybe we'd pull over for a second, breathing it in and contemplating the waves as they softly crashed against a still-deserted beach. Then we'd get back on the road, intensely excited, and from there on out the coast would always be there on our left. The coast, bordered by a snaking ribbon of sand, for as far as the eye could see. Barely half an hour later, we'd arrive at the Cap, with our tank almost empty and our complexions looking gray; I'd say to myself, "Fuck, I don't know how we did it, but we're here"—and then what?

We'd park the car by the roadside, and we'd take the little lanes passing between the houses to reach the beach. And it would only be a few yards before we landed at the spot where Alex had placed her towel, and we could stand there behind a cluster of boulders without ever being seen. There were boulders throughout the area, enough that you couldn't enter the water without your plastic sandals on. Alex was used to this, but it always threw me off feeling that superfluous weight around my feet; I preferred clearer ground, eventually always wading somewhere else alone, because Alex was too lazy to follow. The house was up above, with a staircase leading from the yard down to the beach. It was always a conundrum deciding where to set up for the day. The sun felt blazing in the yard, which had little to no tree shelter, and down below the winds were always hellish. Generally speaking, we stayed up above, roasting for as long as we could take it before heading downstairs for a soak, and then sometimes, if the wind wasn't too strong, we would spend some serious time down there. So we'd have to hope that they were there, and that by some miracle Inès would be alone. It felt possible: Alex would always wander back upstairs looking for things from the house. But even so, what would Inès do when the time came? Smile at me, triumphant, and blurt out, "Kidnapping me? What a swell idea—hold on, I'll go and get my bag." Yeah, maybe that was it. After all, if someone had just hoofed it almost five hundred miles looking for me, I think I would go, just for the sheer romance of it all. But there was still a strong chance she'd first give me this dumb expression, seeing me without seeing me, refusing to accept that I could actually be standing there. Or that I'd start making my way forward, or that she'd get up to meet me, hazarding a comment about how nice I was to make the trip and all, but her decision had been made. Maybe she'd burst out laughing, too, if she really was the bitch that everyone wanted me to think she was . . .

And what would I do next? Would I start begging, or would I walk away without a word? I'd head back in the opposite direction, without even waiting for François, still hidden behind his screen of boulders looking earnestly distraught. From behind, I would look drunk the way my feet sank in the spongy sand. Maybe I'd choose to remove my shoes and socks, and the sand would be burning, diverting me somewhere harder and cooler. All around me, the din of waves as they shattered against the boulders, sending up jets of foam, and then a second later it would just be the sand and the waves now calmly lapping. There I'd be, like some idiot, with my shoes in one hand and the hem of my jeans rolled up around my calves, walking straight ahead of me, praying I might already be out of Inès's sight. Eventually François would catch up, and he'd start walking beside me in silence. But then maybe he'd start talking all of a sudden, saying I should quit girls, that it wasn't good for me, that I should go with him, for example. We'd maneuver toward a lane leading back to the main road, and he'd keep talking. We'd spy the car, and he'd keep talking. And all at once, incensed by his monologue, I'd start grabbing him by the hair and smashing his head against the steering wheel. The blood would start to flow, but I'd keep going, more and more, until fat globs of it were spurting from his mouth, to shut him up for good. Then I'd bend over and open the driver's-side door, preparing to kick him out, until I remembered that this was his car, and then I'd hop out and try to get as far away as possible. But where next? Hitchhiking to the train station in Montpellier? And then what . . .

The door slammed.

"Ready?" he asked, tightening his seat belt.

"No, I'm not ready," I said, averting my eyes. "I give up."

chapter eleven

what doesn't kill you makes you stronger?

1.

In the afternoon the next day, when I got home, I inserted the key into the lock, turned the knob, the door barely cracked, and then nothing—it resisted. Was Pallas actually pressing the door to prevent me coming in?! No, there were four men obstructing it, one of whom, who looked like landed gentry, was raising a glass to his mouth when my shoulder bumped it, spilling the contents all over his loafers. All I needed was a glimpse of the glass to know that I had barged into Alice's showing. I flatly apologized for his shoes, and then I scurried to my bedroom. Still no blinking from my answering machine. I pulled off my jean jacket after grabbing the smokes, then I dropped to the bed and crawled over to the window, which was open behind the shutters. A powerful whiff of dog shit was rising from the sidewalk, which was blazing in the sun. I lit a cigarette and pulled off my shades to massage my sinuses, my eyes studiously avoiding the boxes I'd bought with Jessie. Through the partition separating me from the living room, I could only hear the music, Suede's "Beautiful People," Alice's ongoing obsession. Back when she still lived with us, she had a life-size standee of Brett Anderson, the singer. So sexy . . . The buzzer sounded in the entry. It would go on like this all afternoon. I couldn't fathom how anyone still went to these showings. The first to arrive had time to take stock of the displays, but as soon as they were really pouring in, Alice would start ordering people to sit on the floor so they wouldn't conceal the hangings, and not to sit just anywhere but specifically lined up along the walls. And as a result, the next to arrive would be faced with a row of silent eyes, and rather than casting even the most cursory glance at the exhibit, they would slink in beside someone they knew, hoping to escape the penetrating glares. I laughed to myself picturing some girl squatting in the bathroom, the way I did when Alex dragged me to visit people I didn't want to; for a while I'd disappear, poring over the inevitable flyer-collage on the wall, before moving on to the cleaning products, even the fine print. And then there was Alice's tea fixation: Ceylon, jasmine, vanilla, Chinese teas, Russian tea, impossible to refuse without risking her annoyance. She would be the only person standing, parading around with two thermoses and traveling back and forth to the kitchen to put on more hot water. She served it in any vessel she could get her hands on: mismatched cups, mugs, glasses, I even saw people sipping from Pallas's cheese ramekins—all of which would be cluttering the sink before long. But not this time, I prayed, loosening the shutter cord to drop my cigarette outside.

I needed a change of clothes, but I couldn't envision entering the living room. I went to the door and cracked it open. Landed-gentry man was crouched and scraping the carpet with a sponge. Gallant kid. Whatever was on the floor was clearing up.

"Hey, could you find Pallas for me? Do you know Pallas? OK, yeah, if you could."

I shut the door again to take off my shirt. When it reopened, Pallas was there, stone-faced in a new black dress.

"Hey," I said, attempting a smile, "how's it going? Listen, could you grab me some things from the living room? Pretty please? Mauve shirt, black jacket, boots. And some panties too."

She shot me a look like I was really pushing it.

"Fine, forget the panties."

I lit another cigarette while I awaited her return.

"I'm going to Nikki's," I said, taking the clothes and boots she was handing me with outstretched arms. "You couldn't give a shit, I know, but just in case."

This time she was staring with deep indifference, or contempt, but before I could learn which, she was already gone. I removed my jeans, yanked off my panties and shoved them under a pillow, then raced to get dressed. Before going back out, I made sure I had my cigarettes, my debit card, my glasses, and I walked into the hallway tucking my shirttails into my jeans.

Now everyone was seated in the living room, a good thirty of them lined up along the walls in a silence no music could lighten. Glancing at the mail on the tray table, pocketing an envelope with Virgin letterhead, my eyes landed on Jessie, Eva, and Julia, all sitting in their midst. Their eyes were turned away. Alice's too. It honestly felt like the entire crew was looking somewhere else. As if they'd all simply frozen there and now I was the only one breathing. But it didn't jar me, I was the cool one in my seventies clothes; that's the reason their hackles were up. As I reached the landing out front, I remembered Nikki's records, and I turned around to grab the stack from my bedroom.

Through the opening to Pallas's room, I had time enough to notice all the bags that were on her bed. It looked like she was going to leave and never return. Crazy how advice goes out the window the very second you're gone. I ripped open the letter from Virgin as I sprinted downstairs, thinking that even if this were extra-shitty news, I probably wouldn't care. I read it through right as I opened the front door, out into the sun-drenched street. It was just a heads-up that the payment had gone through. No kidding, I muttered, whipping out my sunglasses, and I jammed the letter down the first available trash can.

2.

I spent all week at Nikki's. The Sunday I arrived, we spent ages hashing things out. Not Inès per se—about her, he could only say: horrible idea, but it'll pass—no, we mostly talked about music. Or I should say: he talked about his music hoping to revive my desire for mine. The next day was a studio day for him, and sure enough it triggered something watching him set up with his Vox, his Junior, and his twelve-string. It made me want to go back to my machines, my latest treasures. Per Nikki: channeling what you're feeling into something productive. He had a point, I think. I just needed a chance to breathe first.

So I stayed there all week. I spent my days on the couch watching TV, and then at night, when Nikki returned, I crawled into his room to go to bed. We slept glued at the hip, but we didn't have sex even once. We just kissed occasionally, and even then, when we did, we stopped because it made me cry. Nikki got home around two or three at night, would hang around the music room for a bit, and then he'd leave in the morning as soon as he'd ingested some coffee.

No sooner had I walked through the door than he could tell that I was jonesing. But even if he, for his part, had reached the conclusion that something needed to change, he wasn't the type to lash out at other people. It didn't bother him, calling his former dealer on my behalf. Sure, he shot up a couple times, keeping me company, and I felt guilty about that, but I figured he must still do it sometimes. I went to the dealer's on Monday, and that was the only time I stepped foot outside. His offer was beyond anything I could've hoped for—white stuff, four hundred a gram—so I got myself a healthy supply. And I used the opportunity to buy myself a stash of cigs, Coke, and freezer food; naturally, I didn't touch any of it but the Coke. A week of your basic junkie stuff, shooting up and nodding off, but I still set a rule for myself: no way was I going to leave the syringe lying around in a glass somewhere. It wasn't out of respect for Nikki, the trouble I took to bring this stuff to the bathroom instead—it was for my sake, so the slope wouldn't get any slipperier.

Nikki had cable, but his TV was so old that there were only six buttons for the six main channels; for the others, you had to adjust the station by hand, a "vintage" feature. So I typically kept to the main ones that would work with the remote, whose batteries must have been garbage, given how hard you had to press the buttons, but I wasn't taking much in anyway. At this point, I couldn't even watch two people kiss. Even game show celebrations set me off. So I channel surfed incessantly. One time I landed on this galling interview on *Nulle part ailleurs*. Nagui was hosting some girl shooting for "real-life Lara Croft." He was asking if she led a hectic life, and this girl, her skirt and ponytail just like *Tomb Raider*, answered without batting an eye: "You know, I travel a lot, I'm always on assignment, and it's honestly pretty fascinating. Whenever I get to a place, I never know in advance where the enemy's gonna be, or how much ammo's on hand." Interview with a schizoid . . . I also caught the end of some TV movie where a blind woman lived in this apartment with photos all over the walls . . . And then a Lactel ad with a little boy asking his grandmother, "But Nana, what do *you* drink?" And his grandmother says, "I don't drink, I get my fix."

I rewatched a few clips from *Cocksucker Blues*, which I had a copy of at home: the Stones documentary where you actually see roadies fucking girls on a plane, groupies shooting up in hotel rooms, and Keith Richards constantly nodding off. And most of all, there's this one scene where he pretends to touch himself through his tight silver pants before he straight-up slips his hand inside. Oddly enough, this didn't bring up Inès. It made me think of Nikki, seeing him in the studio again, getting things set up that first morning in his velvet Levi's, black shirt, and boots. Now I was back to dressing like that, too, lying slumped in my mauve button-down, with my jacket over the armrest and my boots on the floor. Just like the Stones, right? That's where my head was at again. I couldn't really tell where I was anymore.

A man . . . That probably *was* what I was looking for, all along . . . The Hanson brothers were on M6. The one in the middle—he was amazing. The singer, Taylor. Sixteen? His features so perfect, it bordered on obscene. I pictured Nikki bringing him home to loan him his guitar, and when Nikki went down to buy some beer, the kid stayed behind with his back against the wall, fooling around like Keith Richards had . . . Before long, I was doing it myself, on the couch watching snatches of white cloud slowly drifting through the pale blue sky outside. A second later and it wasn't young Hanson I was seeing but an older, burlier man whose face I couldn't clearly picture. What did it mean to do this without thinking of anyone in particular? Were they the dead, or maybe spirits yet to incarnate?

Mere *entities* who, simply because they needed to come just like anybody else, took hold of our physical forms to achieve it? An ectoplasmic horde permanently hunting for human specimens, fondling them to juice them for sensation. Like in *Liquid Sky*, the '80s New York flick where a flying saucer lands on the roof of a drug pusher's and feeds on male brain secretions after they've shot their wad at her apartment. But seriously: Once it was released, where did the orgasm *go*?

3.

On the eventual comedown, I was left with a heap of questions. Questions that, frankly, weren't that deep but still troubled me, like: why does the ash stay perfectly straight when still attached to the cigarette but tumble apart as soon as it drops? Or, how can the sewer system slink its way into every toilet, in every apartment, on every floor, in every building, on every street, in every neighborhood, in every town, in every country? Or, why could I, unlike so many people, never learn to whistle, or snap my fingers, or blow bubblegum? Or, if I were anywhere else doing anything else, where would I be and what would I be doing? That question yielded the fewest answers. I wanted to put my entire brain on hold. After fifteen minutes of this, every subsequent thought felt trivial.

That Wednesday was Fête de la Musique, and I couldn't even budge. Yet I knew that Alex must have returned, was surely mixing somewhere near Les Halles. I didn't even try Inès, either at her parents' or on her cell. I didn't care to hear that goddamn breathy voice again . . . I couldn't budge when night came either, though half the city must have been at Dépôt for Alex and Jessie, while the other half were surely crammed into Rex for Plastikman and

Laurent Hô. Five in the morning, same thing, even though Nikki still wasn't home, but I didn't want to be seen, not at Gibus where everyone must have migrated for some late-night hard house. No desire to blend into the zombies, mechanically dancing, smashed on MDMA or E.

I couldn't stop thinking about earlier that night, when Nikki came home to change. What a godsend. No other word for it—and I was too fucked up to even see it for what it was . . . It wasn't the Hanson kid coming to borrow a guitar, no, this was a hundred times better. He looked like Nikki thirteen years ago, that day when he headed outside after I'd put on *Threepenny Opera*. Thirty-something, with the face of an angel, long brown hair (naturally), black suit over garnet button-down and Annelio boots. Giving me a slight nod before he followed Nikki into the other room, but time enough for him to notice my outfit and the way my legs were positioned on the couch. I could hear them talking guitars next door. By the time I decided to get up, they were already coming back. The guy in question was carrying a flight case in two hands and clearly had been sizing me up again while I lit myself a cigarette. A minor disturbance before he jolted himself back to reality: "Come on, man, hurry up, I'm playing tonight." Fucking guitar players. But instead of asking them to wait up so I could tag along, I stayed rooted in place like an idiot, wishing them good night. Nikki came back two minutes later to grab what he'd forgotten, and while he was scouring the music room up and down, I had time to ask about him. This guy—his name was Julian; funny how rock and roll transforms Nicolases into Nikkis and Juliens into Julians—he'd had his guitar stolen at the airport. A '59 Gibson TV—*why would you even ask?* He lived in London but was French and had come back to play with David Hallyday. Fair enough, his latest single actually wasn't half bad, a little like Dylan's "Knockin' on Heaven's Door," and the amps in the video looked awesome. His face seemed really familiar, in fact; suddenly I was getting really worked up, wanting to ask Nikki why he'd waited so long to introduce us. But I could anticipate the response: Nikki never thought of anything that wasn't right before his eyes, and this guy lived across the pond . . . Before slipping out, he'd asked me one last time if I really didn't want to come, and since I took too long deciding, he bolted downstairs shouting, just in case, the concert was at Place de la République.

But naturally I didn't move an inch. Two weeks before, this Julian might have been the type I'd give anything for, but that baby bitch's breathy voice was the only thing echoing through my mind.

4.

On Friday night, I cracked—I stuck my head into the Pride kickoff at Dépôt.

The interior had changed completely: the DJ booth was now on a little stage over the back-room stairs; the gangway wasn't visible anymore, concealed behind skeins of black fabric. The place was packed to the gills. Alex was on the decks, and Inès, in a blinding white tee, was the very first person I saw. She was sitting all alone on the handful of steps leading up to the booth, and when she saw me she instantly got up to greet me. She pressed her whole body against me, with her arms around my neck—just like the first time by the entryway at home. I really thought she was going to kiss me in front of everyone, all these people I noticed in the distance with their eyes in our direction. But at the very last moment, her mouth shifted to my cheek, after which she took my hand to calmly drag me away. We forged a path through the crowd. The air was rife with CK One, CK Be, and other faggy scents. We walked to the bar where the music wasn't so loud, and we leaned against a wall so we could sit on our heels. We each pulled out cigarettes; I lit hers. The gleam of the lighter against the underside of her face showcased many sores around her mouth. The kind of cold sores you get when your period comes three times a month . . . She nervously mentioned she was happy to see me, that I might be the only person still talking to her. Everyone else was mad at her, what with everything that had happened. But she wasn't going to slip up anymore. There were days when she hadn't slept. When she tagged along at most. When they just dropped her off somewhere and she couldn't move, too at sea for any decision-making. And Alex? How was that going? She said that things were fine as long as it was just the two of them, then turned to shit as soon as others were around. I scoffed and said she was going to have a hard time cutting ties with Alex's crew, which wouldn't be the same if she were with me. She smiled to suggest that this had crossed her mind. Fuck, was she having second thoughts . . . ? "Listen," I started. "I'm happy to forget. You can always come back, and we'll never discuss it again." "I don't know," she said, "I really don't know." I said she should at least spend the night, for a start, get some rest. We could leave right now: wherever she wanted, somewhere no one would ever come and chew her out. She was staring straight ahead, fidgeting her hands. Some DJ Rush bass was growing audible. Her eyes, her body, they showed no trace of me. She was completely out of it, somewhere else entirely. More distant than when I'd known her, for what little that was worth. She asked if I'd started working on my record. I didn't respond. She was clearly wasted. But you never would have known it staring in her black eyes, and I didn't want to think about it anyway. I watched the people go by, and I understood something: fags love each other too much, dykes don't love each other at all. Our crew was coming closer, preparing to dance at the foot of the steps leading up to the booth. Eva was in a white tee reading *Sharon you're amazing* in black; Gayle, just back in Paris, had *Sharon Stoned* in pink on blue, Julia with *Tintin Tattoos*, white on black; Jessie in *Enjoy Me*, white on red, like *Enjoy Coca-Cola*. Pallas was in a dress, deep in conversation with some girl I didn't know. I thought I saw Bruce Willis go by, but then I realized it was Tintin. I'd never noticed how uncanny the resemblance was. I got a flash image of Brad Pitt in the asylum from *12 Monkeys*. DJ Rush kept going—his "I wanna fuck you all night"—and I could see the moment coming soon when I'd blow a gasket and start blathering like Brad Pitt, reading everyone the riot act . . . "Come on," I repeated. "Stay a couple days, get some rest, see how it goes, and if you're not feeling it, you can leave." "Not tonight. Alex and I have stuff tomorrow. But maybe I'll call you later?" I stood. She did, too. "I'm leaving," I said. "Come on." "I'll call," she repeated, her hands on her lower back. A total stranger. I crushed my cigarette beneath my shoe, then moved off to say hi-and-bye to everyone else. Eva, Gayle, Jessie, Julia, I gave them each a kiss that brought smiles all around, at once awkward and a little sad. Pallas I ignored, and when I turned my eyes, I found Alex staring at me from high up in the booth. I had just enough time to catch her T-shirt—*Heroin Kills Only Rock Stars*—and for a second it made me want to go up there and punch her in the face for hooking Inès on heroin. Then Inès's hand found mine amid the crowd: "I'll walk you to the door." Despite all the people, we reached the exit far too quickly. I tried to slow us to a crawl, convinced that if I lingered long enough to hug her, or kiss her, then she wouldn't push me away. At coat check, she assumed I had something to collect, and she waited for me there. Eventually I asked if she was really going to call. Staring at me, looking utterly hopeless, *finally* she seemed all there. Now was the chance, I needed to play my final card. "Listen," I said, grabbing her shoulder to move us away from the little crowd jostling around at coat check. "You and I are the real deal. It's the mess around us that's got you so confused. You need to drop all that, give us another chance, we deserve it, dammit. You can't leave me," I threw in there, "I can't live without you." Pallas appeared and instantly tugged at her elbow, saying she was really restraining herself right now, what with all the people present. "But we're talking!" I shouted. "Sure you are," Pallas shot back, and she dragged Inès away, who offered me a gesture like: resistance is futile.

I couldn't leave like that. At least not right away. So I, too, returned to the dance floor, feeling my wobbly legs giving way, trying to look like I had a destination in mind. Our crew had shifted places, and Inès clearly wasn't back at her seat by the bar. I swept the room. I ran into Eva. "Any new jokes for me?" I hollered, forcing myself to sound jubilant. She shook her head, then moved her mouth to my ear so she wouldn't have to holler back, "I think I'm gonna need a little time to forget," and she wandered off. I could have asked her what the trouble was, but I knew: from the outside, this must have looked like basic dyke shit, and she was disappointed that I would stoop to that level. Eventually I climbed into the booth and leaned back beside a table where Alex had arranged her two flight cases. I proceeded to stay there for at least half an hour, watching her mix from behind. At regular intervals, she turned around to stow one record and pull out another; at regular intervals, she gestured for me to light her a cigarette from her pack. But not once did she try to meet my gaze. I knew she didn't blame me. She had done the same too many times with other people to not have the elegance to take it. But she did seem visibly affected, a certain slowness in her motions, the impression that she was in a hurry to call it off for the night so she could get home and go to bed. I felt something graze my arm, and it was Inès standing below me on the steps. She waved for me to bend over, which I did, and she asked if I wanted to head to the back room. She said it was open to girls tonight. I would have traveled the lengths of the world for her, but not there, not right behind Alex's back while she was working, and with any number of our crew liable to show up. So I said no. At my place, sure, but not here. Her eyes traveled downward and she departed. I stayed behind for a bit, watching the crowd outside the booth. Half of them must have been tripping—E, MDMA, acid, poppers, lines of coke . . . Many of them probably had a little bottle of Stérimar in their bag, a miracle seawater spray for clearing your nostrils. How had Alex put it: When you've had too much to sniff, Stérimar's there in a jiff? Where was her Inès tattoo? I expected her to turn around and shake her head goodbye, but she didn't, so I finally went back down.

I'd still never ventured to the basement—all I knew was that it was huge. At the base of the stairs, a hallway trailed off on either side. I took the one to the left. It was lined with girls conversing in groups, glasses in their hands. They were dreaming if they thought they were about to see something wild, no men would be around if the likes of them were being admitted. I wandered past a string of small, doorless stalls, lit with feeble yellow glows, empty except for the last one where two girls were kissing. There was nothing in the hallway on the right, but then came another right, and it was only when I made a second turn that I reached two dark portals. I walked through the first one and found myself in a wide, circular room. At its center, a row of doors. I walked over and gently turned a handle, discovering a stall with a one-way mirror, peering into another space, this one even rounder and more cramped, where just a single man could stand, there for you to ogle him doing god knows what. I left and tried the other portal, this one leading to a bar bathed in reddish twilight. Ten or so girls were ambling about, like they were visiting a museum. There was yet another opening at the back, but this one was blocked behind a chain. If Inès had come to see the sights down here, I must have missed her. I left and headed for the stairs until I found a final opening. The only light came from the hallway—the back room. I could just barely make out three silhouettes a few yards ahead, everything else was blackness. I walked forward, trying to see what they were looking at, and then I instantly shut my eyes—a reflex—something inside me broke. That was my girl. My seventeen-year-old girl, nude, limbs splayed, getting eaten out.

Bare-breasted with her pants around her ankles, she was being handled by two girls while a man with his head shaved was on his knees before her. The girls were holding her from behind, their hands roaming over her chest, her throat, her mouth, while the man held her hips. And she—she had her head thrown back and to the side, the tendon in her neck looking ready to explode, and she was greedily sucking the tongue of one girl. Her hands—she was using her hands to finger them both. Straight down their open jeans. There was no music, just the sounds from the hallway and the clearly audible moaning. One of the girls must have had a finger back behind given how her legs were bowed. She was writhing around, like this was happening against her will; it was clear she couldn't take much more. I was completely terrified—what would happen if her eyes looked straight ahead and discovered me standing there—but it felt like I was paralyzed. She violently screamed as she came, practically swallowing the jaw of the girl she was kissing. The man stood up and pulled his dick out. The girls kept their hold on her, then one of them slid her hand between her thighs before wiping it against her face. Inès instantly started licking her hand, then pulled one of her own from a girl's pants to grab the man's dick instead. She only needed to lift her head to see me barely three feet behind him, but her eyes were looking down. She was looking at the dick—this dick she was going to lightly jerk off. Clearly he was straight, so now there were a number of possibilities: he was going to take her from the front, from behind, or get sucked off and jizz down her throat or over her face. But I couldn't stay and find out.

When I went back upstairs, I stumbled into Pallas and the other girl sitting on the steps. Pallas was crying, mascara streaming down her face.

"What's with her?" I asked, sounding utterly disgusted.

"She got her tongue pierced," said the girl, "and it hurts."

Ah . . .

The dribbling mascara looked absurd on her, like Frank-N-Furter in *The Rocky Horror Picture Show* when Riff Raff's about to kill him. Pallas raised her eyes, and finding me standing there before her, she instantly recoiled. How did it go again, that scene where Dr. Scott rolls up right as everyone's caught Susan Sarandon fucking the main hunk?

"Janet! Dr. Scott! Janet! Brad! Rocky!"

I repeated the line three times, like they do in the movie. All with this tinge of pure insanity, while horror slowly dawned across Pallas's face. I wanted to add, You're exposed, you asshole! We always knew you were in love with her, too! But I didn't take the trouble to add another word. I simply mounted the stairs; I kept my cool, following the flow to the exits; I slipped out the door and turned the corner onto Boulevard Sébastopol; I staggered to the gutter, I bent down, and I puked.

chapter twelve

gay pride / sinéad o'connor / other complications

1.

"Alright, so Cubase—you're familiar with Cubase, but with the 24, look, you've got loads of extra shit."

Same old, same old, like Jessie 2.0. Did people *honestly* think I hoarded gear I had no handle on? I bit my tongue and nodded along. If you counted my "hello" buzzing him in and my "hurry up" upon waking to find Pallas ensconced in the bathroom, I had spoken three whole words since exiting the Dépôt back room, and that suited me just fine.

The dude at my computer—at my sleek-as-hell, translucent-silver G4 console, complete with matching monitor—I had never seen him before. A friend of a friend of a friend, some guy from this collective in Lille who was passing through Paris for the weekend and who kindly agreed to waste a couple hours installing fifty thousand bucks of plug-ins for free. Why exactly, when he wasn't even making a pass at me, I hadn't the slightest idea. But by now I was used to the boy-scout contingent in techno: they danced to music that made you want to fuck, gobbled down E that magnified that feeling tenfold, and then they didn't make a move. This one looked like all the rest: short, scruffy hair, shapeless clothes; he might as well have been in Daft Punk. That was the thing with home studios: people had stopped bothering to fix their hair and put on clothes in the morning, they just put on some coffee and got down to business.

Slouching there beside him, my eyes occasionally drifted to the television, running as always, and currently on LCI. Every fifteen minutes, they had reports about the latest Pride developments, but every time they flashed back to them, at least for the moment, they only did so through shots of the opening ceremonies, which had already taken place hours ago. The one o'clock news on every channel had trotted out montages from the previous year, especially the Pulp and Dépôt floats, featuring a slew of familiar faces. I never went to Pride. The whole idea had nothing to offer. I'd never fallen in love with a small-town baker-woman I could only visit on the sly. I'd never worked for a company where you had to invent yourself a boyfriend to scare off lunkheads hanging around the coffee maker. And I'd never suffered physical or verbal assault for kissing another girl in public. Nor did I live a lie around my parents—nor had I lost their support when they cottoned on. So, nothing to offer me.

Except that this time, I was going to go. I had an appointment with Nikki's dealer at six, but I'd show face for a bit at the end. Alex had a set around République, and I wanted to see Inès. It would be our last time, assuming these were normal circumstances and the two of them were still leaving tomorrow. Could that change? I needed to find out.

2.

République was swarming with cops and riot vans. I barely missed getting hit by one as I zigzagged in a brain fog, and suddenly I realized: I might not look like an out-and-out druggie anymore, but that didn't protect me from getting frisked. I forked onto a neighboring street to dump my spoon and syringe, but the dope? Never. Even corralled by a thousand pigs, no one was going to chuck a gram of white worth 45K, plus some excellent coke. So I took my boot off and shoved the baggies inside.

I still wanted to find Inès, but aided by the dope and heat, it was starting to feel less urgent. I decided to make three rounds of the premises, and if I didn't run into her, that was my sign I shouldn't see her. The parade hadn't arrived, but there were already DJs mixing under a big-top facing the Boulevard du Temple. It wouldn't be long before Alex's turn, going by the FG schedule. I knew exactly how her set would begin, and since Inès wasn't one for camping out around the decks, that meant she'd be elsewhere, flitting about.

The square was already jammed. People were calling out to one another and running over to catch up. The air was steeped in the smell of fries and merguez wafting from little trailers, now invisible behind dense smoke. Guys from Techno+ were distributing leaflets about drug safety, others were selling ghastly little rainbow flags. The loudspeakers were belching house music that wasn't awful, but the sound levels and crush of people were making my heart race regardless. I had cold sweats whenever I clocked a man in uniform. It was my third go-round, and I was just about to drop it when I noticed Alex's intro, and almost immediately I spotted her behind the barricade in a blinding white T-shirt.

I took my time to reach her. In her trademark bird stance, she broke into a smile at my jacket and boots, a smile that turned shy as if to say, "This still can't happen." Her shades had been pushed into her hair; mine remained in place. I lifted my leg to hop the barrier, but instantly a big Black guy with a walkie-talkie came over, asking me where I thought I was going. A bizarre thing to hear when I'd spent three years going anywhere I wanted to with Alex.

"Can I get back here if I leave?" Inès asked him, before I offered her my hand to help her across the barrier.

She walked in front, clearing a path for us through the crowd. Eventually, she took my hand. Hers was clammy, but I wouldn't have dropped it for the world. Her arms weren't tan—she and Alex must have been more focused on *rekindling* . . . At the intersection with Rue du Gibus, we let go of each other and hooked a right. The music grew fainter behind us as we started trudging forward, hands in our back pockets. Our eyes were on the ground. From time to time my pace slowed even further, almost so much I lost my balance. I wished I could have stopped and hugged her then and there. But I couldn't, I couldn't take a single action. At the end of the street, we had a choice: turn left and head a little farther, take a right and go back to the square, or return the way we came. We returned the way we came. I felt like a moron staying silent, so eventually I started talking. I said I'd only wanted to make three loops of the square and then clear out if I didn't see her. I said I visited the back room and didn't like what I saw. But I was too chicken to look over and gauge her reaction. I said I had come this close to making the trip down south. That I'd been right on the verge of it and then dropped the idea as we were filling up the tank. Still too chicken to meet her gaze. Eventually I asked if she knew where we were, and I turned my head to face her. She stopped—she didn't understand the question. I explained: if we kept going straight, in five minutes we'd be at my door. I held her gaze, asked if she wanted to, and she held mine, gently asking what for. For another chance in each other's arms, kissing in peace, talking things over, nothing major. Here she was again, here her body was again, this body I'd held, her eyes plunging into mine again. She smiled like this wasn't a good idea. I started walking, then realized she wasn't following, so I doubled back to where she waited with her hand out; I grabbed it again, we set off together in silence again, looking at the ground again. Her hand was still clammy; at times her fingers slipped a little, spontaneously searching for a better grip. The music was still blaring as we emerged onto the square again. I released her to steer us toward the barrier, wondering how long she'd have held on if I hadn't. I leaned back against the barrier, and her body did the same, lingering millimeters away. It felt good to have a surface there to support me—I had taken too large a dose. She looked out of it, too. I was starting to see the blackness in her eyes. I was the kind who needed extremes in order to feel something, but she—she was still in the early stages, when a single line could last a whole day. I was envious, but at the same time I felt a twinge of worry at the thought of her experiencing that.

"You're really beautiful," she purred.

Me, beautiful? She was the amazing one. And despite what I'd witnessed the night before, she was like a full-on kid again. But still, something was different about her now, something both horrifying and sexy, indefensibly sexy.

"Come home with me," I offered, meekly. "You can come back here later, I promise I'll let you leave."

"What's the use?" she sighed. "You know if I come we'll get clingy—that's not good."

"Why avoid it if you want it? You wanted it yesterday, right?"

"You're really beautiful," she said again.

Her face was so close I could feel her breath on my mouth. Those lips as soft as ever. I felt like a baby around her, like her lips were a goddamn bottle. I was lost without the warmth of her arms, without the smell of her skin. My eyes were filled with tears, and fuck, hers were focused on my mouth, concentrating, beseeching, just like the first time. Why was she acting like this if, at the end of the day, she still had feelings? It was ridiculous to me. We were restraining ourselves from kissing, but anyone would have been certain, seeing us from afar, that that was what we were doing. I wanted to ask how long she'd been using heroin. And what was the deal with that guy the other night, but even just thinking about it . . .

I finally asked, "Know what we look like? Six in the afternoon, both of us drugged."

She furrowed her eyebrows like she was trying to deny it, her lips on the verge of quivering, and I could tell that for a few seconds, she wanted to ask if I had any left. Her eyes veered off behind me. The music had changed; she must have thought Alex would start looking for her soon. I pictured myself saying that if she would only follow me, I'd slip her everything in my shoe. But I imagined Jessie yelling, "You're fucking pathetic!" and my toes curled tight around the baggies, mustering the strength to keep my trap shut.

"I've gotta head back," she said.

"Are you going out tonight?" I asked, keeping things banal.

"Well, Alex is mixing at Dépôt, Bataclan, Pulp, and then this other thing I forget where. You gonna come?"

I shrugged.

"I think Pallas is on the lists," she added, "try coming with her."

Oh sure, piece of cake.

"I gotta go," she said, lightly kissing me on the cheek.

"Was it nice down south?" I asked, forcing myself to ignore her mouth, her sweet mouth.

"Yeah, it was amazing!" she blurted out, then caught herself sounding too enthused, so she added, "I needed some rest, it did me a lot of good."

Then I remembered. I grabbed her wrist as she was starting to turn away.

"Are you still heading down there tomorrow?"

"Yeah," she mumbled, seemingly apologetic.

I was the first to walk away, repeating what I'd told myself a thousand times before—"Don't turn around"—but when I reached the sidewalk, I couldn't help it. She was trailing off, serene, her hands on her lower back and her elbows jutting out. She entered the crowd, and I could've kept watching that white shirt for ages. On her way to the barricaded big-top in the distance, on her way back to Alex. But I forced myself to leave, sticking close to every passing bus shelter so Alex wouldn't see me if she looked in my direction. Sometimes, the consequences of our actions take forever to settle; sometimes, they're immediate. I had hurt myself just now. I shouldn't have pulled her aside if nothing would amount from it. I shouldn't have lingered at the barrier so long. And I'd only said things that I didn't want to say, and none of what I wanted. Now here I was, gaining distance from the place where she—where she remained. Same as if I'd actually gone down south . . . I had hurt myself a lot just now, and I shouldn't have.

3.

I did eventually call Pallas on her cell, and as if nothing were the matter, I asked what she was thinking for tonight. "Is that some kind of joke?" she lisped in response. Her tongue, right, I'd forgotten . . .

Ignoring the hateful tone, I calmly replied that I was hungry and I just wanted to know where she was having dinner. She said she didn't really see how that was any of my business. I repeated myself, I was just hungry, we wouldn't have to talk or anything—truce, OK? She scoffed, she and Alice were at our typical Japanese place in the Marais, but if I showed up, they'd piss right off. "Even better," I sighed, "more room for me."

When I got there twenty minutes later, they were in the middle of deciding what was next. Alice wanted to hear Alex open for Green Velvet at Bataclan, and Pallas said there was no way she'd miss Jessie play Rex with Jeff Mills. Pallas who had never given a shit about Rex *or* Jeff Mills—who did that cow think she was? She had on yet another new dress, black with a slit in back down to her ass crack. But craziest of all, Guillaume was there. *My* Guillaume. Maybe Alice didn't know I wasn't seeing him anymore, but Pallas . . . I waited to catch her eye so I could flaunt my consternation, but naturally she wouldn't give me the time of day. And neither would Guillaume. They were content to shoot furtive glances at the T-shirt under my velour jacket. I had thrown it on at home, a simple, white T-shirt with black writing, reading:

Life's a bitch
And then you die
And you know it

To think, it was only a year ago . . . when it felt like centuries. Soon, very soon it seemed, I'd be looking in the paper for the first available apartment. I'd be ditching Pallas before she had time to twist it around on me. Clearly, there was no other way for this end, and there was nothing I could do about it.

Meanwhile, all three of them were fiddling with their forks through their meals—but not me, I hadn't ordered anything after all. Which finally earned me a glance from Pallas, a look of disgust; she must have figured I'd done some more dope, and goddammit, she was right—and that was one point in my favor! Guillaume was questioning Pallas about her vocal approach. Apparently she'd been telling him about the trip-hop track she'd made a year ago, and now it seemed she was committed to pursuing it further. Great. I wanted to tell Guillaume how nice it was to see him, but I realized with a shock that Pallas was hitting on him. She was hitting on the guy she always used to criticize when I had been seeing him: suburban hick, retarded pug-face, I could go on . . . He looked uneasy about it happening right in front of me, but he was letting it happen all the same. I could have said something, but hearing my voice felt beyond me at the moment. I chose instead to keep the same vertiginous distance I'd maintained since the night before, ever since Dépôt. But it would have felt great to tell Pallas she had a problem. A serious problem. She'd become a real sack of shit, and she was seventeen thousand in the hole, which I knew from the bank statement in the entryway. Alice had a problem, too. Her neediness ate at her, and now she was scaring people shitless. Plus, her bulimia made her swell so much that her head, with her bangs cut even shorter than Pallas's, was starting to look like Down syndrome. Pathetic, the both of them. I felt my blood run cold, wondering if I'd just said this stuff out loud or if I'd merely thought it. But Pallas kept right on talking to Guillaume, and Alice was looking straight through me. I got up to use the bathroom, thinking of that scene in *Pandora and the Flying Dutchman* when Marius Goring is listening to Ava Gardner at the piano; he's just taken poison, he knows he only has a few seconds to live, he turns around to everyone at the nearby tables, and just before he collapses, he yells, "Any way so I were out of your whispering!"

As I descended the stairs to the restroom, I saw a pair of legs appear and then the back of a girl hunched over the sink, drinking from it, and I had a heart attack. Not the exact haircut, not even the same face once she stood up to dry her mouth on the back of her hand, but the same clothes, the same adolescent indifference. She stepped away with a nervous smile to let me into the bathroom. I quietly closed the door behind me, aware that Inès had loads of lookalikes: really cute, really sweet, really young. Loads and loads of them. By the gates of every high school. And come summer, they'd be everywhere you looked, at every rave, on every beach from Biarritz to Montpellier. I either needed to find myself another one or renounce them altogether, because now I knew I had really lost her. I crouched and emptied my jacket pockets on the tiles, looking for a scrap of paper to use as a straw. Maybe Pallas and Alice were also, at that very moment, remarking about how poorly I was doing. But I was doing just fine, thank you very much. Sure, I was ready for it to be tomorrow already. And sure, I was a little shook to think that tonight Inès would be visiting four separate locations and I wouldn't be at any of them. It wasn't any use, nothing would get any further than it had this afternoon, and maybe I already knew that by the time I'd left République. I had been such a fool throwing all my gear away, the pharmacies would obviously be closed. What a waste, and now, on top of that, it was going to make me puke. Dope left a wretched taste in my throat, but I cut myself another line, with a second stripe of coke right above it. Then I balled the goods back in my pockets, and sitting on my heels, with my back against the wall, I lit myself a cigarette, unfazed by the evident impatience on the other side of the door. I waited over the toilet bowl, waited for the mess inside me to come rocketing back up. And afterward I felt better—or a little better, at least.

4.

I leaned against the wall outside the artist entrance at Rex, hoping I wouldn't fall flat on my face, I was so wasted. I wearily eyed Pallas, who had just fainted at the security guard's feet, her body contorted in her brand-new dress, which didn't hide much.

We had first patiently waited outside the main entrance for a long, long time, and like the two hundred expectant others, we had a hell of a time getting in; they had stopped admitting people because the room was already full. Guillaume embarrassed us, screaming that we were on the list, and all two hundred others piped up in unison behind us: "WE ARE TOO!" Then he tried again by the artist entrance a little farther down:

"Don't you realize who we are?"

Alice kept telling the door guy that he should track down Jessie, but he didn't want to hear it, and all of a sudden, Pallas blew a fuse. She started howling abuse in that lisping voice, saying how could anyone be such an idiot, that all he had to do was check if they were expecting us, it was as simple as that. On the opposite sidewalk, a brawl had broken out: two guys whaling on a third guy on the ground. None of the bouncers at the first entrance crossed the street to intervene. We could hear his bones breaking, Pallas went right on shouting, and the results were equally comical and appalling. Sort of like Sinéad O'Connor at that Dylan tribute show: getting shouted off by the audience, she started reeling off this crazy monologue before, overawed by her own aggression, she started puking all over herself. And that's just what happened to Pallas. Her sushi started spewing out sideways. After which we watched as her knees bowed and her body caved like a puppet whose strings had been dropped.

And now the security guy was slapping her back to reality; I, meanwhile, was getting fed up with all the nonsense. Alice's cell phone rang. She hastily started rifling through her bag, and I wanted to ask her, what was the problem if you just let it keep ringing for once. When I noticed it was her brother, I removed myself from the wall and snatched the phone right out of her hands. Nikki was at some performance piece. I told him to stay put, stay right there, and I handed Alice the phone back and summoned all the energy I had for the march to the nearby taxi stand, turning around to shout at Pallas: at least Sinéad O'Connor can actually sing! Alice joined me as I collapsed into the back seat.

Alice kept her face turned to the sidewalks racing past, but I could tell her eyes were fully glistening. I should have said something, but what? That she'd have been better off rejecting me that night when she'd picked me up at L'Entracte? How late even was it? Where was Inès right now? Did she know I wouldn't show? Had she already known I wouldn't when I left Pride? The radio was playing R.E.M., "Everybody Hurts." Not a song that reminded me of anything or anyone in particular, but depressing as hell all the same.

5.

The room was cloaked in shadow. On a short, underlit stage, a guy with a shaved head was lying buck-naked in a dentist's chair. It sounded like a humming engine room in the background. I was sweating in my velour jacket, but I didn't want to take it off for fear I might lose it. Alice had disappeared and Nikki was standing right behind me, his arms around my waist and his chin on my shoulder to explain things into my ear: something about a guy who got hit by a train and had ended up in paradise. Then he met this girl who handed him an apple, which he bit into of course, but that caused a massive toothache, and the girl (some chick with a green mohawk), who just so happened to be a dental hygienist, suggested she could treat him—and that's where we were.

Green Mohawk was fastening some sort of bib around the guy, who was writhing in pain and spitting up apple chunks galore. I'd heard this saying somewhere that kept running through my head: "Life goes fast, so enjoy the journey." I couldn't bring myself to believe Inès had been screwing with me, no one had enough time on their hands to waste it doing something like that . . . Onstage, a second guy with a shaved head, this one dressed like a dentist, emerged from the shadows. He was armed with a syringe the size of his forearm. When the other guy noticed, he immediately jolted up, but Mohawk had strapped his ankles, wrists, and head to the chair in no time flat. He started yowling as this hyperbolic needle sank into his stomach, spurting a vertical stream of blood. Mohawk clamped his nose closed, inducing him to shut up if he wanted to keep breathing. I turned my face to Nikki, asking if I could spend the night. He whispered yes. A simple, unhesitant yes—it felt good. The Dentist rummaged through the guy's mouth with some pincers; the blood continued spurting. He forsook the pincers, chucking them aside and seizing a drill. Drill noise on the soundtrack. I gently removed myself from Nikki's embrace and left to find the bathroom.

As I sat on the toilet, with one finger tracing a line across my cigarette pack, Inès's image took shape in the distance, kicking down doors and crying. Weeping that Alex could wreck her health all she wanted, but not me. She combed through the entire city, kicking down rows and rows of shitter stalls and repeating "not you," but each door softly boomeranged back against its measly partition, her choked voice echoing over checkered floors, each one of them deserted . . . Tears fogged my eyes; no, I was the one kicking down doors . . . I hurried back to the main room.

The guy in the chair had fainted. His legs were splayed to the max, and the Dentist had one arm plunged up to the elbow in the depths of what must have been some kind of hole in the chair but was meant to be the guy's anus. The blood kept vertically spurting and incessant vomit kicked in, steady jets that started forming a fucking pool. Finally, the Dentist extracted an enormous rotting molar. This huge disgusting thing the size of a soccer ball, and the audience let out a potent "AAAAH." Nikki was cracking up around my ear; his arms were squeezing me a little too tightly. Green Mohawk untied the guy, who slowly came to his senses. She and the Dentist helped him stand, and then they threw him to the ground and started pummeling him with kicks. The guy tried crawling away, leaving long trails of blood behind him. I remembered Jessie's *Reservoir Dogs* T-shirt and wondered if she was still at Rex or had already left for Loco; I assumed she was scheduled for the after-party. No idea what time. I turned my head to Nikki to say I wanted to go home. The crowd parted to expel us, and Nikki only barely maintained his grip. The guy had just flung himself into the audience, was grasping at sleeves and collars, begging anyone to help him, covering everyone he touched in blood. The soundtrack suggested an oncoming train whistle, and then the lights came up. Onstage, Mohawk was working a mop. Alice was right in front of us:

"A little cleanup before act two?"

Which confused me. Again I told Nikki I wanted to go. Hands on her hips, Alice fired back: we had only just arrived, there were other performances coming up. Then, sensing I might tell her to fuck off, she turned to her brother and asked if he wanted to say hi to Sylvain, the guy from the performance. Nikki slipped an arm around my neck. "Come on, it won't be long." When we got to the stage, I didn't have the energy to object anymore, so I let them drag me through the back curtain.

The Sylvain in question was down on his knees, still naked and covered in blood, clutching his neck. Mohawk informed us he drank some bleach by mistake. She pointed to a plastic cup on the makeup counter.

"Wait, how does one drink bleach by mistake?" I mumbled to no one.

"We could have used that in the show," said Mohawk, coldly. "To disinfect the piercing equipment."

Someone had alerted them that paramedics were on their way. Nikki warded off the rubberneckers trying to lift the curtain. Alice had disappeared. I told Nikki I was going home, but I didn't budge. My eyes slid across Sylvain's body as he sat in the chair trying to breathe. His skin, beneath the blood, looked incredibly white. I recoiled against the wall. This guy had piercings everywhere. On his brow, between his eyes, between his nostrils, down his ears, on his chin and both nipples, but oddly enough not his penis. Alex had a whole phalanx of piercings, from her nostril to her tongue to her chin to her vagina, and now the only thing left was her navel. Inès had pierced her tongue and navel. Pallas had pierced her navel and now her tongue. I flashed back to Julia getting started on her dragon tattoo. Eva flaunting her "Gayle." My name on Alex's stomach. Alex's name on mine. Her name on Inès's crotch. Inès's somewhere on Alex . . . The room started spinning, and I let myself slide onto my heels. Nikki grabbed me under the arm to lift me up; he said the paramedics were running late, we needed to take a car. I wanted to object, saying it wasn't my place to go with them, but nothing came out. The crowd had left me behind. Nikki and the Dentist were supporting Sylvain by his armpits while, out in front, Mohawk was shouting to make room. By the entrance, Nikki asked someone to call the paramedics again, at least to learn which hospital to try . . . The Dentist said he'd meet us there after settling up with the venue. On the sidewalk, Nikki couldn't remember where he'd parked his car, which wasn't a laughing matter right now. But I started giggling anyway, because if we had to take a taxi, I could tell right now, anyone who slowed down for us was going to speed off again as soon as they saw Sylvain dribbling blood.

6.

We wound up at Bichat, or so I read when the car raced toward the emergency room entrance. The lobby was completely full. A dozen occupied chairs and just as many guys with their backs against the wall. Immigrants for the most part, with blood on their hands or brow line. No one offered us a seat. Everyone was carefully avoiding looking at Sylvain, as if seeing all that blood risked aggravating their own condition even further, but the next time a nurse opened the door, they all agreed to let him cut to the front. I really wanted to know how he was going to explain all that stage blood. Nikki left in search of a snack machine, leaving me and Mohawk alone together. I took a few steps away, and without even checking to make sure it was safe to do so, I sniffed directly from my stash.

"You got some coke?" Mohawk whispered when I came back over.

"Not anymore," I said, not even trying to sound convincing.

I beheld the entire waiting room, wondering if other ERs, in less outlying areas, were teeming with fags who got punched in the face. Here, nothing would've suggested that tonight was Gay Pride. I flashed back to Pallas getting home from last year's, covered in severe sunburns that kept her locked in bed for three days straight. Where was she now? Still at Rex, or back home shredding my clothes with giant scissors like in that film, I can't remember which? Nikki returned in a huff, pissed that the latest batch of Crunch bars had squares that didn't break in a straight line. The nurse reappeared and informed us there was no point in staying, he was going to be looked after. We waited until she'd faded down the hall, and then we snuck into the room. Sylvain was on a drip, hooked to some device providing an interior mockup of his esophagus. He looked dejected. My eyes roamed over his stretcher, the sheets already bright red, and again I wondered how he'd accounted for all the "blood."

"They want me to see the shrink," he said. "They think it's a cry for help."

By the way he averted his gaze, it seemed like maybe that's what it was. His voice sounded so frail, a funny contrast to what we'd seen from his performance.

"Dumbasses," said Mohawk, and suddenly I missed Jessie's dog, my back straightening at the very mention of his name.

Again the door opened behind us, but it was only the Dentist, accompanied by a third man with a shaved head. "Ho. Ly. Shit! What. The. Fuck!" said the Dentist, approaching the device Sylvain was hooked to. He whipped out a camcorder, while the other guy started flicking the observation lamp on and off like a strobe. I whispered to Nikki that we should really get a move on.

"Listen," he said, pulling me aside, "be patient for five minutes—shit, that's my buddy right there."

I wanted to open my mouth and call him a name—just what, who even knows—but again my eyes fell over the stretcher and the blood-soaked sheets. I flashed back to my own sheets, stained in Inès's blood, and that was all I needed to tear myself away.

Following the gleam of streetlights in the parking lot, I sheltered between two parked cars, intending to do a little more coke, hoping to wake myself up enough for the trip back home. But what I grabbed instead, in that crouched position, was another line of heroin, and then another, until I dribbled out a thin stream of bile.

My heart was on the blink, missing every other beat. I clung to a parking meter, dry-mouthed. I stared at fake plates of sushi through the window of some Japanese place. It wasn't even a restaurant . . . I could hear people laughing, hooligans heckling. I staggered away, and my knee slammed into the bumper of a parked car. The pain surged through my thigh, taking my breath away and instantly bringing tears to my eyes. I bent down and locked my hand around it, a stupidly reassuring reflex, as if the mere contact could ever mean relief. Dawn was breaking in a bluish haze. I knew this corresponded to a specific hour of the day, but I wasn't sure which. I had just stepped out of a taxi—strange, because I didn't remember stepping into it in the first place. I seemed to be around the corner from Loco, but Jessie might not have arrived yet, or else it had already ended ages ago.

"Fucking pisses me off!" came a voice.

I knew that voice. A group was approaching, and Eva clearly among them. I straightened up, grimacing in pain.

"Fuck, I'm pissed!" She pulled off her backpack, rifled through it, pulled out a flashlight, lit it and rifled through some more. She offered me a cigarette, which I refused, realizing I already had one. "It's so pissy—Jessie was on a heater when these gasbags came and told her to shut it all down! It wasn't supposed to end before ten!"

The rest of the group walked over. Just some guys. Faces I recognized, that I'd seen in passing a number of times before, but no one I really knew. Eva unscrewed the cap from a little water bottle. "So there's this blonde who . . ." but the rest of the sentence just hung there while she drank. The sun was breaking through the clear skies above. I dropped my cigarette butt when it scorched my fingers.

". . . who gets fired on Christmas Eve. She gets back home and finds . . ." Again Eva cut out, but this time it was because she suddenly remembered having said she didn't want to talk to me for a while . . . I shrugged, too disgusted to make a comeback. She gave me a sad smile.

"She gets back home and finds that her man's up and left her. So she hops in her ride for a drive when she has this major accident, her ride's bent in two, you know? So she decides to walk to the Tour Montparnasse, go all the way to the top, and throw herself off, because she's thinking, hey, my life's gotten pretty rotten. And just as she's about to jump, she hears this voice behind her saying not to do it. She turns around and, wouldn't you know it, it's Santa Claus. So she explains: you don't understand, I lost my job, my fiancé, and my car, all in one day. So Santa goes: well, since it's Christmas, how about a gift? When you go downstairs, you're going to find a brand-new car; when you get back home, your fiancé is going to leap into your arms; and then tomorrow, at the office, it'll be like nothing ever happened. So the blonde, she's astounded, like how awesome is that—so what can I do to thank you? Well, you know, when I'm up there with my reindeer, I sometimes get to feeling all alone, so how about a little blow job? The blonde, I mean, she doesn't really want to, but in light of everything he's just done for her, and seeing how she hasn't seen anyone else up there ever since she reached the tower roof, she thinks: you know, all things considered, why not . . . So she gets on her knees, and she slips under Santa's robe. And, you know, he's starting to stroke her hair, and he asks: By the way, what's your name? And the blonde, her mouth's full, she says: I'm Pamela. Santa keeps stroking her hair, and he asks: And how old are you, Pamela? And the blonde, her mouth's still full, she says: I'm thirty-two. And Santa goes: so Pamela, you're thirty-two and you still believe in Santa Claus?"

Eva was laughing so hard, you couldn't hear anything else in the street. All of a sudden she turned chalk-white, ultimately realizing her shit was hitting a little too close to home . . . She walked over and gave me a hug—"Take a vacation or something"—then she walked away to join the others who had been wandering off.

I could see Inès and Alex by the sea . . . I could see the pearly surface of the waves, dripping with sunlight, Inès submerged up to her shoulders, holding Alex, who had her thighs wrapped around her, both of them roaring with laughter, merrily splashing each other. We had had no time—NO TIME AT ALL, DAMMIT.

I pulled out the postcard from my back pocket; I ripped it in half and watched it fall.

And then I felt a girl's arm looping around mine. At first I thought it was Jessie, emerging from her set at Loco, but no, this one actually had hair, and she was rail-thin.

"Fucking Inès," I pleaded.

"Let it go," said the girl, "Inès isn't there."

Yet my entire upper body was trying to turn to face Loco's giant marquee as we left it all behind. I was certain she was there and I would see her coming out any second now. But the girl gently pushed me into a back seat, my knee producing another painful grimace as it bent, then she dropped down beside me, and with a subtle jolt, the taxi set off down the street.

chapter thirteen

special k

1.

Maybe it was a matter of smell. Who knows what that meant, but that's the sentence I had stuck in my head when I opened my eyes. I seemed to have maintained my initial crash position. I was prostrate on my back on some sort of thin futon mattress rolled directly onto the floor, fully clothed beneath one small sliver of a nylon blue sleeping bag, with nothing under my head and with my right leg hanging off the bed. I stirred only slightly and the pain instantly awoke. The room was stifling in the sunlight. There was a lovely, seductive piano tune rising through an open window. That and the tasty aroma of fried potatoes. But that wasn't coming from here. Here there was only a vague coffee scent. From my diagonal position, I trained my eyes on the VCR, for as long as it took to decipher the numbers, 15:09; then I propped myself up on my elbows and observed a figure in the near distance. Behind a countertop, somewhat similar to Jessie's, a short-haired brunette, viewed from the back, was rummaging up high in a closet. The bottom of her khaki T-shirt was exposing her lower back, offering a glimpse of tanned skin. She turned around revealing two cups in her hands that she placed on the counter; her face told me nothing. This living room, this apartment, they felt utterly unfamiliar, a little like Jessie's but much smaller, with the hallway starting on the right instead of the left. I got all the way into a seated position, which triggered another painful grimace on account of my knee.

"Good night's sleep?" asked the girl, walking over with her steaming cups.

I signaled yes and watched as she placed them on the coffee table. Coffee table? No, just a delivery pallet that hadn't even been repainted, left as is, piss-yellow with splinters sticking out. That and the couch were the only furniture in the room. Everything else—TV, VCR, and ghetto-blaster, plus a handful of CDs and videotapes—were scattered at random across an oatmeal-colored carpet. On the wall, a small poster from some German hardcore festival was hanging by a single thumbtack, an ominous color photo of an empty, muddy field. But the most depressing feature was the coffee cups. They were both effigies to Lady Di; that smile of hers had fuck-all to do with this place, with the surrounding decor. I looked back at the girl herself, who had assumed a position atop a mountain of cushions and was lacing up some black sneakers. Turkish maybe, or something like that—she had olive skin with a waxy glaze underneath. She was neither ugly nor beautiful, just very, very masculine, with the gauntest face and no tits under her form-fitting khaki tee, which had *Clit Control* overlaid in black, with matchstick thighs clad in some tight, faded jeans. She must have been about twenty-two, and aside from looking a total homo—or, more accurately, completely unsexed—she looked like one of those kids you always saw at "teknivals," the kind who get really grimy stringing together sleepless nights and sucking down anything they can get their hands on. How I'd wound up crashing at her place—or wherever it was she was squatting, since there was only the couch to sleep on—I hadn't the faintest idea.

She grabbed a cup and gestured to the other one with her chin.

"Thanks, but I don't drink coffee," I said, stretching warily.

"Yeah, but you could really use some," she replied, her voice none too beautiful either.

Why was she acting like a remixed Jessie? Besides my knee pain, the simple fact of bending to one side to try and grab my boots made my head spin. I decided to give it a few seconds before my next attempt. The pain had sapped my energy for anything more demanding than sitting up straight. The girl was staring at my T-shirt. She must have thought it looked super-cool, and why not—this shirt hit all the right buttons. But her speaking voice was already starting to weigh on me. I eyed the pack of Craven As on the table, wondering if there were still any cigs in my jacket or if she'd already had her way with them. I maintained my stare on those smokes for a while, because the girl wound up reaching for one, which she shoved into the corner of her mouth before lighting it up for me. What was she thinking, that just because she'd plucked me off the sidewalk, now she'd have to spoon-feed me too?

"Sorry," I said, amused, "but who *are* you?"

"Ariane," she said, visibly put out. "I'm Inès's best friend. You still got any left?"

"Huh?" I asked, not catching the reference.

"I mean, it seemed like you had a whole stash on you this morning . . ."

I didn't need to rifle through my pockets to know the coke baggie and heroin baggie had been cleaned out, but even if there had been some, I'm not a hundred percent certain what I'd have said to her.

"There's gotta be something lying around," she said, standing up. "Feel free to take a shower if you want," she added, walking away.

I watched her disappear down the hall, trying to remember if this was the same girl who'd said hi to Inès at Pulp. Her best friend . . . but . . . I decided I wouldn't even try to understand. Once more I bent over to grab my boots and slip them on, hoping to avoid flexing my knee too much, and I stood up, leaning my back against the wall. Once I seemed capable of letting go, I slowly crossed the room toward my jacket, which I'd spotted on a chair.

"You're freaking beautiful," she said.

At least that's what it seemed like I heard behind me. But when I turned around to finish putting on my jacket, she wasn't looking in my direction. She had resumed sitting on the cushions with her cup in her hands and now was finally starting to drink.

"I really need to go," I said, fixing my collar. "Thanks for this morning."

She set her cup down but still wouldn't look at me. She lit another cigarette in that masculine way, so ugly when girls do it, shrinking her head between her shoulders and enclosing the flame with her hand at the same time, after which she let herself fall backward onto her elbows, and then said:

"What about if I find us something that'll get us really, really high? We could rent a bunch of movies, order some awesome pizza, and just fuck around watching TV."

She said this with total conviction, like this was the usual habit, and maybe it was; something about her felt filthy, and fucking noxious. I could have told her that I frankly couldn't care less about spending any more time with her. Or I could have replied I was in no state for anything else. But I think some kind of fever was propelling me onward. And I knew what she was thinking.

She was thinking Special K. Which just means ketamine. Now I remembered: Inès said her best friend had a hookup for that. Only problem was I didn't have my debit card.

"You can go and find it or whatever," said Ariane, "I'll front the money, and we can meet back here in two hours."

Before I slipped out the door, I grabbed a phone and dialed Pallas on her cell. One of these days, if she kept refusing to get a landline like everyone else, people would stop calling her because it was getting too expensive. But deep down I knew it was the inverse: everyone would end up settling for a cell phone. Tough break for all the paupers out there who couldn't manage it, anyone for whom it cost an arm and a leg.

"Hey. You home?"

"Why?"

"Because I'm coming through and I don't want to see you."

"Well, sucks to be you."

My irony was supposed to sound playful, but Pallas's irony was ice-cold.

When I left, I realized I was in upper Belleville—around the corner from the Place des Fêtes, speaking of dire shitholes. I couldn't imagine ever coming back here, to hell with the ketamine. Or, I would only come back here if my home situation felt too unnerving.

2.

The home situation was, as Jessie had put it, Ambience 2000. Slamming doors and exasperated sighs, with Guillaume massaging his hands in the kitchen all the while, super uneasy about me seeing him there. Pallas's attitude didn't bother me much, because to me it just felt forced. For real, because even if she hadn't spoken one word to me the night before, she hadn't pissed off when I got there either, like she'd said she would.

By the time I rang Ariane's doorbell, she had changed, now wearing a white button-down tucked into beltless jeans. She had tried to pretty herself up for me and had failed abominably; I couldn't even find it touching. She approved of the bag of Coke cans I placed on the coffee table, and I wanted to ask what made her think I'd let her drink one. She had rented four movies whose titles I couldn't make out, what with their being upside-down, all except for *The Silence of the Lambs*, whose lettering I knew by heart—add me to the list of those who looked straight past Anthony Hopkins, obsessed instead with Jodie Foster, who allegedly was into women—and she had the Pizza Hut flyer all ready to go, with the telephone in easy reach. She had folded up the futon, as well, and had tidied up some of her crap, but everything still looked awful in here. My eyes landed on a magazine strewn with the cut-off ends of McDonald's straws and two little baggies. The first one, a transparent Ziplock with white powder inside, must have been the ketamine (who told me it looked like little pills?), but the other one, the white paper one, was that coke or heroin? She said it cost five hundred apiece, and I pulled out my cash. Parents who pay for their brats' studios or apartment-shares after graduating would be seeing red if they knew how often the grocery allowance went toward getting stoned.

I pulled out my freshly purchased Steribox, took off my jacket and placed it on the back of the couch, and I sat down, careful how I flexed my knee. Now that I saw the contents of the little white baggie she'd just unfurled for us, I couldn't tell if it was going to mean sweet relief or inevitable disappointment: it was heroin, for sure, but looked like the most disgusting brown imaginable. Before putting on the first movie, she suggested we watch a little *Party Zone* that she'd recorded off MTV. It reminded me of Jessie's mix for MCM. I'd known her for a lot less time than the others, but I was going to miss her just as much. I got up to find a water glass and an actual spoon. The sink was full of dirty dishes, and as I washed myself a glass, I expected to see a cockroach skitter past. The video she'd put on was nothing but terrible trance music with two-bit CGI: colorful winding intestines, writhing molecules, and multidimensional geometric desertscapes, vomiting out a horrid series of hills and plains. But fuck it, soon enough all our consciousness would be on our little cooking project. Ariane seemed to be struggling with the right proportions, tracing and retracing lines with her phone card. For me, it was a walk in the park: aspirate, garrote, shoot up. After which I let the syringe soak in the water glass as I folded up my arm, letting myself droop backward on the couch. Ariane still couldn't manage a perfect line. Eventually she got up and headed for the kitchen, returning with some tinfoil. So I guess there were people still chasing the dragon these days. I shouldn't have stared, because it only made her want to push things further. She decanted her powder but didn't know what she was doing, holding the lighter much too far beneath the foil. Why was I staring at her anyway? Was I trying to make her uncomfortable? Eventually she managed it, and her eyes immediately started tearing up, just as her jaws started clenching to restrain the puke, which was surely surging up. Ooh baby, that's a killer method, sure enough, but you really have to know how to take it.

"How long do we wait?" she asked, as if in total control.

"No idea," I said, smirking. "Fifteen minutes or so?"

We waited, smoking and rubbing our faces, glaring in the vague direction of the TV, rooted to the spot for fifteen minutes solid. Ariane was sitting a little too tall on her cushions, her jaw still tense, and just as I was wondering how long she planned to stay like that, she abruptly stood and disappeared to the end of the hall. Why were things going like this? Why hadn't I stumbled onto some nice girl instead, someone who wasn't so seedy? I should've gone home, I shouldn't have stayed. But a Special K hookup wasn't easily refused. I was just starting to feel the first blush of dope, unsure how it would react to the ketamine. Ariane came back, looking green, while I nodded off . . . I left for a white, sandy beach. Some tropical country but with no vegetation or any deadly sunshine. I was sitting at the apex of a boulder with my arms around my knees, which I'd pulled up to my chest, and I watched as a ball gently bobbed on the cresting waves. A large inflatable ball with multi-colored panels. I didn't need to number them to know that there were twelve of them, like the twelve astrological signs. And every panel was some rare color, or rare in this context (topaz, aquamarine, ruby-red), and on every panel, emerging through the colorful, crystalline reflections, there were words taking shape. I couldn't make any of them out, but I understood that they each bore the name of a track for my record. As soon as I realized it, the ball swerved in a sudden arc and set sail for the open seas . . .

I opened my eyes and found Ariane sprawled on the cushions. I straightened up for a better view of the table, grimacing slightly from my tingling knee, then I pulled over a magazine so I could empty the ketamine baggie on top. Ariane was pouting at me, looking nauseated. I carefully divided my little mound in two, then started to heat it. It turned a milky white but seemed to dissolve well. Ariane finally straightened up and started tracing herself a line. Silly girl couldn't stop trying to wow me.

"You sure you want to do it like this?" she asked, a little nervous.

"Yes," I muttered under my breath, "I'm sure."

Once you've shot cough syrup, you can shoot anything you want. I lowered the cotton wad, and it was instant absorption. Apparently, that did the trick. Again I wrapped the handkerchief around, I clenched my fist, and the vein puffed up; I thought about how no one I knew had ever fixed like this before, and yet I stuck it in regardless, drawing a dot of blood, and started slowly pumping. I scarcely had time to extract the needle before the stuff was already racing through me, ramming into my heart.

I kept my arm bent, a little breathless. I tried to stand, and I was quaking.

"You OK?" came Ariane's voice from far away.

"Yeah, I . . . I'll hand you . . . hand you the bag," I gurgled.

The bag, sweet Jesus, the bag I'd brought those cans in. Nausea was foaming around my lips. Fuck. I crawled away on all fours. Over to the corner that seemed least risky.

I was in Alex's car in the middle of a traffic jam. Inès was in the back, hunched forward between our two front seats with her arms around the headrests. Alex was so out of it that she had to continually pump the brakes to keep from hitting the car in front of us. Inès was out of it, too. Turns out both of them were dosed. Their arms were still bare, the better to admire the little dried blood bubbles at the crooks of their elbows. When I finally couldn't take it anymore, I yelled at Alex to stop. Cut the engine. Get out of the car. You too, Inès, get out. I opened the trunk, pulled out both her flight cases, then skirted around the car to pocket the keys. Alex could barely stand. The hell are you doing, I'm supposed to be mixing soon. What the hell am *I* doing, I barked. I've got a fucking record to make so there's no way I'm gonna die tonight. And Inès is only seventeen so the same goes for her, no way is she dying tonight either, you just need to get a cab! No, you've gone ballistic or something, give me the keys. Over on the curb, Inès was in stitches. This isn't funny, Inès. Fucking shit, give me the keys right now. Inès, don't get in the car. You fucking leave her alone, this isn't your problem. But actually THIS IS MY PROBLEM—the sound of my own voice made my eyes open.

Tears were streaming into my ears. Pain was throbbing through my heart. I was trying to suck in air, but only microscopic amounts were coming through. The room was lit by just the weak gleam of the TV, which was still playing at low volume. Muggy, zero airflow. Ariane on her back atop her cushions. Her profile bathed in blue. Her eyes seemingly open.

"Hey," I managed.

She was having a hard time swallowing, was running her tongue across her lips.

"Hey, can you hear me?"

I raised a leaden arm in her direction. I felt a ten-ton weight crushing my rib cage. The couch was so squishy, I was sinking into it and could see the other end rising above me. Again I shot my arm out, over to the table for a can. I opened it, then tried bringing it to my lips without raising my head. I downed a lukewarm gulp of it. I drank a little more, and a violent spasm wrenched through my stomach, doubling me over. With one hand I held my stomach, while the other groped for a place to set the can on the floor. Some Coke ebbed back into my throat. My lips were squeezed shut, my tongue plastered to my palate to block anything that wanted to come up. I attempted some shallow breathing through my nose. When it finally died down, I swallowed a little more. Gazing toward my chest, I could make out the upside-down inscription of my T-shirt, which I hadn't had time to change at home: life's a bitch . . . I wanted to take it off. But after all, wasn't that the truth? Wasn't life the biggest bitch of all, sequestering me here when all I wanted was to hold Inès's hand on a beach somewhere, not stoned, not nothing? On-screen, the Stones were craning their entire bodies over miniature city blocks. I started laughing, thinking of how Keith Richards had been onto something when he got his blood swapped out in Switzerland. Everyone assumed that he'd done it to stay young or something, but that wasn't it at all: it was so he wouldn't feel the loss so acutely when he decided to kick the habit. I couldn't fucking tell anymore if the tears pooling in my ears were from laughter or despair. Again I could hear Marilyn Manson's crooning, how the pretty ones want to get you high to leave you low . . . She probably never even realized, wasn't shrewd enough to sing those words' true meaning. She didn't deserve to be a Scorpio, her only specialty was acting dumb. A ruse without an ounce of subtlety: just a little lost teen. And what about me, who wanted her name tattooed? I laughed even more—must have been true what I'd heard about ketamine: horse tranquilizers!

3.

Every now and then, the light in the stairwell came on and illuminated the courtyard. A radio alarm wouldn't stop blaring somewhere in the distance. With that counter at the other end of the room, it felt like I was at Jessie's, it felt like when Jessie and I had vegged out watching television. Except that over there I'd felt fine . . . It would have been nice to sit up and look for the remote, any way that I could to dodge the Britney video. But I could barely manage to prop myself up on one elbow before the weight in my head started dragging me down again. I had a flashback of Guillaume at the house, so proud of how fast he could clean the dishes. Pallas could always find someone to handle her dirty work. Hitting on some guy she'd always found so blah when I was the one seeing him? More power to her. She could hit on Inès, too, if she ever got the chance. But try it at your own risk, honey, try it at your own damn risk! And the other one—she could have all of Paris run game on her if it appealed to her so much. Cupping my face in my hands: how could I lie to you when you look at me like that. I love you, I love you, I'm leaving her tomorrow. The pain stabbed my chest again. I noticed Ariane on all fours over by the television. She was trying to insert a tape into the VCR. To do so, she'd have to remove the one already in it. She wound up crawling back to her cushions, collapsing yet again. Inès, with her eyes drifting downward to make her words sound that much deeper: something in here feels right to me. I know I'm only seventeen but I want to be with you. For a long time. For years. Maybe my whole life even . . . I love you, I love you, I'm leaving her tomorrow . . . They must've been on the road by now. That guy at Dépôt—what was that all about? Where were they heading to like that? Their whole deal was fucked. I turned to face Ariane:

"There was this man with Inès at Dépôt . . ."

"Shaved head? David? That's just some dude Alex wanted to watch bang Inès. Alex, you know, when she wants Inès to do something, she goes hint-hint and Inès just follows along. I mean, David, she slipped that guy a grand. Me, I've fucked those two countless times, but hey, I don't need a payoff to bang Inès!"

With incredible effort, ignoring the darts in my knee, I pulled myself up into a sitting position. A little more effort and I had dragged the table over. I felt stuck, leaden, and at the same time like I had shed my corporeal form. I felt the metal spoon between my thumb and forefinger, but the rest of my body was absent somehow. It took a little while for me to take stock of Ariane's expression, the half-smile on her face:

"Listen," she started saying. "Inès told me some of the things you did together—I mean, if you're interested, you know, I'm free right now, so . . ."

"No, you listen," I cut her off. "You look fucking filthy, which I doubt you even intended, so just can it, OK?"

I dumped the leftover heroin into the spoon, careful not to spill it. Yeah, I know it was a little harsh, but that girl didn't deserve my politeness. Might she have even been one of the girls restraining Inès in the back room? The temperature was so hot, my veins were protruding unassisted. I was thinking about Inès. Nothing in particular. Just her face, laughing in the presence of others. One day I might run into her and my indifference would stun even me. I love you. I love you. I'm leaving her tomorrow. Screw you, I muttered, feeling the world grow distant.

"Screw you," I repeated a little louder, this time to Ariane, and the room went suddenly white.

chapter fourteen

goodbye and thanks

1.

When I awoke, the room was as cold as the gray sky outside, and you could hear a pin drop in the apartment. Nothing but the rain bouncing off the roof. Ariane had left her cushions behind. I shuddered, curled up in the fetal position. The VCR showed 06:35. I was in no hurry, but I knew that the more I waited, the harder it would be to get up. Like when the bathwater's gotten cold and, stupidly, we wait and we wait until we finally, finally get out. I warily sat up to assess the damage, but there didn't seem to be any. Aside from my knee, which was still suffering from its encounter with the bumper, there was no nausea, no debilitating headache, no real aches to speak of. Just the faint taste of blood in my mouth and a strong nicotine smell from my yellow fingers. I stood up to put on my jacket, which had landed somewhere far away. As I walked over to it, I noticed the little nook where I had puked, nothing too dramatic, just a little liquid that hadn't yet absorbed into the beige carpeting. I came back to sit down and put on my boots, which I no longer remembered taking off. Aside from a stain, which was luckily odorless, the mess on the coffee table was no more apocalyptic than any other stoned morning-after. Ashtrays overflowing, a half-dozen cans, two of which had spilled on the carpet, straw tips, ash everywhere, and the syringe and spoon soaking in the glass of pink water. Now that—that was something I wasn't used to seeing anymore . . . There was a little coke left. I considered pocketing it, but I didn't want any, so the other girl was going to have to keep the rest. She must have rallied her strength enough to wander to the bedroom, but a little voice in my head, whispering in my ear, told me she could just as easily have been on the bathroom floor, or on the floor only halfway down the hall. Maybe she had bumped her head as she fell; maybe she'd straight-up had a heart attack. I smiled and chased away any vague anxieties, thinking that if this heralded the beginning of some new life for me, how revolting would it be if this was how the previous life ended? Did that bother me? Of course it felt sad on account of her age, but I'd lived through so many drug fiascos that I had fully incorporated their lesson: at the end of the day, everyone's got to handle their own shit. It looked cold outside. My eyes fell on a gray sweat-suit top, and I took off my jacket to stick it on. Then I pocketed the handkerchief and syringe so the other chick wouldn't fool around with them. I checked my jeans to make sure my debit card was still in my back pocket, I put on my sunglasses, I collected my cigarettes, and I cut bait and ran.

Outside, the rain was like piss. I shoved the syringe into a trash can, the handkerchief too, and I pulled up the hood on the sweat suit. I felt stupid wearing this thing under my jacket. The hood was ginormous, and I had that ridiculous jingle for Chaussée aux Moines cheese stuck in my head. And it smelled like Calvin Klein, reminding me of this nutcase from the club who once tried to whop me in the face because I didn't want to go home with her. Supposedly I'd been ogling her all night and I had some nerve to keep her hanging there for nothing. I couldn't help it if she'd been dawdling around for hours, just because I was there, too, watching Alex mix. Pathetic. Those kinds of situations just kept happening to me.

I stopped at the first newsstand I saw, waited for him to finish cutting the strings around the bundles, grabbed *Le Figaro* and *France Soir*, and found myself a seat at a café. I started marking things with x's while drinking one Coke after another. Then I searched for a tabac where I could buy a phone card and opened the first booth I passed en route. The first two numbers reached busy signals, while the third one picked up. The guy said I could come over right away.

I took my time reaching République. My shoulders had started cramping, and my nose was running, but I bypassed every pharmacy I saw. A week of dope sadness wasn't going to have me racing for the codeine. Meanwhile, my knee was throbbing even worse than the night before; it must have doubled in size. The first car horns were starting to honk in jammed traffic. People waiting at bus stops took a step back whenever a car drove past, sending up giant jets of water. I thought about how, as soon as September rolled around, teens would start flooding this place again. Sitting on benches or standing in little groups in the middle of the sidewalk, dragging on cigs and loudly heckling one another. Flooding the place, yes—outside the gates of every high school and tutoring center and university in town. There wouldn't be a single place I could walk without the risk of running into one, and even the dullest egghead was going to remind me of Inès. Inès, who'd surely be at a café somewhere near the Sorbonne, hunched over books or lecture notes, advancing into a life that didn't include me. That said, now that she was gone . . . The rain intensified, but I didn't care. I threw off the hood, telling it go ahead, just wash this shit off me. And, at the same time, I said: Those two? Yeah, go ahead, ruin their trip.

It felt strange crossing a square that two days before had been overrun for Pride. But passing where Inès and I had only recently been, it didn't depress me, it just left a bad taste in my mouth, and if I'd been a man I would have spat it on the ground. When I reached my destination, my jeans were clinging to my thighs. The guy giggled at the sight of my dripping sunglasses, and I knew: if this spot worked for me, it worked for him. It was spotless, fully renovated with white walls and dark gray carpets. The living room looked out over a courtyard; the bedroom could only fit a bed but it had closets down one wall; the tub was a decent size, and the kitchen was well-equipped. The courtyard was the deciding factor. A big paved courtyard from the eighteenth century, leading into six different buildings, with a fountain, three-hundred-year-old trees at the center of a rectangular flower garden, and ivy creepers wherever you looked. As the guy explained, it wasn't exactly soundproof; his parents had bought it for his eighteenth birthday, and back in those days he used to play guitar. While he took a call on his cell, I pictured us sitting on the carpeted floor, here in this empty room, discussing music. I would've told him about Nikki, about me, about Alex, about the sounds that we all made, and about the crisis I was having. But I also knew that in the heat of the moment, a whole heap of confessions would tumble forth, not the kind of things to drop on one's future landlord.

He had a car; I asked if he had time to pop over to my place, to handle my paperwork as quickly as possible. He waited in the car. Upstairs, Pallas was asleep, and I wondered how things would go when I returned. We headed to a café so we could do it somewhere comfortable, and I handed him what little I had: my contract, the letter that went with it, and my last bank statement showing the deposit. He asked if it was convenient for me to meet him back at the apartment later that afternoon. I asked him to repeat that twice. He said he didn't just think I was pretty or something; he felt good about me, that's all. I wanted to grab his face and kiss him, I wanted to suggest getting drunk to celebrate, but once again, I was scared of acting inappropriately.

On the way back, he dropped me off at République again, and I made a lap of the surrounding area. The place was on a street off the Boulevard Magenta, barely two hundred yards from the square. Plenty of tabacs, some bakeries, a supermarket, lots of Arabs, and an ATM for my bank. And on the square itself, my very own McMorning assembly line . . . The cramps kept gnawing at my back, and I was constantly having to wipe my nose, but I still wasn't trying to use a pharmacy. The rest of the morning, I popped between the Darty and Habitat shops on the square. From the former, I grabbed a toaster, a juicer, and a stash of cassettes for the DAT. From the latter, two ashtrays, two plates, two glasses, two mugs, a teakettle, a frying pan, a pot, and a serving tray. I knew I could find this stuff much cheaper elsewhere, but shit, I still had almost thirty thousand. Then I visited the address once again. I didn't have the entry code and I'd have to wait a while for anyone to come out. I buzzed the super, who had seen me earlier when the guy was around; I asked if she could watch my bags until that night, which she agreed to. By the time I left, the rain had stopped, so I took off the sweatshirt and dumped it in a trash can.

Heading home, I took a detour through the Galeries Lafayette. I picked out two pairs of white sheets, two duvet covers, two pillowcases, two towels, the least expensive mattress they had, and I asked them to deliver it all to me the following day. I had to remember to stop at the supermarket to grab some boxes, and then the hardware store down the street for a big roll of tape.

2.

Back home, I found Pallas getting dressed outside the living room closet. There was steel in her eyes, so I kicked the front door closed without even saying hello. I headed straight for my bedroom and let out a deep sigh when I got there, finally releasing the dozen boxes I had squeezed under each arm, which wouldn't stop slipping the entire way home from the supermarket. I pulled off my jacket and chucked it on the bed, then walked to my machines and started switching them off, one by one. Pallas had planted herself in the doorway, pondering my heap of boxes.

"You can't do that," she said, sounding frosty.

I didn't respond and continued unplugging my hardware. If she didn't get it by now, then I wasn't going to explain myself. I was already working with enough grievances, given how long it was going to take to hook my shit up again. More than a hundred cables, a number of which looked perfectly identical but weren't. Any wrong moves could spell disaster. And their settings—even just switching them off risked killing the settings, *all* of them. I heard the front door slam.

I was missing bubble wrap, but when I saw my bed, that seemed good enough. No way could I use the bloody sheets, but I tugged out the comforter, leaving the slipcover intact, and I started gleefully tearing away strips. I took out the original packaging for the electronics, which I had left folded behind the trestle table; I put them back together and reinforced their bottoms with tape, then did the same for every box I'd brought home. Next came the hardware itself.

First laying it all on the ground to remove the slab and trestles, then doing the same for the turntables and stereo on the other slab. It had been a good impulse, keeping the box for the G4. That need I had—being able to pack up at a moment's notice—that wasn't going away anytime soon.

From the living room closets, I didn't know what to take. Something told me I'd regret it, but at the same time, looking it over, I felt: bare minimum. I pulled out my T-shirt pile, and I selected half a dozen. From the sweaters, I culled a measly two. From the wash, I chose two button-downs, Nikki's and the plum one. From the hangers, I grabbed my other pair of 505s, my black dress, untouched since L'Entracte the previous year, and my jean jacket. Tennis shoes, I grabbed my red-and-white Gazelles and my blue-and-yellow Pumas, plus the set of heels to match the dress. Next, I went through the overnight bags up top, pulling down the three of them I owned. A ridiculously large black nylon, a small white-leather Adidas, and a medium-size blue-leather Puma. I chose the last of them, with the animal leaping over its inscription, just like the floor mat in Alex's car. Our bags, our tees, even our skin had stuff written on it . . . Everything fit in one bag. I went to the kitchen for some trash bags, and I returned to start cramming them full of everything I was leaving behind. Pallas arrived as I was lining the second trash bag against the wall. Clearly she had just bought some cigarettes. I myself was out, and I could have really used a smoke, but I'd have rather died than ask.

"What's that?" she asked, pointing at the bags.

"Stuff I'm leaving behind," I said, as calmly as possible. "I don't know if there's anything you'd want, but if not, I don't know, make someone's day or something—give them away, sell them, I don't care."

"Uh, I don't have time for that shit," Pallas scoffed, incensed.

And I had thought it might make her happy . . .

"Alright then," I said, slipping an overnight bag under each arm before securing my grip on the trash bags.

I set them all on one side in my room so I wouldn't mix them up with everything I was taking, and then I tackled the rest. Packed the TV, the VCR, managed to fill multiple boxes of CDs. The pillows went in a trash bag, the comforter in another. The mattress belonged to Pallas; Inès's blood thankfully hadn't seeped into it. Even the sheets might have been pristine if I'd only taken the trouble to wash them. That postcard in the gutter—maybe that, too, had been written in invisible ink. Nothing remained. Just her final message, still on the answering machine . . . Next came the boxes piled up along the window. I didn't touch the three that had my books and *Keyboard* magazines. I opened only one of the four with my videos, extracting only *Cocksucker Blues*, and then I dumped the contents of the last box, the knickknack box, to retrieve a single case from the bottom: a silver jewelry case that had come down to me through my grandmother, which I never used, though it meant a lot to me. The rest I jammed helter-skelter into a trash bag. Alex's E.T. piggy bank, a couple of empty frames, some broken Walkmen, shades I'd stopped wearing, and some jumbled photos and letters, but even those—or those most of all—I didn't want anymore. I still took one photo of Alex and an envelope with all of Nikki's. I deflated the one-eyed alien and folded it up—my New York souvenir . . . Pallas had planted herself in the doorway once again. Now she was staring at the bloody sheets, which looked naked without the comforter.

"I'm leaving you a month's rent," I said, not even trying to meet her gaze. "Plus the security deposit so you're not waiting for someone to cover it."

No thank-you, no nothing. I was about to do the answering machine and telephone when it started ringing. I crouched over the device as I listened to Jessie's apologetic voice.

"Hey, hope you're doing OK. Listen, I wanted to say that I think it'd be better if we don't see each other for a while. It'd be complicated with Alex and all . . . Anyway, that's all, just please don't be mad, I'll call you back."

I unhooked the voicemail and telephone, and I stuffed them in a box; I dried my nose on the back of my hand and started grouping everything together. Everything I was taking with me on one side, everything I was leaving on the other. The club chair included . . . Gauging the separate stacks, I was taking more than I was leaving. But factoring out the hardware, I'd have little more than a bed and a bag of clothes. Which is just what I wanted. Like a hotel room. I started tallying the boxes of electronics, and I realized the sheer impossibility of it all. There were already a dozen of them, not counting the three synths and my huge mixing deck, which weren't packed yet; two slabs, four trestles, a computer chair, synth stands, and my unboxed 12-inches. Even with a seven-seater, an Espace or something, no taxi driver was ever going to agree to multiple trips. I wanted to sit on the floor and start crying, but I pulled myself together. At worst, it'd take a day or two to find a van, and probably I'd have to sleep at Nikki's for the time being, but at least everything would be ready to go. I went to grab the tape and started closing up the boxes. Pallas, who had since left, now came back with a lit cigarette and an ashtray held beneath it. Behind her mask of contempt, this must have felt like doomsday: what would happen to the dishes and chores? . . . I wished I could have told her all was well, that she'd find someone cool, someone I'm sure she would handle much better than me. But nothing about her attitude made me want to be nice.

"All of this, I'm leaving," I said, gesturing toward the other side of the room. "Do you want to inspect it, or is it going straight in the trash?"

"No, no," she sighed, "leave it, I'll take a look."

Was she opening a door for a back-and-forth? Maybe. But on second thought, I wasn't up for it. I couldn't find anything to say. This had all gone much too far. She had knowingly wished to hurt me, and it wasn't like she'd apologized in the time since. Now, added to the grudges and disillusionment was a limitless distrust that might never go away. I was like a cat: once you've hit us, we never forget it.

"Alright then," I said, hoping to conclude the conversation, and I went back to taping my boxes, trying to weigh whether I still had enough for the vinyl or if I'd need to head out for more.

"You're a real bitch," Pallas said abruptly. "You're intentionally fucking me over."

I took a deep breath.

"Don't you think you could have thought of this before?" I asked, as gently as possible.

"*I* didn't do anything."

She was rooted to the spot, hollowing her dimples in contempt. I slowly walked over.

"You didn't do anything?" I asked, putting my hands on my hips, an inch away from laughter. "Are you joking? It's been three weeks of you giving me grief. For ten days, you were so awful I had to find other places to sleep. And the other day, you were—honestly, I don't even know the right word for it . . . And all for what? All because you didn't have the guts to tell the truth. Yeah, the truth: you were in love with her too."

"You're hallucinating, babe!"

"Oh yeah? Well what's your problem then, you're in love with *me*?"

"Hell no!"

"Then why are you meddling? Why have you been trying to stir shit up from day one? It was none of your business, she wasn't your girlfriend or anything! What did you care, huh? Huh???"

Hands on my hips, I walked away to calm down a little.

"You were supposed to be my best friend," I said. "You should have said something. Maybe nothing would be different now but at least I'd have understood, and we could have tried to find some solutions. You think I've got nothing better to do than move out? I've got a goddamn record to make!"

"No one's forcing you to leave," she said.

"Oh yeah? And how do you figure that?"

"I've done nothing," she said again.

Psychotically stubborn: there was no other way to put it.

"Alright, listen," I said, as blank as possible, "as far as I'm concerned, you've turned into a whole other person that I'd rather not know, so you should just piss off because I've got a lot of things to do," and when she wouldn't budge, staring at me with a vague, sarcastic smile, I grabbed her by the elbow and pushed her into the hallway.

3.

When I got back from signing the lease, Pallas wasn't there anymore. I didn't find a note saying good luck or fuck off or anything, so I didn't write to her either. I was just there to take a final look at what

I was leaving. It made me queasy, but I already had so many things to take away. The videos that it had taken me years to hoard . . . I went back and reopened all four boxes, then flipped them out on the floor one after the other, hastily refilling one of them with the tapes I liked the most.

The guy who showed up—two hours behind schedule—was frankly unpleasant. One of Nikki's friends, a sound engineer with a van. I said I was ready to pay whatever he wanted for the help, but apparently he had back issues. Still, absurd that the guy couldn't even carry a chair. And not one peep the entire trip. Just "what's the code?" when we got to the front door, which he still only held for me. But I honestly didn't care; as soon as I'd set down a box, I went right back for another. My knee hurt, but I just avoided flexing it too much. First I put everything under the front stoop so the guy would stop shouting at the honking cars behind him, then I slipped him a bill for five hundred francs and didn't return his "see you around." On the final trip, the super emerged from her lodge to hand me my bags and welcome me. A ton of different odors were wafting through the courtyard, all of them delicious. A ton of different music was feebly escaping through the open windows, all of it listenable. I drank a little something by the fountain, completely exhausted, but I told myself that here, this place, would be just fine.

Once everything had finally made it inside, I lay down on the living room floor. The surface was hard; all around me lay bare. But this was my house. I had taken a real risk: if I hadn't found someone, all my stuff from the Galeries Lafayette might have evaporated by the following morning. As hectic as things had become, I had forgotten all my toiletries. I got up to drink from the tap in the kitchen, and then I took a tour of the place. Everything seemed a little less perfect than the first time. The skylights in the three left-hand rooms—the kitchen, bathroom, and bedroom—only had a view of a stone wall, with no end to it in sight, so things were always going to be dark, and then the back section under the eaves was going to mean plenty of bumped heads. The sliding bedroom closets were coming off their hinges, the faucets in the bathroom and the kitchen had pitiful flow, and the living room window didn't actually overlook the courtyard, so you really had to contort your body to one side if you wanted to catch even a shred of greenery. But those nitpicks were nothing compared to the torture I'd have faced if I hadn't found something quick.

Lying on the floor again, my eyes fell upon my purchases from that morning, the Habitat bags with all the things I'd bought in pairs. I thought of Inès, who would probably never set foot here. I thought of her torn-up postcard, surely drifting through some sewer—the postcard, I shouldn't have done that to the postcard. I opened the box with my answering machine and then looked for my Walkman, put the recording inside it, listened as she left me again, and cried.

4.

Later, it was dark out, and without electricity, I had no way of knowing the time. The candle I'd bought from the Arab guy downstairs was now peacefully flickering over the walls. Sitting on a cardboard box, I ate off my knees from a new plate. I ate some slightly stale Savane marble cake that I cut using my grandmother's utensils, washing it down with a warm Coke. I could feel the shits coming on and had to keep wiping my nose, but killing my brain cells with Neo-Codion wasn't in the cards this time around. Somehow, feeling off was giving me the strength to be alone. It gave me something to fight against. When I walked to the toilet and dropped trou, I let out a pretty little whistle seeing the state of my knee. There was a bruise covering the whole thing, a circle of violet and yellow. But in spite of the pain, which wasn't dying down, it made me laugh: if this was going to be it, the only trace I'd keep from it all, then a week would be enough for it to all go away . . .

Still, I regretted not having taken the club chair. Sitting in it wasn't going to make me think about Inès forever. But I wanted minimalism to the maximum, and now I had it.

Who was going to take my place on the Rue du Chemin-Vert? Surely someone who could handle Pallas's housework . . . Maybe someday soon I would learn that she married some guy, someone who knew how to keep her under control, who had her living on easy street. I wished her well if that was really what she wanted, even if I'd rather she start slogging: waitressing by day, preparing art shows by night, or maybe a record if she wanted, but en route for success all the same. As for Alice, I wished a resolution to her problems. For Eva, I wished a long life with Gayle, who really needed to settle in Paris by now. Anything for Eva to go on being the way she was: the most complete human being I'd ever known. And for Jessie and Alex, I wished an amazing, blockbuster record—a record of their own. For Alex, I also wished she wouldn't get addicted again. And as for the other side of her life, why should I worry if she wasn't worried . . . But two things were clear: my Notre-Dame fixation was getting a little stale; and beware of oases in the desert. Beware unsigned postcards, too.

I didn't know what they, what any of them, would retain of me after enough time had passed for them to think back on it all with zero animosity. Surely there would come a day when some of them would want to catch up. Ultimately, other than Pallas, none of them were *actually* mad. It was just a matter of time. Certainly, without them, there was going to be a fucking void in my life, a mega-void like I'd never experienced, but possibly I'd get used to that. It was possible that the day would come when they'd be ready to reconnect whereas I would be the one who didn't want to. Once you've lost someone, does that necessarily mean you want to see them again? You've stitched up your wounds and now you'd risk reopening them? Maybe we'd get back together, who knows, but it couldn't be the same anymore. I could never be part of a crew, never again.

Inès—I could picture her on her first day of college, anonymous in a mass of students her own age. Or maybe not anonymous. Maybe still the most irresistible, the most mysterious. Was that really her? Or was it only the way I saw her that made her special . . . ? That wasn't my problem anymore.

My problem was tracking down Julian again, Nikki's Julian. The guy who'd come for a concert on the square, barely two hundred yards away . . . And my problem, my more immediate problem, was finding the energy to reinstall my hardware. Rehooking all the connections. I was going to put it all in the bedroom and make the bedroom into the living room.

But before that, I was going to spend my first moments here lying flat on the floor with my jean jacket folded up for a pillow, the candle my only company. Its flame that kept peacefully flickering, casting its shadow on the wall, soothing compared to what I'd seen quivering on the walls at Chemin-Vert, the very first night I'd spent there . . . Those shadows saying, "Get out while you still can"—I hadn't listened.

I felt good, here in my new home, with a little cash advance and no scores to settle. I just regretted not having a good tape for my Walkman. I really wanted to listen to something. To anything at all.

epilogue

superstars

Forty-eight hours later, all my hardware had found its spot in the bedroom-turned-office. Everything hooked back up. It had taken me the entire previous afternoon, but every cable had eventually reached its destination, and by some miracle, none of the settings were askew. Together stationed on the left-hand side of the room, they resumed their inverted L formation beneath the skylight, with the master synth in easy reach from the computer, and with both the others arranged behind my chair, like three sides of a square. All the rest—my mess of DAT equipment, manuals, computer magazines, and thirty-odd videos I'd salvaged—could be found heaped up beneath the tables, just like before. The records and CDs were on the right. As for the living room, it had become the bedroom I'd always dreamed of: I had gone out to buy a second TV, same size as the one I had, so now I could expand certain images or watch MTV and MCM at the same time. The room was nothing but both TVs stacked one atop the other, the VCR, a pink lava lamp I found at Dom, a big glass ashtray from Habitat, and the bed—the white bed.

Forty-eight hours later, with the electricity restored and my address updated for welfare, I had a telephone now, too. When it rang, it had to be Nikki: I hadn't given the number to anyone else yet. I hunkered over the answering machine to listen as he apologized for being so late in stopping by. He was still in the studio and couldn't come before this weekend. In the meantime, he hoped I was doing well getting set up and back to work. He added, like always, that at the end of the day, the work was all that mattered. A few minutes later, another ring. I figured he'd forgotten something and this time I picked up. It was Inès. She said she was in a phone booth, not very far away. I wanted to ask how she'd found me, but instead, coldly, I let slip:

"So?"

"So can I come by?"

It had taken her convincing Pallas to call Nikki, that he had needed to give her the number, presumably for some leftover nonsense at my old apartment. That didn't explain why he'd given her the address, though. I guess it was a kindness on Pallas's part, some way of trying to mend things . . .

"No, don't come by," I said after a beat.

"Why?" she asked, practically begging.

"Please, don't call me back."

"Wait, don't hang up. I'm sorry. I just wanted you to know."

"Well, that's great, I know."

"Wait. I'm sure you've heard a lot of bullshit, and probably some of that's from me, but I panicked, OK? Let me come up, just five minutes. I left Alex."

I was silent for a minute, pondering some crack in the wall. I could have stayed like that for hours, weighing my options. But it was just like everything else. I had to get it over with, simple as that. So I gave her the code, the directions from the courtyard, and I hung up.

While I waited, with my back against the wall near the intercom, I started feeling sick to my stomach, just like the first time. Afraid I was going to blush, or that I wouldn't know what to say, and I was so disheveled, in a rumpled white T-shirt stained with traces of black that my hands had left behind, ceaselessly wiping them as I unpacked all the hardware. The intercom buzzed, so shrilly that I jumped. I was about to unhook the receiver when I realized I wasn't blushing, not even a little. No accelerated heartbeat. Just a sudden weariness at the thought of having to hear her unspool everything she needed to say. The intercom buzzed for a second time. I wasn't going to let her in. I just wasn't. It rang again, and this time I unhooked the receiver and left it hanging in mid-air.

Lying on my bed, I could hear her calling through the open window, but with my hands behind my neck I simply gazed sideways toward the leaves in the trees, gently swaying in the breeze. From this angle, you could actually see some green and a vast field of sky. A fucking marvelous blue sky, as electric blue as a trash bag. Aside from the sound of my name popping up at regular intervals, there wasn't any other noise in the courtyard. It felt like a hotel. My lifelong dream. I didn't know how long I would live here. I only knew I'd make a record here.

And I knew I'd keep an eye out for the next time Nikki's friend was around. Girls were in the past. No more headaches finding pretty ones that weren't straight. No more yeast infections, like: What's the deal, girls, all the time? And no more "what's-her-name said." Now I knew what was good for me, or at least what wasn't good for me anymore. That was the thing: girls weren't good for me anymore. Like dope, in a way: something that made me happier than anything in the world but that also ate me up inside. So maybe someday, if I fell for another girl, I would simply act like it was dope: as long as you tried to resist the temptation, it would go back from whence it came. Given time, you get into a groove, and after that, it's smooth sailing.

There in that moment, the important thing would be diving into the record, giving it everything I had. Afterward, whatever happened, happened. With a little luck, it would sell enough I could afford a little butter for my pasta. With a little more luck, it would sell so much I could start tackling the next one. And with an insane amount of luck, it would sell tons and tons, could get me out of this shithole country taking sixty percent off the top as soon as you got good enough. Then, with different luck, I'd see Julian soon. And if it couldn't be him, then there would be another, I'm sure. A god with a Gibson TV, but game to be eclectic. Because obviously that's where I was heading: an electro record with lots of rock in it.

And that was it: I'd put out this killer fucking album, as Jessie would put it, but to do that properly, Alex and the others were going to need their own fucking hit, too. That was all that mattered: doing what we loved with the means to be left in peace. And we would get there in the end, to the place Alex wanted all of us to get to. We'd be superstars just like she said. And if we got there separately, no big deal . . . Our pads would be to die for, enough cars and cash that we wouldn't know what to do with it all. But most of all, we'd be proud of ourselves, proud of doing things that mattered. Life was finally going to start shaping up.

I got up and leaned out the window. Three floors down, Inès was still shouting her lungs out in a red suede coat.

"What the hell are you doing?" she asked when she saw me.

"Get lost!" I laughed, and I closed the window.

AVAILABLE AND COMING SOON FROM PUSHKIN PRESS

Pushkin Press was founded in 1997, and publishes novels, essays, memoirs, children's books—everything from timeless classics to the urgent and contemporary.

Our books represent exciting, high-quality writing from around the world: we publish some of the twentieth century's most widely acclaimed, brilliant authors such as Stefan Zweig, Yasushi Inoue, Teffi, Antal Szerb, Gerard Reve and Elsa Morante, as well as compelling and award-winning contemporary writers, including Dorthe Nors, Edith Pearlman, Perumal Murugan, Ayelet Gundar-Goshen and Chigozie Obioma.

Pushkin Press publishes the world's best stories, to be read and read again. To discover more, visit www.pushkinpress.com.

THE PASSENGER
ULRICH ALEXANDER BOSCHWITZ

TENDER IS THE FLESH
NINETEEN CLAWS AND A BLACK BIRD
THE UNWORTHY
AGUSTINA BAZTERRICA

SOLENOID
MIRCEA CĂRTĂRESCU

THE WIZARD OF THE KREMLIN
GIULIANO DA EMPOLI

AT NIGHT ALL BLOOD IS BLACK
BEYOND THE DOOR OF NO RETURN
DAVID DIOP

WHEN WE CEASE TO UNDERSTAND THE WORLD

THE MANIAC

BENJAMÍN LABATUT

NO PLACE TO LAY ONE'S HEAD

FRANÇOISE FRENKEL

FORBIDDEN NOTEBOOK

ALBA DE CÉSPEDES

COLLECTED WORKS: A NOVEL

LYDIA SANDGREN

MY MEN

VICTORIA KIELLAND

AS RICH AS THE KING

ABIGAIL ASSOR

LAND OF SNOW AND ASHES

PETRA RAUTIAINEN

LUCKY BREAKS

YEVGENIA BELORUSETS

THE WOLF HUNT

AYELET GUNDAR-GOSHEN

MISS ICELAND

AUDUR AVA ÓLAFSDÓTTIR

MIRROR, SHOULDER, SIGNAL

DORTHE NORS

THE WONDERS

ELENA MEDEL

GROWN UPS

MARIE AUBERT

LEARNING TO TALK TO PLANTS
MARTA ORRIOLS

THE RABBIT BACK LITERATURE SOCIETY
PASI ILMARI JÄÄSKELÄINEN

BINOCULAR VISION
EDITH PEARLMAN

MY BROTHER
KARIN SMIRNOFF

ISLAND
SIRI RANVA HJELM JACOBSEN

ARTURO'S ISLAND
ELSA MORANTE

PYRE
PERUMAL MURUGAN

RED DOG
WILLEM ANKER

AN UNTOUCHED HOUSE
WILLEM FREDERIK HERMANS

WILL
JEROEN OLYSLAEGERS

MY CAT YUGOSLAVIA
PAJTIM STATOVCI

BEAUTY IS A WOUND
EKA KURNIAWAN

BONITA AVENUE
PETER BUWALDA

IN THE BEGINNING WAS THE SEA
TOMÁS GONZÁLEZ